For Michel, my gentle, loving husband, as always. Also a salute to my wonderful agent and friend, Jonathan Lloyd at Curtis Brown. Jonathan, you are the most supportive of men.

Thank you both for being the wings in my life, and helping me to learn to fly.

'I think it's perfectly possible to be a good man Monday to Friday and then, one terrible Saturday, to do something bad that haunts you for the rest of your life.'

Philip Kerr

'Bliss was it in that dawn to be alive, But to be young was very heaven!'

William Wordsworth

The Present

Late May, departure

Frenzied activity.

Calls, shouts, giggles echoing along the corridor, bouncing off the whitewashed walls and finding their way into sunlit room after sunlit room. Plimsolls, muddied socks, semi-damp swimming togs forgotten beneath the beds or abandoned on the stairs beyond the guest bedrooms. Taps running, loos flushing. Doors opening and closing. Feet charging to and fro.

'Hurry with your washbag, please, Trish! I'm closing up your case. *Now.*'

'MUM! Get it together! I gave it to you twenty minutes ago.'

I was in the hallway, one foot poised on the second step, listening, feeling sad about their departure. 'Sam!' I called up the stairs to one of my two step-daughters, while noticing that the walls all the way to the first-floor landing had been scuffed by the children's comings and goings. Toe marks, fingerprints. Traces of their days on the beach. Grains of fallen sand crushed into the wooden steps.

'Sorry, what did you say, Grace? Just leave that, Trish, please. I'll pack it last.'

'You were going to give me your reservation number so we can print out your tickets.'

'Damn, I forgot. Sorry, Grace, can you give me five more minutes?'

'Whenever you're ready. You've got bags of time.' I returned to the kitchen where I was preparing a stack of sandwiches. My fingers were greased with butter and streaks of fat from the salami I'd been slicing. Two rolls of tinfoil, three paper carrier bags, two loaves, pre-sliced by the baker, a Thermos flask of black coffee, a boiling kettle, which I had switched on and forgotten for whatever reason, and several cartons of fruit juice greeted me.

Peter was out on the veranda, or so I had assumed, but when I walked through into the living room to ask him to turn on the printer, I couldn't find him. 'Peter, *chéri*,' I called softly, not wanting to wake him if he had nodded off in the shade somewhere. I knew he was feeling down-hearted at the prospect of the imminent departure of one of his daughters, along with three of his beloved grandchildren. The medley of emotions he must be facing, along with his inability to handle them, frequently sent him to his desk behind a firmly closed door or somewhere else quiet where he could brood without being observed. He might have gone for a walk. It was a beautiful morning, with nothing to disturb the equanimity of the rich blue sky.

Yes, he'd possibly set off for some gentle exercise along the clifftop.

'Harry! Harry!' Samantha was calling from one of the first-floor rooms to the youngest of her three. 'Grace, have you seen Harry?'

'No, sorry.' I yelled up to her again. 'Last time I spotted him he was coming down the stairs, all dressed, ready to go. It must have been about half an hour ago. Forty-five minutes, maybe. Might he be down at the beach with Jenny and her two?'

'I hope not. He'll need another shower if he is. Harry!'

I could hear the tension rising in her voice. None of us wanted her to leave, to return to England, and it was a long journey alone with her three youngsters. The timing was unfortunate, what with her father's heart surgery looming, but she had her career and a husband in London, patiently awaiting the overdue return of his family. Initially, she had intended to stay just a week.

'I'll go and have a look outside,' I called up the stairs. 'You've hours till the train, Sam. No need to worry.'

'Why does he always go missing when . . . ?'

'I'll have a scout about. He won't have gone far.'

If Peter had set off on a walk, he might have taken his grandson with him. Neither he nor Harry was on the veranda as I passed through and stepped outside onto the narrow ledge of grass, bright with wildflowers and carpenter bees, that led to the roughly hewn flight of steps that swept zigzag down to the beach. I hung back at the top and waved to Jenny, Sam's twin sister. She was wading out of the sea, squeezing the water out of her long curly hair. Her two girls were sitting cross-legged on towels, making daisy chains, necklaces and tiaras out of the flowers they had been picking earlier in the morning. I signalled again to Jenny who, glancing upwards, caught sight of me.

'Have you seen your dad?' I was cupping my hands to make a megaphone with them. 'Or Harry? He seems to have wandered off somewhere.'

Jenny shook her head as she bent low for a towel.

Where could the pair of them have got to? It was then I noticed that *Phaedra*, our boat, was missing. Our little seafaring yacht. In the season, it was always moored in the cove directly in front of the villa, anchored and bobbing just beyond the shoreline, and that was where I had abandoned it two days earlier. Surely Peter and Harry hadn't taken it out.

Due to Peter's health problems, the boat had not been used all that frequently this year, except by me, of course, but the family knew nothing of my illicit early-morning trip along the coast. Might I have forgotten to take out the keys? I'd been alone, at a little after dawn in the soft violet light, in an emotionally unstable state, freaked by the threats I was facing, the veiled blackmail. Had I left them in the ignition? I scanned the sparkling sea vista in all directions. There was no sign of the boat on the calm water. Where could it have got to? Had it somehow become untethered and drifted out to sea, unnoticed from the bay, or was it trapped in a rock crevice? Had I, in my distress, been careless in parking it?

The keys must have remained in the boat for the last couple of days and no one the wiser. I was puzzled, trying mentally to retrace my movements, and momentarily forgot that I was supposed to be searching for Harry.

Harry. The youngest of my grandchildren and, yes, the apple of my eye.

And who knew that?

Who knew that if I refused to do his bidding . . .

One other explanation crept into my mind. Might *he* have stolen the boat? Might he also have cajoled my grandson, charmed or threatened the unsuspecting child into setting off on an expedition with him?

'Harry!' I yelled, with fierce force from lungs trained to project. 'Harry, can you hear me?'

I had to find Peter.

Could I have been so foolish, so scatter-brained, as to have moored the boat within wading distance of the beach and then, the following morning, left the keys in it? I spun on my heels, hurrying back into the house to confirm whether they were in the cupboard or not. As I did so, I stopped short, thinking I'd caught sight of Harry. Out of the corner of my eye, possibly half a kilometre distant, standing inland of the edge of the high cliff face. That summit zone was a national beauty spot. It towered perilously above sea level.

I was puzzled. Was it Harry? Oh, God, yes, yes, it was, and far too close to the rim for safety. Sam had already dressed her six-year-old for travelling. There he was in his neatly pressed shorts and the new dusty-red flexi-trainers he and I had purchased together at the market in La Ciotat a few days earlier. His feet planted firmly on the limestone surface, his back to me, his head was lifted. He appeared to be listening, transfixed. Semi-hidden behind one of the giant boulders, was the silhouette of a man. *Him.* It was him. No doubt about it. Where had he appeared from?

He must have been waiting for this opportunity. Hanging about, close to our property, spying on us, biding his time . . . Living in our shadow.

'What the . . . ?'

The man was wearing a Panama hat and dark sunglasses. It was late May. Even so, the Van Morrison lookalike was in his flimsy black raincoat and was engaged in conversation with my grandson. Peter's grandson. I felt a sharp pain tighten around my chest. Every muscle, every nerve in my body contracted.

'You bastard,' I screeched. My curse was lost on the air. 'Harry!' I yelled.

Both boy and man were too far from me to hear my calls. The sound dissipated on the breeze and drifted, unanswered, out to sea.

I backed up and started running round the side of the house to gain the cliff-side path. I stumbled, losing my footing in my determination not to take my eyes off the pair.

'Harry, if you can hear me . . .'

The man raised a finger as though about to perform a magic trick. Harry lifted his arms to applaud and then, quick as a flash, the man locked both his hands round our grandson's wrists and began to pull – drag – the child towards the precipice.

'Dear God, no!'

Harry appeared to be resisting, tugging himself free. He had shoved his face into George's left leg and was swinging his small squat body from side to side. He stamped his feet and let out a muffled cry, which I could only just make out.

I yelled his name again – 'Hold on, Harry, I'm coming!' I was running for dear life. The ascent was steep. The man latched more forcefully onto my darling boy and swung him off the ground into his arms. Harry was kicking his feet, beating his fists. His resilience was remarkable.

I lost sight of them as I rounded shrubs, then boulders and leaped upwards to gain the limestone path. By the time they were within my view again something had happened.

The man was backing up towards the craggy brink, dangling Harry in his arms.

'Stop!'

He danced towards the cliff edge, then pulled back, jogging on the spot. Was this a game? Was he intending to jump and take my grandson with him? Or throw the boy over?

Something bad.

This was no game.

I was screaming, hoarse with fear and anger. I had wings on my feet. One purpose. To reach Harry. Nothing else.

I sped up the ascent, far from the house, hit the dust trail, thrashing my way beyond our boundary fence into what, for some years now, had been designated national parkland. There, I pounded the sand track that led to the highest point, a well-known beauty spot where hikers, tourists, pause to admire the magnificent surroundings.

As I drew close, so close to the edge, glimpsing the rocks and the drop to the swirling sea, the gaping, shocking space, my head began to spin.

'George,' I roared. 'It's Grace. I'm here.'

The man, George, registered my arrival and clutched Harry tighter.

'Give me the boy, George.'

I moved in closer. Stealthy gestures. George took a step backwards. He was perilously close to the edge, the yawning crevice.

7

'I'm taking my grandson, George. Just hand him over to me, and then we can talk if you want to. Just you and I, quietly.'

'Nanny Two,' whimpered our child. His nose was running. I wanted to wipe it. I reached out gingerly for Harry as an arm, the back side of a hand, slapped me away.

'You let me down, Grace.'

I stumbled, lost my balance, head smarting, sickened by the distance to the rocks and the sea.

Fury powered me. 'If you harm one hair . . .'

I lifted myself up to my full height again, flesh stinging, and charged at the man. 'Give me the boy,' I was bellowing. My arms were pulling at Harry. I was trying to gain a purchase on my grandson, whose round eyes were chasms of terror.

'Come to me, Harry, don't be scared.'

Harry, with a presence of mind and force of will I would never have given him credit for, somehow kicked himself free and dropped like a log to the scree-faced ground, inches from the edge, scrambling to safety, as the interloper, the man who called himself George, moved to me, looming over me, dribbling and sweating, furious.

My petrified features were mirrored in his sunglasses.

'Listen, we can talk . . .'

A fist rose to smack me again. An image, a memory, came to me from long ago. My father's hand raised in anger.

In self-defence, I jumped a step backwards. 'If you come near us again, I'll kill you.'

Breathless, I swung towards the ground, lurching for my grandson. I grabbed his arm. 'Don't be frightened, sweetheart, we're going back to the house.' Harry staggered to his feet.

George came after us.

I spun around, letting go of the boy. 'Run on ahead, Harry. I'm right behind you.' I nudged Harry onwards, and he headed off obediently. I stood my ground, facing George, whose fist was still menacing me.

'You lied to me, Grace. Just deserts, remember?' With a lizard's speed he gripped my wrist.

'Let me go!'

Tears of rage stung and blinded me as I struggled with my opponent, attempting to wrench myself free. 'You're mad – you're out of your mind.'

Before I knew what was happening, George was staggering sideways. He was bent double, as though he'd suffered a blow to his abdomen, as though I'd punched him. Had I? Had I punched him? He seemed to be deflating, spent of strength and purpose. Stones underfoot shifted and slid. He was losing his footing. One of his old trainers slipped loose and rolled away. Shoulders pitched forwards, George let out a curious gurgle, then a rasping sound, like a low-pitched rattle.

I tried to grab him, to pull him upright, to help him regain his balance. What was happening? 'George!' My fingers were gripping his coat. I was attempting to pull him towards me, but eventually I was obliged to let go or the power of him would have knocked me off balance and sent me over the cliff-face.

'Nanny Two! Nanny Two!' my grandson was screaming. I spun in the direction of our land, towards the child. The line of dark pine-forest mountains rose up behind us towards a bright spring sky. I was too distant to comfort him and took uncertain steps in his direction. 'I'm on my way, Harry, keep going.'

I glanced back to George to confirm he wouldn't come after us, but he had disappeared. Vanished. Nowhere to be seen. Only one sneaker remained in the dust and stones. I stared out, horrified, towards the horizon. 'George!' I yelled.

Heaving in the salted air, choking on phlegm, bent low from the waist, I gazed down upon the distant rocks and crashing waves. No one in sight. I swung round. Was he hiding behind a rock, readying to pounce on me? The clean scent of resin sharpened the air. Stillness, high-altitude trees and scrub, but not a soul in sight besides one anxious boy thirty metres removed who desperately needed me. I was alone on the cliff at the edge of the world. George had vanished.

Was the nightmare finally over?

Two Weeks Earlier

Beyond gently billowing muslin curtains, the windows were open wide, exposing a waxing crescent moon hanging midway in the sky. It was a little after five in the morning, and I was awake. My head resting on Peter's chest, I tuned in to his heartbeat. Its speed was alarming. In spite of his daily medication, it still beat disconcertingly fast. By comparison, my ticker is an old plodder. I lifted myself to a sitting position. Peter was sleeping, sighing and moaning. 'My darling, please get well.'

I have always been in the habit of rising early. When the house is silent, I slip out for a long walk and a swim, like a full-sail galleon scudding across a cloudless sky, leaving my cares behind me. But during these anxious days, these fretful days of waiting for Peter's operation, once out of bed I dally, hang back before heading for the beach, watching over my husband until I feel secure about leaving him.

This early-May morning, my knees tight against his side of the bed frame, I gazed upon him. Peter, my beloved, swathed in a twisted, sweaty sheet. He was fighting for equilibrium. His heart had become his enemy, hammering furiously at him. It pained me to observe his suffering, his visible decline. I bent low to him, stroked his shoulders, reassuring him of my love, while taking care not to disturb him. I crouched, laid my cheek against the fleshy part of his upper arm, softly kissing it. I inhaled him, the night on him. The heat, the worry sweat. He claimed he was not apprehensive about what lay ahead, but I would have argued otherwise. I was witness to his unsettled dreams.

I am the spectator, tuning in to his restlessness.

Throughout his waking hours, I had begun to remark a new expression in Peter's eyes. A fixed stare, glassy, as though his pupils had glazed over or been coated in a thin layer of varnish. This focus disguised his fear, blocked it out, blocked me out. Peter was pushing me away, which, according to his logic, was to protect me. He believed that he was sheltering me from his terror, or sheltering himself from my terror, my inability to confront the worst possible outcome: his death.

I dreaded losing my husband, his heart packing up without warning, 'worn out by strain', in the consultant's ominous words. Snatched from me while he was sleeping or, when the appointed day arrived, while he was under sedation. A being submerged beneath the effects of medication who would never awaken.

I refused to compare it to the past, to the first time I had lost someone, a lover who never resurfaced, the years it had taken me to come to terms with it.

Had Peter made the connection, cast his mind back to 1968, 'our first summer' together at this house, our long, carefree days together on this beach? Until calamity had struck.

It had come as no surprise to me that Peter was diagnosed with atrial or supraventricular tachycardia, SVT. He had lived his life at a supersonic pace, in the turbo lane. He had travelled ceaselessly, worked incessantly, handled and triumphed over high-profile legal cases, which had won him a coveted international reputation and the honour of a CBE. However, alongside the acknowledgements came high stress levels. His caring heart carried the burdens of those less fortunate, those whose liberties he fought for and won. In his juridical field, few reputations, if any, surpassed Peter Soames's.

Long-haul flights were his norm, sometimes once or even twice a week. He was always out of bed by five thirty a.m. no matter when we had turned in the night before. Even after we had stayed up till two watching a movie, he had set his phone alarm for five. And then he'd switch it off and roll over for half an hour, indulging in his 'lie-in'.

I longed for him to slow down. Some days I felt as though I'd never catch hold of him, never pull him by his shirt tails and draw him in slow motion back to me, begging, 'Hey, what's the rush? Bide time with me.'

I turned now from the bedside and pattered to the open window, leaning my elbows on the sill, mesmerized by the swallows dipping and circling above the pink-tinged beach. I loved this time of year, with the first stirrings of summer ahead. I loved this old cliff house built high into its scrubby hillside overlooking the Mediterranean. Heron Heights. Peter had inherited it, this rather splendidly eccentric sunlit villa, from his late aunt, an artist, Agnes Armstrong-Soames. Yes, the painter. The very same.

I loved the privacy, the isolation, the villa's distance from the nearest town. Our lives here have become secluded, our world privileged. The environment has cocooned me, allowed me to feel safe, even from the past. My past. Our past. The tragedy that took place here too long ago to remember. Except that I do remember. I have never allowed myself to forget it, but I have forgiven myself. Forgiven myself for the foolish, brainless role I played in someone's death.

Peter and I never talk about it, never allude to it. That long-ago midsummer night.

Our bedroom is on the second floor in the tower. Once upon a time, this capacious loft was Agnes's studio, her atelier. Today, it is our sunlit sleeping quarters. There remain traces of her paints, smudges and stains, rainbows of glorious colours on the walls and woodwork, which we have never decorated over. Her autograph writ large as a memory, a reminder. I am convinced she lives on here in spirit with us. Agnes Armstrong-Soames, our guardian angel.

This airy space faces out to the beach and the sea. Often, at this early hour, there is a tanker or two to be seen far distant, navigating the silvery-blue line of the horizon, way beyond the four small islands visible from the seashore, ploughing westwards, towards the modern port of Marseille. Since we settled here in the mid-nineties, giant cruise ships have begun to invade these waters. We catch sight of them more and more frequently. They drop anchor for an overnight in one of the large resort cities along this coastline, Cannes, Villefranche, Sète, then steam on east to Italy or in a westerly direction to Barcelona and the Balearic Islands of Spain.

Reassured that Peter was sleeping soundly, I tugged on my bathers and shorts, my espadrilles awaiting me beyond the sliding glass doors of the veranda. My early-morning ritual always takes me to the beach.

I skipped down the steep zigzag track – passing the terracotta pots of tumbling geraniums to be watered on my way back – to the foot of the land, where I reached jagged rock and the hand-hewn set of steps that leads to our strip of beach, our 'hidden' cove. Ours is a coastline of creeks, shingled bays, hilltop paths and underwater caves decorated with Neolithic art, which only the most skilled of divers can access and survive.

The bay, our bay, was deserted, as it always is. It is really only reachable by boat or from our cloistered plot of land. Little visited and more or less private. I could walk for miles clambering over boulders, balancing on rocky ledges, toes licked by the sea, picking my path to the next inlet or cove and, during the out-of-season months, never encounter a soul.

I am no longer tormented by the past, the tragedy that wrecked my youth. The secrets I kept out of the light, hugged tight against my bruised heart. Peter and this house have healed me.

I paused to catch my breath, perched against one of the great granite stones that encircle us, and watched the early-dawn return of the first of the small fleets of fishing boats. Motoring slowly towards shore, with their deep knowledge of the sea and the wealth of their overnight catch, they were too distant yet for me to identify who was aboard.

Later, I might drive to the village and buy half a dozen red mullet or a shovel-load of shellfish for dinner, choosing directly from the boatmen's catch. My purchase would be our supper, which I would enjoy cooking. We have no help, only Geneviève, who drives up from Cassis two mornings a week to help with the domestic chores – the cleaning of rooms, the airing and changing of our bed. Apart from her, there is no one to trouble us or intrude upon our lives. Few guests. Peter has twin daughters from his first marriage, I no children. (Childlessness was part of the price I paid for 'my sin'.) And I'd had no previous marriage, just this one to Peter.

Since Peter retired, we have spent less time in London, preferring to base ourselves here, by the sea, relishing the solitude, our endlessly carefree days in one another's company. While I garden, Peter devotes long hours to writing his memoirs, locked away upstairs in his den. It gives him a purpose and, lately, has served as a distraction from his upcoming operation.

My time is spent idly, pottering, keeping myself busy with cooking and decorating, house maintenance, tending the vegetable patches. Fingers dirty, no make-up, sloppy old clothes. I revel in it, the anonymity, the release. I don't miss the world of stage and film any more, although I'm still employed if I choose to be. Surprisingly, the offers of work still trickle in for me and occasionally something comes along that excites me. However, until Peter's operation is over and we have been assured that his convalescence is on course, I have taken myself off the market. No more acting for the present.

Fortunately, we are not without funds. Peter's career has rewarded him handsomely, as has mine, and Agnes's generosity, along with her ever-increasing posthumous eminence, has been our silver lining.

Two decades after what we still refer to as 'that first

summer', Peter found me again. Out of the blue, he stepped back into my life. By then, I had healed and I was ready for him, open to his love, a love that he asserts had always been waiting for me.

Even to this day, he swears it was love at first sight. Peter, the uncompromising romantic. In that, he hasn't changed. It goes with the territory: the idealist who wooed me into his life, his Utopia. It was Peter's magnetism and conviction, his noble mind, that fired me with passion for his cause, during those heady Paris days of 1968.

Before the fall.

Peter never allowed my behaviour of that first summer to stand between us. It was me who occasioned the rift. He had forgiven me before I even knew I was grateful for and in need of his forgiveness.

I had not long blown out the candles on my sixteenth birthday cake when Peter and I first met. A callow, eager girl looking for thrills. Fifty years ago. How many heart-beats does that equate to? I am attempting a calculation.

Peter's weakened, troubled heart was firing at a hundred and twenty beats a minute. Twice the pace of a healthy heart, it was a ticking bomb. In one hour that adds up to 7,200 heartbeats. In one day . . . My brain is going fuzzy: it's too early for mathematics. The sun is still rising, dawn barely broken.

In one day, 172,800 heartbeats. One hundred and seventy-two thousand, eight hundred beats of his heart. A formidable amount of work for such a small muscle. And there was no tea-break, no let-up, no summer holiday from its commitment to pumping. His heart was set to keep on at such a frantic rate until it stopped, worn out. Expired.

'We'll beat this,' Peter encouraged me, when he saw the black cloud of misgiving furrow my brow, when he knew, because we read one another as swiftly as shorthand, that the fears were rising within me again, plaguing me.

My dread of losing him. Peter gone. No more.

'We'll find a way.'

And then a miracle, a promise of respite, modern medicine offering a solution.

Peter's upcoming operation will be a state-of-the-art affair, which could last several hours. His surgeon is a rhythmologist, one of only a handful in the world who specialize in this adolescent branch of medicine: the rhythms of the heart.

I had never heard of it before.

'We go in,' the consultant informed us calmly, a pencil entwined between his delicate well-manicured fingers, 'and we choose the heartbeats to conserve while the rogue over-enthusiastic devils we extinguish.'

I closed my eyes while he described the procedure.

The operation is achieved without opening the body, without peeling away the flesh on Peter's breast plate. 'A small instrument, something not dissimilar to a tracking craft on a space ship, sets off through the veins, sailing the blood flows. Its objective: to make contact with the electrical pulses of the heart, to identify and annihilate those that are beating out of time with the principal heartbeat. These are false pumpers, abnormal, and they need to be killed off.'

What if they target the wrong pump? I was silently asking myself.

'Of course there are risks. No physician would kid you

otherwise, and it's my duty to warn you of them. Notwithstanding, we carry out this procedure four or five times a week here at this Marseille clinic and there has not been a problem so far.'

I made no comment. Tight-lipped and terrified.

What are the perils? A haemorrhage? Heart failure? I tamped down the army of questions assembling within me. My own heart had upped its rhythm as a result of the challenge that lay ahead, and my anxiety in the face of it.

'What do you think?' I asked my husband, half under my breath, while fingering for his hand.

Peter gave it a second's consideration, then nodded. 'We'll give it a try.'

And so it was decided. Forms were signed. We needed only to await the date for the operation, which, we were promised, would take place within six to seven weeks.

That was almost four weeks ago.

Until the set date, our lives were to continue as normal. As long as we took no risks, as long as Peter did not overtax himself, was not subjected to unnecessary stress or shock, all should be fine.

So, a gentle existence was set to be ours for the interim, cruising through the days until the operation and convalescence had been successfully achieved.

'Will you inform the girls?' I asked him, during our homebound drive from the clinic. The 'girls', his daughters. Adult women with families of their own. Five grandchildren in total.

Yes, he confirmed that he would, and he did.

'Oh, Daddy, let us come,' begged Samantha. 'I'll organize it with Jenny. We'll be there as soon as we can.'

'No rush, my darling.' His voice was calm. Always the pillar of strength.

Why was I going back over all this again? Why did I feel a nagging rush of cold air brush up against me? As though a ghost was rising from the depths.

I walked to the village most mornings. It's not a walk, it's a fair old hike. Either I made my way negotiating the sandy bays and coves, or I chose the mountain trail with its powerful scents of herbs – juniper, thyme, rosemary, bay laurel – and mellifluous wild flowers. From the high track, I cut down to the coast at the last dusty pass and wended my steep, winding way from there. Either route took me the best part of an hour, but I delighted in the exercise and fresh air. I looked forward to it and it kept me trim.

If Peter was in good spirits and hard at work in his study, I frequently lingered, sitting outside one of the several cafés in our small fishing village. I bought our morning paper, *Le Monde*, or read a book while sipping my cappuccino. Out of season, I was familiar with the majority of the faces, all of whom nodded, *Bonjour.* I took pleasure in observing the fishermen as they hauled in their boats, dragged out their laden nets, crouching low along the diminutive quay to rinse their loads before offering their catch to passing shoppers. Two or even three times a week I'd exchange a handful of euros for a plump rainbow-skinned sea bass or a delicate John Dory – two of Peter's favourites – or I'd opt for a shimmering kilo of the small Mediterranean sardines, glinting and shiny, like newly minted sixpences, succulent to grill on the barbecue when the weather was fine and we were planning to dine on the terrace. My routine was simple. Our lives were unembellished and I was at peace with the undemanding existence we had carved out for ourselves. It soothed me, was curative.

Today was the beginning of the second week of May – the tenth, according to my phone. I was seated at Chez Clément, one of my preferred cafés down by the small harbour. Aside from the Easter onslaught, which had been and gone, it was too early for anything more than a dribble of tourists, which meant that any newcomer along the cobbled front would automatically draw my attention.

I glanced up from the novel I was reading and gazed vacantly at a man, a stranger, passing in front of me before returning to the pages of Isabel Allende's *The Japanese Lover*. With the sun bouncing off the water, blinding me with its direct light, the silhouette was little more than an outline lacking detail and form. But hadn't he walked by once already?

Without really being conscious of it, I raised my head again. The rising sun was causing me to squint, added to which my mind was distracted. Was I lost in the story I was reading or was I thinking a million other irrelevant thoughts? Perhaps I was worrying about Peter's health. Still, even in my abstracted frame of mind, I had vaguely noticed the passer-by. I focused on him now because he struck me as odd. Out of place. He was wearing a suit, a rather ill-fitting cheaply cut grey one, which was unusual attire for this part of the world and even more curious in this weather. Along with it he sported, not carried, a lightweight, silky raincoat. He was a little portly, not fat, and was wearing sunglasses and a Panama with a wide brim. A bizarre ensemble. He ambled to the quay's edge, looked out beyond the station of berthed boats towards the open sea, hands in his pockets. There he remained, striking this seaward pose, his back to me.

I suppose I would have lost interest in him about then anyway, but my phone began to ring and my concentration was immediately drawn to it. It was rare for anyone to call me so it immediately caused me to think the worst. Something amiss with Peter's health? I glanced at the screen. It was Peter. He had rung off too soon. I pressed Call Back. He answered within seconds. My heart somersaulted.

'All well?' I was attempting to keep the edge out of my voice. I jumped too easily, these days, over nothing.

'Yes, and you?'

'I'm in the village, down near the dock. Do you need anything?'

There was a moment's hesitation. 'Are you bringing fish?'

I glanced upwards towards the quay where the man in the hat had turned his attention from the sea. His back was to the water now and he was facing the small esplanade of shops and bars where I was seated at a table on the pavement. I quickly scanned the quayside. No fishermen in their boats were in sight.

'I can, if you fancy some. I'd considered red mullet but I think François must have already sold his load or he's offering his catch in Cassis today. I haven't seen him here this morning but I wasn't really paying attention.'

The man in the hat and shades was strolling in my direction. I dropped my gaze, uninterested in him, concerned by this call. 'Peter, is everything fine?'

'Sam phoned. Change of plan. She and Jen are bringing the children and arriving today. They'll be on the five-twenty train into Marseille from Paris this afternoon. I thought it would be fun to serve a big baked fish. Or a bouillabaisse.'

Why this sudden change of programme? Did they know something I didn't?

'I'll head back right now, pick up the car and drive to La Ciotat.'

'No need to fuss, darling. Just a thought. See you when you return. *Je t'aime.*'

And the phone went dead. I was staring at a blank screen, a tad puzzled, concerned about whether there might or might not be a reason for the girls to have shifted their plans forward by a week. Until I calmed myself with the reminder that I was Peter's wife. Do other second wives react in this way? Even after all these years? Do they forget that they are the next of kin, the primary port of call? If there was an emergency, I would be the first to be informed, not his daughters, no matter how close they were.

I rummaged in my shoulder bag, dug out my purse and coins for my coffee. I slid three euros fifty onto the table beneath my half-finished cup, stuffed my book and that morning's newspaper into my bag, hoisted the strap over my shoulder and stood up, kicking the circulation in my legs back into life. The man in the Panama was hovering. He appeared to be watching out for someone, awaiting their arrival from my direction. He stood about thirty metres from me, staring. I turned my back on him, thinking no more about him other than to remark silently that he seemed out of place. At that stage, I hadn't the slightest clue that I was the object of his attentions. In fact, once I was on my way home, I forgot about him altogether.

I was deliberating on my route and decided it would be preferable to take the mountain path. It was a stickier, more challenging climb, even with the high breezes coming in off the sea to cool me but, although it was also marginally longer, it was a more straightforward trek than skipping and hopping the rocky coves. Another bonus: there were occasional cars passing along the upper road, which might mean the chance of a lift, if I was lucky.

I felt an urgent desire to reach home as soon as possible, to be reassured that all was well and that Peter was not fobbing me off with excuses when in reality he had need of me and was too proud or protective of me to ask outright. As I stepped away from the table, the yellow van belonging to Jacques, our postman, was turning and reversing at the far end of the small square. Having delivered letters to the Hôtel Restanjou, no doubt. I glanced at my watch and calculated that Jacques was almost certainly heading in our direction. Our mail was usually with us a little before lunch. I began to wave and hurried along the quay in his direction.

'Jacques!' I called. A woman with two small children and a tan short-haired wiry dog was entering the cobbled *place*. Her terrier ran to the rear of the La Poste van, yapping, causing the postman to brake hard. That proved to be my good fortune. I reached the stationary vehicle and popped my head through the open passenger window. 'Are you on your way to us? If so, can I grab a lift?'

Jacques smiled, leaning over to unlatch the passenger door. 'You're in luck, Madame. Jump in. If it hadn't been for that blasted dog I would have been up the hill already. All well with Monsieur Soames? We hear he's due for an op.'

I climbed in and our young postman skidded off almost before I had slammed the door. His cab smelt of peppermints and rosemary, a sprig of which hung from the rear-view mirror. He switched off the radio, a morning news programme. 'There's post for you. It's top of the pile right behind you. Mostly bills. You can dig it out yourself, if you like. It'll save me going right to your front door, if that's fine with you. I'm a little behind schedule. It's been one of those mornings, and I need to finish smack on time today. I'm driving the missus to La Ciotat for her check-up. It's to be a boy. Did she tell you?'

I shook my head. 'Congratulations. Claudine must be thrilled. I know she said she was praying for a boy.'

'We both were, and we both are. Thrilled. Third time lucky, eh?'

I glanced out of the window towards the open water beyond a stately château hidden behind palm trees and olives, and renowned for its fine wines grown on a sea-facing vineyard. Far out on the glittering water, a trio of tankers broke the line of the horizon. The hot morning gleamed beneath them, like a silver plate. Gulls were wheeling and mewing overhead in a sky of uninterrupted blue. It was an idyllic scene. I worshipped days like this, never-ending spring feeding me with optimism.

'I swear it's getting hotter. I don't remember a May when it's been so clammy. The air-conditioning in this bloody banger isn't up to much. I keep complaining about it to the powers that be, but no one does anything. Will you be staying here throughout the summer, Madame? You usually do, don't you?'

I nodded, trying to recall. We had so rarely travelled away from here during the summer months since we first moved into the house in the mid-nineties that I was rather surprised by Jacques's question.

'Of course, you're well protected from all the holiday-makers up there on your private plot. Few sightseers, not even the curious or your most ardent fans, will want to stagger up to Heron Heights in the sweltering months. It must be a relief to be so isolated, and at that altitude when the heat waves hit. The tourists are a curse as much as a blessing. Or that's what we locals feel most of the time.'

Jacques braked hard and pulled the van over at the junction where our stony track rose up to meet the road. I swung round and lifted out the top pile of letters held together with an elastic band. 'Thank you so much. Good luck at the clinic this afternoon and say hello to Claudine from me. It's splendid news.' I stepped out and shut the tinny old door. My espadrilles dislodged a spattering of dust, which expanded to a great cloud as the wheels of Jacques' van spun and clawed at the unmade path.

I stood a moment, watching the disappearing jalopy, daydreaming about nothing in particular, listening to the skylarks and drinking in the view with the swallows gathering in swelling flocks. Bliss.

The sea was so still. It glinted turquoise close to the shore and grew in depth of colour to an intense emerald and peacock blue the further out I cast my eyes. What could be more perfect? I decided I'd go for another swim later, once I was confident that all was well with Peter. I'd prepare him a light lunch beneath the shade of one of the fig trees that had shot up from wild in the garden, and then I'd drive to La Ciotat and buy us all some delicious fish. I breathed in the rich scent of broom, in full crocus-yellow blossom, across the hillsides to the rear of the house. It was a flawless day and I was looking forward to a pleasant hour alone before the arrival of Peter's daughters and rumbustious grandchildren.

Later the same day
Jubilation at the Marseille Saint-Charles
railway station

'Nanny Two! Nanny Two! Nanny Two!'

Still wearing his duffel coat, buttons undone, front flying open as he moved, Harry was haring across the concourse as though the place was on fire, his face broken by a toothy grin as broad as the white cliffs of Dover. I was on my haunches, the bag hanging from my shoulder scuffing the floor, arms outstretched to welcome my favourite lad. I think it was no secret that Harry was the caramel-eyed child of my heart. I loved them all with a passion, all five, of course, and one should never have favourites even among those who are not your flesh and blood, but Harry, at just six years old, had stolen my heart.

Whoomph.

The force of his squat, muscular frame bulleting into mine almost sent me toppling backwards. His arms were wrapped about my neck, gripping too tight.

'Hello, Nanny Two,' he gurgled in my ear, as though confirming the validity, the physical reality of my existence. I inhaled him, his smooth downy flesh. He smelt of chocolate and something delicate and soapy, like a lavender-scented shampoo.

'Hello, big boy. Good to see you. How's life?'

'We came on the train.'

'Yes.' I attempted to pick him up and carry him in my arms as I struggled for balance and rocked myself to a standing position. 'My, you've grown. You're getting too big for all this lifting,' I laughed.

'I am one hundred and seventeen centimetres tall and I weigh twenty-one point five kilograms. The doctor, Mrs Jennings, she told Mummy that I'm big for my age and getting cleverer and cleverer. I'm almost a giant.'

'I think you're just perfect. Come on, let's find Mummy and the rest of the gang.'

Harry was Sam's youngest. She had two more, Marcus and Trish, twins. Jenny had two girls.

'There they are!'

The new arrivals were waving, jumping up and down in an untidy huddle – souvenir selfies snapped on smartphones. I grasped Harry's podgy trusting hand and we skipped towards them.

Only later, when I looked back over the entire sequence of George's arrival in our lives and the terrifying events that followed, did I recall a man, a lone silhouette, late fifties, early sixties – older? – balding, in a dark ill-cut suit. He was poised in three-quarter profile beneath the station clock, which read thirty-six minutes past five. He was wearing dark glasses. I couldn't see his eyes, but it was possible that his attention was levelled on me as I hurried by him, clutching my grandson. I didn't fully note him at the time and even today I cannot be certain that it was him . . .

I herded the family outside. We swooped down the steps, hurrying round to the rear of the station where I had parked my Renault Espace. We were struggling with the luggage, gabbling and shouting over one another, overexcited, everyone recounting anecdotes from their journey, while Peter's daughters were firing questions at me, digging for facts about their father's health. Harry, gripping tight to my fingers and skipping in front of me, was walking backwards, pausing suddenly to quiz me with endless questions, counting out loud, almost knocking me over.

'One hundred and four.' He grinned.

'One hundred and four what, Harry?'

'Steps leading down from the station. See how well I can count, Nanny Two.'

Harry was spot on. There were precisely one hundred and four steps. I remembered counting them myself as I descended from the station in the company of Peter on my maiden visit.

As we bustled into the car, a memory returned of Agnes in one of her multi-coloured frocks with purple beads the size of golf balls. She was waiting at almost the same spot as I had just now been waiting in the station. She was there to collect her beloved nephew, Peter, who was proudly escorting me, welcoming me into his aunt's world. 'Peter's new friend,' she'd said. 'What a pleasure, my dear.'

My very first trip to Marseille, to the South of France.

It was hard to believe how long ago that was. June 1968. A year, a summer, that had marked me for ever.

'Hello, my sweethearts. All my sweethearts together!'

'Here we are!'

'Hi, Dad.'

'It's so good to see you, my darlings.'

'I want to hug Granddad first! Let me, please!'

'No, me first.'

'No pushing, please.'

Peter had been keeping himself busy in the kitchen during my absence. Our arrival was greeted with shouts and cheers, hugs and kisses, bodies bumping amiably against one another, and the scents of sorrel, dill and fish bubbling in a pot. How Peter loved to cook. Champagne was on ice while small feet clumped up the stairs to the bedrooms on the first floor.

I had left the tribe to choose between themselves which beds they wanted in the guestrooms. Sam and Jenny flung themselves into rockers on the veranda, kicked off shoes, peeled off cardigans and scarves, their city attire, and dragged their half-reluctant father by both arms to seat him at their sides.

'It's good to be back,' cried Sam. As, literally, a tear fell. 'Oh, Dad, I'm so happy to see you.'

'How are you, Dad?' begged Jenny.

I pottered in the kitchen, discreetly taking some distance.

The kids above were hollering and pattering from room to room. Doors were slamming.

'I'm putting on my bathers.'

'It's too late for swimming, silly. The sharks will get you!'

'I'm hungry.'

'Nanny Two bought a cake – she told me. It's a secret.'

Peter was assuring his daughters of his ongoing good health, remaining placid, while they interrogated him relentlessly about the impending operation. I uncorked the champagne and carried it, along with tray, glasses and a bowl of salted nuts – not for Peter, who had been warned to avoid salt – out to the veranda.

'Sam, Jenny, when the kids come down, there are fruit juices in the fridge and a couple of tubs of Häagen-Dazs, chocolate, in the freezer.'

No one appeared to have heard or registered my words. Two young women, with earnest expressions, were locked onto their father's every syllable. Their anxieties paralleled mine. Ah, it was going to be a joy to be in the company of women.

I poured myself a glass of champagne, slipped off my sandals and wandered out onto the grass in my bare feet to the flight of steps that descended to the beach. Halfway down the decline of fifty-four, I settled. There I perched, gazing out at the waves, contemplating the movement of the sea, listening to the plaintive calls of a pair of cinnamon-chested hoopoes hiding in the brush somewhere to the east side of the house. It was too early for sunset. Even so, I loved this time of day. The slow shift, the melting and mixing of colours from intense to pastel that accompanied twilight. I glanced at my watch. It was ten past seven. The days were getting longer.

The bay was empty, not a footprint in sight. I loved the fact that we could almost claim this bay as ours, so few passed this way. Our yacht, *Phaedra*, was rocking rhythmically in the shallow waters, inactive for a few weeks. We could take the kids out in it over the weekend. If Peter didn't feel up to the trip, I could skipper her. That'd be fun. They'd enjoy that.

So why did the prospect of such a day out not swell my heart with gladness?

Some inner fret was badgering me.

Images, black and white, hoary, indistinct, were flashing in and out of my mind's eye. I could not grasp or identify them and I had no clear notion of what was triggering my unease. Today of all days, when I had not been mournful or idle or nostalgic but had been actively occupied with the arrival of Peter's family, excited at the prospect of their company. I sipped my champagne and closed my eyes.

What was there? A vestige of what?

A sketchy portrait, grainy, like scuffed fragments of an incomplete timeworn photograph. The images were dancing and circling, rising and flickering, swinging in and out of my subconscious, but they faded before I could grab hold of anything specific, piece it together and recognize what my anguish was about.

I was beginning to feel sick with a presentiment I could not put my finger on. It was not about the girls' early arrival, which had been triggered by nothing more sinister than a switch in exam dates for one of their offspring.

I was counting the days till Peter's wretched operation was behind us. Surely my unsettled mood was caused by the drawn-out waiting, the anxiety as to whether or not my husband would survive the ordeal. That had to be the shadow lurking over me.

'Grace!' I spun round to see Peter high above me on the grass, waving. Lord, how drawn he looked, how frail, his face a little sunken, his hair almost white. Was that how the girls had viewed him, not having set eyes on him for months? He had grown so fragile in a way I hadn't noticed before, as though the gleam, the essence was slowly leaking out of him. He looked aged, and . . . and frighteningly mortal.

'Please, don't let me lose him,' I whispered to no one, to the falling evening air.

I lifted my arm to acknowledge his call and managed a perfect smile. 'Coming!' I trilled. The accomplished actress that I am.

He nodded, padded out of sight.

Was I taking sufficient care of him? Was he eating enough, getting plenty of sleep? The girls were here now. They would lend a hand and chide me for my incessant worrying.

The ghosts within me had taken fright, vanished. I rose to my full height, brushed the sand off my clothes and ascended the steps to join my husband and his daughters for *apéritifs* and a delicious fish dinner.

The depth of my disquiet was illogical.

Peter's check-up was booked for eleven the following morning at his regular clinic in Marseille. Ordinarily, I would have chauffeured him into the city, but Sam was suggesting that on this occasion she and her sister accompany him, tackle the traffic, while I stayed behind with the brood. Secretly, I think they both wished to be assured by a professional source that Peter's rather flippant delivery of the gravity of his predicament was accurate. They had a string of questions requiring in-depth answers, particularly Sam, always the more exacting of the pair. She never let anything escape until she had scratched the bottom of the barrel, unearthed and examined every final detail. She hadn't qualified as an investigative journalist for nothing.

I was more than delighted to accept beach-patrol duty. Hours alone with the youngsters were a rare gift for me and I was enjoying the prospect of taking on the responsibility, leaving father and daughters to a day on their own. After Peter's appointment, they were planning to lunch at one of the many excellent fish restaurants circling the old port, while Jenny was keen to visit the recent museum addition, the MuCEM, which I had been raving about over our meal the previous evening. I was told to expect them back for drinks before dinner.

We ate an early breakfast together, without the children, adults *en famille*. Sam was updating me on the developments of her three, priming me of their needs. She reeled off facts as lists.

'Marcus and Trish are swimming easily. No fears of the water at all. Harry can manage without armbands in the shallow end of our local pool when I'm with him, but you should definitely make sure he wears them if he wants to paddle in the sea, which he will. Marcus will watch over him. He's good with his younger brother. Very patient.'

Pale-skinned Jenny, on the other hand, was silently sipping her black coffee, not yet entirely awake. A packet of cigarettes had been placed on the table alongside her untouched plate. She ate like a sparrow, smoked too much, was getting rather skinny and was two marriages down.

'Any special instructions for the girls?' I asked her, with a smile.

She shook her head. Anna and Christine, eleven and eight (different fathers, neither of whom was in the picture now), were both strong swimmers, she assured me, and both fully aware of their looks and budding femininity. Sam's three were definitely more boisterous, even Trish, a tomboy at heart, except when she was in the company of her two rather feline cousins. Then she begged use of, or even 'borrowed', my lipsticks and blushers, tottered about in my high heels and wrapped herself in some of the more glittery choices from my wardrobe.

And I was fine about it.

'They have sarongs and sunblock and will lie in the sun or wander off in search of shells to make bracelets and necklaces. Anna is big on handmade jewellery at present. It's her latest "thing", her passion, and, I have to say, she's rather talented at it.'

I sipped my coffee, sliced open a kiwi fruit and listened attentively, making mental notes, keen to get it all right.

It was two years since the girls, Peter's daughters – why do we still refer to them as girls when they will soon be approaching forty? – had been here together with their full squad of children.

'Listen, neither of you has anything to feel concerned about,' I promised, with a laugh. 'My day will be totally dedicated to doling out ice creams and Offspring Watch.'

'No more than one ice cream each, please.' Sam's command.

I was in one of the bathrooms along the guest landing, unloading beach towels from an airing cupboard, readying my load for the day. Six towels with a few smaller ones in reserve. Sam and Jenny were in one or other of the bedrooms, unpacking bathers and flippers, throwing together all the paraphernalia required for the children's hours at the beach.

'Should I make sandwiches and take them along with bottles of squash or should I march them all back up to the house for a spot of lunch, a drink and perhaps a shower?'

'A snack in the kitchen will work fine,' shouted Sam. 'Maybe take some apples with you to the beach and a couple of cartons of juice. Don't let them dehydrate.'

'Nobody needs a nap in the afternoon?' I called through the walls, noting previous instructions, ticking them off my mental list.

'No,' was the response in unison from both mothers.

Harry appeared, like a rabbit popping out of a hat, at my side, snuffling close.

'Nanny Two?' he began, his voice soft and conspiratorial, while nudging his frame against my thighs, sucking his thumb.

'Yes, my darling?'

'I can swim super-well without my armbands. Mummy's just fusspotting.'

'Good boy, that's excellent news.' I was counting seven towels now balanced on my knee and two small bathrobes with hoods, although the likelihood of anyone catching cold in May along this Mediterranean coast was highly improbable. For the past two weeks we had been enjoying an unseasonably warm spring, which frequently pre-empted stupendous storms, but none had yet been forecast.

I was rooting in the cupboard for comfort clothing – baggy T-shirts, fleecy zip-up blousons – should there be a water incident. Or . . . Lord, I didn't know. Water up the nose, a fall on the sand, an argument that led to tears. I was being over-cautious in the way only a non-parent could be.

'Will you come in the sea with me and I can show you? Breaststroke and crawl, I can do whole widths of both, although I'm less good at crawl.'

'Yes, of course. We'll have a dip together.'

'Marcus wants me to wear my armbands because then he's the big boy, the swimming champ, and I'm the baby. But I'm not, Nanny Two. I'm six.'

'I know you are, and isn't it splendid to be six? Mummy told us last night that you had a lovely party.'

He stared at me, his head thrown back, light toffee-brown owl-eyes beneath a frowning brow. 'Have you ever been six?'

'A long time ago.'

I began to edge to the side of him to pass by. I would

have ruffled his hair but my arms were full. 'Grab your swimming bag and I'll see you in the kitchen. Tell the others to get a move on. Sam!' I called through the walls. 'You and Jenny need to get on the road or you'll be late.'

'Can I leave my armbands in my room, please?'

'No, Harry, bring them with you.'

'Oh, Nanny Two,' he whined.

'Maybe we'll wear one each. How does that sound?'

Once Sam, Jenny and Peter were on their way, I began the almost insurmountable task of rounding up the kids to assemble on the veranda and we headed in a crocodile – Marcus at the front while I brought up the rear – carefully down the steps to the beach where we laid out our little station, 'our camp', for the day. Towels were placed neatly one alongside another in a row, like a brightly coloured picket fence.

Marcus and Anna had both pointed out to me that I had forgotten to pack parasols. Oversight corrected, the boys were erecting and opening them while the girls were fussing over their costumes and the colours of the slides they would be using to pin up their hair. I was flagging, and the day had barely begun. Glancing at my watch, I saw that it was already close to midday. By the time all was in place and we were settled, it would be time to start handing out the sandwiches, which, in spite of Sam's advice, I had hastily slapped together.

Marcus and Trish had decided to go swimming. Harry was jumping up and down at his brother's side, eager to accompany them.

'Not without your armbands,' insisted Marcus, a tad bossily. Harry swung to me for support.

'First swim with them,' I pronounced, 'and later we'll see.'

'No, no, no!' Tears were forthcoming. Cheeks reddening.

'Harry,' I insisted. 'First you swim with them and we'll reconsider the situation for the next dip after lunch, okay?' My voice was firm, bridging no refusal.

He glared at me, shocked by what he perceived as my unexpected lack of support. Then he acquiesced, with little grace, fretting and complaining, whimpering like a chained dog. Marcus took his hand, appeasing him, and the three of them, Sam's delightful family, set off together into the water. Squeals as a toe, then a foot followed by another white limb breached the deliciously inviting water. The sea was calm. Turquoise blue flecked with a snowy silver, it caught the bright sunlight, like yards of unrolled silk.

There seemed no danger so close to the shore, although I knew better than anyone that you could never count on that. Drowning happens in seconds. A body swept out to sea, never to be recovered.

I stifled the retrospection and settled myself on my towel, leaned back on my elbows, outstretched legs bare beneath beige Max Mara shorts, to observe the high jinks and larricking in the roll of gentle waves.

Harry was jumping up and down, showing off, beckoning to me, both arms aloft. I lifted a hand, unbalancing myself, and waggled my fingers to return his salutation.

'May I borrow your comb, please, Granny?' Anna purred, at my side. She was so ladylike, so polite. I wished she wasn't, wished that she was a little more rough-and-tumble, edgy perhaps, more like her cousins.

'Aren't you two going in the sea?' I urged. I turned my head and took in the exquisite beauty of the pair of them. China dolls. Skin like candle wax. Both so different, genes from their fathers, yet still with Jenny's fine bone structure and natural refinement. They might have been off to a ballet class.

'First we need to put our hair up in ponytails and buns and rub in some cream. I don't want to go red.'

'And I don't want to peel and look all scaly like a horrid lizard,' shrieked little Christine, with an earnest pouty expression. She had lost one of her front teeth and was lisping a little.

I burst out laughing. 'Lizards eat the mosquitoes that bite you and make you red and itchy, as well as the flies that congregate in the kitchen. They're anything but horrid. I think you'll be fine with a little cream if you keep out of the full heat. We haven't reached midsummer temperatures yet. My comb is in the green plastic *pochette*. Help yourself.'

A scream from the sea caused me to jump. I was on my feet in seconds, scanning the view. Marcus and Trish were in sight, but . . .

'Where's Harry?' I yelled, exposing unnecessary anxiety.

'I'm here,' he whooped, mouth wide open, popping up like a slippery seal from beneath the shallow waves. 'I was looking at the fish, all shiny like moving spoons. There are squillions of them, Nanny Two. I'm going to count them and you can guess how many.'

'You can't, silly. There are shoals of them, but not millions. Not even thousands,' corrected Marcus. 'Will you throw the beach ball, please, Granny?'

I bent to the towels and reached for a large lightweight multi-coloured ball, which I hurled towards the sea. It fell wide of its mark and rolled and bumped carelessly towards the water. Marcus loped from his turquoise bath, scooped it from the sand and lifted it above his head, arms outstretched and dripping. Aiming it horizon-wards, he pitched it with skill. Trish and Harry jumped and squealed, while I settled myself back on my towel and rolled over onto my stomach, digging into my bag for my book, *Tender Is the Night*. Having finished *The Japanese Lover*, I was now on my biannual rereading of my favourite Fitzgerald.

Jenny's two girls were creaming each other's back, small nail-varnished fingers stroking and kneading in perfect circles, a fair-skinned twosome. Both were clad in striped bikini bottoms but only Anna sported her matching top. Both were flat-chested, but Anna was already self-conscious about her nipples, her budding breasts and developing girly figure.

I smiled. 'When you've done that, go and play ball with your cousins,' I encouraged them.

The sunblock neatly repacked in their shared toiletries bag, they slipped their hands together, like a pair of delicate angels, and took flight for the sea. Peace descended, not that I objected one iota to the children's energies and attentions. Quite the opposite. I lifted my gaze upwards towards the house and suddenly, freakily, I heard clearly the barking of a dog. It sent a shiver through me. It sounded just like Bruce, Agnes's dog. Bruce, yapping and frenetic. His frenzied barking that fateful night. My sixteen-year-old self bent double, crippled with cramp, shock and misery.

Where is he, Peter?

I don't know.

He's not coming back, is he? He's drowned, hasn't he?

Why these memories rising? Why this haunting?

It had been a long time since I had allowed my thoughts to drift back to that summer, to that harrowing August night. Whenever they did, I dismissed the images forcefully. However, since yesterday, since the family had arrived or even before that, an amorphous shadow was nudging up against me, pushing its way to the surface of my mind, and I was unable to shrug it off or pinpoint what might have seeded it.

Was it connected in some way to Peter's impending operation? The vulnerabilities of our lives? The face of death? The apprehension that if the risk, that minuscule risk, kicked in and Peter didn't recover, didn't regain consciousness, I would be facing the rest of my days widowed and alone? I had spent so many years without Peter, running from him, that the few we had shared and savoured were so precious.

'Nanny Two, what time can we eat our sandwiches and chocolate cake, please?'

I lifted my gaze to the small drenched boy, his hair standing on end, chewing at his towel. His presence washed over me, a comfort as big as the world. 'Who told you it's chocolate?'

'You always buy chocolate cos you know it's my favourite and Mummy says you like to spoil me.'

After our sandwiches and gallons of squash, which prompted the children to traipse one after another back to the house to wee because I adamantly refused to allow them to urinate in the sea or in the shadows of the mighty boulders that enclose our bay, we settled to books or puzzles or, in the case of Anna, threading a sparkly necklace of translucent aquamarine beads. Trish was singing to herself, drawing boats and clouds with a stick in the sand.

The barking of that ghost dog erupted again. I glanced up, scanned the length of the sand dunes as far as the cliff top, convinced someone was there – a trespasser, a phantom – but at each raising of my head, I confirmed the grounds were empty. No man, woman or beast was prowling our hillside.

This was absurd, irrational and absurd, and I was spooking myself over nothing. I had to get over it.

My phone rang.

It was my agent, Ken. His telephone call had come out of the blue, and with it a rather enticing offer. A leading role in a new play destined for London's West End. My immediate refusal, my desire to be at Peter's side for the foreseeable future, certainly throughout the upcoming months, took an explanation that ignited questions. After Ken had accepted my decision, we chatted and gossiped about inconsequential matters and I invited him, with his lovely wife, to fly over for a few days during the late summer season for a long overdue weekend of wine and jollity.

When Peter was better. When he was cured.

My skin was getting lightly bronzed, toasted in the gentle heat. I had temporarily forgotten the activities and exuberance of the youngsters: they had not broken into my conversation. It was out of character for me to spend so long on the phone. How long I didn't know, but the sun had moved west by the time I said goodbye and switched off the call. It was still high above the horizon but noticeably to our right when I sat up and gazed out towards the water. A wispy cloud or two had entered the scene and there was a dimming of the light. I hoped this was not the first harbinger of change, of an incoming storm.

I glanced to either side of me. Anna, on the left, was wearing her handmade necklace. It swung from her throat long and loose, reaching snakelike to the towel beneath her. She was lying on her stomach, facing away from the sea with her legs dangling in the air and her ankles crossed one around the other. Her concentration was buried in what I mistakenly took to be a picture book. In fact, it was a jewellery instruction manual.

'Those beads look fabulous,' I said.

She glanced in my direction and lifted her left hand up to stroke them, all blues and turquoise. 'My sea necklace,' she cooed, beaming with pride. 'Would you like me to make one for you as well, Nanny Two?'

'Oh, that would be splendid! Yes, please. Thank you, sweetheart.'

Beyond her, curled up on her side like a shell and facing her, was Trish. She was staring at herself in a mirror, making faces, pouting her lips, which had been striped ruby red with lipstick. Mine, no doubt. Christine was drinking lemonade from a bottle through a straw. Reaching the dregs, the air-sucking noise she was making was loud and rather disgusting.

'Christine!' screeched her older sister. 'You are gross!'

I wanted to tell them that Peter and I no longer used straws and alert them to the danger to sea creatures caused by all the plastic we humans were discarding, but before I could do so, Marcus had approached and was standing over my shoulders, dripping with sea water, creating a shadow between the sun and us females. He loomed large.

An uncomfortable memory returned. Marseille 1968.

I rolled fast towards him. 'What is it, Marcus? You're masking the sun from all us ladies.'

'I can't find Harry,' he said. I couldn't read the expression on his face because the sun was behind him, but his voice was solemn. I sat up directly.

'Can't find him? What do you mean?' I knew I mustn't snap. Keep control.

'He and I were playing catch together in the sea. I hit the ball really hard with my hand and it went spinning far onto the beach. Harry went after it, and while he did, I had a quick dip. When I lifted my head from the water he'd disappeared.'

'How long ago?'

Marcus shrugged his shoulders. 'Ten minutes.'

'Jesus.' I looked from left to right along the sea front. No sign of anyone there. No small boy to be spotted anywhere.

I jumped to my feet, spinning and turning in every direction. 'Might he have gone up to the house to the loo?

Did any of you girls see Harry go past?' I asked. They shook their heads, puzzled by my consternation.

'Anna, run up and have a look, please. Try his room too. Marcus, in which direction did you hit the ball?'

My eyes were scouring the length of the beach. The bay was completely empty, save for us. A few birds at the water's edge. Gulls overhead. No other life.

'Over that way. But I ran to the boulders to see if he was hiding there and he wasn't.'

The tide was coming in. There was a muddle of footprints close to the water's edge: some were spreading, losing shape, soggy, filling with bubbly water, but there were none that had wandered further in any direction from our little encampment. To the sea and back, or up to the steps ascending to the house and down again.

'No sign of the ball?'

Marcus shook his head. His shoulders were rising towards his ears.

'Trish, take Christine and walk up to the dunes. He might have headed off in that direction.'

It was a wild chance without any footprints to follow. The only other possibility, where there would be no tracks at all, was seawards. Had Harry ventured into the sea, out of his depth, panicked and . . . ? Marcus, with his head underwater, might have missed his cry for help.

I had missed his cry for help.

'Did any of you hear Harry calling? Was he still wearing his armbands?'

That night, all those decades back, we'd heard no call, no cry, no final attempt to be saved, to warn us of the last gasping breath of a drowning man.

Each child stared at me solemnly and shook their head. The alarm rising within me was causing my saliva to dry up. My mouth felt glued, paralysed. My phone was back in my beach bag. Should I call Peter and his daughters, or should I wait until we'd found Harry? *Because we were going to find him, weren't we?* Harry hadn't gone and drowned silently, had he? Should I call the Lifeboat?

Yes. I knew all too well I should call it immediately. Now. I grabbed my bag, fumbling, all thumbs, for my phone.

'Maybe he got talking to the man,' offered Marcus, nervously.

'Which man?' I was digging for my wretched telephone, hands shaking. Had I left it on the sand?

'There was a man sitting on the rocks over there.'

I twisted round. The clouds shadowing the rocks caused them to look like a herd of hunched black bison. They were no longer glistening white salt crystals in the sunlight. There was no one there, no silhouette I could make out.

'You saw a man over on the rocks. Are you sure? There's no one there now, Marcus.' This seemed an unlikely explanation. This place was always deserted.

Marcus confirmed that he couldn't see anyone now but he had done earlier.

'I'm going over there. Marcus, gather up our things here, please – don't leave any litter, take it with you – and carry everything back up to the house. If Harry is there with Anna, shout down to me. I'll listen out for your call. Otherwise, stay there. Give a yell to Trish and Christine to join you back at the house. Then, none of you go out from the villa till I get back. Do you understand me? Stay in the house. You are in charge till I return.'

The eldest boy nodded gravely.

'Point to me precisely where the man was.'

'Sitting there, up on that high rock. That one. He wasn't doing anything spooky, not watching us or anything, just looking at the sea and smoking.'

'What did he look like?'

Marcus shrugged. 'I couldn't see his face. I d-don't know, Granny. I wasn't paying attention.'

'Was he there for a long time?' I was beginning to feel physically sick, dread washing through me. My hands and knees were shaking. How had I let this happen on my watch? A stranger on our beach, a child missing, and I'd been oblivious to it because I had been gossiping on the fucking telephone when I was meant to be taking charge of the young ones. Where was my phone?

'Where the hell is my phone?'

The girls had all disappeared off to their various points. Marcus stood stiffly, staring at me. His face expressed a slow gathering horror. His features were almost frozen.

'I j-just had a quick dip,' he sobbed, tears welling like puddles in his eyes. 'I was sticky from the ball game. I thought Harry would be there with the ball. Is this my fault, Granny?'

'No, my darling, of course not.' I stopped rummaging, took a deep breath and wrapped my arms around his solid stock-still frame. I hugged him tightly. 'We'll find him. Hurry with all of the stuff. Go and take care of the girls. I'll be back shortly.' I turned to run off, then dipped into my bag and miraculously pulled out my phone where it had been all the time. 'Marcus, if you can carry every-thing, take my bag too, please. Good chap.'

Should I call Peter? What could they do? This would unnerve them, put stress on Peter's heart. Peter's heart. Jesus. If anything had happened to Harry . . . I was clutch-ing the phone in my right hand and running towards the rocks. 'Harry,' I was yelling. 'Harry.'

The distance was a matter of a few hundred metres, but I was retching for breath when I reached the rocky barri-cade that enclosed the eastern wing of our bay from the one that neighboured us. 'Harry.' I clambered up onto one of the rocks. They were slippery. At the menace of my shadow, a small flesh-pink crab fled for cover, disappear-ing like magic into a defect, a fissure in the rock.

'HARRY!'

I must have called five or six times without any response. Only the sound of the waves behind me. And then, from somewhere beyond the flat echo of my voice, I heard a frail murmur.

'Here.'

'Harry! Oh, my God – Harry?'

Silence. Had I imagined his answer, his husky reply?

'For God's sake, where are you, darling?'

'In here.'

'Where, Harry?'

I shoved my phone into my shorts pocket, freeing both hands. I was climbing clumsily on all fours, cutting and scratching my legs, peering between the unrelenting rigidity of the rocks, dark and austere.

And then, buried low in a crater between two mighty granite stones, was my grandson. 'Oh, thank God.' His tear-stained face was staring up at me. He was as pale as death, the colour exaggerated by the darkness of the rocks, and he was shivering, teeth chattering.

'I slipped and twisted my ankle.' He sobbed. 'And I've burst Marcus's ball and lost my armbands.'

Alongside him, squashed, punctured between his shoulder and one of the stone surfaces that were imprisoning him, was the deflated beach ball. Harry's shoulder was bleeding.

I scrambled over the rock and lay on my stomach in an attempt to reach him.

'Give me your hand,' I ordered, reaching down into the crevice. But either because his arms were too short or he was wedged so deep that it hampered his movement, his fingers could not grasp mine. I inched my splayed body closer to the rock's edge – I feared falling, tumbling in and landing on top of him.

'Try again,' I huffed, extending both arms to the limit of my reach. 'Can you stand up, Harry? Can you lift yourself up?'

He shook his head and started to cry. 'I've gone to the toilet in my trunks, Nanny Two.'

'It doesn't matter, darling. Let's just get you out of here. Can you lift yourself up a little bit and try to take hold of my hands?'

The distance between us was not so great but it made the difference. We tried again, stretching for those extra inches. Still, he could not reach me and I dared not lean my flattened self further into the rock hole.

I was trying to think, think fast. I needed a rope, or a stick, a branch. Something solid for the boy to latch on to.

There was no chance that the tide would travel this far inland but I had no idea what poisonous life or other dangers might be lurking close by. A sea urchin beneath him. His legs might cramp – he must already be getting cold and paralysed. How long had he been stuck there? I had to get him out of the cleft but I couldn't manage it alone. If I ran back to the house for Marcus? But I didn't want to abandon Harry, leave him trapped. I began to scrabble my prostrate body into a crawling position. I was deliberating about what to do next, deciding that my best plan was to telephone for *les pompiers*, a fire-brigade rescue, when a shadow gathered to my left and paused, poised above me.

Marcus?

My gaze settled on a pair of shoes, scuffed navy-blue trainers, adult size, planted on a boulder a few metres from the one I was squatting on.

'Do you need help?' The question was asked in English, a male voice, gruff, throaty. I drew myself to a squatting position and looked up. An older man in sunglasses was staring down at me. Where had he come from?

'Hello . . . My grandson has slipped between the rocks and I can't lever him out.'

'Let me try.'

'You're very kind.' I clambered backwards out of the way, vacating the space for the stranger. Although he was overweight, beer tubby more than fat, he stepped lithely across the rocks, dipped down and plunged both arms into the hollow where Harry was trapped.

'Take my hands, Harry, and hold on tight, there's a good lad.'

Harry? How did he know the boy's name? He must

have heard me calling, must have been within the vicinity. Was this the fellow Marcus had spoken of? Must be. Had he been there all the time? If so, why hadn't he come to Harry's rescue before now?

I glanced across to the bay on the eastern side of ours and was astonished to see several small groups of people dotted here and there on the beach, children and adults. Several were sunbathing, others wading and jumping in and out of the sea. Holidaymakers or locals enjoying a day out. A couple of German Shepherds were capering in the waves at the water's edge. No doubt, it had been one of those I had heard barking earlier. How perfectly daft of me to have imagined it to be Agnes's Bruce, gone for decades. Groans drew my attention back to the present. Harry was being raised by his armpits to light and safety.

'There you are, lad, safe and sound,' said the man, planting him on a curved rock, holding him steady because he seemed a little faint or dizzy. 'Nothing to fear now.'

The stranger's accent was northern. It sent a shiver through me. I bent low and wrapped my arms about my grandson, hugging him far too enthusiastically. 'Thank God you're safe.'

'Ouch,' he mewed.

'Come on, let's get you back up to the house and clean you up. Thank you so much. Say thank you, Harry, to this kind gentleman.'

Harry obeyed with a shy inaudible word.

'What a stroke of good fortune that you were close by.' I was addressing Harry's saviour, whose mirrored sunglasses hid his eyes but, disconcertingly, reflected mine. Dressed in urban clothes, certainly not beach attire, his outfit struck me as odd, ill-fitting and out of place. I had an idea I'd seen him before but I couldn't place him. I stared at him to the point of rudeness as though I . . . There was a familiar note that nagged at me but I could not put my finger on it.

'Have we . . . ?'

As we stood facing one another, he lifted a calloused hand and removed his shades. It was a slow, rather affected gesture, which exposed his naked face.

'Oh . . .' My reaction was out before I could contain it.

An ugly scar exploded from his balding head, running like an arrow to the mid-point of his cheek, disfiguring the placement of his left eye, which was semi-closed and crooked. The revelation was unexpected, shocking. Too intimate. Dare I admit it? Repellent. I instantly dropped my gaze, feeling the urge to swing away from him, but pulled myself together, quickly realizing the rudeness of my behaviour.

'We really are most grateful, Mr . . . er . . . May I – may I offer you something?' My whole body was trembling.

'Like what?' he snapped back. 'Were you thinking of giving me money? Or did you have it in mind to invite me up to your villa for a cup of tea? And then we could chat.'

The forthright nature of his questions took me aback. I wanted to look up, to read his meaning in his features, search beyond the damage, but I kept my eyes lowered, to avoid staring at him in the way he was staring at – into – me. His attitude was intimidating, as though he were challenging me. After a few moments he replaced his glasses, masking his injury.

I was struggling for words but could form none.

Harry pressed himself against my leg, trembling, arms grasping my thigh.

'Forgive me, I – I must get the boy home, into a hot bath. I don't know. I meant . . .' I had no idea what I had intended, certainly not money or an invitation into our home. 'Perhaps you need a lift somewhere?' My proposal was ludicrous, an inept attempt to rectify my rudeness, cover my awkwardness.

I was desperate to be gone. However, the Englishman had saved my grandson further trauma and discomfort. I owed him courtesy, at the very least, but there was a presence about him, a tenor, that was rattling me. He was standing directly in front of me now, an inch too close, invading my personal space, as though attempting to trigger some manner of reaction in me.

Why had he taken off those glasses and revealed himself in such a theatrical fashion? What had he expected of me?

'Look, I – I really must get my grandson home.' I was repeating myself. 'Come on, Harry. Thank you so much. If I can . . . if there's anything . . . Goodbye. Enjoy the rest of your holiday.'

I was nudging Harry forward. 'Can you walk? Nothing broken? Take care as you climb down not to slip and fall.' I was fussing, maladroit.

At my words, the man leaped, almost vaulted, onto the sand on our bay side and held out his arms to ferry Harry to safety. Harry must have picked up on my discomfort for when he landed on *terra firma* he skidded off at a lick, bad ankle or not, heading for the safety of the house without a glance backwards.

I jumped to the sand, nodded stiffly at the man and sped away with equally bad grace.

Trish and Anna took Harry off to bath him while Marcus brewed tea. I discreetly helped myself to a large whisky from the drinks cabinet on the veranda after I had telephoned our local GP to know whether I should drive Harry over to see him for a check-up.

'Anything broken?'

'I don't think so. He was running on the beach the moment he was free.'

'That sounds positive. Let's see how he is tomorrow. If necessary we can organize X-rays then.'

When I'd replaced the receiver I stepped outside with my glass onto the grass to look over towards the eastern bay. There was not a soul in sight, no sign of the Englishman. I let out a sigh. He had not hung about as I was dreading he might.

I realized that it was gone five o'clock and I needed to gain some semblance of composure before Peter returned with his daughters. Of all the events that had woven through the afternoon, I couldn't work out which had most thrown me. One phone call, a quarter of an hour of neglect, and I had nearly lost us a child. I was appalled at myself. Accidents happen in the blink of an eye: such a platitude. Even so, nothing altered the fact that, without a stroke of good fortune and quick thinking on Marcus's part, Harry might have come to far greater harm. Visitors were such a rare occurrence at this time of year. The tourist — with that northern accent, that northern accent — knew

Harry's name. Most likely he heard me calling. It must have been my alarmed cries that had alerted him to the fact there was a problem and a child was in danger. Why else would he have been on the spot?

Whisky downed, I ran up the stairs and along the corridor to the second guest bathroom, where there was a bath as well as a shower. Here Trish and Anna were tending their youngest relative. The girls were singing softly. I knocked before entering.

'It's Nanny Two,' I whispered into the wood, hoping they would all forgive me and love me as they had done in the past. 'May I come in, please?'

Anna opened the door. 'He's all scratched,' she informed me, with a solemn adult bearing, 'but we think he'll be fine.'

Harry was in the bath, covered with bubbles, excitedly holding aloft a model of a wooden sailing ship he must have purloined from the windowsill. Peter's. Its sails were soaked and drooping, but Harry appeared restored, full of good spirits. Relief swam through me.

'Hello, big boy,' I said, as I bent low over the lip of the bath. 'All good?'

He nodded a little bashfully but his eyes were shining bright. The resilience of the little ones, I was thinking. Thank God for it.

'Will Mummy be cross with me because I burst Marcus's ball?' he asked. 'And lost my horrid armbands.'

I shook my head. 'No one will be cross with you. Nanny is the naughty one. I shouldn't have let you wander off so far on your own. I'm sorry, Harry, that you fell when I wasn't there to help you and you were frightened.'

He stared at me curiously, eyes scanning my face. 'There were crabs in the rocks,' he remembered, 'walking about sideways, like crabs do, then popping out of sight. I was frightened they'd bite me or pinch me, or a snake would come out of one of the big holes and gobble up my willy.'

Anna, behind me, hooted.

'A snake? Lord, I never thought of that.' I laughed nervously. 'I don't think there are any snakes on this beach. Aren't we lucky, eh?'

'After I've dried myself properly, please can I have ice cream and the rest of the chocolate cake?'

I lay awake almost the entire night, tossing, turning, getting up, pacing, staring out of the window at the rocks, then back into bed. Sam, understandably, had been mad as hell with me, at the revelation of the day's events. She'd ripped into me about my lack of responsibility. My 'lack of prudent guardianship'.

She and Jenny had spoken with their father and the consultant, and no doubt her concern for her father's impending operation exacerbated her explosive reaction. Even so, her anger shocked and grieved me.

'I'm so sorry,' I repeated, like a fool.

'Sorry! For Heaven's sake, Grace, he could have died.' There were tears of frustration in her furious, puffed features.

The children were in bed. Sam had been stewing with her mood, waiting to tear a strip off me, but she had held back until after dinner, until we four adults had been settling to a nightcap on the veranda. I noticed that during the meal she had downed more wine than was her habit. Usually she was a temperate drinker.

'But he didn't, Sam,' interrupted Peter. 'Harry is right as rain. Hunky-dory, except for a scratch or two. Within a couple of days he'll have forgotten about it, so let's not overexcite ourselves, please.' There was an emphasis in my husband's voice, an even keel, that I knew was for me. He was supporting me, sending out his love as he always had done, even in the years before I had appreciated it.

That night, and every night, I loved him for the loyalty he had always shown me. Even when, once upon a time, I had so uncaringly rejected him.

I turned now in my insomnia and stroked his shoulder. Nothing comes between Peter and his sleep. 'I love you so.' I mouthed the words so I didn't disturb him. He seemed peaceful and I was grateful. If it were me facing the challenging operation that lay ahead for him, I would be terrified.

Thunder growled from the hinterland, curdling in the mountains. On this night with its gathering banks of clouds masking the stars, the misgivings that were keeping me awake, that wouldn't go away, did not only concern Peter's future. It was the past, rising up to ensnare me.

The man who'd rescued Harry: had his presence been fortuitous, or had he been on those rocks for a purpose? To watch us, stalk us, to gain entry into our lives? He, with his partially crushed face and awkward questions. I had been rude to him, ungracious, but that was not the qualm that was preventing my sleep.

I closed my eyes, allowing my memory to trawl back in time. He had addressed me in English. He spoke with a trace of a northern accent. Those twisted, battered features, how had they looked in youth? A few wisps of hair remained on his bald head. Had it once been blond hair? Lustrous locks of blond hair. Wet from the sea, embedded with sand.

Why had he removed his sunglasses? The act was a disclosure. Was he silently saying, 'Look at me, Grace? Remember who I am?'

I couldn't look. Couldn't meet his eyes.

What if he had been revealing not his scar but his face? What if he had counted on my recognizing him? Was that it? Was it? Or were these hour-of-the-wolf anguishes feeding a hypothesis too outlandish to contemplate?

But why else would he presume even for one second that I might have invited him into our home? Unless, unless . . . And then the question I had been asking myself since the afternoon's encounter . . . But, no, it was preposterous. It was beyond plausibility, beyond any measure of credibility. Yet still the question returned to taunt me. People don't rise from the dead, do they?

1968

Grace at Sixteen:
Arrival in Paris

Spring, those first bud-leaf days of April. I had won a scholarship to a drama school in north London, a three-year course commencing mid-September, so with time on my hands, I was off to Paris. Paris. To begin there and then, if my meagre finances lasted or other opportunities came my way, I'd explore further afield. Others of my generation – school chums a couple of years older than me, pals from our local youth club – had set their sights on more remote locations. Plans were under way for following in the footsteps of the Beatles, learning transcendental meditation by the river Ganges. Others were off to Nepal, Tibet, while one girl was travelling overland to Australia and another to South America.

But I was sublimely content with Paris, for its book-shops, cinemas, galleries. The city of love. The City of Light, La Ville Lumière. Leading up to the French Revolution, it had been the nerve centre for ideas, philosophy, literary salons. Who could not dream of Paris?

In my opinion, it beat flying to India to find God and coming home with dysentery.

I was sixteen and green as unripe fruit.

My home life, my childhood, had been turbulent. I seldom spoke about it. Even today I rarely revisit the years of my adolescence. I loved my parents, both of them, don't misunderstand me, but they were wrestling with their chains, struggling within a marriage that was suffocating them, and of course I couldn't save them. Anger, accusations, violence ensued. Domestic violence. It wears away at your soul because you don't talk about it, and so, without ever intending to, you collude. You bury the pain, swallow the anger. You don't disclose it because you don't admit that it's happening.

Witnessing it first-hand – as I did, as well as being its victim – eats at your self-esteem, until you start to perceive yourself as worthless. That was me back then. The teenage Grace. Five, nearly six years of domestic unhappiness had influenced my personality, seeded insecurity, a tendency towards negativity. I couldn't see the young woman I was blossoming into.

Peter was the first to awaken me to my potential, and then I turned my back on him, handing myself to another, far less worthy. Pierre.

But that was later. After Paris.

One or two of my school chums had an inkling of what my domestic life was like, although they never uttered a word about it to me. On one mortifying occasion Jess, one of my classmates, accompanied me to my home to pick up the sandwiches I had made that morning for our lunch, then had left, forgotten, on the kitchen table. We were on our way to play tennis. As we rounded the house by the side path, I heard Dad's transistor radio playing a vocal. It was Frank Sinatra singing 'Try A Little Tenderness'. Looking back, I see the irony right there.

Jess, who was humming, was right behind me. We slipped in through the kitchen door, and there, smack-bang in front of us, a full domestic. It might have been a scene from a kitchen-sink drama. Metal flashed, caught by sunlight. A bread knife wielded, glistening, blood smeared along its sharp edge. I was frozen rigid, until I heard Jess, alongside me, let out a cry.

'Shit! Don't look.' I swung about to shield her from the scene. My first instinct was not my mother's wellbeing but to get Jess out of there. No one at school must know.

I shook her, pulling at her shoulders as though awakening her from a trance before she shot out of the door and threw up into a bed of full-headed blossoming daisies. My mother's pride and joy, those flowers were. I ran after Jess, trying to quieten her. I pulled at her cardigan. 'Don't say anything, for God's sake. Promise not to tell anyone. Promise!'

She nodded, globs of sick on her chin, shrugged herself free and beat a hasty retreat up the lane, tennis racquet in hand. I hung back, watching her disappear.

'Please don't say anything,' I yelled after her, but she didn't react. She wouldn't have heard me. She was well out of earshot.

I trudged back inside.

My mother was rinsing her hand under the cold tap, dabbing at it with a blood-stained tea towel, while my father was seated at the table, face buried in his hands. He was crying. Loud sobs. My handsome young dad, heaving with guilt and remorse. I didn't know how to handle this. I hated him for what he had done. I wanted to strike out and hit him, but I loved him too. Achingly so. It was a mess. Neither of them said a word. And neither did I.

Were they even aware that I was there, bleeding inside? Who knows? Our family life. I loved them both. It tore at my guts to see this unhappiness, this inability to resolve their differences. My dad wasn't a cruel man. He had a quick, sparky temper, but he was good and kind underneath, and my mum might have taunted him occasionally.

But sometimes I just wanted to run at him, grab him by the arms, anything to stop the violence. In earlier times I had attempted to intervene, but not any more. It seemed to exacerbate Dad's anger, Mum's secret weeping. 'I wish I was dead,' she said to me once, gulping the words with saliva bubbling out of her lips.

'Don't say that, Mum. Oh, God, please don't. What about me? What would I do if you were gone?'

'Oh, Grace . . .' She dragged her damp fingers across my tear-stained cheek.

More than anything in the world I wanted to protect my mum.

Would they eventually separate, leave one another in peace, stop tearing at each other, if they didn't have me to feed and attend to? Should I run away? Was that the best solution? Yes, I should. So many students were planning a pre-university trip. I should too, even if I was younger. Just go, Grace. Do it. Yet to vamoose felt like the worst act of abandonment.

Like someone craving water, I craved new beginnings. I craved the unfolding, the awakening of my self. The sloughing of my damaged shell. I watched the hippie revolution unfolding on the television in our sitting room.

I watched the 'boys', the American soldiers in Vietnam. I saw others burning their draft cards. I dreamed of adventure, of changing the world. Love, sex, rock and roll. *No more violence.* It was the age of Flower Power, of Jimi Hendrix and Janis Joplin. I leaned more towards heavier rock than the Beatles. It was the age of free love and hallucinogens, psychotropic drugs. None of which I had taken, of course. I was the proverbial virgin who had never puffed a cigarette, never got tiddly on anything more lethal than a half of cider. I was raw as a cabbage and 'green in judgement'. I was damaged, needy, ripe for exploits, hungry for adventure. Indiscriminate.

And so to Paris I set my modest compass.

A motherless child.

I took the night ferry train, from platform two at London's Victoria station to Dover Marine.

Freedom. Freedom.

I can still recall the salty pre-dawn stink of Calais. The acridity of diesel fumes, of congealing blood on gutted fish. The cry of invisible gulls. The air was chilly and damp, drizzling, and I was heavy-eyed, sluggish, after a truncated night. My spirits lifted when, shuffling along with a line of other passengers, I stepped aboard the waiting train, La Flèche d'Or, our Golden Arrow to Paris. My magic coach flew through the northern French dawn, rattling me to the capital. Then, hey presto, I was in Gay Paree. Liberated, unchained, ready for anything and everything, ready to change the world.

Change the world?

My boundaries and dreams knew no limits. Face turned upwards, looking outwards, oozing willingness and a fresh, earthy smile that – even though I say it myself – could light up a room.

Foolish girl.

I had eighty pounds in cash, earned from cleaning houses – vacuuming, scrubbing floors, changing beds – part-time jobs achieved in the evenings after school or Saturday mornings. My hard-earned banknotes were stuffed into the cups of my bra – forty in the left cup and forty in the right. Later, for comfort and a better silhouette, I wedged my stash beneath my clothes at the bottom of my rucksack. It was the largest sum of money I had ever been in possession of and I felt *rich*. And full-bosomed. The cash had to last me through to the autumn, to my return to London and to drama school.

I had visited Paris once before, with my mum and dad when I was eleven. Now, at the tender age of sixteen, on Friday, 5 April 1968, I stepped off the train at the Gare du Nord. It was nine in the morning. The station was bustling. My backpack was cutting into my shoulders. I needed to offload it. The banknotes in my bra were itching my boobs. I wandered aimlessly for a while, breathing in the ambience, quelling my excitement and a dollop of rising uncertainty. I had no bed booked for that first night or any beyond it. No place to stay.

My sights were set on the Left Bank. The Sorbonne University district in particular. I thought if I could touch base with students they would point me in the direction of a youth hostel. My French was passable. I had gained an A at O level and at home had devoured French literature. The classics. I was yet to become acquainted with Boris Vian, Simone de Beauvoir, Marguerite Duras, and their contemporaries. I was a fan of Jacques Prévert because I was already a passionate enthusiast of French cinema, *Les Enfants du paradis* was one of my favourites. More recently the *nouvelle vague,* Truffaut, *Les Quatre cents coups.* (Did I relate so viscerally to this film because in part it was a reprise of my own story?) *Jules et Jim*: I loved that picture best of all and had seen it three times. Jeanne Moreau. Those eyes, that smile. Such sexiness. I wanted to *be* Jeanne Moreau, to slide inside her skin. Or was it the role of Catherine I longed to embody? Catherine, who loved so freely, without guilt, without commitment. Loved two men at the same time. Wasn't such a female the embodiment of the sixties?

I paused to buy a map of the city. The station newsstand was decked out with copies of the latest French *Vogue*, the April issue, on its glossy front cover a leggy model wearing an apple-green tunic dress topped with a full-brimmed hat hung with pink tulips. It was gushy, unrealistic, and yet it was the incarnation of springtime. Or so it seemed to me on that introductory morning. Yes, this was Paris. My new life for the next few months.

I took the Métro, Line 4, from Gare du Nord to Odéon, on the Left Bank, and from there I began to walk eastwards along the boulevard Saint-Germain. Black tobacco smoke, drivers hooting impatiently, car fumes, dark brown dribbles of concentrated coffee from espresso machines releasing clouds of steam. I inhaled it all, every cliché, breathed it in in great gulps, as though my life depended on it. This was the beginning of living. My first tentative step into the vast undiscovered cathedral of my own existence.

I turned off Saint-Germain onto boulevard Saint-Michel and headed down a few narrow streets in the general direction of the Panthéon. It must have been raining earlier because the pavements were damp and the cloud cover was low and grey. I was wearing Levi Strauss jeans, blue suede hiking boots and a leather motorcycle jacket I had picked up from a second-hand stall at the Petticoat Lane market in the East End of London. I had dubbed it 'my *Rebel Without a Cause* look'. My auburn hair, coppery after a recent shampoo with henna, was hanging long and loose. I thought I was the epitome of *cool*. Françoise Hardy, watch out. In my rucksack were several mini skirts, skimpy tops and other feminine accessories. I was ready for every occasion, as I climbed towards the Sorbonne district. The heart of Paris's university life.

It was midday. Church bells began to peal, mingling with the less harmonious sounds of hooters, and a siren call. The summons to workers to down tools, and eat lunch. (You didn't hear that in Bromley!) Youngsters, three or four years my senior, were seated on the café terraces that lined the lanes, smoking, immersed in serious discussions, sipping shots of coffee. Several of the guys were sporting black-framed reading glasses that reminded me of Hank Marvin or the late great Buddy Holly. They were deeply engrossed in their newspapers. *Libération* seemed to be the popular choice.

Liberation.

Here and there, sheets and tablecloths had been hung from the façades of the old buildings. I thought it was laundry drying but they were scrawled with messages in bold black lettering: *NON à la bureaucratie* or *Presse libre*. I had no idea what they were about. I supposed it was to do with the anti-Vietnam marches taking place all over the world, but I wasn't clued up on any finer issues at that stage.

I met Peter Armstrong-Soames on that very first day. Talk about good fortune. I'd been wandering about for a couple of hours by the time I got into conversation with him. I was hungry, energy flagging, and asking myself rather too frequently where I was going to sleep. The intrepid girl abroad was languishing a little, sinking into uncertainty.

I sat myself down for a *grand crème*, a large frothy coffee with milk, at one of the many coffee bars to be found on every corner, and unfolded my map. With my index finger, I was tracing out that fifth arrondissement *quartier* when a soft voice broke my concentration: 'Are you lost?'

I had been vaguely aware that someone was at the next table, but I hadn't paid him any attention. In fact, I don't think I had even registered that my neighbour was male. I lifted my head and saw that he was staring at me. Intently. Quizzically. Smiling. Warmly. Good-looking.

He had spoken in English. It took me a moment to register this, and then it disappointed me.

'Lost? *Moi? Mais non, merci beaucoup.*'

If he had been French, I might have tried out my Jeanne Moreau flutter. He had remarkable eyes, more violet than blue. His black hair was cut short in a conventional style and he had rather perfect ears, which was not something I would normally notice – I don't have an ear fetish – but his ears were . . . well, perfect. Not too big and sitting neatly to his head.

'*Non, je ne suis pas* lost.' Best French accent accompanied by a carefree laugh. Nonchalant. I was not lost. I knew which street I was in. I was at a loose end, you might say.

'Well, you're studying a map, so I assumed . . . Can I help in some way? I know the city well.'

'I'm looking for a bed.'

His smile widened into a broad grin.

'No, no, *excusez-moi*, I mean . . .' My cheeks began to pink. Lobster, not the most flattering colour. I felt like a right fool. 'What I mean is, I'm searching for cheap digs.'

'There are several *pensions* in the vicinity. Finish your coffee, I'll show you the way. What's your name?' He threw coins on his table for both our orders and stood up, not waiting to learn my name or to allow me to finish my coffee. He was taller than I had expected, elegant, well-turned-out even in denims. Someone had ironed that shirt, and even his dungaree jacket was immaculate. Crisp. My mother would have described him as 'expensive-looking'.

'Let me take that.'

Without another word, he drew my rucksack from the chair opposite and hooked it over his shoulders. I hastily folded my map and stuck it into the back pocket of my jeans. He set off on the pavement beyond the boundary of the café and turned left. I followed a step or two behind, watching my belongings being borne along the street by a stranger. If he disappeared with everything I owned, I still had my savings. I had no idea where we were going but he seemed confident and kind, so I allowed myself to trust and be led.

He steered me through narrow, winding lanes to two

lodging houses, situated on opposite sides of the same street. Both landladies shook their heads. *Complet.*

The young *anglais* bowed his head, frowned and harrumphed. 'I felt sure one of the two would have a spare room.'

'Please don't worry,' I said. 'I'll find somewhere.' I was feeling awkward about putting him to any further inconvenience. 'Honestly, I'll sort it out. It's just a case of trial and error. I probably should have booked . . .'

Peter was not listening to me. He had turned on his heels and was descending the street, weaving his way in and out of the sauntering populace with the ease of one who was comfortable within his body and probably did lots of sport. 'There's a small hotel I know,' he called over his shoulder, 'not far from where my parents live. It's about a kilometre from here. It costs a few francs more . . .'

But when we arrived the establishment had the same notice hung in its window. *Complet.*

I glanced upwards. This place was definitely a cut above the other two. Its exterior was pretty, with bright red and pink geraniums in window boxes. 'I couldn't have afforded it in any case. Tight budget.' I shrugged, making light of my slender means. My hand was raised to offer my thanks. He was scrutinizing me again with those percipient eyes. His facial skin was soft, not many years advanced beyond the downy stage, surely tender to touch, yet there was muscle about him, strength and intelligence. On second observation, he was seriously dishy.

'You've been very kind. I . . .'

Somewhere, a church bell tolled. Twice. Two o'clock.

'It's getting late. Come on, I have another idea.'

'There's really no need . . .'

'Let's go.'

My companion was residing, he said, with his parents in the sixth arrondissement. It was a bit of a hike, beyond l'Odéon, turning at the famous theatre, south along rue de Vaugirard, right towards the church of Saint-Sulpice until our arrival, nudging rue de Rennes, at a Haussmann-style apartment building. Its austere entrance was exactly that: austere. Not even a caretaker. How come? Every French film located in Paris had a caretaker peering, scowling from within a cramped cubicle.

The lift, landings and corridors were spotlessly clean, maintained to a gleam, with sparkling railings and brass doorknobs. I knew right then that I was out of my class.

Peter pressed a finger to a bell on the third floor and slipped a key into the lock of a sturdy oak door. He encouraged me into the hall, which was impressive, daunting. At first glance I appraised it to be about the size of my bedroom in Kent. The open space, with its pristine white walls, spoke of silence, of absence, and smelt, discreetly, deliciously, of beeswax. There was no warmth, no clues to family intimacy or quotidian comings and goings; no wellingtons, overcoats, umbrellas, slippers, dog or cat baskets to make you feel real life was close at hand and you were welcome. I could have been entering a rather grand set of offices. My companion dropped his keys on a half-moon table set against the wall and called, 'Paola?'

A female voice trilled a lighthearted *Je suis dans la cuisine.*

'There won't be anyone else here for lunch. Father's at the embassy. You must be hungry. I am.'

I was stomach-growling ravenous, but I shook my head. 'Honestly, I'm fine, really. I should be thinking about . . .'

Peter slid my rucksack to the floor – 'That's damned heavy' – and took my hand. An unexpected familiarity. We still had not exchanged full names but I was enjoying the mystery of this escapade and his company, even if I had nowhere yet to sleep.

The kitchen was a bright, light space clouded by steam rising from boiling pots and with condensation running down the windows. Across a generous-sized rectangular wooden table was a petite woman, back to us, in a maid's uniform.

I had never before encountered a real person in a maid's uniform. Only in hotels and theatre farces.

'Paola,' announced my companion, '*nous allons crever de faim.*'

When she spun towards us from the sink and chopping boards, the maid was sticky with perspiration. She beamed at me, her brown eyes lined with heavy mascara, and gestured us to the table. Speaking with a thick Portuguese accent, she ordered Peter to lay cutlery and plates. Within moments, oval serving dishes were set before us. They were adorned with wafer-thin slices of *charcuterie* and slabs and pyramids of white and cream cheeses. A green salad was hastily thrown together, crisp and delicious, a half-bottle of red wine appeared, along with glasses, a baguette, and a chunk of pâté with a dish of cornichons alongside it.

'Help yourself.'

Peter poured the wine.

'Wow, this is groovy.'

That was the first meal I consumed with the man who

was eventually to become my husband. Oh, but that was so much later. A lifetime, much loss and sadness later.

'Paola, none of Mum and Pop's insufferable colleagues are staying in the spare rooms, are they?'

We were rounding off our delicious *déjeuner* with dollops of ice cream served in glass dishes.

Paola winked at my companion. 'Not even sufferable ones, Monsieur Peter. The blue and rose rooms are both available. Take your pick.'

'My father, with my mother as the loyal hostess at his side, is in the diplomatic service. A life replete with social activities and booze.' Peter had turned his attention to me. 'Since George resigned, we've been hosting one British emissary after another. Britain is still pandering to de Gaulle, angling to be accepted into the EEC. Brown favours Britain's entry, but not every other politician does.'

I nodded, dumbstruck, trying to get my head round the fact that Peter was referring to Britain's erstwhile foreign secretary, George Brown, and he had called him by his Christian name.

'Stay here with us, why don't you?'

'But what will your parents say?'

'They won't care. They possibly won't even notice. There are plenty of rooms. You can go for days without bumping into anyone, unless they're drunk, of course, and have passed out in the corridor.'

I tried not to be shocked. Not at what my new friend had confided but that he would openly admit to family shortcomings, while I had gone to such pains to bury our gremlins.

'We should ask your mother first, don't you think?'

'Is she here?'

Paola was now stacking the dirty dishes in a machine while a pot of coffee bubbled on the stove. This was the first dishwasher I had ever set eyes on.

She shook her head. 'An afternoon meeting at number sixty-five.'

'My mother's attending an AA meeting at the famous American church.'

Alcoholics Anonymous. I'd heard of it but had never met anyone who had actually signed up for its programme. 'Is she . . . ?'

'She attends, she declares, on behalf of Father and his cronies. It's nonsense, of course. Papa wouldn't be seen dead in such company. Paola, we'll take the rose room, if that's convenient. What do you say? I can introduce you to all my favourite haunts in Paris.' He turned to me with such a winning smile, I almost fell off the chair. 'Will you stay with us?'

I pondered the invitation for less than a second, then nodded shyly, murmuring my thanks to Paola, who strode off purposefully to prepare my room.

Why not, I said to myself, at least for one night until I'd found somewhere else? It would save me a few francs, but aside from that, Peter was great company and his family intrigued me. I was dying to clap eyes on his parents and, with luck, bump into someone famous in the bathroom – Harold Wilson in striped pyjamas or Edward Heath cleaning his teeth. I'd brag about it for ever.

I had a bed. I had a room, my own fabulously ornate suite with draped pale rose curtains and burgundy wallpaper, *and* I had my own bathroom. It was modest in size, but it was for my exclusive use. And it was in Paris. This exceeded my expectations by some distance.

The room looked out upon a courtyard cluttered with climbing plants. From there, voices rose and sang and belly-laughed. I stretched my arms wide, embracing my new life, even if it was only for the interim.

I pulled off my boots and socks and tossed them to the carpet, intending to take a shower in my very own bathroom. Anonymous me, suburban me, had made it to Paris and fallen firmly on her feet. I threw myself down onto the capacious bed, lifted my legs into the air and tugged off my jeans. This was happiness, this was freedom. This was me triggering my very own destiny. Later, I'd send a postcard home. *Dearest Mum and Dad, I'm here and safe. Please take care of yourselves. Be kind to one another. Love from your Grace in Paris. X*

The Present

Stormy weather

The weather had taken a turn for the worse. Overnight, or around dawn, about when I was finally drifting off to sleep, a storm began to blow in. Within no time it was hammering at the windows. Such a tempest was unexpected, certainly not forecast, and it was wild. It lashed against the panes, spilling and flooding in rivulets to the ground. At around seven thirty while Peter was still sleeping, I climbed out of bed. I was shattered after such a restless night. Before me was a gathered mass of iron-dark clouds, a sea that looked black as tar from lack of light, and a wind that was whipping and bullying the plants and the structure of this hillside house.

Such a force of wind occasionally brought trees down, closing off the road, impeding our passage out. Shutting us in. Locking out the world. Stranded. Victims of the storm.

I sat on the foot of our bed, staring out at the unheralded angry morning. The wind was lifting the sand in sideways drifts while the waves were exploding in highrises of white foam. It felt ominous, arriving after days and days of perfect calm and early-summer heat. I was still trying to rid myself of the ignominy I felt for my inefficient care of the grandchildren and the foolish hauntings that had kept me awake. My sleepless night had left me frazzled, edgy, riddled with irrational fears, spooked by memories from a past of so long ago, buried so deep. A past that Peter and I had, in a beforetime, agreed to lay to rest.

For how many years had I tried to convince myself that that night, that episode, had never happened? If you speak it frequently enough, or if you eschew mentioning it altogether, can you erase an act in actuality? Can you strike it out of existence?

The torrential storm meant the children were stuck in the house, curled up on the floor in their pyjamas playing Monopoly, flicking the TV from one channel to the next, ransacking the shelves for DVDs, drinking endless glasses of squash, eating every packet of biscuits I had stocked for them in the cupboards and, in the case of Jenny's girls, stringing beads that rolled and got crushed underfoot, leaving smithereens of glass to be brushed up. They were forever up and down the stairs and I feared they might disturb Peter. Marcus and Anna were on their iPads. Nobody could go to the beach – you'd be dragged out to sea by the waves – and by the middle of the afternoon, they were getting overexcited and quarrelsome.

Harry had shown no signs of damage from his fall, save for a few feathery scratches and two mighty bruises that were developing into advancing stains of deep red and purple, with a streak of spring green thrown in for good measure around his thighs, on his right buttock and one on his shoulder blade. He said they resembled tattoos and was mightily proud of them, hoping they'd stay.

His jaunty frame of mind did nothing to offset Sam's

brooding resentment towards me. I was attempting to deal with her hostility: I put it down to her concerns for her father's health because she and I had never shared a cross word before, not in twenty-five years. Ever since they were thirteen years old, Peter's girls had been in my life. Rarely had any antagonism passed between us. Once the fact that Peter and I were sharing our lives had been accepted, that he would no longer be living in their family home, we had found our way, had muddled forwards, building a new and different unit. They had spent fun weekends in my London duplex. Step-ma and Dad's girls. I felt now that I had badly disappointed her.

By the following morning we were out of milk and fresh bread. The biscuits, never usually in stock *chez nous*, were essential now to keep the imprisoned troops satisfied. Someone had to shop for them. Peter was upstairs, enclosed in his office at work on his manuscript and I didn't want to trouble him. I volunteered, glad to release myself for a short while from the vibes in the pent-up house, even though I was hesitant about driving in the storm and hoped the road would still be open, not closed by fallen vegetation.

When I struggled out of the kitchen door to take the car to Cassis, I was blown back by the force of the wind. It was operating like reverse suction. We hadn't seen such weather in a very long while and never to my knowledge during the late spring. The last time, two Februarys back, it had brought down several pine trees, sealing off our exit path, but that was winter. In May, and under the present circumstances, it felt like a curse.

I considered walking, but it was too far on such a day. I

would get soaked to the skin if I wasn't blown off the cliff. I splashed my way to Peter's car, battled with opening the door and slid myself into the dryness and calm of its interior. The engine started without a hitch and I rolled out of the carport in reverse gear, then inched my way forward with caution. If the wind proved too powerful, to hell with it, we'd manage without provisions.

'Let them eat brioche,' I said aloud, making a pathetic joke in an attempt to cheer myself up.

I moved up into second gear as I began the lane's ascent. The trees were whipping and dancing, like frenzied participants at a voodoo ritual. At lane's end I turned left, ascending towards the upper route, which linked with the higher summit road, the route des Crêtes. It was then that I caught sight of a dark shape, not a tree but a being, in the distance, planted at the intersection that took me right, onto the upper road towards La Ciotat, or left, to lead me to the village and, eventually, past Cassis, to the motorway for Marseille.

The figure, looked at from my lower perspective, loomed large as a giant. A forbidding menhir, a menacing silhouette in black. Static save for its clothes.

His outer garments were spinning about him in the rain and wind. Occasionally in summer, we might come across a party of hikers or, more rarely, a lone adventurer trekking along the coastline by one of these upper, more solitary, paths. But in this season and this weather, this individual was an implausible sight. Was he lost? Had his transport broken down? Had he been involved in an accident? I feared to continue but knew that I must. If someone needed assistance . . . I pressed my foot hard on the accelerator, forgetting my own circumspection, my apprehension about this outing, concerned for the stranger who must be in trouble. I flashed my headlights twice to alert him to my arrival.

If he saw me, he made no signal, offered no reaction. I was alongside him in two, maximum three minutes. As I drew close, I pressed the switch to partially lower my window, careful to protect myself against a sharp incursion of wind. 'Can I help you?' An intake of breath. I recognized him immediately, though sodden now and with whatever little hair he still owned hanging in darkened stripes across his face, partially obscuring his disfigured features.

'Hello again,' I began tentatively, regretting that I was there and that I'd stopped. 'Are you . . . ?' Lost, no. How could he be lost? He had been on the beach alongside ours only the day before yesterday. *Had he been here overnight? Was he illegally camping on the beach? Sleeping in a car?*

'Are you in need of help? It looks as though it might be my turn to return your good deed.' I was doing my best at normality.

He made no immediate answer.

I spoke a little louder against the force of the wind. 'Do you need a lift?'

'Which way are you going?'

'Only as far as Cassis. To the grocery. I could go to La Ciotat, if that is more convenient for you. Where's your car?' I glanced in both directions. Nothing but a dense flinty mist beyond windows bespattered with rain. No vehicle was visible. His outer clothing, his silky black raincoat, kicked and twisted about him, making a sound like rolls of thunder. His hands were deep in his pockets.

The salt rain against his misshapen features gave him a polished, tessellated look. Mesmerizing. His skin was mottled and pink, like a baby's. His lopsided eye had closed with the force of the rain. His other was almost bleached of colour, not transparent but cloudy, marbled. He really did have an otherworldly countenance, alabaster. Yes, like someone not quite of this life. He drew a hand from his pocket and scooped the water from his good eye, and I was suddenly rocked with fright.

No one rises from the dead. Not even him.

1968

Discovering Paris

After I'd taken my shower – lashings of hot water – and carefully secreted my eighty pounds of crumpled notes inside one of the crisp cotton pillowcases, Peter and I were back outside, him guiding me about the city while the day still offered light. The fresh spring air was perfumed with hyacinths, while chestnut and cherry trees unfolded into blossom. The sun had come out. The afternoon was sublime. I was in seventh heaven.

'What do you want to do next?'

'Anything. Walk, look, stroll, conquer the town. Be a part of it.'

We were at the highest lookout point of the Eiffel Tower. A must, Peter had said, for a first-timer. I was not a first-timer but, hey, what did it matter? I was here.

It was heady and lofty, of course, and made my brain swim. The view, and the amazing day I was having. The Seine, a khaki green reptile far beneath our feet. And the French voices on the streets, but not up here. Here there were tourists of every race and creed. When I turned my head Peter, behind me, was smiling right at me, his penetrating eyes speaking volumes. 'I think you're lovely and I'm so enjoying your company.'

His generosity, his evident pleasure, was infectious. It ignited laughter within me, and a newly discovered lightheartedness. 'Thanks for this.' I grinned back at him. 'For the bed and, you know, the guided tour and everything.'

'My pleasure.'

He was in love with me right from that first day, he claimed later. I was not ready, too damaged, to appreciate the depth of such emotion. My love came later.

When he thought I'd had my fill of Paris from the sky, he led me back down to earth. If it were possible on that first day to land back on earth. I was sky-high with joy, with my good fortune. Miss Serendipity. Not yet centre stage but skipping on from the wings like a can-can dancer making her debut, with lots of swirling skirts and petticoats. Trumpet fanfare.

We exchanged few words. I was full of 'gosh' and awe-struck grins, which seemed to be sufficient for my handsome escort.

'How about the Louvre? It'll still be open for a while. A quick glimpse of the *Mona Lisa*?'

'Not today,' I was smiling, 'not this afternoon. It's too late. It's past teatime.'

Teatime! What was I thinking? Gone was England, for the present at least. Gone was teatime. This was the glorious present, and soon it would be *l'heure de l'apéritif.*

'So, tell me about yourself.' His chin in the cup of his hand, elbow on the table, observing me. Had I even given him my full name by then? Should I make one up, befitting the role I was playing: the ever-so-modern miss? The embodiment of a liberated French mademoiselle.

Tous les garçons et les filles . . . I loved that LP. *Yé-yé* . . .

We were seated outside a café, the round tables barely bigger than dinner plates, pushed tight against one another. Behind us was sliding glass to the animated interior. Here, city fumes mixed with the intoxicating scent of new growth, spring-green leaves. Our shoulders were brushing against one another and I was silently wondering whether Peter was intending to make a pass at me later and, if so, would I let him? Would I offer up my virginity to the dashing young Englishman whose lips seemed pretty kissable at that moment? And then would I slip away, disappear somewhere in the city, back to the life of the poor girl, without having revealed to him my full name? Just like in a film.

Now, it was the hour of the *apéritif.*

Beyond the terrace where we were sitting, the streets were milling with people, mostly young, moving purposefully in many directions. Or dawdling, holding hands, pausing to embrace, to kiss – serious kissing in broad daylight – sharing secrets. In Bromley we called it 'snogging'. Such an ugly word. In Paris, it was definitely smooching, which was much sexier.

Was Peter also aware of the lovers?

A fleeting romance in Paris would be cool. Quite the thing.

'What would you like?'

'Sorry?'

He didn't wait for my response, as he hadn't waited to

learn my name. He ordered two *coupes*. Cups of champagne. His French was impeccable. His accent, almost without trace, was swoony sexy. The tall slender flutes were set down before us with a white porcelain dish of salted peanuts. I lifted up my first ever glass of champagne.

Bubbles effervesced into my nostrils. Oh, it was delicious, beyond sophisticated. My fingers wrapped about the chilled glass, imprinted the condensation.

'Welcome to Paris, Grace.'

I nodded, blushing, swept off my feet by a young Cary Grant.

The street smelt of evening, of sweet chestnuts coming into blossom. Of expensive perfumes, a cornucopia emanating from bodies pressed all about me. Of traffic fumes. Of Peter, who was so elegant and sophisticated. Totally out of my league, but I must be ready for everything. I wanted to *be*. This was the sixties – not simply the sixties but the Sixties. I was here for *all of it*. Before I returned home to start my drama-school training I needed to experience life, a skinful of *growing up*. Free love. Romance. Drugs. Psychedelia. LSD. Well, maybe not LSD. But then again, why not?

His voice broke into my reflections.

'Where are you from, Grace? England, yes, of course, I realize that, but whereabouts?'

Should I confide enough to keep his curiosity bated, spill the beans on my relatively humble upbringing? Three up, three down, and much strife. Not the ugly stuff, not that.

'My dad's a musician.'

'Really? Jazz?'

'Bass and guitar. Trad jazz. Has his own dance band.'

Out all hours. God knew with whom. Women. Obviously. Lipstick smudged against cotton sleeves – residue of carmine – and that cloying perfume on his evening shirt. Sugary. Cheap. 'Like the tarts he keeps company with,' my mother might have sniped, as she tossed his soiled laundry into the washing basket. She thought I didn't know. She tried to protect me.

'I should take you to some of my favourite jazz clubs. The city's full of them.'

My head was bowed, and I was staring at my fingers intertwined on the table. I didn't recount the horrors from home. I was not sharing any of my domestic ordeals with Peter. No way. I was there to forget my troubles, to re-invent myself.

'Hey, Grace, where are you from?'

'Kent,' I replied. 'And you?'

He frowned, but made no further comment on my straying thoughts. 'We've lived so rarely in the UK but when we did it was in Knightsbridge with my grandparents. Father's family. I was born there.'

'Knightsbridge. You mean near Harrods?'

He nodded.

Posh. Like the apartment where he lived in Paris. 'Resides', he'd said, not 'lives'. People like him reside. With a maid. I glanced about me at the bustling boulevards spreading outwards to form a star configuration. Gatherings of people smoking, heads close, engrossed in chatter. Queues across the street for the cinema.

'I wonder what's playing there? I love the cinema.'

Throughout my early adolescent years, I had wiled away whole afternoons and evenings at our local playhouse. The fleapit. Dreaming of my future on celluloid, all pearly white and gleaming. Minty teeth. No decay. Sequin frocks. Ginger Rogers. Satiny, like the imagined pumps on my delicate feet. Hollywood or Paris? I'll take Paris. Truffaut. Brigitte. BB, who studied dance. Ballet. My mum had nurtured grand notions of me becoming a ballerina. I was at ballet classes from the age of four. 'It teaches you poise,' she used to encourage me. I loved to dance and I wasn't bad at it.

The only place I had ever seen couples kissing like they do on the streets in Paris was in the cinema, in the dark, the back row. Snogging and fumbling. Not for me. My ambitions were classier.

Peter glanced across the street, following my eyeline. 'So you like the cinema, do you?' he asked me then. A new thought that might offer a clue to the identity of his rather reticent companion. I wondered if he picked girls up in cafés as routine. Did it matter? This was Paris, after all, and tomorrow I'd be gone, back to my own level, a cramped room in a grubby *pension* somewhere on the outskirts. And Peter would have forgotten me.

'I'm going to be an actress.' I grinned.

'You're pretty enough.'

My elation sank. I wanted to be scintillating in sexy tights and feather boas. Cinch-waist corsets. Drop-dead gorgeous.

'Very, very pretty.'

I wanted my smile to break hearts, for men to die from unrequited love. I lifted my glass and swigged back the remainder of my champagne. It sang as it zipped down my throat.

'You remind me of Anouk Aimée,' he whispered.

A Man and a Woman. I gasped, replaying the soundtrack in my head, the famous carousel tracking shot, almost choking on the swallowed champagne. Anouk Aimée, Jeanne Moreau, Françoise Hardy, Audrey Hepburn: I'd have settled for any of them. And stardom.

'Shall I order us another?'

'Ooh, yes, please.'

The Present

'Yes, I need a lift . . .' His response seemed to be addressed to the weather, not me. He wasn't looking at me. 'We can talk together.'

I was about to throw the car into reverse and allow it to roll back down the incline.

'Cassis suits me fine,' he replied; before he strode round the bonnet of the car and pulled hard to open the passenger door. As he climbed in, a host of ghosts, of wind-blown, messed-up phantoms, took their places in the vehicle alongside me.

He slammed the door and we sat a moment in silence, the engine purring. It was the only docile sound in a hostile late morning.

For a moment I was incapacitated, brain out of synch, couldn't think how to engage Peter's old banger into gear. My hands were trembling. I was numb. No, not numb. Overwhelmed by the amalgam of emotions this man's presence was provoking.

'Would you prefer I took the wheel?' he offered. His voice was unexpectedly soft. Tame, hypnotizing, the lilt of his northern accent apparent. The same almost indiscernible trace was still there after all these years.

How could this be?

For years I had pictured him decomposing at the

bottom of the sea. For years I'd remembered him, yearned to be perched alongside him again in his open-top Cadillac.

I shook my head.

Little doubt remained in my mind that I was in the presence of . . . my past.

What do you want? What are you doing here?

Have you risen up with this tempestuous weather, been disgorged by an angry unforgiving sea? Have you come in search of me? Been waiting for me? To punish and harm me?

A surfeit of questions surfaced within me. Perhaps uppermost now in my thoughts was: should I get out of the car, battle my way back to the house and fetch Peter? Peter, who is sick, whose heart is weakened and must not be shocked or strained. No, that was out of the question. Such a revelation, resurrection, could kill him, freeze his heart for ever.

Why did I fear this man so, perceive him as malevolent? Was it my own guilt?

If I handed over the wheel to him, where would he take me? Was I relinquishing control? To be kidnapped, murdered, driven and disposed of somewhere? Indubitably, I judged his presence as a threat. Why? Because I had walked away, turned my back on him? I had not saved him. I had done precious little to rescue him or save his life.

I took a deep breath, slung the gearstick into first and released the brake.

'Cassis then,' I mumbled, my voice rasping with terror.

Once on the upper road, where the wind seemed,

inexplicably, illogically, to be a little calmer, I pressed the first question. 'Are you . . . ?' I was unable to finish the sentence. I took a breath. 'We used to know someone who was called Pierre . . .'

An intake.

'We thought Pierre was . . . Are you Pierre?'

'Pierre? Fancy that.' The man at my side let out a guffaw, a bitter half-laugh. 'Yes, you could say that. Yes, I'm Pierre.' Soft and yet savage. 'I thought you'd've forgotten all about Pierre. Thought I might be obliged to jog your memory.'

I wrapped the palm of my hand tight over the gearstick. The sweat locked like glue.

'That little affair, thought it meant nothing to you. Given how your life's turned out. Famous and successful.'

'Pierre, list—'

'George,' he said flatly. 'It's easier if you call me George.'

'Sorry? So, you're not Pierre?'

For one insane, exhilarating moment, I believed him. I believed I had been mistaken. Mistaken identity. Lack of sleep, too many nightmares from the past that had resurfaced and squatted in my present, then the dread of losing Harry, or Peter, his ill-health, bleeding into my sanity.

'I made it up, spur of the moment.' He clicked his rain-wet thumb and finger.

'Made what up?'

'All those years ago. Told you I was Pierre. I am Pierre, yes, but my name's George Gissing.'

'You mean you gave me . . . Why would you have done that?'

He thought about this for a moment, then shrugged. 'We were in France. Pierre sounded more French than George.'

I let this change of his identity sink in. So, I hadn't been mistaken. Whatever his name, it was him, and he had returned. 'Pierre, very well. If you prefer, I will call you George.'

'Gissing.'

'I see.' How many times over those long ago summer months, with their false emblems of happiness, had I wondered about Pierre's surname, which I had never known?

'And I came to find you.'

'Me?'

'Yes, you, Grace. And him. You married him, right? That bloke you were with back then, right? I read about it, your wedding, in the newspapers. We got given newspapers, not every day but . . . I liked to catch up with the news. See the stars, the TV personalities, who was doing what. Kept me daydreaming. I saw your picture. I watched you on the telly from time to time, and then when you were in that series that was playing every week, I was glued to the screen. Couldn't take my eyes off you. Beautiful. Wanted to touch you, hankered to be close to you, feel your skin. You haven't changed that much. A few wrinkles, broader of beam but not that much. Still sexy. To touch you, feel your skin.' His voice was flat, unemotional, which made his words all the more unnerving as he stared straight ahead, out of the rain-splattered window, his hands inert in his damp lap. The wipers were slapping back and forth in a careless, messy fashion.

Dear God, what was he after?

The passion I had felt back then was long gone, irretrievable. Surely he didn't expect that we could pick up where we'd left off all those decades ago.

I felt the urge to pull over. To force him out of the car but . . . there were remnants from that summer. His voice, that accent. I had mourned this man's death, through lonely, aching years. Now I felt fear and a sense of dread.

'So, Pi– George, if you came to find me, is there something you want, something we' – I emphasised *we* – 'can help you with?' I had to keep a level head, a restrained demeanour.

'I'm the Revenant, right. George Gissing. That'll be a bit tricky for you, eh? Did you see that film, *The Revenant*? We watched films sometimes. There were occasional screenings. Once a week, actually, in the visitors' room. I didn't go every week but I enjoyed that one, *The Revenant*. It was one of the last I saw before they . . . That kid, Harry, he's your grandson, yes?'

'No, no, he's not my grandson.'

And if you hurt one hair on his head, I wanted to add, *I will kill you. Kill you, do you hear me?*

But this man, whom I had loved with a treacherous intensity, Pierre or George, was the man who had lifted my darling Harry to safety out of the rock crater. Why was I assuming he meant me or Harry harm?

Because he had come back to find me.

For what reason?

Because we had run out on him, left him for dead?

I pulled the car to the side and switched off the engine. Too shaken to continue onwards. This route, deserted today, was little better than a dust track cut through the bracken and brush, this 'upper road', as we had christened it, all the way back to Agnes's days. Even after all these years it had never been tarmacked and we preferred it so. It kept our corner of the world hidden, inaccessible, kept the prying eyes of tourists that bit further out of our precinct in summer. Encroaching strangers, like the person sitting alongside me in my car.

He, this man, reincarnated as George, was a stranger. Too many years had passed for it to be otherwise. Pierre, the young golden Adonis I had loved beyond reason, was gone. The drenched figure at my side was no longer the young man whose death I had mourned for more years than I cared to count. A man to whom I had so foolishly, recklessly, selfishly given myself. Before leaving him to his fate.

Hot tears were rolling down my cheeks. They seemed to burn a deep blue, like flames searing, scorching my flesh.

What sort of a life had he led? What had happened to his face? It was not young Pierre's, which had been unspeakably beautiful.

When had Pierre been transformed into this ugly creature, whose real name was George?

Wet through, like a soaked, abandoned cur out in the rain. His nails were chewed, I noticed now. No rings, no jewellery, a cheap watch with a frayed black strap. The long fine fingers that had so skilfully whittled a fishing rod had grown stubbier, bitten away. Nothing about him had flowered, had grown into the potential I would have wagered upon. The charisma that had caused me to sin. Was it a sin? Yes: the pain I had caused Peter was beyond cruel. But I had been a girl. Sixteen. Little more than a child.

The ignorance and callousness of youth.

'So, if you've come looking for me . . .' I coughed, clearing my throat, attempting to bring some resonance, steadiness to my voice. My trained vocal cords. 'Do you want something from me or . . .' I let out a laugh, a pathetic gurgling '. . . or is it . . . ?'

Did I dare ask him if it was money he was after? Hadn't he mentioned money out there on the rocks after he had pulled Harry to safety? He didn't give off an air of someone well-heeled.

'Retribution,' he replied, without hesitating. 'My just deserts. Poetic justice.'

'Sorry?'

'What is a life worth? Have you ever asked yourself the question? What – is – my – life – worth? What's to regret, what's left to live for?'

I shook my head. I was reaching back to a winter long buried while staring through teary pupils at my hands wringing in my lap.

'I have, Grace. I have spent a great deal of time cogitating – some might say too much time, day in, day out, but then I had time on my hands and to spare evaluating the question. The worth of my life. My life, a man's life. How many years are we talking about here? Fifty, give or take a few months. The pitiful sum of a grand a year equals fifty thousand. Ten grand for every twelve months? Half a million. You see, it soon tots up.'

'So, you're asking f–'

'However, Grace, there are other measures and those are not financial. The lack of children, for example.'

I let out a deep-rooted sigh.

He'd had no children.

He kept talking while I brushed away a tear from the tip of my nose.

'The opportunities snatched from a man, the chance of raising a family, having kids of one's own. A faithful partner, loving wife. A loving wife, Grace. Not some whore who couldn't give a shit. To have known love, real love, Grace. To have been loved, caressed, wanted. So, what would you say? One child, two? There are so many ways to balance the scales, you see. Do you see, Grace?'

Pierre's child.

He turned his head towards me. His eyes were glassy, his gaze zealous, almost delirious. 'Do you see where this is going?'

'The loss of children,' I repeated. Another tear rolled off my nose.

'You have none. I have none. But your husband there, posh Peter, he has two. Both girls, right? And they have — how many? — five between them?'

How had he acquired all this information? He appeared to know everything about our lives. This realization set alarm bells ringing. Was I being set up, taken for a fool?

Was this man George, who was claiming to be the love of my youth, merely a stalker, an imposter? Had he somehow dug into my past, found information that few, if anyone, could know and was now using it to threaten me? I was confused. And yet that voice, his accent, it resonated with so many distant memories. The shadow of a gesture flashed me back to those sweltering days, those lovesick nights. Even so . . . there was little else to persuade me that this was the same young man to whom I had given myself with such abandon. Whoever he was, whatever he wanted, I had to pull myself together. Drive him to Cassis, get him out of the car and, if necessary, register this with the police.

'Mr Gissing, you mentioned money. Or are you making some form of veiled threat against my – my husband's grandchildren?'

'Calculations,' he murmured. 'Suppositions. Let's suppose it had been me you'd married, let's just imagine you'd married a Gissing, me, and not the toff. How different our lives, mine, might have been.'

I closed my eyes, spooling back in time, picturing myself lying on the beach in the arms of the young Pierre. Striking, swashbuckling Pierre.

'Let's suppose there had been no jealousy, no violence and no attempted murder . . .'

'Murder? What are you saying . . . ?'

'Attempting to drown a man, leaving him for dead?'

'There was no attempted murder, George. We – we didn't leave anybody for dead. We searched for you!' There was rage, panic mounting in my voice. 'What nonsense are you concocting?'

'Drugged out of your pretty little brains. Wasn't that how it was, Grace? What do you know of the truth? Your posh husband could have told you anything and you'd have believed him. What can you remember? Quite a sensation, eh? Think of the headlines. The murky past of Grace Soames. That would put a dent in your squeaky clean image.'

So, I was in the presence of a blackmailer. And a liar. And possibly an imposter. But if he wasn't Pierre – Pierre risen from the dead – how could he be so intimate with my fragile memories?

'Just tell me what you want.'

'Grace Gissing. It has a ring to it, wouldn't you say? Those two Gs, they fit nicely together. They were made for one another. Like us.'

I leaned forward and started the engine, surreptitiously checking the time on my watch. Two twenty. The police station would be opening again shortly, after its closure for lunch. Or. Or. There was a point further along, this side of Cassis, where the road, this muddy lane, ran perilously close to a *falaise*, a sheer rock drop. It would take little more than the twist of my wrists to spin the small car in the merciless wind over the edge and plummet us both into the raging sea.

Back into the water whence this beast, this lunatic, had risen.

But I did neither.

1968

Paris

The next day dawned and I didn't move out of the Armstrong-Soameses' apartment. Instead, I was introduced to Peter's parents, who behaved as though they were rather grateful for my presence in as much as they displayed any interest in me at all.

'You're very welcome to stay with us unless you're a Red.'

'Sorry?'

'Your political affiliation?' His father, Sir Roderick, cross-examined me in the kitchen over a pot of tea after Peter had left for the Sorbonne. 'We hope you're not here as an accomplice, a stirrer?'

'I'm on holiday. I'm going to be an actress.'

'An actress – well, you're certainly pretty enough.'

'That's what Peter said.'

'My son has a good eye. Well, then, during your holiday, you can keep our young Peter occupied, away from politics and his foolish talk of revolution. Fill his head with sex. Tire him out.'

'Roddy. She's just a girl.'

Peter was studying political sciences at the Sorbonne. He was involved with 'certain groups' his father vociferously disapproved of, dismissing them as 'dangerous Reds', and one student leader, Daniel Cohn-Bendit, as 'an undesirable Jew', which sent Peter into a furious spin. With reason. Even so, Peter struck me as the most unlikely of 'Reds'. But what did I know?

Peter's activities left me with plenty of free time to do with as I pleased. By the time I woke, Peter had left for college. I bumped into his mother occasionally, a distant, preoccupied woman in a satin housecoat and high-heeled slippers with fur trimmings shaped like pom-poms. She had legs that went on for ever, like Cyd Charisse.

'Do you like dancing?' I asked her.

She gazed at me as though she had never set eyes on me before. She smoked incessantly, drank endless cups of black coffee and seldom uttered a word. Each time I pottered into the kitchen, her head would turn in surprise and she'd look me up and down as though she knew she had met me somewhere before but couldn't quite recall where. 'Peter's little friend?' She was confirming the fact to herself.

I'd nod and turn tail. I had no desire to be rude. I felt sorry for her. Once she mentioned in passing that she attended her A A meetings to have somewhere to go, to pass her afternoons with people she could converse with, who didn't harp on incessantly about the state of the world and 'British bloody politics' in particular.

'I don't mind listening to their tales of woe,' she'd mutter, between long drags on her cigarette – she frequently had two on the go at once, one locked between her nicotine-stained fingers, the other smoking in an ashtray somewhere. If I was in the apartment in the early evening, having returned from an afternoon at the cinema, I would sometimes run into her in the kitchen. Still wearing her coat, she was home from her AA meeting. Head in the fridge, scrabbling for ice cubes, scooping them up with her manicured fingernails, to chill the large gin and tonic she had poured for herself.

She never remembered my name. I sometimes asked myself whether she could even recall her own.

Peter's father was a different kettle of fish altogether. Unlike his wife, he was sharp of mind. He missed nothing, was keen to hear what was going on, as though his diplomatic role was to sound out the points of view of Youth versus State. I could handle the questions, but not the other thing. He was lecherous. If I changed my perfume, he commented on it. No one else noticed. He negotiated me into darkened corners, private moments between the pair of us, engaging me in some trumped-up debate about the state of affairs in France and what I, as a young student, might have gleaned or overheard. All the while, he was leaning over me, never quite touching me, except with his hot breath on my neck. Yet I always felt when we separated as though he had spread his hands all over me, coating me in an invisible webbing of sordidness.

'Trust our young Peter to have unearthed a gem like you. How old are you? Stay as long as you like. And if you're at a loose end for lunch, pop into the embassy and ask them to buzz me . . .'

It goes without saying that I never did. And I never mentioned these rather unsavoury exchanges to Peter.

Saturday, 6 April 1968

MARTIN LUTHER KING KILLED BY
SNIPER'S BULLET

While we were out strolling by the Seine, Peter's attention was drawn to these headlines. He hurried to a kiosk and bought a copy of *Le Monde*, which we took to a café.

'"On the evening of 4 April at a hotel in Memphis . . ."' Peter read the news aloud. '". . . The evolution of the situation in Vietnam has been eclipsed by the murder, on Thursday evening, of the pastor Martin Luther King, killed by a single bullet to the head. Race riots have broken out in several American towns. The President, Lyndon Johnson, has postponed his trip to Honolulu for an indefinite period. America is shocked and sad."'

Peter placed the paper silently on the table.

My eyes welled with tears. I wasn't as *au fait* with politics as Peter, but I certainly knew that King was one of the good guys.

9 April

Sir Roderick and Peter's mum were glued to the evening news when I arrived back on the evening of 9 April. The TV channel was transmitting the funeral of Martin Luther King. I would have liked to watch it, but felt awkward.

'Where's Peter?'

I shook my head.

'Come in, sit down.' I shuffled into the living room, hovered uncertainly. Sir Roderick was patting the sofa cushion alongside him.

'Has my son mentioned anything to you about Daniel Cohn-Bendit, an anarchist currently residing in Paris?'

'Nope,' I replied, and made a dash for my room. I hated the way he tried to coerce me into telling tales. I knew nothing about the anarchist, but even if I had, I wouldn't have spilled the beans.

I had bought a beret that afternoon and wanted to try it on. It looked groovy, I decided. I bunched up my hair and stood gazing at myself in the mirror. Bonnie Parker. Maybe I could be a sixties Bonnie Parker, though I wasn't willowy like Faye Dunaway.

Peter's parents were more screwed-up than mine. Maybe I should think about moving on.

12 April

Peter and I attended a solidarity demonstration in support of a German student, Rudi Dutschke, otherwise known as Red Rudi, who had been shot in the head by an anti-Communist, Josef Bachmann, in Germany. I wore my new black beret. Afterwards, I accompanied Peter and a group of fellow students to a bar that, late in the evenings, was transformed into a really lively club, Chez George, 11 rue des Canettes, on the Left Bank. This was the first time Peter had introduced me to any of his friends. We drank ice-cold beers, and everyone was smoking heavily, except Peter and me. I think we were the only two people in the entire city who didn't smoke. Peter talked lucidly about politics, the state of the world and what could feasibly be achieved. His friends listened to his words with respect. They seemed to hold him in such high regard. I was also surprised but rather chuffed that several of them assumed we were a couple.

They discussed the philosopher Herbert Marcuse and Daniel Cohn-Bendit. Lionel, one of the students, told the table that Cohn-Bendit had been ordered to Paris from Nanterre University to appear before a disciplinary committee. He referred to Cohn-Bendit as Dany and it dawned on me then that this was the 'anarchist' Peter's father had quizzed me about. None of the others had heard this news, except Peter, who seemed to have a keen antenna for the arc of events unfolding and the as-yet-unpainted political landscape.

'The sixth of May,' he confirmed. 'We ought to be there to protest against the hearing, to show our support for him and his colleagues.'

And I, along with everyone else, raised a hand. Comrades together.

That spring, I spent most of my days mooching about on the Left Bank, walking miles, gazing into shop windows – sexy lingerie way beyond my budget – munching on *jambon* baguette sandwiches in the Luxembourg Park. I tried to keep out of the apartment when Peter wasn't there. His father was getting too amorous. He'd tried to kiss me in the doorway to my room. Seriously creepy.

It was the evenings I looked forward to most, discovering new places with Peter. Our outings were almost always spent engaged in political debate, and I was beginning to take an interest, especially as his father was asking me questions about so many people I had never heard of.

The mood most evenings was optimistic, sometimes volcanic, and I was rubbing shoulders with their fire, their determination to finish off de Gaulle and herald a new order. I couldn't deny that their passion was electrifying, their ambition daunting: to bring down the system. But I was on the outside looking in, not actually participating.

If I got bored of all the theoretical speeches or I couldn't follow or understand what was being discussed, I wandered over to the lovely old jukebox that glowed in the corner of the bar we frequented, slipped in a centime or two and danced dreamily by myself. Occasionally a guy – no one from 'our' group – would saunter over and offer to buy me a beer. I always declined. I had the feeling that Peter, no matter his commitment to his cause, was observing me. His focus was partially tuned to my whereabouts and what I was up to. I thrilled to his attention. I really liked him, but that was as far as it had gone. We were just pals.

One evening, after the gathering of comrades had broken up, Peter and I left the bar in the rue Saint-André-des-Arts, and strolled along boulevard Saint-Michel hand in hand. It was a perfect spring evening. I was beginning to feel very French and was fired with the optimism that had imbued the evening. I so hoped Peter was feeling that passion, too, and that he would pause, lean me against one of the statues in the place Saint-Michel – the black dragon spouting water, for example – and kiss me. One of those lingering French kisses that make you weak at the knees. But he didn't. He never did.

That night I lay in bed, disappointed. I wanted more.

Peter cared for me, made me laugh, caused me to think deeply about the world, and he watched over me like the best brother but, I deduced, he didn't fancy me. His world was taken up with politics, change, revolution.

There were lighter moments. My friend seemed to be acquainted with every single club on the Left Bank. The best places to start the evening, the late-night spots for music, for dancing, socializing, bebopping. To my surprise, I discovered that Peter was an excellent dancer, very agile.

Right up until his present heart condition, Peter has always loved to dance.

Most of those candlelit evenings in Paris, '68, were taken up with endless discussions over countless bottles of wine. While we talked, protests were erupting both in and beyond the capital. They had been breaking out, in minor ways, since January, Peter told me. Petty outbursts, minor groups at first, but the fire was being stoked. The common spirit was swelling with dreams of rebellion. Even I picked up on the outrage aimed at the establishment. It radiated outwards from every club and coffee bar we visited. Topple de Gaulle, bring down the government, change the education system: these were the objectives. Limitless possibilities for everyone, no matter their class: these were the dreams of the young in '68.

And we were young.

La Révolution arrive.

Such slogans daubed across doorways and walls brought an embittered smile to the face of Peter's father.

'"The revolution is coming"? Over my dead body,'

he'd scoff at his son. 'In my day you obeyed your parents. Listened to their wisdom. You young think you know everything but you know nothing, except how to make a noise. Riots! If this is what paying for a private education and a top-notch university delivers, I would have done better to send you out to work. You'll be joining the long-hairs and peaceniks next, participating at sit-ins. Cowards, the lot of you. It will all come to nothing.'

When Peter ignored him, his father turned to me. 'Did my son tell you that he was on the anti-war march on Valentine's Day, marching against the Vietnam War? When I was his age, I spent Valentine's Day trying to get my leg over.'

I stormed out of the room. Foul man.

It was time to do my own thing, maybe move out.

The third of May was a cold, blustery day. Students were gathering in the front square outside the main building of the Sorbonne. There was a mood of solemnity in the air. We were there to protest against the previous day's lock-out at the Sorbonne's sister university in the Paris suburb of Nanterre, and now closed for an indefinite period. Peter had invited me along.

At the outset, the students numbered about three hundred. They were calling for changes to what they described as an 'outmoded education system'. The majority were undergraduates from Nanterre, and activist colleagues of Cohn-Bendit. As the day wore on, the crowd began to swell. People were calling, jeering, but it was harmless. There was no violence. In spite of this, and for no apparent reason, the rector of the Sorbonne or one of his associates called in the police. They pulled up in vans and began to surround the university buildings. The atmosphere changed instantly to threatening, scary, confrontational. Peter and his comrades remained calm so I kept my fears to myself. I closed my eyes. No violence, I prayed. I stepped tight to Peter, who was deep in conversation with a couple of bearded guys I hadn't seen before.

By four in the afternoon, the college was ringed by police and CRS officers, the French riot brigade. There was the odd skirmish when a student shouted at them, '*Foutez le camp*! Get lost!' but little other trouble. Even so, the police began to arrest people for no reason, or for stupid trumped-up stuff. I watched as perfectly affable demonstrators were taken away. Understandably, this provoked outrage.

'Are the *flics*, the police, trying to create a situation?' I asked. I was amazed. Everyone had been cool, peaceful. The university was against its own scholars, and was inciting anger, anarchy. The mood of the day had shifted to Us and Them. The undergraduates were being warned that to protest was unacceptable. As word of this spread, others – students, young people, intellectuals, ordinary Parisians – began to pour in from all over the city, offering support to the demonstrators.

Eventually – inevitable by then – pockets of fighting broke out, and the Sorbonne rector declared the university closed. The doors were bolted. Just like that. No one could gain access.

Had that been the intention from the outset?

'Hey, my research material's inside.'

'My books.'

'We have rights!'

'You have no charter to bar us from our college.'

Raised voices. Raised fists. A few were determined to gain entry, but as soon as they took a step, the riot police closed in. Up to a point, their presence quelled the brewing animosity. No one wanted trouble. Still, many, Peter included, were now unable to access their belongings: their lockers with files, clothes, study material.

'This is only the second time in seven hundred years the Sorbonne has shut up shop,' Peter informed me. 'The other occasion was in 1940 when the Nazis took control of Paris. So, you can see, it's pretty serious.'

As an immediate response to the closure of their seat of learning, l'Union Nationale des Étudiants called a strike, effective forthwith. They issued the following demands:

Reopen the Sorbonne
Withdraw the police
Release those arrested

The gap between college officials and students was widening as discontent spread. The mood was inflammatory. The immediate consequence was for certain political bodies to take advantage, to incite further unrest, playing on the situation to bolster their own ideologies, or so argued Peter. The entire city was now engaged on one side or the other. Me, too. I was with Peter.

The moment we walked into the hallway at the Armstrong-Soameses' residence, a row broke out between Peter and his father. The upshot was that Peter was forbidden to attend any more rallies. Worse, his father threatened to lock him in his room if he disobeyed orders one more time.

That was seriously outrageous.

Peter, understandably, hit the roof. He was twenty. Perhaps in legal terms not yet an adult, but still far too old to be told what to think or do.

I slid off to my quarters. I wanted no part of the row. I overheard my name being bandied back and forth. Peter was defending me against I knew not what accusations. I stayed where I was while his father yelled at him, 'Pack your bags, and take your sweetheart with you.'

This was followed by the slamming of doors, another round of verbal abuse, incoherent words. I couldn't follow most of it.

I remained in my room.

One of the reasons I had left England was to escape family disputes and I didn't want to become embroiled in this one. No matter my affection for Peter.

I was beginning to think that soon it would be time to quit Paris, to head south, although I had no specific destination in mind. The climate in the city was nerve-racking. People in shops were edgy. Peter's friends were tense, smoking heavily. It could explode at any moment. On the other hand, the idealism was infectious. It swept you along, and part of me wanted to stay, to witness history, to play my part in what was beginning to feel like something truly momentous.

There was energy, resistance, a sense that the cauldron would soon boil over. Everybody was as mad as hell about the closure of the Sorbonne. People, not only the students but the majority of citizens, were waiting to know what would happen next. What position de Gaulle would take.

I craved new experiences and I longed to be included.

However, the current situation made me feel very uncomfortable. I abhorred violence. But I also abhorred injustice and I had witnessed examples of it during the rally outside the Sorbonne, so my emotions on whether to stay or leave were seesawing back and forth.

I was stuffing my belongings into my rucksack when I heard a soft knock on the door. I hesitated. I was in my nightdress. I opened the door a crack. I had taken to turning the key whenever I was in the room to protect myself against Peter's father.

It was Peter. I let out a deep sigh.

'You look awful,' I whispered. He was pale, eyes red-rimmed. For a moment I thought he'd been crying, or possibly drinking.

'May I come in?'

I nodded and opened the door, checking as I did that his parents weren't spying on us. Peter had never entered my room before. He slipped in, secured the lock and made his way to the desk at the window where my diary was open with a pen placed on the page of today's date, 4 May 1968.

He glanced at it without registering it, peered out into the courtyard and swung back towards me. It was then he noticed my clothes piled on the bed and my rucksack on the floor at the foot. He frowned. 'What are you doing?'

I shrugged guiltily. A part of me felt as though I was deserting my friend, making a run for it to save my own skin, skipping off, like I'd done from home. Leaving my mum . . . 'I think I should be on the road.' My tone was apologetic.

'At this groundbreaking moment?'

'I'd always intended to spend the summer in the south, get some sun, get fit before I start college. We never discussed it, and well . . .' Peter was staring at me with an expression of incredulity as though I had lost my marbles.

I babbled till I ran out of steam.

He crossed from the window, lifted his hands and settled them firmly on my shoulders. 'There's no reason for you to leave. Please. I'm sorry you had to hear such an ugly exchange. He's a pig. Narrow-minded, anti-Semitic, and beyond conservative. And, what's worse, he wants to cast me in the same mould. I hope you understand?'

'Of course I understand, but . . .' But this was not my fight. I didn't want to get further implicated. Yet these people, this upper class, out-of-my-league family, had welcomed me into their home, given me a bed and a jolly comfortable one at that.

'Please don't leave. Fight at my side. I need you. We're changing the world, Grace.'

I was speechless. I stared at Peter gormlessly. He was asking me to fight at his side. Suddenly this was real. The revolution wasn't just something people were debating in coffee bars.

Obviously, like everyone else with half a brain, I wanted the US to get out of Vietnam and was willing to demonstrate for it, and I hated to see people working for next to nothing and all of that, but I was sixteen. I was there for my own experiences. Selfish? Yes, totally selfish. Aren't we all at sixteen? I wanted to change the world, like most of my generation. The idealism was thrilling, infectious, potent as any drug, but was I prepared to engage in the violence it seemed to be demanding?

Make love not war. That was my motto, even if I was still a virgin.

Peter was watching me intently, his eyes moving from side to side, his frown set like tram lines on his forehead. He looked puzzled. 'What are you thinking?'

'It's better I go. Honestly, I'm a bit –'

'What?'

'Out of my depth.'

'We'll leave together. How about that?'

'Don't be daft! You can't do that. This is your dream.'

'Where do you want to go to? That's what I came in here to tell you – we're staying with Pascal tonight.'

'Who's Pascal?'

'You've met him several times, a friend, fellow student. We spent an evening at Aux Trois Mailletz, remember?'

I nodded.

'I'm not sleeping one more night under the same roof as my father.'

'Okay, I'll leave with you and . . . I'll find a hotel for tonight and tomorrow I'll hit the road.'

His body tensed. His face was earnest and pained. I couldn't bear to spurn him, if that was what I was about to do.

'You're going south?'

I nodded.

'My aunt Agnes – she's an artist and absolutely nothing like my father. In fact, it's hard to believe they're brother and sister. She has a house on the coast close to Marseille. I'll telephone her. What do you say? It stands on a cliff overlooking the Mediterranean. You'll love it. Tonight we'll get out of here, and at the end of the month, we'll go south together.'

I didn't need a house. I wanted to be free, to be my own person again. I had allowed myself to be swallowed into a world not of my own making. 'It's a terrific offer, Peter, but . . .'

'But?'

'I think I should be making tracks. We'll stay in touch, of course we will, and I'm immensely grateful for everything you've offered me. You've been the best pal and your parents have been so generous. Even your dad –'

The rest of my sentence was lost as Peter pulled me clumsily, rather more roughly than I was prepared for, into his arms. I was taken aback. This was the first real physical overture he had made towards me, aside from holding hands. I had taken it for granted that he had filed me in the box that said 'friend', 'comrade', that he was not attracted to me in any sexual way, and that had been fine because I had no idea what I felt about him, besides really liking him, caring for him, looking forward to our evenings together and respecting him as a person. Although I was dead keen to lose my virginity, we had been so busy discovering Paris together and the worlds of jazz, student revolution, political thinking and all the rest that I had put the sex bit to the back of my mind. Well, not quite. We'd been having a tremendous time. Now, he was holding me so tight I thought I would suffocate.

'Peter, you're hur–'

My arms hung loosely at my sides. I could smell the sweetness of his sweat, his body odour heightened after the arguments and high emotional tension. It wasn't unpleasant. On the contrary. His skin, the skin of his neck, which was pressed against my lips as he held onto me in his bear-hug, was smooth. His shirt rubbed against me, my upper arms, which were bare because my night-dress was sleeveless, and it was possibly see-through. From where he had been positioned at the window look-ing across to me standing by the bed with the light on just behind me had, no doubt, illuminated my flimsy clothing. The shape of my naked silhouette beneath my nightdress must have been revealed. Tits, nipples, the auburn trian-gular shadow of pubic hair.

He bent his knees, dropping in height, and his right hand slipped up under my gown. I gasped. A tingling in my down-there privates followed. The sensation was more galvanizing than I would have expected. I let out a cry. My reaction encouraged him. He nudged the right side of my clothing higher, to waist level, baring my inti-mate self. His hand slid upwards to my thigh, my buttock and across to the lower part of my abdomen, just above my pubic hair. So many physical sensations within me seemed to have been activated, as though a light show had been switched on and it was going bonkers all at once. I felt juice between my legs. Mine. Peter gently negotiated my body so that the backs of my knees were pressed against the bed and slowly he tilted me backwards, fold-ing me down upon the mattress. I was now lying rather uncomfortably at an angle on top of the layers of clothes I had stacked there earlier. The studs on my leather jacket dug into my shoulder. My legs were spread loose. I had slid them apart as he fiddled urgently with his belt and flung it to the carpet. I watched, mesmerized by the peeling of clothes and the revelation of his body, which was muscular and a little more downy than I had envisaged when I had imagined him in the buff, which I had. Often.

His body was beautiful. Well crafted, like a Rodin sculpture. His erection impressive, daunting – would it fit? – as he stood over me, touching himself, enjoying the moment before bending forward to enter me. A quandary grabbed hold of me. Protocol. Was it my duty to let him know I was a virgin? Clearly, he wasn't. Was there an etiquette to this? Like the correct knife and fork to use for the appropriate dish. I shouldn't be thinking about table manners now. Not during sex.

I wished I was someone else, someone with skills and sophistication. Jeanne Moreau.

'W-wait a minute,' I stammered.

Peter paused for the briefest of seconds, then lowered himself onto me gently. I felt the power of him, of his nudging genitals.

He began to push himself, the tip of his penis like a big blind worm, against me and inside me. It pierced, stung, seemed to tear me. I felt as though I was all stitched up and it took him several attempts to gain any access.

'I haven't done this before,' I confessed. 'I'm a b-bit scared.'

'Don't be. I won't hurt you.'

'But you are,' I nearly screamed at one point, until he rested his fingers over my mouth.

'Let's not excite my father.' He chuckled in my ear. And then he was inside me – it had happened. It was all at once easier, slippery, lacking in resistance, and he was beginning to ride me. I closed my eyes and, once the stinging pain had subsided, I tried to relax my muscles, dissolve the anxiety and fear and surrender to the experience, make the most of it. It was my first time. This was it, I was having sex, and it would never, ever, be my first time again. I should give myself over to the pleasures of it, yes, because it would be an occasion that one day I was sure to look back on, confide to others. The loss of my virginity. One of those 'How did you lose yours?' conversations.

Peter began to moan in my ear. His body was trembling, almost shivering. He was coming. At the very last moment he pulled himself out of me. I opened my eyes and there he was on his knees over me. His penis, moistened, dripping, was beginning to deflate.

He lowered himself onto the bed alongside me and drew me into his arms, beaming, wrapping a leg over my sticky stomach. I smelt different, of him, his seed, like newly mown grass or freshly crushed almonds.

'Wait till the end of the month,' he whispered. 'We'll have won our revolution by then, and we'll leave together, you and I. We'll make our way south to Agnes's. She'll be delighted. I can't wait to introduce you to her and Heron Heights. Stay with me. We'll do this together. I want you with me.'

I was committed.

The Present

With Gissing at my side, I drove in terse silence. I refused to engage further in any form of discussion with him. He offered a few sentences but I remained tight-lipped, obdurate. I couldn't stomach the realization that 'Pierre' had transformed into this 'George'. It was not his physical appearance, although that was sufficiently shocking, but his bitterness. The sordid calculations. The cloaked threats. The wretchedness of him.

I deposited him in the main square in Cassis close to the quay, which was, understandably, eerily deserted, given the weather. His parting words were, 'I'll be in contact with you again soon and I expect you to give me your time. No arguments. We have matters to discuss, to finalize. You know that, don't you, Grace?'

I made no response, turning away from him standing there, coat flapping, sopping wet, at the half-open door.

'I won't let you off the hook, Grace. Not now I've come this far.'

Without looking back, I scudded off, taking myself to the small grocery store on the opposite, north-facing, corner. Here I parked directly outside and hurried through the door clutching my purse.

I had offered to drop him wherever he was staying but he had sidestepped any answer, clearly not happy to reveal to me his holiday address. Holiday? I wondered how long he had been in the small fishing town, if this was indeed where he was lodged. It was not yet full season, way off by a couple of months, so strangers are more noticeable among the rest of us regular inhabitants. I recalled then the man I'd seen several days earlier when I'd been sitting in the sunshine at a café and Peter had telephoned to let me know the girls were arriving sooner than had been planned. Of course. That was where I had seen Gissing before. George Gissing. Was that all there was about him that had seemed familiar? A man passing by me in the street? Was I being hoodwinked into ...? And yet his velvet voice, his Yorkshire accent, certain gestures, his knowledge of my, our, secret past. It had to be him. But I couldn't bear to equate him with the lover of my younger days. It was heart-breaking to accept that this was the same human being.

He might have been better off dead.

Had George been watching me, following and scrutinizing us, our lives, movements, for some time now, or had he recently arrived? How structured was his plot, his scheme? What 'deserts' was he after? Should I go to the police? Should I have delivered him to them now? But on what grounds could I report him? For menacing me, veiled threats of blackmail – my word against his – for lifting my grandson to safety when he had fallen?

I was shaking, distracted, as I grabbed a loaf off the shelves, a baguette wrapped in plastic, which Peter and I had agreed not to buy any more – no more plastic – but that afternoon I couldn't face making a stop at the *boulangerie* as well as the grocery. I wanted to get back on the road and to the sanctuary of home, behind locked doors as quickly as possible. I craved the love and physical presence of my sane, well-balanced husband.

Was I intending to impart to Peter the reappearance of this visitor? What would I say? A man, a ghost from our past, has walked back into our lives? Such improbable information and the worry it could cause might kick-start a malfunctioning, an acceleration of the rhythms of Peter's heart, which was precisely what we were working to protect him against. On the other hand, if George Gissing turned up at our villa, rang the bell, forced an entry when I was out or down at the beach, swimming, and Peter answered, or one of his daughters . . . Such a scenario did not bear contemplation.

How, in Heaven's name, could 'Pierre' have survived? And why had he waited so long to make contact? Had something triggered his emergence now? No, no, Gissing's claim was implausible.

I was arguing in circles with myself until, with one swipe of my baguette, I clumsily knocked the entire load of stacked bread sticks to the floor. The units tumbled and rolled as I bent low to pick up the first. The young store owner, Ali, ran to my assistance.

'Please don't worry about them, Madame Soames.' He was kneeling at my side. 'I will gather them up in a jiffy. I stacked them in a hurry. My fault.'

His grace as always was endearing.

'I'm having a bungling day,' I fretted, trying to make light of my clumsiness. 'It's this damn wind, makes me a little edgy. I'm so sorry. If any are damaged, I'll take them, or pay for them at least.'

'No damage. Yes, this wind is fierce, fiercer than usual,

I agree. Level seven, the newscaster announced. It does jangle the nerves, doesn't it? You know, here in Provence, in the past when these winds gathered such force, it was when married people murdered their spouses and they did not have to face prison sentences because the wind was given as an extenuating circumstance.'

I laughed.

Outside, a metal sign advertising Magnum chocolate lollies, swinging on its pedestal, took off and was whipped across the square, bouncing, bumping its way noisily and clumsily along the cobbles towards the water's edge. A grocer ran, arms open wide, to save it. An elderly lady with a small dog, a frantically barking spaniel, was turning in circles, trying to redirect herself.

'Look at the force of that,' I remarked, as I emptied my purse in search of small coins.

'Will you be safe to drive back? Crossing over the hill in this wind is more than dangerous, in my opinion.'

I was silently wondering the same, but I had no desire to hang around the little town today.

'It's due to calm – according to the Météo man on this morning's breakfast television – soon after lunch. You'd be better to sit in a café and wait it out for a short while. I could telephone Monsieur Soames for you if you don't have your mobile with you. Forewarn him that you won't be back till it calms down a bit.'

Stay with me for a while, Gissing had asked, while I was driving the car over here, gripping tightly to the steering wheel, overcoming my desire to plunge us both over the cliff-side into the sea.

Keep me company.

It was impossible to explain even to myself, to comprehend, why dying, a self-induced end, with Gissing seemed to be the least complicated option. For how many years had I wished 'Pierre' hadn't drowned? Now I wanted nothing more than to thrust his ghost back to the bottom of the sea.

But surely to God this man was not Pierre. How could he have survived? It was a fact that no trace of his body had ever been recovered. If I went to the police station in town, would they have retained the records? Or was it all too long ago?

'Madame?'

I spun back to the till to where gaunt-faced Ali with his tobacco-grilled voice was calling to me. 'Sorry, Ali, yes?'

'You have forgotten your shopping.' He was holding a white plastic bag between two fingers, swinging it lightly back and forth. 'You see how this wind affects the mind. We are not responsible for our actions when the mistral takes hold. Shall I telephone your husband for you?'

'Please don't worry, Ali, I can do it, but thank you for the offer and your concern.'

I sat alone in the Café du Port for almost an hour, biding my time. It was currently occupied by four people, including myself, aside from the proprietor-barman, Thierry. The trio of male customers was hunched over the bar, *le zinc*, downing shots of cognac. I recognized the face of one, and could tell from their weathered skin and features that they were all local fishermen. They must have returned to shore at some point in the middle of the night if they had wished to avoid being caught out at sea in this foul weather. I hoped for their sakes none of their comrades were still out there. I was at a table by the window, looking out at the bleak wet afternoon. In my haste to pick up the shopping and return home, I hadn't paid attention to the direction Gissing had taken when he had stepped out of the car.

The wind was lessening, as Ali had predicted. The force of the storm was abating. I closed my eyes in a form of prayer, wishing that the phantom from my past might also dissipate.

I glanced towards the bar where the three men remained almost static. Immense broad shoulders, the muscles only in movement when glasses were lifted or placed back on the counter. Gone were the days when they would light cigarettes and fug up this space. For one fleeting moment, I recalled Paris in '68 and the smoky bars Peter and I used to inhabit.

That heady month before Pierre walked into our lives, before I caused so much damage.

Now, for the pleasure of a smoke, the fishermen were obliged to saunter outside. If any of them did so, I would ask the question, but none moved, backs to the weather, backs to their rigorous lives beyond this snug. I caught Thierry's eye. As barmen always seemed to be, he was drying glasses, tea towel tossed over one shoulder. I made a signal for my bill. Two coffees during the space of an hour. Thierry nodded and I returned my attention to the empty square, then sent a swift text to Peter to say I would be back shortly.

Thierry was in front of me, lowering the saucer with my bill to the small wooden table. 'Quite a storm, eh, Madame?'

I nodded. 'Business too quiet. Keeps the customers away, eh?'

'*Mais oui.*'

'Are there many tourists about at the moment?'

Thierry shook his big head. 'My flat's rented upstairs on an annual lease to a German family, but they're not here at present. We're expecting them back early June, or so they wrote to the missus. A couple of the houses along the Strand, towards the Cap Cable, have been taken. But it's not good, Madame. Business has been quieter all round since the attacks. The Nice one damaged southern tourism badly. Slowly, the foreigners are coming back in dribs and drabs. Except for the Brits, of course, with their Brexit concerns. What a madness that is, eh?'

'Any idea who's taken the houses along the Strand?' I probed, drawing coins from my purse while trying to hit a nonchalant note.

'François might know. One of the properties belongs to his wife's family. François!' The barman swung back to the men at the counter, all still in their tall rubber boots.

François turned and nodded in my direction. We knew one another. I had bought fish from his landed skiff on many a fair morning. 'You looking for somewhere to rent then, Madame?'

I shrugged. 'A friend was asking. She's thinking of coming over from the UK for a few weeks a bit later in the season,' I lied, hating myself for offering any false financial hope to these hardworking men.

'My sister-in-law's rented hers,' he said. 'The man doesn't know how long he'll be staying. Indefinite, he said, so I wouldn't like to promise anything there. I can ask her, though, to give you a call. Or she can talk to one or two of the other proprietors in the street for you.

Cheaper than doing it through one of the agencies in La Ciotat.'

I nodded, caught at the sentence about the man who was in residence indefinitely. 'Her rental is alongside the house she lives in. Is that correct?'

François nodded. 'Number eleven, that's right.'

'Don't worry.' I smiled. 'I'll drive over there and have a word. Thanks so much.'

I lifted myself from the table, my limbs still trembling. The men, Thierry and François, were watching me, not with any suspicion but simply because there wasn't very much else to concentrate on and I had brought a moment of diversion to the boredom of the afternoon. Their second day grounded, without hope for a catch.

'Tell all your English friends, Madame, to come and spend the summer here.' Thierry smiled when I reached the door. The bell clanged as I opened it and stepped outside.

Number eleven, along with all the other pastel-coloured terraced houses along the Strand – once the abodes of the local fishing community – faced out to the sea, which was gradually growing calmer. Its hue was a manganese turquoise. I loved the casts and tones of the water after a heavy storm, when the sands had been roiled and nothing was tranquil or limpid.

I was in the car, inching forwards at a snail's pace, checking every now and then that no one was behind me, growing impatient. I was keen to avoid a waspish driver, whose hooting and ill temper would draw attention to my presence. I had decided that to walk this strip, which in any case was too blustery, would leave me wide open to the view of anyone within the houses looking out of the windows or seated on a terrace. If it was Gissing who had rented François's sister-in-law's place, and I was guessing it was, the last thing I wanted was that he knew I was out looking for him. That he had successfully spooked me.

And when I had confirmed that Gissing was staying there, what was I intending to do? I had no answer to that question. It was one step too far ahead. My objectives were plain to me: to make certain he never came close to our house again, nowhere near the grandchildren, above all, and that either with money, persuasion or threat, I didn't know which yet, I could somehow prevail upon him to decamp. It seemed a tall order, mostly because I had no inkling of the level of sanity of the mind I was dealing with.

Was he violent? Fanciful? His mention of murder? Was that some fantastical nonsense he was intending to use to construct a blackmail threat against us? Was extortion his game? Did he believe any of his trumped-up story? Did I? How much money was he after? And who was George Gissing? What nature of man had he, 'Pierre', become?

I had reached number eleven. I crawled forwards the distance of another two houses and then, outside number fourteen, I drew to a halt. That particular property was shuttered and sported a sign, *A Louer – To Rent*, attached to a post in the front garden. Number thirteen was also closed up, but numbers twelve, eleven and, by the look of it, ten were all open, not shuttered, so probably occupied.

My telephone pinged a text. I glanced across to the

passenger seat where the mobile was lying. A message from Peter: *Where are you? I thought you were on your way back.*

I picked it up and typed: *Stayed and drank a coffee, waited for storm to die down. Back shortly. Please don't worry. X*

I had disengaged the gearstick but not switched off the engine. I should head off, be on my way. There was nothing more I could achieve here in the immediate future, not unless I aimed to go knocking on the doors demanding certainty, and that was not my intention. Not yet. First, I wanted to know where he was stationed and what I was dealing with. From there on, I would formulate a master plan. I pushed the car into first, crept forward, swung the Renault across the street to make a U-turn, now facing the sea and the narrow strip of beach sullied with bracken and driftwood, then turned the wheel for the town and from there the upper road to home.

Reflection must be my strategy. And afterwards a clearly formulated counter-attack.

An unnerving silence ensued. I heard no more. There were no more sightings of Gissing. The storm endured, settling for an hour or two before erupting once more. On it belted for more than seventy-two hours. Afterwards, the bright days returned, as though a switch had been flicked, back to their spring glory, which meant the youngsters returned to the beach. Peter's operation drew closer. Just one or two more weeks. I spent my free hours walking in the hills, swimming in the early mornings before the household was out of bed, reading, contemplating and remembering, jotting down memories, reliving my past. My encounter with Gissing, I had disclosed to no one. Better to keep the interview to myself until I knew what we were up against. I felt a deep-seated swell of grieving in the pit of my stomach.

I forced myself not to return to the Strand to verify whether or not Gissing was still in residence. I tried to persuade myself that our meeting had been all he needed, that he had been appeased. I talked myself into believing that once he had seen me, spoken to me face to face, threatened me and observed the fright he had caused me, he was satisfied, had enjoyed his petty thrill, and would return to his own life back in England. Back in England? I didn't even know that for a fact. And if his fantasies had not been gratified, what was I to expect? I had no precise idea what I was waiting for, or up against, what menace would be served up next. And why this silence when he had clearly said, threatened, that he would be in touch?

What if I were to fly back to England, to accept the role in the play Ken, my agent, had telephoned me about? Would that take the heat, the spotlight off Peter's family? Would I be refocusing Gissing's crazed mind on me and only me? I could promise to meet him in London. Would I release the children from any dangers they might be in the line of? The downside of this plot was that if I committed myself to the play's six-month run I would be absent throughout the summer and I would not be here to support Peter, to see him through his operation, to be at his side – my hand holding his – when he regained consciousness. And it was that I desired more than anything else. To be with the man I loved when we learned that his operation had been a success and his life was no longer endangered by a defective heart.

What an irony. Peter, of all men, had no emotional defects of the heart. No one was kinder, more amorous or loyal. Peter's heart was so full of generosity and concern for others.

Those were the options, the arguments, the points of defence that turned over and over in my mind as I hiked or strolled the hills and observed the May days inching towards June and early summer. Buds unfolding, scents deepening. The *maquis*, the Mediterranean scrubland that climbed the mountainous elevations directly behind Heron Heights, was reaching its aromatic zenith. A cornucopia of perfumes wafted around our isolated house, enveloping it, lulling me into a false sense of security. *He is silent because he has packed up and gone.* Lounging on the veranda of an evening, when the perfumes were at their most potent as the sun set, was almost like imbibing a drug.

Drugged out of your pretty little brains. Wasn't that how it was? That's the story. What do you know of the truth? What can you possibly remember?

1968

The May Riots

We were outside in the street awaiting the arrival of Daniel Cohn-Bendit along with seven of his fellow students from Nanterre for their disciplinary meeting at the Sorbonne.

'There he is.' Peter pointed. 'That's Cohn-Bendit. The ginger-haired fellow.'

'Good luck, Dany!' Voices hailed him.

We watched as the group of eight passed through a police cordon, voices raised in a rousing chorus of 'L'Internationale'. I glanced about me at the clusters of students lining the pavements, waving their arms and chanting, *'Debout, les damnés de la terre'*, lyrics from the first stanza of the famous left-wing anthem written in 1871.

I couldn't follow everything because there was so much shouting and cheering. Peter had his left arm hanging loosely over my shoulders. Since we'd quit the luxury of his parents' pad, we'd been sleeping on Pascal's floor by the stove. Our standard of living had certainly nose-dived, but we were happy. In any case, I was getting excited at the prospect of leaving the city shortly and moving south.

My Summer of Possibilities had taken a major leap forward.

The revolution was the big story, of course, but while

Peter, his friends and comrades discussed, *ad infinitum*, strategies, philosophical concepts, I was coming to terms with my new status. Womanhood. I wiled away time in the toilet cubicle at Pascal's, staring into the broken strip of mirror hanging from a nail above the stained sink. I was searching for signs, tracing the contours of my face, hoping to spot some indefinable transformation shining out from within me, but as far as I could see, I was the same old young Grace.

Peter's chocolate-brown wool scarf flapped in my face as his right arm was held aloft in a salute. The mood was upbeat, in spite of the police presence, and I felt elated. So many of my generation surrounded us, calling for a better, fairer world. Peter's words: 'the demise of capitalist greed'. I was being drawn into his cause although I didn't fully understand the demands, and I certainly wasn't prepared for the brutality that attended us when Paris was transformed into a battlefield.

In my dreamy, growing-up state of mind, I didn't see what was coming. I had never taken part in any demonstrations before, not even peaceful ones. It was only another couple of days before the aspirations of the young spiralled out of control and were transformed into something seriously ugly.

And, unwittingly, I found myself caught in the eye of the storm.

Once Dany and his comrades had disappeared from sight there was a bit of a lull, as though no one knew what to do next. Then a male voice, deep and rusty, from within the crowd, bellowed, '*Allons-y.*'

He was bidding his fellow protesters to start marching,

waving their banners. Cries of approval rang out and we began to shuffle through the streets of the Left Bank. Peter took my hand. It was too easy to get jostled and lose one another. Basically, we were moving in the direction of l'Odéon. Peter shouted in my ear that we'd keep step with the crowds for a bit and, later, catch up with a few of his gang back at Pascal's.

Little worked out as planned.

When the demonstrators arrived in rue Saint-Jacques, we came face to face with a battalion of police officers. They were waiting for us, lined up along the pavements and street. They had rigged up lengths of temporary fencing, a railing to block our route forward. Students called out to them, 'Let us pass.' A few others, I admit, yelled more provocative comments. These caused the *gendarmerie* to raise their shields and step towards us. It was not a goose-step exactly, but it was threatening and brought to my mind images I'd seen of Hitler marching in victory in Berlin in 1933. This was on a smaller scale, I agree, but when ranks of armed, uniformed men, trained for combat, are trooping towards you with weapons . . . Well, it scared the living daylights out of me.

Someone hurled a stone. It might have been a brick – I couldn't see. We were too far back in the lines and, at five foot five, I'm not that tall. The police were prepared for defensive action with their batons at the ready. As a unit they began to advance in earnest. On the offensive. An order was called and tear gas was shot into the crowds.

It didn't happen at once, the response. It was almost like a slow-motion clip from a film, as though the gas was frozen in mid-air before it reached us, its target. Our lines began to break up – many had been walking with arms linked until this point. Now chaos was unleashed. Half the demonstrators, those in the front rows, began to cough. Those same protesters were temporarily blinded, hands pressed up to their faces, or tears running down their cheeks. I was able to get a fuller picture now because the ranks had been divided.

'Shit, man! I'm burning!'

'Help!'

'I'm on fire!'

'My eyes!'

'Fuck it, I can't see.'

The provocative language escalated. People were running to and fro, back and forth. They scattered, shouting, swearing, some hysterical, running, turning in circles. A few became aggressive, attempted to counter-attack, but without weapons . . . This incited the police. Our front ranks were stumbling, pushed backwards, losing footing. I twisted my ankle while attempting to stay upright as bodies fell over me. Peter and I dropped hands. I think he was covering his face.

'Hide your eyes, Grace!' he shouted, from behind fingers pressed to his. 'Take my scarf.'

I felt sick, woozy. I was desperate to get away, to escape as fast as possible – this was too vicious for me – but we were hemmed in, blocked, encircled within animated panic.

I assumed it was over, that the police had made their point, but, no, this was just the beginning. The law must have called for reinforcements because, within no time, crocodiles of navy-clad officers appeared, piling out of vans, arriving from around street corners. I will never forget the incessant thud of marching boots. There were dozens and dozens and dozens of them. All flaunting weaponry. In Britain, the police were rarely if ever equipped with arms, nothing besides truncheons. To stand face to face with so many handguns and rifles put the fear of God into me.

The National Police and the crowd control unit, the CRS, were wearing tin helmets with visors down to protect themselves against the gas and smoke they were spraying on us. They were brandishing shields and batons. I spotted assault rifles, which freaked me. The air was opaque with clouds of tear gas. It created an eerie, haunting atmosphere, apocalyptic, and it became almost impossible to follow, with any clarity, what was going on.

People were in all directions, shouting, bleating, handkerchiefs pressed over mouths and noses, or arms stretched, like distress signals, above their heads. The street was raining bodies. Another round of tear gas was released. I was standing in a fog sound-tracked by yelping, coughing, wheezing.

I had lost sight of Peter, lost him altogether. I yelled his name, coughed, spluttered it again. I spun in blind circles, bodies banging up against me, knocking me this way and that. Scared doesn't describe it. I wanted Away From Here Now. This was terrifying. Suddenly an image of my parents fighting, tearing at one another, flooded my brain. I screamed, pressed my knuckles into my eyes ... They were stinging, weeping, burned by gas. My vision was deteriorating.

Close by, students began pulling up paving stones. Others behind me were heaving a parked Citroën, rocking the black car until it was upright, balanced precariously on its back bumper, engine pointing skywards, until it lost balance, spun fast and crashed onto its roof, sending whorls of dust and broken parts in all directions. Metal, mirrors smashed and splintered. People were jumping out of range of the shards of glass. I didn't understand what this senseless destruction was about until I clocked that the students were creating their own blockade to protect themselves against the police.

'Peter!' I screamed.

I was desperate to escape the mayhem.

All my belongings, my squirrelled-away savings were at Pascal's. I had about ten francs in loose change in my pocket. I couldn't even pay for a *pension*, a room to hide in till the pandemonium blew over.

I roared Peter's name again, but my cry was stifled by others.

Violence was what I had fled from.

Then, ahead of me, close up to the barricade line, I spotted a pair of guys I recognized. We had spent an evening together in a bar with Peter. I shouldered my way through the crowds, trying to remember their names and praying they would help me.

Pascal had been arrested, I learned from Peter late that same evening when I finally managed to catch up with him.

'Will they charge him?'

Peter feared they would. The education authorities had announced faculty expulsions for students arrested and accused of leading or inciting riots.

'That's atrocious!' I cried. 'It's not ethical. What happened to freedom of speech?'

Peter nodded gravely, then winked at me. 'You're getting the hang of this, eh, Grace?'

The Sorbonne remained closed, awaiting further orders from the college rector, who was not sympathetic to his undergraduates' requests.

The headline of *France-Soir*, the evening journal, read: *The Sorbonne is surrounded by a large police presence.*

'All of France is reading this,' I reminded Peter. 'That'll go in your favour.'

When I awoke the following morning, Peter was not at my side. I threw clothes on and hurried down to our usual bar for a coffee, hoping he might be there. Disappointed, I bought a newspaper and took it back to the café, to await Peter. Thousands of citizens, I read triumphantly, had expressed shock and disgust at the violence displayed by the police towards France's younger generation. Some were calling upon de Gaulle to calm the situation while others believed the president was determined to see the agitators punished. He was a soldier after all.

I caught sight of several small groups marching in the streets. Ordinary folk, middle-class members of society, they were adding their voice to the *lutte*, the battle.

'*Vive la révolution*,' I cried out to them.

When I returned to Pascal's, Peter was there. 'Where have you been? I was getting worried. We don't want you arrested. The government has ceded two points, did you hear?'

I shook my head. 'They must have read this.' I handed him the newspaper.

'The Sorbonne is to reopen,' he told me. 'And the

authorities have promised to pull back on police involvement, but they're adamantly refusing to release the arrested "rioters". The punishments to be meted out will be harsh. Pascal is among those awaiting trial.'

I was shocked.

That morning, Peter had been to visit his friend to offer support. He had tried to get him released, but without luck.

It seemed wrong that we were using Pascal's studio, making love, having fun, while he was in a cell, but we had nowhere else to crash until it was time to leave the city, and Peter saw no problem with us being there. Even with just the two of us, though, it was cramped. I was dreaming of beaches and the sunny south.

We hardly slept. The pickets and protests were now continuing around the clock.

Over five hundred students and demonstrators had been arrested. Days ran into nights and nights into days. I had been working non-stop building barricades since four the previous afternoon, in rue Gay-Lussac a few doors up from Pascal's. Peter had been posted elsewhere. I got nattering to a chap in his fifties, with thinning sandy hair. He was a bank manager at the Crédit Lyonnais, and was out in his pyjamas and a duffel coat.

'I was just off to bed,' he said, as he heaved stones, 'when I heard the kerfuffle below. I peered out the window and watched you all for a few minutes and then, well, I couldn't just go to bed, as though the revolution was not marching by my doorstep. In any case, the noise would have kept me awake. I was young once, with dreams of a better future. That's what our republic is built on. The man in the street.'

I grinned and straightened to ease my nagging back. I was wilting. I turned my head and watched the industry of the human chain, all the way down the street. Dedicated citizens, all shapes and sizes, who had chosen to stand with the student struggle.

Cool.

They were passing stones and lumps of rock from one to the next while engaging their neighbours in discussion. Any bit of debris was handed along to secure the barricades. I felt such a surge of pride. I couldn't imagine this happening in Kent. Digging up the high street in Bromley? I didn't think so.

From open windows along the narrow *rue*, kindly folk had left their radios playing. They were transmitting Europe One and Radio Luxembourg. These radio stations were our opportunity to keep abreast of the situation, to forewarn us of danger. The television stations were controlled by the government and they were dispatching anti-student stories, blackening our reputation, calling us all 'Reds'.

'Sssh, quiet, everybody, listen,' came the gentle call from a young male student.

'Although the government has yielded two points,' a newsreader informed us, 'they still refuse to release the arrested demonstrators.'

'*Libérez nos camarades!*' Boos and hisses rang out while others worked on silently.

I was part of a team of seven, all French students except me, instructed to build two barricades. One, a metre high, was constructed almost entirely of cobbles pulled up from abutting streets. The second wall, some twenty yards distant, stood almost three metres. It was a creation of dustbins, upturned cars, stones, lampposts, broken chairs. There were wheelbarrows, metal drums, steel girders, cement mixers and several massive blocks of concrete. I had no idea where all this material had been filched from. A nearby building site, I suppose.

One old girl, all in black, like a Greek widow, was heaving a country chair through the door of her ground-floor flat. 'Lend a hand, someone!'

A young lad ran to her aid.

'I've done this before,' her raspy voice cried jubilantly. 'Remember liberating Paris from the Nazis? *Vive la France*,' she croaked. Everybody cheered. Such a sense of camaraderie. It ran through my blood, felt stupendous. I was alive and I belonged there.

'Hush! Hush! Hear that!' a female voice called.

'Quiet, everyone,' laughed another. An expectant lull fell. Feet shuffled on the spot. A small pebble rolled. The tip of a drawn cigarette reddened. Someone coughed lightly. And then a collective silence. Tuning in, we heard from somewhere out of sight, from among the broken bricks and bicycle spokes, a nightingale.

A nightingale was singing.

'How about that?'

'God bless us all,' sobbed my friend the bank manager.

His words hung in the night, like a talisman for our future.

'*Vive la révolution*,' another bloke, several doors along, roared proudly, and everyone in that dusty pre-dawn street raised their filthy sweat-stained arms and cheered with every ounce of breath in their lungs, '*Vive la France.*'

The exultations echoed and bounded off the walls for what seemed to be minutes. I lifted my head to the almost non-existent stars and grinned like a loony. I felt energized, integrated. I was participating in something important. The Hand of History.

France's revolution for better education, equality, was under way. The state was being challenged for its conservatism, its outmoded attitudes towards sex, women's liberation, freedom of expression and for the standard of its teaching. University reforms were what we were fighting for, improvements in student rights. Sexual freedom. We were changing the world, or we were about to. Peter and his comrades were calling for reformation of the French constitution. And I was there. I was a part of it. Playing my minuscule role, but participating. This was living. I was sixteen, bursting with life and sap and hope and possibility. Freedom, I cried into the night softly.

It sure beat jiving to Gerry and the Pacemakers at our less than groovy youth club back home in Bromley.

The Present

While I was still tormenting myself with far-fetched scenarios about Gissing and what had become of him, on an afternoon when there was a spattering of cloud cover to lessen the temperature, Peter suggested we take the children on a nature trail.

Nests were sometimes to be found in the *maquis*, discreetly secreted among its diverse and highly aromatic vegetation. In olden days, Agnes had told me many years earlier, lynxes and giant tortoises had roamed those peaks and their lairs and dens were buried in the thick density of evergreen bushes. Nests, if ever we sighted any, should be left alone. 'You wouldn't want someone poking about in your house, would you? Let's leave them in peace.'

'You go,' I countered. 'All of you. I'll stay here in case . . .'

'In case, what, Grace?'

'The clinic might call with a date for –'

'Grace, what has got into you? They have our mobile numbers. You mustn't let this weigh on you so. It will do you the world of good to lighten up for a bit. Hiking boots everyone, please.'

We had only been out for twenty minutes, Peter and I holding hands, gently leading the climb, no over-exertion, when Harry shouted triumphantly that he had tripped over a skull.

I felt myself freeze.

'I've kicked someone's head,' the child cried. 'It's got no skin.'

'Don't touch it,' cautioned Peter. 'Let me see it first. Stand back a step, Harry, there's a good lad.'

Peter bent to his haunches, dividing a path in the dense growth of bushes as he did so. The children scrambled to poke their faces and fingers among the mass of prickly or broad-leaved evergreens. And there it was. Bodiless, a decapitation, overgrown by feculent roots and vegetation. It was small and desiccated but well preserved.

'Sharp eyes, Harry, well spotted.'

He beamed at his grandfather's praise.

Anna begged to be given it to make necklaces from its parts.

'What is it, Nanny Two? Is it a squashed man?'

'A fox or cat, I would think, Harry.'

'Let me have a closer look, please, Harry.'

We gathered tightly round the bones held now in the palm of Peter's hand. 'I'd say it's a badger.'

'How do you know, Granddad?'

'See how the eye sockets are far forward? Teeth of different sizes – look at these. Notice how long and sharp they are.'

The children stared in wonder.

'Those teeth identify the creature as a carnivore, not a herbivore. It's the skull of a hunting creature. Yes, a badger, I'm reasonably sure.'

'What are carni for?'

I took a deep breath, inhaling the magnificence of the view.

It was then that I recalled the drugs. Pierre's stash.

A day – or was it two? – after Pierre had drowned, fearing the police would search Agnes's house and Pierre's car and uncover the contraband, I stuffed everything I could find of his into a bag and buried the haul somewhere up here within the maquis. I dreaded we would be charged for possession of hard drugs, that Peter and sweet Agnes would be incriminated. I deserved whatever was to come to me, but Peter and Agnes were innocent.

I was sweating as I'd climbed, as I'd dug dementedly, displacing gnarled roots, with a garden spade, scratching, grubbing at the ungiving rocky soil until my nails split and my fingers bled. Tears streamed down my cheeks. I was grief-crazed and terror-stricken, haunted by the possibility that Peter would find me, discover my illicit act.

Hadn't I caused sufficient damage?

I glanced now at the man at my side, hair turned grey, his strength diminishing but soon to return, I prayed, surrounded by a troupe of entranced children, sharing with them his love of this magical landscape. Could I remember now, if I were obliged to, where I had buried that bag of illicit substances? I had stuffed everything deep into an abandoned badgers' sett on these hills, somewhere high above the house. Nothing of Pierre's possessions would have survived, of course, not after so many decades. The substances would have rotted, disintegrated into the soil. Or might there be the tiniest residue, a sunken trace of his trade, to use as evidence against him, the Gissing man, should it become a necessity? Should I be forced to defend my family against the unthinkable.

*

Slowly, as one day rolled into the next, my psyche began to split. I was inhabiting two time zones. At one moment I was sixteen again, living dangerously, recklessly, in Paris with my young hero, Peter, fighting alongside him for the revolution, and then, once we had escaped the capital and landed here, at his aunt Agnes's, I was soon betraying him with Pierre.

The next hour, I was returned to myself in the present: a sixty-something actress and a granny, Grace Soames, of the present, strung up inside, waiting. Waiting for what? Gissing's next move. The menace I feared.

The minutes, the hours ticked by, hammering at my head.

I became withdrawn, confused, without even being aware of my changing state. The others noticed. One morning before breakfast, Sam approached me in the kitchen. With an empty coffee cup in hand, I was padding about in a sarong and socks, still not fully awake, having missed my early-morning swim. She wrapped her arms around me and hugged me hard, all tight and squeezy.

'I'm sorry,' she whispered in my ear. 'Jen and I both know how much you love the children and that you'd never do anything to harm them. I was ratty and uptight because I was dealing with the scary news from the specialist, and the prospect of Dad's operation, the risks involved.'

I nodded, half asleep, nonplussed.

'Is it me who's made you so unhappy, Grace?' she pressed.

I shook my head. 'No, no, I . . .'

'Then what? What's troubling you so?'

'I . . . I've been offered a play. I was mulling over whether I . . .'

Peter had stepped into the kitchen behind me without my noticing. 'Grace, if you want to accept the play, then you must. I'll manage. We'll manage. Jenny has offered to stay on with the girls, even if Sam needs to leave and get back to the UK.'

'No, no,' I protested. I had been digging for an excuse to explain my antisocial preoccupied behaviour. Now it was backfiring. 'I need coffee,' I yelled jokily. 'And I've already turned the play down. No more discussion. Let's have breakfast.'

Later, alone, Peter took me in his arms as I was donning my trainers. 'It's a fact that you have been a little remote of late. We've all remarked it. All well? Nothing up, my darling?'

I shook my head. I wanted more than anything in the world to reciprocate, to hang my arms around his neck, rest my head against his chest and unburden myself of Gissing – our past, the younger man's untimely death – but Peter's health stayed any disclosure.

I was trawling through my bank and savings statements on the internet, jotting down calculations. In preparation. Finances were not my strong suit, but if it came to blackmail and I emptied all my accounts, I could offer him everything I had access to. In the car, on the road to Cassis, Gissing had hinted at half a million. It had been a casually proposed figure, but might it be the number he had in mind? I couldn't raise that sum, not without assistance from Peter and, with his assent, us tapping into Agnes's invested capital. But I could give him everything I had in ready money, pray it would satisfy him and buy him out of our lives.

On the other hand, what was the extent of Gissing's financial resources? Could he afford to rent an entire holiday house throughout the high-season months? Or might lack of funds send him on his way? *If he was still here.* In which case, no matter what threats he made, it would be ill-advised to agree to give him one single euro. And who knew? With any luck he might already have upped sticks and gone on his way.

If not, why was he so reticent? *It was the silence that was driving me up the wall.*

Three more days passed, and the silence continued, but I was using my time fruitfully, even if agitated. I had avoided all visits to Cassis, accomplishing the minimal amount of shopping we required, which was predominantly the fresh stuff, at the market in La Ciotat. The drive was a little further and sinuous along the summit route, but I had no desire to bump into Gissing until I was ready to face him again.

I had been surfing the internet on my laptop, searching for his name. There appeared to be dozens of them, the GGs. Many were on Facebook, Twitter, LinkedIn, Tinder and other social-media spaces I had never frequented.

Before I made a move, if I made any, I preferred to have to hand whatever background information I could dig up. This required eliminating the GGs one by one, methodically. I began with those resident in the north of England, given his accent. Those displaying photographs that bore no resemblance to the man I knew as Gissing, which was all of them to date, were instantly deleted. The others, the faceless ones, were more awkward because, to get to know them, I needed to approach them and I had no intention of signing up to be linked in, to request friendship, a dating possibility, with a stranger who might prove to be my potential enemy.

When I was not spending hours on the beach with the youngsters, I tried to do whatever was necessary – from scouring the internet to peeling potatoes – seated in a chair out on the verge beyond the veranda where I had more than a 180-degree bird's-eye view, a vantage point for every ingress to the property, except the rear. Should Gissing approach the family on the beach from any of the neighbouring bays or from the sea, I would almost certainly spot him before anyone else did. I had allocated myself the role of watchdog.

If, as before, he returned and waited in the rear lane, I would still be the most likely one to discover him. Peter rarely went out, these days, except for brief walks, and these we tried to enjoy together, while Sam and Jenny spent blissful, recreational hours jumping in and out of the sea with their children.

By day five, I was growing suspicious, puzzled. Had Gissing left? Should I drive to Cassis and try to find out? Was the potential horror story over? Or was he being incommunicative in an attempt to jangle my nerves, to up the ante? My hopes were just beginning to rise that this had been little beyond an extended nightmare when a letter arrived addressed to me in bold biro, scrawled lettering. Its stamp was from Cassis. Fortunately I was the one to collect the mail from the box along the track. I tore open the envelope before I returned to the house with the rest of the post. It was, as I had suspected, from him.

I have been ill. Caught bronchitis in the storm. (My health is vulnerable.)
Hence my silence. But I am still here, and I am waiting for you.

You know where I am staying. You do, don't you? I have been
expecting you to come and find me, talk to me. Be kind to me and
keep me company. I am still expecting you. Or would you prefer I
come to the house and have a quiet chat with you and introduce
myself to your husband?

How about I teach the children to dive? Your young Harry,
he'd come with me.

What are you waiting for, Grace?

G

'Teach the children to dive'? 'Young Harry'? My heart
went cold. Pierre had been an accomplished diver. Who
else would know that, after all these years?

It was gone eleven a.m. To set off before lunch would
provoke too many questions. I would return to Cassis in
the afternoon. No need for an explanation. Peter frequently took a short nap after lunch. It was a recently
acquired habit. His heart's strenuous activity was tiring
him. The others would return to the beach.

Later, during lunch, Sam announced that she was
intending to take out *Phaedra*, unless Peter or I had any
objections. 'We'll be leaving soon, and now that the weather's fine again, I thought it would be a fun afternoon
outing. Do you mind, Dad?'

Peter shook his head. 'Not at all. Why would I? Be
careful, is all I have to say. Keep this side of the underwater shelf and don't let the children swim out of their
depth. Are you all going?'

That would be seven in the boat.

I wondered why they should want to make this excursion today. I was surprised by the idea but could offer no sensible objection. I kept silent. The boat had hardly been used this year. 'I suppose it's in good working order?' I threw a glance to Peter, who nodded and winked.

Tomas at the shipyard in the old port of La Ciotat always took care of *Phaedra* for us and frequently kept her dry-docked over the winter. It was during the colder months that he carried out the servicing and any necessary repairs.

'Will you come with us, Grace?' Jenny asked, as she poured wine. I shook my head, refusing the wine and as a response to her question. 'No, thank you. I'm going out for a while a bit later and eight with three adults is pushing it for that little vessel.' I smiled.

'Nonsense, our cruiser can squeeze everyone in comfortably. You know that, Grace. It's well suited to a family like ours.' Peter grinned. 'Are you off anywhere exciting, darling?'

'The hairdresser,' I lied.

The lunch conversation had given me an idea.

The Strand in the early-season light was all any tourist could wish for, and that afternoon the beach and the street that lined it were peaceful and practically deserted. Two or three cars were parked in front of the terrace of fishermen's homes. Two old geezers were perched on a boulder with rods bobbing in the sea and a lone woman on the beach was exercising a dog off the lead. The yellow Labrador was scooting in and out of the foam, shaking itself, throwing off silvery plumes of seawater, and wagging its tail. I had written a note in response to Gissing's. I felt queasy at the prospect of being alone in his cottage with him – I needed to keep distance and the upper hand. Neutral territory.

> *If you have something to say to me, meet me on the beach at the calanque d'En-Vau. You can walk there, close to the entrance of the Calanques Park. Before breakfast tomorrow morning. Around 6 a.m.*
>
> *You remember where it is?*
> *No need to respond. I will be waiting.*
>
> *Grace*

1968

May, Paris
La Lutte Continue . . . *The fight goes on*

I barely set eyes on Peter during those extraordinary days, our last hours in Paris before we were forced to flee. Today was Friday. I was so dog tired I had to stop and think about it. Yes, Friday, 10 May.

Word was spreading that the entire country, and above all the capital, was now engaged in the student struggle. High-school kids were among us. Middle-class white-collar workers, as well as the working class. Some of the faculty professors had joined our side, which was a real boost to the morale of all those students who had felt betrayed by their lecturers. Even the Communists were waking up to the fact that they were better with the fight than printing leaflets to criticize it.

Peter and I were on our knees. So little sleep. Woke late. Barely time to drag ourselves out of our makeshift bed to grab a coffee along rue Gay-Lussac. Quick shower, gobbled two croissants on the run and gathered with thousands of others at place Denfert-Rochereau. While waiting for the march to get under way, a handful of students passed through the expectant crowds distributing handkerchiefs soaked in baking powder.

'What's it for?' I asked a pretty girl.

'Helps protect against the gas,' she answered, before moving along the line.

'Helps stave off the choking,' added Peter, at my side.

I felt a rod of ice run up my spine.

We were on the move.

'*Egalité, liberté, sexualité.*' A voice from the sea of heads. Others laughed at the joke and cheered, raised aloft their arms. I glanced about me. Several young men were giving piggybacks to young women bearing banners above their heads. Their faces shone brightly, as though they were having a fine day out. There was no malice or anger in their expressions – determination, resolution to effect change, yes, but neither hate nor violence.

As we made headway, the numbers swelled. More joined the rally, all welcomed with jubilant cries. We were embracing everyone in our path. With every step, the mass of humanity was spreading out into the adjacent lanes and avenues of the sixth arrondissement all the way up to the boulevard Saint-Germain, which, word on the grapevine was reporting, was now chock-a-block with protesters of every age and class.

Yes!

Meanwhile, the roads around us were being cordoned off by police, penning us in, forcing us tighter together. I feared a stampede, but just when I thought we were in trouble, we were on the move again.

I needed to pause a minute, catch my breath, get some sense of the size of this *manifestation*, but I was like a sapling being torn from its roots. More than thirty thousand students had rallied, I learned later. I turned my head to smile at Peter. We had dropped hands because it was sticky, and we needed fluidity of movement. As I glanced left, beyond my friend, a hideous scene caught my attention. I tried to hold back, stop walking to get a better look, verify it, but the force of movement shunted me onwards. I used my arms as though swimming in water to steady myself.

A pregnant woman was being battered, yes, battered, and brutally manhandled, by a police officer. I was beyond appalled.

'Stop!' I roared. The perpetrators were too distant to hear me.

'Let me through.' I was elbowing my way to the left, out on a flank. Why was no one intervening? The woman's legs buckled beneath her as she fell. Now she was being hauled by her shoulders and dragged backwards, like an oversized rag doll.

'Stop that!' I screamed. 'Leave her.'

In my mind's eye I could see my mother, cowering.

I feared the crowd might just march over the woman, such was the force of its movement.

'Stop!' I screamed again, sick with impotency. There were so many raised voices all about me that no one took any notice. I had to reach her, had to help. About the same time, several others had clocked what was going on. They were also challenging the police violence. I broke away from the line, broke away from Peter, pushing myself frantically against the flow of the marchers, struggling to reach the abused woman to end her distress. It was like swimming against a tidal wave. And as I pushed, struggled and heaved, I was losing sight of her. I hollered repeatedly, at the top of my voice. 'Someone help that lady, for God's sake.'

Where were the others who had gone to her assistance? Where was she?

Nobody was listening. Everybody was lost in their own revolution, marching to victory. The pregnant woman had disappeared. Was she on the ground? Injured, traumatized? My sense of direction was askew. Where had she vanished to? I jostled and shouldered but was knocked off balance. I needed an overview of what was going on behind me, in front, in every direction. Panic was breaking out all around me and its energy was spreading. What was happening? Something had spooked people. What?

And then, close by me, a police officer lifted his arm above his head. I registered the padded uniform, the thick black gloves clutching an object not much larger than a tennis ball, which he tossed into the crowd. It was a grenade whistling above our heads, a CS grenade. And before we knew what was happening, another whistled our way. And another. Gas. The air about me was thick and cloudy. My eyes were on fire, my throat burning. Choking, coughing, spluttering. And while we were struggling for breath, raised batons began to beat the marchers, slapping, cracking against skulls. Have you ever heard a skull crack? As long as I live, I will never forget that sound.

The screams and shrieks were deafening. Inexcusable brutality. Blood. It was Armageddon. It was Picasso's *Guernica*, Goya's *The Third of May*. If the students had believed, and they had, that this march was about standing in solidarity, making clear their position to de Gaulle, they had been cruelly misled.

This was showdown time.

Then, before I knew what had hit me, literally hit me, a

large body, the weight of a satchel, an arm, a limb, the pole of a banner, a rifle, the toe of a large black boot, whose, what, I never knew, smacked me hard across the face. Whack. Aaargh. Something cracked, broke. For a moment, I was stunned, seeing stars, dazed. A figure in a comic cartoon. The blow winded me, threw me off balance. A real zonking punch to my jaw. I stumbled and reeled, offering a fair imitation of drunken Kid Shelleen in the movie *Cat Ballou*. I thought my teeth had been knocked out, and the impact of that had caused me to bite my gum. I tasted the metallic tang of blood as I went dancing backwards, kicking up a jig before I hit the ground, smashing my head and upper back against a recently uplifted stone. With that, I lost consciousness. For how long, seconds, minutes, I couldn't have said.

The next I knew, a stranger was hauling me to my feet. A big red face shoved close to mine, spitting words. I had no idea where I was or what the surrounding noises were about or where the putrid smell was coming from. It was the tear gas, acrid, sulphurous, but I was too out of it to make sense of the events. I was now on my feet being manhandled by two uniformed officers. They began to drag me, still semi-conscious, backwards. I soon got my wits about me. Was I being arrested? 'I'm not French,' I yelled. 'You have no authority over me.' I kicked out a foot. It targeted one of them in the side. He recoiled in pain. What a fool I was.

Assault of a police officer. Even in self-defence, a serious crime.

At least sixty of those arrested during that week carried foreign passports. It made no difference to the lawmen.

They had their own agenda: no one was getting off lightly, and now they had a case against me.

I had to get myself free.

I wriggled and resisted, beat with clenched fists, intending to make a run for it but they grabbed me tight, squeezing viciously into the flesh of my upper arms until they crippled me with pain. I cried out some more, writhing, resisting, like a trapped fish. They dragged me by my arms and my long loose hair down a side street, then threw me to the ground. I rolled over onto my bleeding knees, scrabbling on all fours. A tooth fell from my mouth to the unearthed paving stones. Then another. A spurt of blood followed. I was coughing, I lifted my head. It thumped with pain. I could see the police van ahead of me already jammed with captured students. 'This isn't my fight,' I spat at the two men in English. 'I'm not a student. You can't arrest me.' I thought it better to speak English because then they would get it through their thick heads that I was a foreigner and caught up in this by accident.

They grabbed me by the shoulders and heaved me forwards. I had little strength left for resistance.

The van was slammed shut, metal clanged. Darkness. The windows were barred. We rolled through damaged streets, sightless, to our destination. I stared at the steel cage that separated me from the officers in the front cab.

Escape was the only thought on my mind.

The journey was short. The doors were unlocked; we were frog-marched one at a time and hustled into the Commissariat of the fifth arrondissement. My heart was thudding like Big Ben at midday. Within the station, huddles of young people were waiting to be charged and relieved of their identity papers. Once their names had been logged, they were systematically handcuffed and led below to the basement where, I presumed, were cells. I was shoved forward to a desk where a member of the force was writing down names and confiscating the *cartes d'identité* of the offenders. My passport was stored at Pascal's, along with my money and the rest of my gear.

I was terrified.

'*Votre nom?*' the staff sergeant barked, pen at the ready. He must have voiced this question more than a hundred times already today. 'What is your name? Give me your identity card now, please.'

'I need to *faire pi-pi*,' I pleaded, attempting a smile but my mouth was too swollen. Lips like a rubber doughnut.

'How old are you?'

'Sixteen. I need to pee.' One of the two sous-officers from the van pushed his way to the front and elbowed me to the side, to the left of the space I'd been occupying. The bodies surged forward into the gap and I found myself, fortuitously, out of the line of investigation. This was my opportunity. It was now or never. I shuffled a step backwards. My eyes were scanning in every direction, appraising the possibilities. People surged more tightly around me. At the desk, a new fracas was breaking out, hogging the limelight. I edged crab-like further to my left. I could see the door, ajar. I could see light. Freedom. I had to make a run for it. Well, not a run; that was impossible with so many bodies around me.

I dipped down, not quite as low as to my haunches but to be out of sight. A couple of others who had been in the same transport van must have cottoned on to what I was up to. A bloke with a nice smile and rather wild hair, who had been squashed up against me in the Black Maria, was beside me again now. He glanced down at me and nudged his comrade. One laughed, both eased themselves away from me, creating the opening to a pathway. The first called out to the room, 'Who's serving the refreshments, then?' It caused a titter of laughter but not sufficient to help me. Then the second lobbed a small sharp object – his lighter? – towards the window. The sound of it cracking or spinning against the glass caused all heads to turn in that direction, leaving me free to skedaddle.

I pushed with my shoulders, waddling, like a duck or a Groucho Marx stunt double, and before I knew it I was at the door. A swift glance. No officer in sight. I rose to my full height and legged it, stumbling along the street, running, hopping, limping, a desperate, demented figure. As I was all but clear of the locality I heard a male voice from behind roar, 'You there! Halt! You are under arrest.'

Oh, no, not on your nelly.

I was dust. I rounded a corner, then another and one more, scuttling into a rather pretty courtyard with forests of plants growing in old tin canisters. There I hid, pressing myself up against a closed door while struggling to control my huffing and puffing. From somewhere, a man's voice began angrily shouting. I shoved myself sheer against the building's frontage in the hope of becoming invisible. As I did so, I accidentally kicked over two zinc buckets filled with water, all but drowning a sleeping cat.

Merde.

The sounds of splashing water, metal against cobbles and a hissing feline echoed and bounced, like a siren's call, all around the horseshoe-shaped yard. My breath was coming in gulps and heaves and I was beginning to hiccup. I thought I was going to wet myself, I was so deranged by fear. The door with the overturned buckets outside it opened and the cat flew inside. An old lady hobbled forwards and frowned at me. 'Who are you? What do you want?' she snapped, staring at me with a confused, suspicious expression.

'May I use your toilet, please?'

To my amazement she ushered me inside, accompanied me to her dingy but clean lavatory, then poured me a cup of rather burned coffee from the stove.

'Student?' she asked, when I was seated and she was across from me at the lace-cloth-covered table.

I nodded.

'But not French?'

I nodded again. I still hadn't properly caught my breath and my voice was tight, high-pitched and thin from tension, grating like a wrong note played on a violin.

'Do you know that your face is covered in blood?'

I lifted a hand to my mouth. My lips were burning as though they'd been scalded. They felt fat and puffy and there was a soft liquid cavity in my mouth into which I poked my tongue. I slipped a finger along my gums, and confirmed that I had lost two teeth. Fortunately not front ones.

My wrinkled hostess pulled a handkerchief from her pocket and tossed it across to me. 'Use that. Don't worry, no germs. It's clean.'

'*Merci*.' I began to dab at my face. It stung like hell.

'You know something?' the old girl began, as she rose to boil some water in an aluminium saucepan and chucked a handful of salt into it. 'Here, gargle with this. You know, if I was younger I would have been out there today with you, cheering you along, stepping with you. I've been watching the events on the television. You're a brave young missy. I've seen two wars in this city and I did my bit for France during both of them. I lost my husband in the last one. He was in the Résistance. A neighbour ratted on him, the bastard. The Germans arrested him and executed him in a firing squad. De Gaulle was our hero back then. He's a soldier, not a statesman, and he's making a right royal mess of this calamity. It should never have reached this level of unrest. If I can help you, just tell me and then I'll feel I'm still doing my bit for the population of France. Democratic demonstrations are a part of our constitution. This clampdown is a disgrace. We are not Fascists beating up our young. When you're my age, you will look back on all this and be proud of yourself. You'll always be able to say "I was there, May 'sixty-eight." What's your name?'

And I confided to her the information I had held back from the police.

'Have you got a bed?'

'Yes, thanks, and I'd better be on my way. *Merci beaucoup* for your kindness.'

She rose to her feet a little unsteadily and kissed my cheek. 'I pray that both my little granddaughters will prove to be as brave as you when they are old enough to make choices for themselves. *Bonne chance*, young lady.'

In place Maubert, I stopped at a café, had another pee, and ordered a glass of white wine to steady the tremors. It stung as I slurped. I could barely swallow. My mouth was bruised, lips puffy, distended. My gums tasted of blood and felt like jelly. I must have bitten my inner cheeks and cut myself in several places.

I was more than lucky to have made a successful getaway. It was a miracle. If I ever encountered the fellow who had lobbed his lighter to distract the police, I'd plant such a kiss on him.

Back out on the street at a kiosk, I purchased a copy of the following day's *Le Monde*, for sale as always the evening before. The front page reported that many students had been convicted. The numbers were in the hundreds. Many had been injured too. Orders, it seemed, not only from the university rector but possibly from the minister of Education or even, highly likely, the Élysée Palace itself.

Mercifully, I found Peter that evening in a small bar on the Left Bank where I'd guessed he might be holed up – Chez Georges, in the Mabillon *quartier*. He was downstairs in the cellar, huddled tight with a small group of earnest-faced friends. In the background, Dylan on the jukebox was intoning for change. Thankfully, it was dark in the cellar. Candles were the illumination, and Peter barely noticed the condition of my face. He frowned when I sat next to him, shifting close for protection. 'Where have you been?' he whispered.

'I'll tell you later.'

The events of the afternoon were beginning to bite. I downed a slug of the rough wine in Peter's tumbler. I needed to flee Paris. I wasn't a coward, but I didn't want any more trouble. I was haunted by images of my mother weeping, head cut open. My parents' violence, and that pregnant woman being trounced on the ground by those men . . . Had anybody found her? Had the attack against her been reported? Was her unborn child safe? I found no account of the incident in *Le Monde*.

Back at Pascal's I told Peter I was leaving.

'We'll go together,' he assured me, 'at the end of the month.'

I shook my head, adamant. 'If the same police team, or one of them, recognizes me, I'll be arrested again. I don't want to go to prison. You stay. I'll be fine.'

After much debate, Peter insisted on leaving with me.

'You don't have to,' I countered.

'I want to.'

Our plan was to make our way south to his aunt Agnes's home.

How could I have known then that I was not escaping my predicament? I was running headlong towards a different danger, a crueller act of destruction.

How could I have known that Pierre lay ahead?

Peter favoured taking a train to Marseille. I begged to hitch. 'Are you in the habit of hitching?' He was rather shocked.

I shook my head. 'I've never done it before.'

'Then why? I have money for train tickets.'

It struck me as the ideal way to get a sense of how far the revolution had reached and what the rest of the nation felt, or even knew, aside from the news they heard on the independent radio stations, of the student revolt. In 1968, the French television stations were in the hands of the state. Every single item broadcast required clearance from the Palace. If de Gaulle didn't approve, the info was not going to the nation.

I wanted to witness it first-hand. If Peter truly cared about how France judged the student revolts, and where the man in the street stood, then travelling south slowly, thumbing lifts, would give us a ringside seat. I also secretly fancied the adventure but I kept that to myself for fear he wouldn't approve.

My argument won the day.

We made our way out of the city by Porte d'Italie and hoped to pick up a lift to the motorway. We were not lucky. Did drivers fear our youth? Fear the events that had taken place within Paris? Did they consider us delinquents?

Eventually a van took us as far as Sens, a small town a hundred kilometres south of the capital. Sens seemed so quiet, so otherworldly. Both of us were exhausted physically and emotionally. I was glad to be out in the country. It was springtime. I had completely forgotten that while lost in a world of stone-throwing and savagery. We found ourselves a room for the night above a haberdashery. The first question, of course, was one room or two.

'We're not going to pretend to be married, are we?' I whispered, as the old lady who was the proprietor of the store gave us the once-over.

'Brother and sister?' she asked.

Peter hesitated.

'I'll need a look at your papers.'

'We're cousins,' Peter confided softly, 'on our way to stay with my – I mean our aunt. I can give you her telephone number.'

'You're not runaways from the law, from the troubles in Paris, then?'

We shook our heads. I crossed my fingers behind my back.

She nodded. 'It'll be five francs for the night. There's a couch, a bed and a sink with running water. You sort it out yourselves. Pay now.' She held out a gnarled hand with fingernails as yellow as old chalk. Peter handed over the money, and she left us to carry our bags up the narrow wooden stairs.

On the road south

To the astonishment of students and government alike, the French trade unions called for nationwide strikes. No man or woman was left working. They were demanding higher wages, better working conditions. France was grinding to a halt.

Peter read the news aloud and smiled. 'Beleaguered de Gaulle.'

We had barely shaken the dust of the capital off our boots and the country had come to a standstill. Everybody was on strike, as the Communists had promised.

One edition of *Le Monde* printed a photograph of the Gare de Lyon in Paris. A bunch of seated train workers were reading the newspapers that were reporting the strikes while they were striking.

Soutenez les cheminots en grève. Or 'Stand with the railway workers', stated the poster above their heads.

We had reached the Mâcon region. We were staying on a small vineyard, helping with the weeding and general chores. Slowly we were putting Paris behind us, although the newspapers confronted us with daily reminders until they also switched off the printing machines and downed tools. Even the TV station went dark. The fight was far from over. France was adamantly on strike. The trains were parked. Petrol was almost impossible to come by. The roads were empty. Food, the basic produce, was not being transported but when it was, bizarrely, it was cheaper. Direct from producer to consumer. No middle man. It was one of the lessons the unions wanted to impart to their fellow citizens. 'We don't need our employers, the barons, the bosses. We can run this land ourselves without all those who are taking their cut, giving us orders, keeping us the underdogs.'

There was little choice for us but to stay put or walk, make a leisurely affair of it, covering short distances each day, stopping each afternoon in time to find lodgings for the night, sometimes little more than a barn with a hay bed. I felt as if I was starring in a movie of a John Steinbeck novel. It was exhilarating. We were breathing fresh country air, getting plenty of exercise, eating wholesome, mostly home-grown food, making love, walking through varied landscapes, chiefly agricultural, accepting whatever was on offer. I was discovering this rich, complex country. Even on its knees, it had so much to offer. I grew through the experience, gained confidence, put behind me the tensions of Bromley and family life, the brutalities of the capital. The nightmares evaporated. I blossomed, and all the while Peter was falling deeper and deeper in love with me.

And I was soon to betray him.

The students had taken the Sorbonne. Hundreds of them were camping inside the buildings and libraries. The disappointment on Peter's face when he realized he was missing this ground-breaking development caused me guilt.

'Listen, go back. I'll make my own way and link up with you in the south later, whenever you're ready.'

He shook his head and wrapped a hand around mine. He refused to leave my side. 'If anything happened to you,' he said, 'I'd never forgive myself.'

'Peter, I'm fine. I can take care of myself.'

He silenced me with a kiss.

Our most pressing task was to contact Agnes. We found a telephone box in the Burgundy village where we were staying. Peter dialled his aunt's number.

'I've been expecting to hear from you. Your father has been on to me twice. He's all but accused me of hiding you. Are you on your way here?'

'Soon.'

'Excellent news. I'll make up your room. Or should that be two? I gather you might not be on your own.'

The Present

Dawn at the creek

Nobody would be surprised if they woke and discovered my absence from the house. I'm habitually the first out of bed, a solitary wayfarer on the beach. Peter, the family, would assume I had gone swimming and taken a little longer about it than usual. The weather was ideal, with no threatening overtones or hues. At first light, the sea shone like a pearlescent sheet back-dropped by a ghostly grey mist far off in the distance towards the horizon. It caused no threat to me and was burning off as the sun began to rise. The bedside clock read five twenty-five. I slipped from between the sheets silently, not wishing to disturb Peter, grabbed a clean bikini from one of the drawers, pulled on shorts and a T-shirt. My trainers were downstairs inside the main door. The boat key and the knife I had purloined from Peter's toolkit the night before; I had hidden them at the rear of the medicine chest in the downstairs loo. Now I slipped them both into my left pocket.

Outside, a chorus of birdsong greeted me. The key to the boat was jangling lightly against the more pernicious metal object. I was adept at navigating our little vessel, and on that calm morning, the short journey along the coast, motoring close to shore while avoiding the rock constellations both above and below the water's surface, should prove no problem.

The girls had dropped anchor and left the dinghy bobbing in the sea, wading back to the beach. One of them must have carried Harry on their shoulders. Marcus, perhaps. The tide was out so it was easier for me to reach *Phaedra*. I slipped off my trainers, curled up the hem of my shorts and headed into the gentle waves. The water's chilliness at this early hour sent a shiver through me.

I climbed aboard, steadied myself against the rocking – legs apart, bare wet feet planted firmly on the teak deck – and slipped the key into the controls. I pulled out the choke knob fully to allow the motor to warm up, raised the anchor and started the engine with ease. I glanced up towards the house with its broad expanse of windows and glass on the sea-facing side, to confirm that no one had been woken by the turning-over of the engine. None of the children were watching my departure through the many open windows. The boat bucked and took off, heading southwards towards Africa and then, as I tacked skilfully to my right, circling a cluster of outlying rocks towards the next bay in a westerly direction. I knew the geography of these waters relatively well. Not as extensively as Peter, but over the years I had honed the skills, studied the nautical map.

As the boat scudded and bumped, tossing up waves, the dawn palette grew warmer, softer, rosier. The rising sun burning through the curtain of haze was on my back. I felt its heat penetrating my shoulders and neck, releasing tension and encouraging me onwards.

Being out on the open sea, even this close to land,

always filled me with joy and lifted my mood. I could handle this. I sailed past Cassis on teal-coloured water and was approaching the soft whiteness of the limestone cliffs and inlets that constitute the calanques, the ancient escarpments and creeks. In the near distance, like floating humpbacks, our string of miniature islands. Rioul, the largest, was ahead and to the left. The craggy limestone rock formations that made up the coastal front were dotted with pine and juniper bushes. They had taken root with almost no soil base in the rock's natural crevices.

I glanced backwards to estimate the distance I had travelled from Cassis and knew I must be nearing my destination.

When I pushed in the acceleration control, the boat began to drop speed. Letting it idle for a moment or two, I spun the polished mahogany wheel towards the coast and skimmed through chalky turquoise waters. I was scouting the shoreline for the entrance to the creek. Beyond, as I remembered it, was a confined channel, which led to a pebbled beach, an organic harbour where there'd be a safe spot to set down and alight. I needed to confirm by the natural features of the rocks, as the boat inched forwards, that I was heading into the right creek, the one I had suggested to Gissing, and not another. There were so many bays and inlets along this coastline that it could be confusing and it had been a while since I had visited any of them on the Marseille side of Cassis.

A pair of storm petrels was bouncing off the surface of the sea, diving for prey, mackerel or sardines perhaps, to feed a shore nest I could not see. I spotted a couple of dusky groupers moving soundlessly beneath the waves.

They were almost certainly juveniles in waters so shallow.

I was in luck. Not a single fishing boat in sight. I had passed no one, my presence witnessed by not a soul. And luck again. The creek was deep and narrow, with towering organ-pipe rocks on either side, and at its end a perfect cove sloped sharply to the water's edge. I cruised into its channel and negotiated *Phaedra* directly to the buoy line beyond which boats were not allowed to berth, switched off the engine and allowed the vessel to idle and steady. There was no mooring, no tie-up buoys. For my safety's sake, and in case of any struggle or violence, I preferred to fasten the boat as close as possible to the shingled ledge of the cove. I might need a swift getaway. I had no idea yet what I was up against.

I pulled off my shoes, shorts and T-shirt, rolled them into a ball, jumped into the water, keeping my clothes on the deck, waded the last metres to the shore, dragging the boat with me, then tethered it to a jagged rock just yards from the water's edge. Undoubtedly, it was illegal to have passed into the swimming zone – we might be heavily fined, if reported – but at this hour and in this season I argued that I was encroaching on no one's space.

Judging by the sun's trajectory, I assessed the hour to be close to six. I was too early, had been impatient. Time to bide. A swim, then, while I waited, before the arrival of my opponent, might pacify my nerves.

And then?

My heart was ticking like a time bomb. There was an acid taste to my saliva, usually a sign that my anxiety level was high. I took a deep breath. The air was clear, pure.

Steadily, determinedly, I did a visual recce of the cove, position of hazardous below-surface rocks, water depths, channel curves for the smoothest exit. I would be looking for a fast escape.

Without a towel, such a foolish oversight, I would use my clothes to rub myself dry. My garments deposited on the shingled beach, I waded back in – so crystalline I could see my red-painted toenails distorted by the water's movement. I crawled out past the boat, bobbing and then submerging my face and head. An impressive school, almost like a firework display, of teeny green-golden fish – anchovies? – were foraging round the keel. I took a deep breath and dived down. The water was chilly, invigorating and clear as polished glass. Seaweed and yellow gorgonian coral swayed about my limbs. Rocky underfoot, home ground for the corals. Little pollution here. In need of breath I rose back to the surface, kicking my feet, facing shorewards. A figure dressed in black on one of the higher paths was descending to the appointed creek. It was him. Podgy yet lithe. A result of physical work or muscular exercise? How had he spent the ensuing years? He walked with purpose, head lowered, as though watching his step. The surface was scree, easy to lose one's footing and slip. And a fall from such a height would surely end in a fatality. A man – a stranger to these parts who could not foresee the dangers – out walking a lonely path at first light, loses his balance and plummets to his death? It was plausible.

Had he spotted me? Should I take the ascending path and wait for him there? Surprise him?

Towards the summits of the rock faces, where little

grows besides heather, wild roses and Aleppo pines, I counted three or even four *cabanons*, the creek-side cabins owned by locals for their Sunday outings and holidays. I had always fancied one, a romantic hideaway. Were any of them occupied right now? It was impossible for me to ascertain but there lurked, if inhabited, the possibility of a witness. This was an oversight on my part. The presence of the cabins had gone clear out of my mind. If only one person stepped outside into the unfolding morning, I, we, would be in their direct line of vision.

Should I abandon my plan? It was insanity. The boat was in full view.

I kicked hard, and made for the shore, crawling fast. On land, I dressed hurriedly without bothering to rub myself down. The salt water ran in dribbles down my back and from my twisted strands of hair. I threw myself down onto the beach to slip on my trainers and tie the laces. Almost before I had finished, he had arrived, looming behind me. He had moved with speed, more agile than I was giving him credit for. Make a mental note of that.

'I saw the boat.' His greeting. 'Knew it must be you. You're a skilled sailor.'

'What is it you want, George?'

'To talk, to be near you.' He was on the pebbles now, seated to my right and just a fraction to my rear. An angle that spooked me. I shifted my bottom backwards. Tiny stones, like pellets, stuck to my damp legs, indenting my thighs. I brushed them to the ground, suddenly recalling an afternoon from fifty years before when the man at my side, 'Pierre', had been fashioning a fishing rod. The memory stung, brought a lump to my throat. Now we were eye-level alongside one another.

Enemies, not lovers.

'You look pretty stunning wet. Hard to resist you. Still a water baby, eh, my beautiful Grace?'

'Why are you here?'

'I told you already. Just deserts.'

I closed my eyes for a second, confirming the weight in my pocket. Just in case. Breathing in, I picked out the perfumes of the perennials, the bay laurel, the local spiny heather and milk-vetch, all rooted within the fissures of the amphitheatre of towering cliffs encircling us. I tried to concentrate on the purity of the surrounding nature, the pair of groupers, an endangered species now, I'd spotted on my ride here, swimming beneath the boat. I tuned in to the stillness, to the mewling of a gull, the languid slap of the seawater just yards in front of us, scanning the shallows for loggerhead turtles.

I had loved this man so. Blind to his faults, I would have done anything for him. I had made a god of him. Betrayed my truest friend for the thrill of him.

How had the arc delivered us here?

Just deserts.

'Just deserts means what, George?'

'When I go, I'm taking you with me. You know that, don't you? You will leave here with me. We'll begin a different life together, you and I. We'll stay in France, right here if you prefer.'

I must have snorted, or in some physical way expressed my disgust, my sense of the ridiculous because, quick as a flash, he grabbed my arm, his glare furious. His fingers were pressing hard into the veins on my wrist.

'Let go!'

He didn't.

'There was a time,' he said, 'when you had eyes only for me, right?'

I clenched my teeth, biting back the pain he was inflicting on me. 'Do you know how many years ago that was, George? We were different people then. I was just a girl.'

'You'd have left here with me, though, wouldn't you? Like a shot, but he, the toff, persuaded you to leave with him because he told you I was dead, right?'

'No. We waited, Peter and I . . . We waited together for days. We both thought that you had drowned.'

'That's what your husband intended. That's right, isn't it?'

He was gripping me so tight, nails carving into me, embedded within me, cutting my salted skin. His eyes, those eyes, twisted and chalky, were burning into me. Spittle at one side of his face, his cheeks growing flushed. 'He stole my life,' he said. 'Your fucking husband took everything from me. We, you and I, we loved each other. I came out of that sea naked. When I made my way back, there was nothing. The house locked up, the car gone. You owe me, and I want my share.'

'Your share of what?'

'You. The rest of your life for all the time we lost. Your company. Us, together. I have come for you, Grace. Your husband owes Gissing everything.'

I was staring into the face of a madman. A physically threatening one. One who could aggress me or my family. I was searching for vestiges of the young Pierre, the

174

dashing individual who had set my heart spinning and seduced me, for whom I had betrayed so much. There was nothing left of him that was identifiable save for the trace of his accent, an inflection in his voice. Pierre was buried, untraceable, beyond reach. I could not appeal to that past.

'I want some of the happiness you have, Grace. I want a life, maybe a kid too. That's why I'm here.'

He leaned towards me to kiss me. I spun my face away from him, repulsed, distressed, cornered.

'One kiss,' he whispered, 'and I'll go. I'll leave you in peace. The soft touch of a woman,' he mumbled. 'I need that. It's been too long. That kindness you offered in the past, you owe it to me again, now, Grace. Show me some tenderness.'

My head was bent, my breath catching. How much of me did he need before he was satisfied – before he was sated – and would walk away?

'I've watched you.' He was still holding onto me, gripping my left arm while shrugging off his jacket with his shoulders. The acceleration of his breath was growing more pronounced in my ear. 'Your face on the screen. I studied you, so close I thought I could reach through the glass, take hold of you in my arms and stroke your cheeks, like this. See, with the back of my hand. Like this.'

His free hand, dry rough skin, was on my face. My own was tight to my pocket. Now was my opportunity. Now. I remained immobile. Paralysed. Incapable. *Now. Now.* I was silently urging myself.

His fingers continued to rub my cheek. His black jacket dropped to the sand, inert, like a monstrous preying insect. With his left hand he unclipped his belt. Was he going to hit me, rape me? I struggled to wrest myself free of him, to liberate myself, but his grasp was of iron. In response to my attempts, he forced me backwards to a reclining position.

'Let me go!' I beat my free arm against his chest. He started to cough, a hacking, wheezing cough that would not abate. He was sweating. An ill man. I had no free hand now to reach for the knife in my pocket to defend myself. 'George, let me go.'

'Come here, closer, closer.'

He was partially leaning on me, over me, still wheezing, and it was then I realized that his face was damp. He was crying, sobbing into my shoulder. The sobs grew more violent, climaxing in convulsions. I was frozen, at an awkward angle, no longer sitting and not yet supine. He released me, disengaged the force of his hold against me, but remained pressed up close to my body, his head buried in the concavity of my neck. I felt the damp of his tears and perspiration against my shoulder. The intimacy, his anguish, broke my heart while his mawkish purging nauseated me, and yet . . . This might be the price of my liberation. I could smell the stale odour of him, cigarettes on his breath, yesterday's alcohol or a tipple earlier this morning. My hand was free, able to draw out the knife, but I could not bring myself to harm him.

I could not picture this man's life. Pathetic, dangerous or both? A victim or perpetrator, a criminal? I could not tally this creature with the young hero I had once loved beyond all reason.

'There is only you, Grace. You are all that's left. Over the years, I dreamed that when we eventually met, as I always knew we would, you would be the one to unchain me. To make me whole again, to give me back my life.'

I was barely listening, my concentration not on his words but on my escape. I took the opportunity of his outpouring to inch myself along the embankment, creating air, distance between us. He lifted his head and gazed at me from eyes that showed the inner landscape of a man marooned. A spent man with nothing to live for. I felt sorrow, pity and disgust in equal measure.

'George, it's getting late. I must go back. The family will be wondering where I've got to. And then they'll come looking. Someone will glimpse the boat, and our secret will be found out . . . but if it helps you to talk to me, we can meet again, or . . . or if you require the funds for your air ticket home . . .'

At my words, his expression changed, flooded with savagery. 'You think you can buy me off, right? Patronize me. I am not leaving here without you. We are going to do this together. There's nothing else left.'

'Do what, George?' I was lifting myself to my feet. I was shaking, my whole being juddering and heaving, but readying myself for the boat, preparing for flight. But, damn it, I was wearing my shoes and would be weighed down with them as they grew waterlogged. He leaped to his feet, yet again knocking me off guard by his agility. Nifty for one carrying extra kilos, with an expanding beer gut. He had me by both arms and was shaking me. I was petrified. 'Let me go!'

'If your Peter hadn't tried to kill me, you would never have left me. We'd still be together.'

I stared in disbelief. 'What are you saying?'

'Murder, Grace. Attempted murder.'

'You're out of your mind. Nobody tried to kill you, George. It's all a fantasy, a lie.'

'Who did this?' he yelled, letting go for the seconds it necessitated to point to his face. Then he had me in his vice-like grip again. 'The man you married. The fucking lawyer who claims to help those in need. Human rights, my arse.'

I stared at him in horror, at the mess of him. To accuse Peter, loyal, gentle Peter . . .

The sheen of sweat on his brow, the look of lunacy in his fixed stare.

'What you're saying is preposterous. I was the one in the water. Not Peter.'

'You were so fucking smashed you didn't know what was happening.'

'Let me go!'

'That night he followed you. Into the water. He had a rock or a metallic object in his hand.'

'Stop! Stop now. This is all lies, fabrication.'

I was feverishly trying to recall the heavenly starlit night that had metamorphosed into tragedy and a nightmare. Had Peter been carrying anything when I came across him on the beach? Of course he hadn't. Why was I even listening to this? He had been in the sea, yes. He'd admitted as much.

Why had Peter been in the sea? I was trying to recollect, to drag it back to the surface of my mind. The trauma I'd spent a lifetime burying.

Why was I giving credence to any of this, searching for any thread of authenticity woven within these macabre accusations? This man was sick, unhinged. Peter was a good, compassionate human being. He was not capable of killing anybody, certainly not this pathetic creature. Even I could not bring myself to wield the blow.

'I'll help you in any way you need me to, George, but I won't listen to any more of this. Do you understand me? What you are saying is a lie. Nobody tried to kill you.'

'I told you, Grace, I'm not leaving here until I have what I want.'

'Which is what? What? *What do you want?*' I was scream-ing, screaming, out of my wits, my voice echoing round the cavernous theatre of rocks. If there was anyone abroad they would have heard me. I had to pull myself together. Taking deep breaths, leaning forward, I bent low, snatching the opportunity to unlace my shoes. I rose to my full height, heaving, slipping my feet out of my trainers. 'I'm offering to help you if I can. I don't know why you're here . . . butting into our lives, threatening us. I will give . . . give you . . . But I won't listen to false accusations against my husband and I'm not coming with you. I will never, never come with you, George. Do you understand that? Is that clear?'

His face grew agitated. His expression was desperate, one hazel eye dancing, the other lifeless, immobile. 'Grace, don't – don't say that. You're all I've got. I need you. I've waited for this moment, planned for it, dreamed of it . . . Waiting for the day when I . . .'

My feet were bare now and I was gently edging the shoes out of my path with my toes so I wouldn't trip over them as I made a run for it.

'Grace . . . if you don't agree to come with me, I'll have to do something very bad.'

'Bad?'

I felt my blood turning ice cold, yet I broke out in a sweat. What manner of *bad*? 'No, please, George, don't let's either of us do anything bad. We're fr-friends. I'm sorry I shouted. We can talk about whether I come with you.'

'When?'

'The next time we meet. Is that acceptable, George? Agreed?'

He nodded.

'I have to return to the house now.'

'You loved me, loved Pierre, didn't you?'

'Yes, yes, I did, of course I did. I'm going to swim to the boat now. I'm just picking up my shoes.' I bent low, keeping my attention upwards on him in case he tried anything violent, while hooking the shoes onto my fingers.

The knife alongside the keys clinked in my pocket.

I wasn't capable of killing him, wasn't capable of killing anybody. I loathed his presence here with a passion. I wanted him to be gone, disappear, but I was not capable of perpetrating such an act.

'Come back tomorrow. Here, tomorrow. Our hidden place.'

I nodded, swung about to make for the water, but he was too fast and caught my arm again, hauling me to him. My back pressed against his abdomen, he rubbed hard up against me.

'Don't play any tricks, Grace. Our secret, just like you've promised. If you break that promise, I'll come looking for you at your beach house and, who knows, I might get lucky like last time and meet one of the grandchildren.'

I pictured Harry wedged in the cleft of the rock.

'Don't make me lose my temper and hurt someone. I can hurt if I want to.'

'You have my word. Now, please, let me go.' I shrugged myself free and took off into the shallows, lunging forwards, tears coursing down my face, swimming for my life. Once in the yacht, as it bounced and cut its path through the skin of blue, I threw a glance back. He was on the shore, standing stock still in the same place, jacket lying close by. He lifted his arm and waved. Such a normal gesture, as though I was his best friend setting off on a morning's sail. I slipped my hand into my pocket and closed my fist around Peter's Swiss Army knife.

What a fool I had been. I was in the company of a crazed, morbidly deranged mind, and more lives than mine were at stake.

1968

Grace's first arrival at Heron Heights

My face against the railway carriage window was like warm butter. I was melting, liquefied by heat. The sun was forcing my eyes closed. I purred like a dozing cat, content with its lot. The south was another country. I was excited, bubbling over, wanted to see, to note, to imbibe every last image, every inch of the passing landscape, but I was dazed by a stupor brought on by the early-summer sun. My pen and my diary slid from my knees to the carriage floor.

May had been a challenging month but now we were completing the last leg of our journey south by train. The railway workers were back at their posts. Petrol was on sale again. Cars were on the roads. The strikes had been subdued; the strikers had accepted what had been offered. France was on the move again. Calm restored throughout the land, which was not necessarily a positive result. De Gaulle had come out of hiding. On 30 May, yesterday, via a speech on the wireless, he addressed the nation: '*Mes chers compatriotes*, the crisis has been calmed.'

The cunning old devil had called for the dissolution of the National Assembly as a means of restoring order. He promised elections within weeks, but he did not put his job on the line. He was not up for re-election. He had delegated the risk. Let his prime minister, Georges Pompidou, take the hit. The sea change Peter and his allies dreamed of had been stopped in its tracks. De Gaulle was taking back control. I threw quick glances to Peter seated opposite me, engrossed in his newspaper. I knew his head if not his heart was still in the capital, in the battle for the new order, alongside his comrades. He was torn. He loved me but he was torn, and how did I feel?

Less committed than he did.

I was looking forward to meeting Agnes, excited at the prospect, but with trepidation, rising nerves. She was, when all was said and done, the sister of Sir Roderick who, Peter had learned during a rather awkward telephone conversation from a kiosk in a village close to Lyon, was being 'called back to London, quitting Paris before the end of summer'.

'I will be liberated,' he said, 'with only myself to answer to. In the autumn, I will return to Paris to complete my studies and resume the fight.'

Sometime, late morning, the city of Marseille loomed into view. Bricks and church steeples, high-rises, brutalist architecture, then vapour and steamers berthed beyond the sprawling port. And the sea, the broad expanse of deep blue water in sunlight, the Mediterranean. It nudged up against the urban constructions, curved and rounded itself there, like a sleeping shellfish. My first sighting of this coast. A location that was to tint so much of my future life.

Pierre was out there somewhere, and I was yet to discover him.

The train pulled into the Gare de Marseille Saint-Charles,

engine shutting down with a long whistle. Journey's end. After more than three weeks of travel, we had reached the stern of the land.

My first steps on Provençal soil.

I stood up, shook my legs. Peter reached for our luggage as I stepped down onto the quay.

I glanced among the shifting, hurrying crowds. Sailors, many of them, laughing, lounging, smoking cigarettes, eyeing up the girls, including me. I got a few winks and smiled shyly in return. There were holidaymakers, well-heeled families, unloading suitcases. Along the quay towards the exit, I spied members of the railway staff who, until a few days ago, would have been among the strikers. And police. They were present in force, pockets of uniformed men surveying the arriving travellers. Since we'd left Paris, a lingering worry had been growing inside me about my arrest, and subsequent escape. I cast my eyes towards my walking feet, then elsewhere, anywhere but in the direction of the law. A moment's fear and sickness giddied me until my attention was caught by a woman in a bright frock. She was waving her arms madly, like one of those men at airports flagging in the landed planes.

'Look, there's my aunt.'

Agnes, waiting on the concourse. I felt my tummy turn, feeling unexpectedly shy, but I had nothing to fear. She flung wide her arms to greet me, as if I were a long-lost family member. 'Welcome, welcome! I have been so looking forward to this day.'

I took to her instantly.

'Dear girl. Peter's friend, Grace, what a delight. I've heard so much good about you. But, you know, you're even lovelier than the praise has conveyed. Welcome back to the south, Peter. You carry the bags, dear. I want to chat with your enchanting friend, make her acquaintance, and then I want to hear all about your adventures during this turbulent time in Paris and beyond. Peter, my brother says you're the next Danton.'

Phew, she never drew breath.

She was thin as a wheat stalk with muscular arms, her hands and elbows patched with paint. Her laugh was vibrant, horsy, neighing. She wore a broad-brimmed straw hat. Her flowered frock was buttoned up the front from the hem to its V neckline. She wore a chunky purple necklace of big fat beads with a matching bracelet. No rings. Her build was slight but her personality and her attire were vivacious and bold. I might have wrapped my hand around her waist and still had space to wiggle my fingers. Her hair was dark and pinned up beneath her sombrero with a few strays sticking to her face, which was clammy from the heat.

It was very stuffy in the station. The black hands on the huge clock read ten to twelve. High noon. Poor Peter was wrestling with his case, work satchel and my backpack. We paused for him to catch up. Agnes had her arm wrapped firmly round my shoulders. She was bounding with energy. Her smile cracked open her face, exposing even teeth and crow's feet about her shining eyes. Although she was no beauty, she was striking and charismatic. Age? I would have guessed early fifties. Older than her brother.

A sweeping descent from the railway station to reach the car, so many steps, 104, to a well-polished, burgundy open-top into which Peter piled our belongings. He struggled to find space for himself on the back seat, legs squashed up tight to his chest, alongside everything else, including two straw bags stuffed with shopping. Celery sticks and baguettes packed tight against several gin and tonic-water bottles.

'We'll stop at a shop in one of the villages to pick up more provisions.'

We didn't. Agnes was nattering so much I think she forgot the groceries. 'Peter, darling, did Roderick tell you I have an exhibition in Rome at the end of next month?' She was yelling above the engine, and then turning to me, 'And I'm not even halfway done. Do you paint?' Before I could shake my head, she was on to the next subject. It reminded me of how when I'd first met Peter he had asked my name and hadn't waited for a response, and we'd spent almost an entire day together before he learned it. A family trait, then. Peter also shared some of her looks, her lustrous jet black hair. Clear eyes, less violet in colour, more blue. She possessed a gift for extraordinary attention to detail, although her driving might have been the exception. At the wheel, she barely glanced at the roads. Other vehicles were hooting at her, drivers raising fists. It was dizzying and terrifying, given the sheer drop to the sea along the stretch of road before the climb towards the site where her house had been constructed on a lonely promontory of red rock. She waved an arm in the direction of the sea. 'All this marvellous expanse of green and rocks and natural habitat is the national park and beyond it Les Calanques. Alas, no sea route or I would have taken you that way to show off my patch of Paradise. Perfect for walking, climbing, exploring and days at the beach. You'll need sturdy shoes, and if you aren't a strong swimmer, check with Peter that it's safe before you venture in. We don't want any accidents.'

'Have you lived here long?' I managed, while she paused for an intake of breath.

'I fled England when I was little more than a girl, probably not much older than you are now. Seventeen. I dreamed of studying fine art at the Beaux Arts in Paris, living with the Bohemian set, shedding the British class system, its injustices and prejudices. And then I met someone. I fell head over heels, and once in love, so very much in love, there seemed little if any reason to return to the British Isles. Quite the reverse. Best to stay away. I was not their kind of person, you see, never had been. Everything I dreamed of, everything I required to sustain me, spiritually, emotionally, artistically, was in France and, later, here in the south. Since which time, this region, this house, Heron Heights, has been both home and inspiration.'

Peter had not mentioned a husband so I was unsure whether the someone she had spoken of had remained as a constant in her life. I supposed, because she spoke in the singular, she must be divorced or a widow. I supposed I would soon find out.

In fact, it was after Agnes had died, twenty-five years later, that I discovered her story and the identity of her lover.

We were climbing the last kilometre. I glanced out at the widening view, the vast expanse of cliffs and scrubland yellowed with scented broom, the sea twinkling in the distance, and I felt the wind play with my hair. The knot in my stomach was magically melting away.

The South of France.

'Now I must pay some attention. The road is scarped and winding and one false move . . . Oh, but look, look there! Here, see. Here we are.'

My arrival, as Agnes had promised, would be one of the high points of my trip. The ascent was clouded with dust from the unmade road beneath our wheels partially obscuring the natural beauty. It was at the crest as we drew to a halt that my jaw, literally, dropped open. There it was: the sweeping ageless panorama Peter had eulogized, nudging Cap Canaille.

'Wow, this is Paradise indeed,' I murmured, and the wind whispered its assent.

Heron Heights, pale pink, two storeys, with a funny peaked turret to the right side – it boasted an upper floor (now our bedroom) – was set on a bluff beneath a soaring precipice shaped like an upside-down ice-cream cone. 'The highest maritime cliff in Europe, with not another property in sight.'

Beyond my wildest dreams.

The house, in its unique position, was planted upon jagged rose-red rock. It overlooked miles of sandy or shingle beaches, each divided by giant boulders into coves and creeks. To the right, some distance from where Agnes had stopped the car, towered a series of stone palisades, carved by history and time into what looked like the flue pipes of a giant organ. Beyond, though out of sight now, Agnes pointed to dozens of small secluded bays and inlets. 'They are Les Calanques, the creeks.'

The area had a wilderness quality, reminding me of Cornwall rather than my preconceived images of the South of France.

I stepped out of the car. The soft wind billowed my blouse. I stood with my hands on my head, the breeze as my fan, gazing about me in wonder. Dumbstruck. It was one of the most beautiful landscapes, seascapes, I had ever set eyes on.

Agnes was alongside me, hanging on to her hat, eyes dancing excitedly. 'Pretty damn special, eh?'

'Unbelievable. Mind-blowing.'

'Peter has always loved it here, haven't you, darling boy? All his childhood summers were spent here.' My hostess spun for confirmation from her nephew, who was unloading the car. From somewhere – there was nowhere but the house – a dog was barking.

'It does get windy here sometimes, I'll grant you that. Otherwise, calm, peace, isolation, nature, wild creatures, easels, oils and wine. Oh, and I have a dog. That's him letting us know who's boss. A robust hound, a buster of a boy, who'll chew your shoes, hats and fingers. Be warned. His name is Bruce. I hope you like dogs?'

Back at home – home was a faint memory to me now, so removed was it from all that I was seeing and experiencing – we had never owned a dog, but I had always longed for one.

'Bruce,' trilled Agnes. 'The only man in my life,' she jested, with a wink in my direction as a black mastiff, the size of a pony, came bounding towards us.

I was in the company of two new people, two new friends – even Peter, who just a few weeks ago was also a stranger – on a strip of rock facing south, gazing out upon possibly the most stupendous sight with which life had thus far presented me. How fabulous it was.

I took a deep breath. On that day, that sublime afternoon, I believed that my life had been blessed, not cursed. That meeting Peter, his bringing me there, was a gift. How could I have foreseen that I was to be the instrument of calamity, that tragedy lay in waiting just a few short weeks away?

Settling in

The house was full of warm sun. Heat seeped out of every corner, like juice flowing from an orange. Art deco in style, clean lines, angles and curves. White walls, white muslin curtains that billowed in the breeze. The front of the house, the façade that faced the sea, was a patchwork of ravishing reds and purples: bougainvillaea embowered. Its music was the sea, the waves that curled and receded over distant pebbles and sand.

I was in my element. I had landed on my feet yet again.

I slung my crumpled travelling clothes onto the bed, peeled off the underwear that was almost glued to my skin, and slipped into the shower. Savon de Marseille, a square khaki block of olive-oil soap, clumsy and slippery in my hands, lathering my grimy, claggy body. The water was tepid but it was all I needed to refresh myself. I changed into shorts in that room of my own. Slabs of sunlight on the ceiling and *tomette* floor tiles. Bed bathed in sunlight, warming the white linen, giving it a burnished glow. The writing table was decorated with tall sunflowers and several sprigs of lavender, upright in a floral vase. Beneath it, a note on a sheet of pale blue stationery. A watercolour of a sailing ship out on the open sea. *Bienvenue, welcome, chère amie de Peter,* written in bold purple lettering. *Agnes.*

My own compact room with a view, and what a view.

I could hear the sea clearly even from that elevation and distance. Its rhythmic roll, back and forth, licking the beach, slapping the rocks. If I could fly like a bird, I could take off from this window-ledge and dive into it. Seamlessly, Olympic fashion.

I unpacked my bag at a somnolent pace, make-believing that this was my very own private hideaway and I was there to stay. For ever and a day.

I paused, stopped, started, threw myself onto the bed against the plumped-up pillows, inhaled the scents, leaned again on the window-ledge, kicked up one bare leg behind me, watched the dog, big Bruce, gambolling in the sand dunes, rooting and ferreting at the Marram grass. There was a path and steps. Rope and wood, rustic style, with bamboo canes made into hanging oil lights, snaking all the way down to the cove.

I promised myself I'd investigate it all later. I'd need a hat, not my beret. A bolder statement, extravagant, and as smart as Agnes's. Saint-Tropez savvy. If I could paint, I would never leave here either.

She was on her own. There was no companion. The love she had spoken of was not in her present, then. I wondered what had happened to him. Not sad for her, I hoped. Alone, here. It could be perfect, this solitude. Or intimidating.

The door opened after the briefest of tap-taps. I swung from the window and my ruminations. Peter's floppy-haired head peered round the frame. 'Lunch is ready. Agnes says we'll have a ripping dinner tonight. Now we'll snack. Bread, cheese and wine, will that do?'

'It will all do. Thank you so much.' I smiled broadly. Peter nodded. He looked a little more relaxed. I threw my unfolded undies onto the bed, leaving drawers and wardrobe doors wide open. I could complete the unpacking later, whenever. I didn't want to miss a single second of this magical day.

After lunch, a long, languid swim. Feet flipping, turning onto my back, belly exposed to the sun. I was a seal in slow motion. My hair hanging loose, dripping like lengths of seaweed. Salt on my skin. Afterwards, spreadeagled on the beach, not even a towel beneath me. The vast blue sky embraced me. I yielded myself up to the day, to the present, to the perfection of this opportunity. These chance encounters. Peter was still in the water. He was a powerful swimmer, ploughing a crawl through the mild azure waves. I had not expected him, an intellectual, to be such an accomplished athlete. I lifted my head from my golden pillow to look for him, a dot on the horizon, and saw him rising out of the spray, sprinting towards me. He flopped at my side. Droplets of water, crystal grains of sand settled on my face.

'Watch it!' I whooped.

He leaned over me, olive-skinned and shiny, and

brushed his lips against the rounded blade of my salt-encrusted shoulder and smiled, licking me, tongue into the indent of my collar bone. 'Happy to be here?'

'Mmm. And you?'

I caught the briefest trace of a shadow, a heaviness behind his eyes. It had been gathering weight for days now. I missed the mischievous glint in his violet eyes. I knew, though, that he was disappointed with the results in Paris and blamed himself for quitting the fight. Absent when the students had occupied the Sorbonne. Absent for the triumphs and disappointments that had followed. He had left to protect me, putting my safety before his vision. Others in the fight had got out of the city at the same time, I reminded him. 'Cohn-Bendit, for one.'

'He was exiled.'

Peter's disillusion sat between us, even though he did his best to conceal his feelings. I didn't want him to hold it against me. I didn't want it to spoil our friendship. I wanted us to be friends for ever.

Agnes and I assembled for 'sundowners' on the veranda. Chilled alcoholic drinks with buckets of chunky ice cubes. 'Campari and tonic, Bellini, or gin and tonic with lemon? We have a lemon tree in the garden. Actually, it's little more than a yard out the back on this bed of limestone but no shortage of citrus fruits. Cut yourself a slice. Two, if you like your cocktails sharp. Which will you have?'

'Campari, please.' I had never tasted Campari before. It was bitter, yet sticky-sweet. Insanely good. I drank it down almost in one go.

Steady.

We shook up another.

Swing jazz on the gramophone. 'I Got Rhythm'. Love it. 'Django Reinhardt. Have you heard of him?'

I admitted I hadn't.

'Chez Florence atop Montmartre was my canteen, our regular hangout. I could have listened to Django and Stéphane Grappelli play together all night. Well, I did! The club had moved to rue Blanche by the time we settled in that *quartier* in 1930 and we frequently danced there till dawn. In 'thirty-four, they formed a band, the Quintette du Hot Club de France. Ah, my Lord, such memories. I was twenty-four. Poor man died far too young.'

'Your lover?' I was appalled for her.

Agnes stayed her chopping and stared at me with a wry smile. 'My lover? No. That's . . . another story, for later in the summer when we've become the best of friends. I was talking about Reinhardt. Django. I knew him quite well back in those euphoric days before the war.'

I felt my jaw drop and gulped the last sip of my second sexy scarlet drink. So deliciously yummy and scrumptious, and just a bit alcoholic. The melting ice cubes clunked against my upper lip and front teeth and numbed my mouth. I pictured Agnes bopping and jiving to swing jazz at dawn with her lover out on the sloping streets of Montmartre. Too cool for words.

Peter's aunt was putting water on to boil, trickling pinches of salt into the liquid and furiously chopping herbs. She was swinging her hips to the music as she worked. I watched her from the rear and longed to know more about her life, about the man she had loved. Her feet, in brightly striped espadrilles laced up beyond her ankles towards her calves, like climbing ivy, were tapping to the jive.

'Any sign of Peter?'

'He'll join us for dinner. He's working, writing a paper, he says.'

'He never stops. Such a clever, ambitious boy.'

I hunted for plates, and found stacks in the lower cupboard of a restored wooden dresser. I chose chunky enamel ones decorated with fruits in luscious bold colours, all hand-painted. Big purple figs, scarlet cherries, oranges.

'What fab designs. Did you paint these?' I called to Agnes.

'No, dear, a friend of mine.'

'Local ceramics?'

'Well, yes, but she's gone now.'

Knives and forks from a drawer, I laid the table for three outside on a terracotta-tiled terrace abutting the side of the main body of the house. It was an enchanted arbour, shaded by vines and overlooking our expanse of sea, settling to navy now and glinting still beneath the first stars of the evening. The table was already dressed with a cloth printed with bees and cicadas. Candles spluttered in the almost imperceptible breeze. What a gay and jolly welcome the table offered, with its display of fruits and insects.

I sat a moment on one of the rush-seated chairs, happy to drink in the panorama before me. The sun had set but the sea was inviting. A bat overhead swooped by my cheek. I jumped from my seat, emitting a shriek. The creature swung about, nose-diving into our evening, then disappeared.

'Our miniature Draculas, Mediterranean horseshoe bats – they're perfectly harmless. They sleep all day wrapped in their cloak-like wings behind the shutters of the house and venture out at dusk in search of dinner. Their delight is moths, not you, dear, and the blasted mosquitoes. They show no fear and I think they've got used to my company – they accept me now and my guests.' Agnes was approaching with a steaming plate of pasta. Big Bruce padded at her side. I rose to help her.

'Looks scrummy.'

'Nothing fancy. Simple dishes because I have little time. No one has complained yet. How did you meet Peter?'

'He picked me up in a bar.'

My hostess let out a loud roar of delight. 'Good for Peter. He has a fine eye for beauty, just like his aunt.'

I reconsidered my answer, thinking I might have given the wrong impression. 'Well, it was more a café than a bar. Lunchtime. My first day in Paris.'

'Love at first sight, or so Roderick described it.' She grinned, plonking the spaghetti in the centre of the table. Aromas of garlic, unfamiliar spices and freshly snipped green herbs wafted my way.

'Smells delicious.'

'Sit yourself down and pour a glass of wine. There's no ceremony here. Tomorrow evening you can make the cocktails. How about that? You're family now.'

I glanced her way to see whether her face expressed

this sentiment, or whether she was just being flippant, and I believed it did. The candlelight chiselling her features gave her appearance a greater beauty than she owned in reality. She was handsome rather than beautiful, and probably older than I had originally estimated.

'I'm not sure I'm up to making cocktails just yet, but thank you for your kindness and your hospitality. This place is beyond wonderful. Cheers.'

'It's splendid that my nephew has brought you here. I've never seen him in the company of a girlfriend before and he's clearly smitten with you. Dear boy. First big love. As I said, his father remarked on it too. Peter has never spoken to me of any girl in the past but, then, he hasn't visited me for several summers now. He was just a teenager the last time he came. I've missed his friendship and company. In the olden days, when he was a boy, he confided in me about everything and I adored it. He's the closest I have to a child of my own. Then university came along and the attention of his comrades took first place. To be honest, it did cross my mind that perhaps he was homosexual and keeping it to himself, though why he should feel it necessary to conceal it from me I have no idea. His father, I suppose. Roderick would hit the roof, old bigot that he is, so Peter would have felt obliged to hide his preferences. Of course, it's clear now that he hadn't met the right girl. It'll be a challenge for you, though. Peter is dedicated to his work, of course, and' – she lifted her long-fingered hands, still smudged with paint stains, to make inverted commas in the air – '"the cause". He'll make a better ambassador than his father. Kinder nature. Considerate. More of a diplomat.'

I was spinning from Agnes's words. Confused.

'Does Peter want to be an ambassador?' I asked, but that was not the question circling in my head or the one I wanted an answer to.

'I assume so. Why else would he be studying politics and law, like his father?' She slapped the palm of her right hand against her left arm, causing her big bracelets to clink against one another, like the play of billiard balls. 'In spite of the bats, we still have mosquitoes, so be warned. Sit still, Bruce, there's a good chap.' The dog was barking at his mistress's bracelets. 'You'll need a wrap to protect your shoulders in the evenings and a decent anti-bug cream. I can furnish you with both if you're not able to sort them out. You'll find everything you need in one of the spare rooms, or pop into the village and buy what you prefer. I burn citronella – that keeps most of the blighters at bay. Never mind Peter. What are you planning on doing with your life? You're young yet, of course.'

I was pouring Soave into my tumbler. Stopped in my tracks. 'You mean as a career?'

'Have you made up your mind or are you just drifting, looking for inspiration?'

'Mind made up long ago. My dad's a musician. Live entertainment and all that. I want to be an actress.'

'Theatre or cinema or both?'

'Cinema's my passion.'

She bowed her head and made a face, which I couldn't quite read. 'Ambitious. Good girl. To achieve anything you have to be ambitious and slave away at it. I hope you read a great deal. Vital in your line of work. In mine as well. Bruce and I walk in nature every morning before the world is up and about. Study the changing light show, the shadows, tones. I commune with the sea and I read. Do help yourself to whatever you fancy in the library. To borrow, mind, and please, please, don't leave the books out in the sun. The heat unglues their spines, yellows the pages and it drives me doo-lally how some guests abuse them. Oh, and I listen to music. There's a splendid collection of LPs on the two shelves alongside the record player in the study. Otherwise up in my studio. Where is that nephew of mine? The spaghetti will be getting cold. Peter! Peter! Give him a shout, will you please, Grace?'

'I'm right here.'

Peter sauntered onto the vine terrace cradling a full glass of red wine. He was wearing neatly pressed shorts, khaki, almost the colour of the soap in my bathroom, and a crisp open-neck white shirt that no one would have believed had been stuffed and creased in his suitcase for three weeks.

'I thought you were working, not ironing your clothes,' I teased.

He had caught the sun. Burnished-beetroot, even his delicious ears. It was odd but it suited him, gave a Latin dash to his otherwise conventional handsomeness.

During the journey, I had been bothered as to whether Agnes was under the impression that Peter and I were a couple. Not just sleeping together but in the conventional adults' approach to relationships. I was delighted and relieved to have been given my own room.

Now that I'd met her, she didn't strike me as a traditionalist. Still, I was puzzled by her remark that I would need to be patient, that Peter's career would be a challenge for me. I mean, we weren't planning on settling down. We were just having fun.

After dinner we slid across to the veranda 'to stretch out more comfortably'. It was vast and extended the full length of the sea-facing side of the property. There, Peter and his aunt spread themselves on reclining chairs, wine glasses on the floor at their sides, while I opted for one of the old wooden rockers, stuffing an embroidered cushion for comfort beneath my curled-up bare feet. Agnes untied her espadrilles and tossed them to the ground. Bruce snored contentedly at his mistress's side. A scented joss stick was burning in a tall glass on the drinks cabinet behind us. From the record player in the study, piano keys played softly.

'I love this,' I said. 'Mozart's Piano Concerto No. 21 in C major, K 467. Second movement. It's amazing.' I was showing off. Too many glasses of white wine. I knew next to nothing about classical music but I had seen the Swedish film *Elvira Madigan* the previous year at an arty cinema in Oxford Street in London and had fallen in love with the soundtrack. This was it.

Agnes glanced across at me with an amused glint in her heavenly blue eyes, a little surprised. 'Clever girl,' she said. 'Can you identify the pianist?'

I didn't have a clue.

Beyond the cliff's edge, with its dramatic drop to the sea, the sky spread out above us, navy and star-laden. None of us said a word. Even Agnes was silenced in the face of the night's splendours. Its tranquillity. Its perfect harmony. Only the cicadas remained busy, sawing noisily in their quest for love. Peter reached a hand in my direction and curled the tips of his fingers round my wrist. I could feel him nudging me to set off for bed, but I was settled, content where I was. Releasing his grip, I lifted both my arms and gathered up my long hair, twisting it into a knot atop my head, then allowed my hands to fall into my lap.

'Well, that's me done for the day. Leave the table. I'll do the dishes in the morning. I'm always up and about at five. It's the perfect time to get all the chores behind me while I drink my first bowl of coffee before a walk. Come on, Bruce boy.' Agnes bent for her espadrilles and prodded the sleeping dog's haunches with her painted toes. She wore a silver bracelet round her ankle, I noticed then. The dog staggered to his feet and plodded to the door. His paws made clipping sounds against the stripped wood.

'Goodnight, to you both.' Agnes leaned over us one after the other and pecked our foreheads. 'Sleep tight. Peter, put some cream on your skin before you peel like a piece of fruit.' She turned to me. 'Peter will tell you, dear, breakfast is whenever you want it. Coffee always on the go. You organize the rest according to your fancies. Sweet dreams.' With that, she and her hound swept into the main body of the house. I could hear her humming the Mozart, into its third movement now, as she climbed the stairs to the tower, her studio and bedroom. The crown of the house, the bird's-eye view, she'd claimed.

We sat in silence for a time. My head was empty of thought. I was deliciously sated. Food, wine, cocktails, sun and swimming had worked their sorcery. I wanted nothing more than to scramble into bed in my own small cabin-room and be lulled to sleep by the freshness of those lavender-scented pillowcases.

I rose and stretched, a good long yawn, and sauntered to the table. Peter was on his feet too. 'Leave all that – you heard what my aunt said.'

'I'll just take them through and stack them in the sink.'

'There's no need.'

'I want to. In any case, I'm not ready to sleep yet.'

Peter, behind me, wrapped his arms around me locking my spine and buttocks against him. 'Neither am I,' he mumbled in my ear.

I gently extricated myself. 'I'll see you up there.' I was beginning to take on board the intensity of his emotions. Wherever I was, that was where he wanted to be. It made me a little uneasy about what would be expected of me, and a little claustrophobic. I dreaded wounding him, that was the last thing I wanted, but I wasn't up for commitment, not ready for it. However Peter pictured our relationship now and in the future, I felt sure it was not in synch with my vision. Agnes's words had set me thinking, and it was on that evening that I decided I should distance myself from him. Just a bit.

I felt guilty that he had left Paris for me, although I had been, and still was, colossally grateful for his kindnesses. And I was incredibly fond of him. Agnes had referred to me as family, which was a bit far-fetched, although I was super-pleased to be included in their company. I was fascinated by her, a little mesmerized. She was different, odd but attractively so. She was Bohemian, a free spirit. I wanted to emulate her. Bohemian was groovy. She would surely understand that I was not ready for commitment.

Peter upstairs, I was alone in that spectacular environment. It was thrilling. All cares about my parents and my future or the ugliness of events in Paris, about Peter's feelings for me melted to an acceptable softness. Like chocolate in the hot sun. I felt as though I was mistress of this universe. I was tempted to rush barefoot, arms flung wide, to the beach and throw myself naked into the phosphorescent water for a moonlit dip, but as I didn't know the currents, the path had some sharp stones and I was definitely tipsy, I thought better of it.

Agnes had warned me about the dangers of swimming. There was a steep shelf in the water. It fell away within metres. You were out of your depth before you realized it. 'You need to know the bays,' she'd said, 'and the time you choose to swim. On the up side, there are some astounding underwater rock formations, and caves with Neolithic paintings. They're well worth a visit, but I advise against making those discoveries alone. Speak to Peter. He knows every inlet and cove, almost every pebble, along this stretch of coast. You'll be safe with him at your side.'

I finished the clearing up and slipped outside to sit cross-legged for a while. I was beyond the veranda's edge, like a Buddha on the grass, inhaling the nocturnal scents. It was splendorous, too beyond-my-wildest-dreams to find myself there. The pine resin was the perfume most dominant, released into the cooler air after a long hot day. I listened to the crickets, watched the stars, hoping for the white line of a shooter, but saw none. The sky was inky-black now and still.

*

When I climbed the stairs, I put my head round the door of Peter's room. He had left it ajar, waiting for me, his bedside light still illumined. A book of Nietzsche had fallen to the floor. 'Sleep tight, Peter,' I mouthed soundlessly. He was already deep in slumber, without a care in the world. I smiled and tiptoed two doors back to my own blissful abode.

Too excited for sleep, I crossed to the window and leaned out, star-gazing. Still no glittery sprays of white magic. It didn't matter.

As a child, I had watched by my bedroom window for shooting stars. They were harder to see in England because the sky was frequently cloudy or it was raining, unlike this astonishing vista. My dad had told me shooting stars were lucky – everybody believed that, I learned later, it wasn't Dad's magic formula – and when I saw one or caught sight of a meteor shower I should always make a wish. Under such auspicious circumstances, he promised, my wishes were bound to come true. Mum, who brought God into most subjects, said shooting stars were God's way of showering blessings upon us, which is why our dreams come true when we wish upon them.

I closed my eyes. What did I wish for now? First, that my dad would be gentle with my mum and the fighting between them would cease. What else? To stay here? To be as free and independent as Agnes? To be a film star, which had been my most profound wish since I was little, or just to continue as I was at the moment for as long as possible without responsibilities?

I wished that this summer could go on for ever, but as I knew it couldn't, I added an addendum to the wish.

After this was over, I wanted to come back to Heron Heights one day and stand where I was at that moment, looking out at the sea, and have a perfect life.

It was a massive wish, but that's what wishes are, aren't they? Dreaming the impossible, wanting the whole damn caboodle.

Oh, but how soon my carefreeness was to end.

The Present

I never managed to keep my promise to George. It was made in haste, but I had intended to meet him again at the creek, as I had agreed. My non-arrival must have flipped him out. It must have been the turning point.

I rose at five having slept fitfully, dressed quickly, hair not brushed, face splashed with cold water, eyes puffy, hurried down the stairs, picked up the keys to the boat, then descended the beach steps in barely a shaft of light. This had to be the last time, I knew that. Somehow I had to persuade him to leave, go away, but I hadn't yet found a solution, the enticement that would send him on his way.

If I offered him a carrot of hope for the future? Time together in London? But I hated the thought of tricking him. Of such duplicity.

That morning, I'd had the presence of mind to bring a towel and I waded out to the craft in seawater that chilled my flesh. Once on deck, I dried myself and swung back to the house to confirm that I wasn't being observed. The snug world of Peter's family was in dreamland. Oblivious to the danger that awaited them. No one in sight. Perfect. I drew up the anchor, slipped the key in the ignition, gave the motor some choke and turned it over, but it refused to fire. I was puzzled. I tried the key once more but still no luck. It turned over but did not ignite. The battery wasn't flat. Everything had been in good working order the previous morning when I had anchored her. My heart was in my mouth. I had to honour this rendezvous. I had to be there. I could not enrage the man further. Lives depended on it. I wanted no more threats. I wanted him dealt with. A clean break. I was grappling, scrabbling for the torch to try to understand the problem. I feared that numerous attempts at turning the engine would kill the battery, wake someone and serve no real purpose. I was early. I had time. Overhead a gull screeched, making me jump.

I took a deep breath, wiped away the sweat gathering on my brow and in my armpits. There was no reason to get alarmed. I bent low to read the fuel gauge. The boat was not out of diesel. So what was the problem? Was there water or dirt in the system? I checked that the air vents to the fuel tank were open. All fine. Had one of the filters got clogged? I was on my hands and knees crawling in the semi-rising light. I had to fix this. I was whimpering, chuntering to myself. What else could be causing the problem? Why this morning of all mornings? I lifted myself to my haunches, pulled out the choke knob – had I flooded the engine? No. I turned it again. Still no engagement.

'What the –'

Peter would know what to do. He would solve this in seconds. But I couldn't confide in him.

I closed my eyes, hands over my face. I could picture that figure in black plodding, as the sun rose higher, to our appointed meeting place, waiting there on the beach, gazing out to sea, angry and disappointed, plotting his riposte. Plotting his revenge. *Something bad.*

Swimming to the cove was out of the question. It was many more kilometres along the coast than I could manage and time was not on my side. I swung myself up and over the side of the boat, into the water, nearly ricking my ankle, and waded to the shore. 'Promise you'll come,' he'd said, 'or I'll do something bad.'

All I wanted was for him to disappear out of our lives. No more threats.

1968

Late June, meeting Pierre

On the bus to Marseille. A bus of many colours, of reds and blues and sticky-rock dreams. Mountainous sea road. Rounding the curves, the bus swayed and rolled and bounced along its way.

'Where are you going?' Peter had called to me as I set off, hair flying, bag slung over my shoulder.

I nearly answered, 'Morocco.' It was equally exotic here, though. I might have been in Africa. Palm trees leaning towards the horizon. Olives and dates and thick black coffee for breakfast.

'Shall I come with you?' He was trailing a few steps behind me as I set off down the path.

I shook my head and waved without looking back. 'See you later.' I screwed up my eyes. I didn't want to pain him – I didn't want to ill-treat him but I had to claim my independence. 'I'll see you later for a swim.'

Evergreen oaks all bent in on themselves, sharing tribal secrets, lined my route. Sandy inlets, flooded with emerald green sea, beckoned. Nature's molten jewellery.

I was en route to the mighty port city, which stood forty minutes by bus. Through the window, I stared down on tourists slathered in oil, horizontal in the bays or bobbing in the shallows. Matchstick-sized holidaymakers. Crisp white yachts.

From the diesel-reeking bus station bustling with crowds, I strode to the port. Sloe-eyed sailors from the Middle East cast me lascivious looks. It was new to me, the way men looked at me, hanging on me their drooling hunger. I wondered, might it be because I've said farewell to my virginity? Invisible changes had happened, were happening, within me. An aura of womanliness was peeping through and unfamiliar pheromones seeping out. Swarthy dark-haired young men drinking in cafés gave me a wink, a grin, blew kisses with pouted lips. A tongue slipped loose like a lizard's. I turned my glance elsewhere, acting coy, falsely oblivious to the scrutiny, though I confess, deep down, I was flattered by the attention even if I knew I shouldn't be. Peter would not be impressed. But I was not tethered to Peter. I was young and free.

Belle-époque grandeur, buildings you could eat, like oversized wedding cakes, were surrounded by breeze-block hell. Windows open, screaming infants. Pneumatic drills digging up the streets, dredging for space for future skyscrapers. After the quietude of Agnes's hillside, these urban activities were an assault on my senses.

I skipped with a bounce, in plimsolls, cut-off denim shorts and skimpy top. Midriff exposed. Stomach not sufficiently flat. All the wine. Must lose weight before drama school. A tad plump, I foolishly judged myself. The wind from the sea blew my hair. It flew and flapped and sailed. I was in fine fettle, swimming daily, eating healthily. I stopped to buy a postcard and stamp for my folks from a newspaper kiosk. *Left Paris, made it south. Having fun. Don't do anything I wouldn't do. Xx.* My dad's phrase when he was being lighthearted and I was off to the youth club on a Sunday evening.

I re-read it, my biro message, sighed, tore up the card and chucked it into a street-side bin. I'd find a post office, telephone them, speak to them, listen to their voices. Blow the expense. Just a brief exchange. Were they at each other's throats? Was Mum being knocked about? I'd hear the fear, if I spoke to them. I hoped they were missing me, but not too much. I hoped Mum was not on her own, not lonely all the time, that Dad was coming home at nights and being kind to her. I wanted them to be happy so that I could be, so that I could live my own life.

I wanted no cares. Growing up is a selfish process. It's Me time. Discovering Me. Pushing my limits, my boundaries.

A window-cleaner on a ladder leaned dangerously from a second-floor window and gave me a long wolf-whistle. I laughed, preening, strode on, accentuating the swing of my hips.

This was my second solo trip to the metropolis in the three weeks since we'd arrived in the south. I had taken a shine to the muddled old city with its turbaned Arabs, whiskery old hags with gleaming eyes and hawkers screeching from the fish stalls where the *poissons* flapped and gasped to save their expiring lives and would screech, too, if they were able. Lobsters crawled across slabs of salt-soaked wood, their claws tied with string. Marseille stank of the petroleum-polluted sea. It stank of history, imperialism and corruption. I witnessed the disregard for the scrawny North Africans, the maltreatment of them.

The way the police hassled them. I would have weighed in, fought their corner, but I had to keep beneath the radar.

Marseille was the city of illegal drug runs, although I hadn't caught sight of any of this, of mighty vessels and black tobacco, Moroccan water pipes and just a vague whiff of urine from the drunks hoping for a passage on a ship to North Africa.

The prostitutes, many of Semitic and Phoenician extraction, were well padded. Buxom, tawny-skinned and scarlet-lipped. None of that northern European thinness for their clients.

I chose a ringside seat down at the *vieux* port on the street terrace of one of the multitude of cafés. Here, Big Brother and the Holding Company, with lead vocalist Janis Joplin, were rocking 'Down On Me' and I ordered three dollops of ice cream – *coconut* ice cream – and sipped locally pressed lemonade sweetened with sugar. I was idly leafing through a yellowed paperback filched from Agnes's study – André Gide's *Fruits of the Earth* in English. Peter had lent it to me. 'You must,' he said, pressing it into my hands. But feet tapping, my concentration was all over the place. I didn't want to read yet. I was happy to drink in the ambience. I pretended to spot the criminals and smugglers, invent their stories, eyes peeled for covert operations, and jot my reflections in my diary. Action movies. Deep stuff.

I hadn't telephoned my parents since we'd hit the south. I'd promised my mum I would try to ring home at least once every few weeks and I said to myself, as I tapped my feet to Janis, that I would do it today before I took the bus back to Agnes's, where Peter would be waiting for me, impatient for our afternoon dip. He had been on at me to know why I was spending less time with him. I didn't know how to explain that sometimes I wanted to be on my own.

I cared for Peter, and mostly I fancied him, but I wasn't in love.

It was peaceful down at the port, watching the world go by. Until a police car cruised by. It rolled on down to the end of the track, swung about and motored back. My heart was in my mouth as the vehicle drew to a halt, engine idling, a few metres in front of me. My spine, my limbs were tensing. I scuttled my feet in under the table, like a crab, and buried my head, resolute concentration, in the book I was not yet reading. Nobody had taken my picture on that May afternoon in Paris, had they? A creeping doubt that my escape had been archived, that law enforcement was looking for me, continued to harry me.

The officer alongside the driver was peering out of his open window, dancing his head to and fro, like one of those nodding dogs you see in rear windows. The inside of the café appeared to be his focus. Were they hunting someone? Had I, in all innocence, installed myself outside a seedy dealer's joint? I glanced into the darkened interior, searching for the barman to settle my bill and get away. No waiter in sight.

I grabbed my biro and began to scribble nonsense in my notebook. For want of something more interesting, I began with the date – Monday, 24 June 1968.

And then what? Pen hovers over page. *Can that* flic *see my trembling hand? Is he from a local or national squad?* I was scribbling furiously with half my hooded gaze concentrating on the lower section of the patrol car, which remained stationary. Wheels at a standstill. Hot tyres against well-worn tarmac. Close by, tossed in the gutter, a flattened blue packet that had once contained Gitanes. The engine was cut. It settled to stillness.

Merde.

The passenger door was opening. Booted feet, one after the other, hit the grimy street and began to pace in the direction of the bar. No, in my direction. I slid the Gide paperback towards me and started to copy whole sentences from where it had fallen open somewhere in the middle. I pressed hard against the book and felt the spine weaken. Agnes will chastise me for this, if she finds out.

I was attempting the 'buried in work – studious of thought' posture. Student engagement, but my body language was giving me away as I began to shiver. A tinny taste flowed into my mouth. I recalled blood. Instinctively the tip of my tongue settled within the soft, missing-teeth cavity. Police officer, missing teeth. The two were wedded in my memory. The booted feet, polished to a spit, were inches in front of me and, *merde* again, they drew to a halt directly in front of my table.

'*Mademoiselle, excusez-moi?*'

I hesitated, then slowly lifted my head, feigning surprise at the sight of him. I should have slipped my sunglasses on. Too late now. I spotted instantly that he was from Police Nationale, not the local *municipale*. More serious, then. Heavier metal.

'*Oui, Monsieur?*' I smiled, exuding charm.

'Your bag is on the ground. *Malheureusement*, there are

many light-fingered undesirables hanging around the port and this corner is one of the seamiest. Your belongings could be snatched in the blink of an eye and the blackguard gone before you know it. I suggest you keep it on your lap.'

I nodded. My limbs were locked, rusted together, my smile rictus. Lips, a taut piece of string. No words, not even *merci*, were forthcoming. He remained where he was, obscuring the sun, enveloping me in a wide black shadow that had the bulk of Orson Welles. He was eclipsing the heat, the warmth of the sun, shrivelling me.

Was he hanging about to confirm that I had understood him and taken on board his advice? I slid my hand to the ground and, without looking up again, I hooked my satchel strap with my fingers and hauled it to my bare knees. Did my conduct appear suspicious?

'You are not French, is that so?'

I cleared my throat. 'No,' I croaked, 'not French.'

'May I see your identity papers, please?'

Now I was jelly, visibly jittery. Full-on collywobbles. I should have just picked up the stupid bag and he would have sauntered off to get on with his day. Too late.

I fumbled with the zip on my satchel until eventually, clumsily, I drew it open. Inside, tucked, was my passport. I lifted it out and handed it over. Holding my arm steady. A ChapStick dropped into my lap, settling in the cradle of flesh between my locked bare legs. The bulky law man clocked it. Peepers on my thighs. He accepted the document without unfastening his concentration from my limbs. A large mole was growing in the centre of his right cheek. Or might it have been a scar, a healed bullet wound?

He was menacing, like someone who had the upper hand, behaving with the nonchalant certainty of a cop who is on to something.

It would have been almost comical, this clichéd behaviour, if I hadn't been so scared.

Could he smell my fear?

'Travelling alone?'

I nodded.

'You're very young to be here by yourself,' he remarked, as he flipped through the pages, most of them empty, journeys not yet undertaken, of my blue-jacketed passport.

'Sixteen. First time out of Great Britain?'

I shook my head.

'Have you just arrived in Marseille? Disembarked one of this morning's trains?'

I shook my head again.

'Stayed in Paris?'

'Only,' I coughed awkwardly, 'for a few days.' My legs pressed tighter against one another.

'Got somewhere to stay in the city?'

'Outside. With friends, not far from La Ciotat. You want the address?' I was praying he didn't. The last thing I wanted was for lovely Agnes to discover the details of my Parisian incarceration, albeit for less than half a day. Peter wouldn't have mentioned it.

The cop was still turning passport pages, back and forth, calibrating, weighing up whatever unanswered questions remained in his head.

'Do you know what this area of the city is reputed for?'

I held out my hand, encouragingly, expectant that he

would return my travel document. He didn't. His fingers bunched around it more tightly.

I glanced towards the port and, in the distance, hefty rocking vessels. Liners, trading vessels, a barge stating 'Port Police Patrol', pleasure cruisers, fishing boats, their coloured nets hauled to shore and thrown into heaps. The stink of blood and filleted-out innards. 'It's a fish market,' I replied.

He screwed up his features, hardening his resolve.

What was I supposed to answer? That this was one of the most corrupt ports on the planet? That I was hoping to score drugs? Which I was not.

'Are you here to buy fish?' He swung his attention back to the waterfront where, lined up along the water's edge, the stallholders, fishermen in thigh-high wellingtons and oil-stained vests, busy alongside their stocky wives with hands as scrubbed and scoured as Brillo pads, were packing away their wooden crates and the remainder of their morning's catch into Citroën and Renault utility vans. 'If so, you are a little late.' He tossed my passport back onto the table. It landed on my notebook-diary. A spoon clattered and dropped to the ground. A tawny crouching cat, back arched, beneath the next table hissed and took off. Mr Plod's partner fired up the engine. The patrol car was ready.

'How much cash are you carrying?'

'Sorry?'

'It is a legal requirement here in France to keep a certain sum of cash on your person. Otherwise you are classed as a vagrant. How much have you got?' His accent was thick. Provençal, twangy.

I rooted for my purse. The engine, behind him and in front of me, was idling. I slid open the smaller zip and pulled out all that was there. One fifty-franc note. I ignored the few coins and raised the note, like a prize, between my trembling fingers.

He nodded, and a half-smile broke across his podgy face.

'Have a good day, Mademoiselle.' He turned and waddled his large backside to his car. Once seated, he gave a last surly glance in my direction and the black Citroën pulled away. My body went limp. My hand fell to the table with a light thump, fingers loosened, and a gust of wind made off with my blue fifty-franc note.

Damn.

I let it go, too drained to give chase, watching as it danced and streaked towards the sea until a stranger halted its progress with the sole of his sandal, swiped it up from the cobbles, confirmed his *bonne chance* and pocketed it. Someone's lucky day. Not mine. 'There goes the price of my lemonade and ice cream, my bus ticket back to Agnes's, my call to Kent and any shopping I might have felt inclined to indulge in.'

I peered into my purse before stashing it back into my bag, and stuffed the ChapStick back in there too. Sixty centimes was my remaining fortune. The rest was in my room at the villa.

Now they *can* arrest me for vagrancy!

I didn't even know the telephone number back at the house. The walk would take me till tomorrow. I was stymied.

I had no choice but to hitch a lift.

'I'm glad that wasn't me being given the glad eye by that gross brute.'

A male voice from behind me with an English lilt to it. He must have been in the café drinking at the bar out of my line of vision, concealed within the crepuscular light. I swung round and was taken aback by the man smiling down at me. Without exaggeration, he was the most . . . the most gorgeous, sexy, attractive, striking dreamboat I had ever set eyes on. Lean. Large grey eyes that seemed to shift gently between grey and denim blue. Blue-grey. Expressive. He looked as though he had been dipped in gold. Perfect skin, evenly tanned. White teeth. Was I staring? Was I lost for words?

You bet.

In loose pale-blue chinos, open-neck beige-pink, short-sleeved beach shirt. Expensive beige suede loafers, which to my taste were a bit too smart-set-on-the-Riviera show-off. Blond hair. Bleached by the sea? Was he a yachtsman? His hair fell in long, easy curls, like the curls of butter in posh restaurants. He had tied it back in a loose ponytail. My constitution had already been weakened by the encounter with that probing police officer. I was not ready for this.

'May I?' He pulled out a chair from the table where the cat had been napping out of the sun and placed it alongside mine. Straddled it back to front as though riding a horse, leaned his arms, tanned to a golden buff, on its backrest and smiled. 'On the run, are you, darling?'

I shook my head, glancing downwards. He was just too

gorgeous, like staring into the sun. I felt the force of his attention pulsing right through me and I had little resistance left.

'This is the girls' beat. I suppose you knew that?'

'Girls' beat?' I couldn't hide my surprise. No, I hadn't known. 'So he thought I was a hooker?'

'I fear so. Let me buy you another drink.'

I lifted my head and grinned, as though my face would split in two. Salvation. Strands of my hair were pinned to my cheek by the wind. I tugged them loose. 'I tell you what, could I ask you to pay for this one, and the ice cream too, if that's not pushing my luck?' I pointed to the empty dish, its spoon now somewhere beneath the table. 'It would help me out. I have no money. I'll pay you back.'

He nodded. 'What's your name?'

'Grace. And you?'

A split second's reflection, then, 'Pierre.' He laughed.

'Pierre? That's odd.'

He winked.

We were conversing in English and I discerned traces of lengthened syllables, of a Yorkshire accent.

Pierre ordered us a bottle of wine. 'White?'

'Yeah, why not? Thanks.'

Chilled Chablis, a *premier cru*.

Seriously!

'After that grilling you deserve the best.'

Once past our second glass each, and I was feeling a great deal lighter of spirit, Pierre proposed lunch at one of the fish restaurants along the front. The wine was making my head swim. Nothing for breakfast and only ice cream since, I was feeling careless, carefree. I should have been trotting back up the Canebières to the bus stop. At this rate I'd forget where it was. Lose track. Peter and Agnes were expecting me back at some point but, but... I didn't have the price of the bus ticket, didn't know the house phone number. And my stomach was rumbling. I felt the burning sun rouging my skin, scalding my cheeks. I dipped my finger in my wine glass and patted my cheeks with dribbles of liquid to cool them. Licked my finger, frowned, a bit salty. Dabbed behind my ears, playing the fool, giggling. Pierre was watching me, denim eyes hard on me. My legs had changed colour since I'd been sitting there. One was redder than the other, which was funny. The wine coursed through my veins.

Lunch in a fish restaurant in Marseille with this total hunk of a stranger.

Suddenly, my lucky day.

I was deliciously, giddily, effervescently drunk. On the pavement laughing raucously, head thrown back, rocking on my feet, little different from the yachts out on the water, until a church bell chimed four from a tower out of sight.

Four o'clock. No. I must be on my way. I spun about and caught the lace of my sneaker, almost lost my balance. Pierre grabbed my arm. 'Are you running out on me, Cinderella? Where are you staying?'

'Not far from Cassis.'

'Let me give you a lift?'

'Should you be driving? It's a fair distance. Dangerous *cols* up on the high road.'

'*Cols?*'

'Sharp twisty bends.'

'No problem.' He bowed, mock-chivalry. 'Let's go.' He took my arm to guide me a step or two.

Pierre's car was parked outside the old city. We set off on foot from our harbourside diner. It was a strenuous hike and we sweated off lunch, and maybe some of the alcohol we had consumed, as we climbed keeping stride. After some effort and huffing, we found ourselves at a dizzying lookout point with a parking bay, fringing a sweeping drop. Stationed there was one lone car, an open-top the length of an ocean liner. Pearly green.

'This can't be yours?' I was dumbstruck but there was no other vehicle in sight.

He nodded.

I moved to touch it, stroke it. The bodywork burned my fingers. Too long stationed in the midday sun. 'What kind of boogie-woogie wagon is this?'

A 1963 Cadillac-Eldorado-Biarritz. Its body contours were as elegant and sexy as its owner's. Its interior had walnut panelling, and the seats were fitted out in dark green leather that counterpointed the bodywork. Exterior finish in chrome. Hubs, bumpers. It had fins. Fins, and white tyres and a metal grille at the front, like chrome shark's teeth. I circled it, brushing, rubbing, fingering it, not quite certain whether it was real or a mirage. It was supersonic, notorious luxury and surely it could fly off the mountainside. I laughed loudly, wine-fuelled. 'Is it a green dragon or a golden coach?'

My day had taken on a surreal, fairytale aspect. Enchanted. I smiled to myself. Pierre – who was he? – watched me silently.

What a summer.

We were overlooking the city. To the west, the commercial and old city ports whence we had climbed. The Mediterranean of trade and commerce dominated here, both underworld and legitimate. Towards the east, the opposite orientation, was the flight path to Agnes's villa facing out to wide-open waters, a burnished horizon flecked with blue and turquoise, the azure sea, the mauve-rock inlets and canyons of the *calanques*. Gulls were circling in the near distance. Our clandestine playground. Peter's and mine.

Pierre and Peter. The same name. I had only just cottoned on.

Why was a bloke from the north of England called Pierre? Maybe not his real name.

Pierre was unfolding the soft top. He pulled open the passenger door, waiting, like a chauffeur. 'Ready?'

'Sure you don't mind driving me back?'

He dismissed my question with a wave of his hand.

Should his reckless disregard for the rules of the road have alerted me right back then?

I slid in. As spacious as a motorboat, it exuded class, as Mum might have remarked. Damn. I hadn't rung home.

Once in the driver's seat, Pierre thrust the car into gear. The tyres spun, kicking up small stones and pebbles. We reversed and swung out onto the narrow ocean road, all set to navigate the lofty highway. A bird's-eye view. The only way to travel. I was picturing my arrival. Drawing up to the rear of Agnes's house, Bruce growling his disapproval at a nattily turned-out, prosperous-looking stranger in a fancy car. 'Where have you been all day?'

I hadn't sent my folks a postcard and I had been drinking.

'You can ditch me here,' I said, as we approached one of the final turns in the lane that led to my summer residence.

Pierre rounded the corner and drew to a halt, depositing me without a word in what appeared to be the middle of nowhere because I'd requested it. The house was nowhere in sight or any other building – well, there weren't any. Who was to say where this deserted lane led? Still, he didn't question my request to be set down in this out-of-the-way spot. He expressed no concern for my safety. He took me at my word.

I hesitated before opening the door.

When will I see you again?

'Thanks for lunch,' I was spinning out the moment, elongating it. 'And thanks for jollying up my afternoon.'

'It was fun, Grace. I hope the rest of your holiday is a blast.'

I unstuck myself like Elastoplast from the passenger seat and smiled with an all's-well face, struggling against my disappointment. Was this it?

I lingered, watching him, anticipating, eager for a last-minute invitation. His elegant yet cherub-featured face. His beauty was not symmetrical. His features were not even. Still, in my eyes, he was perfection, except he hadn't asked to see me again.

I raised my arm to offer a little wave. How coy, pathetic. How stupid and girlish of me, to wait there for him to invite me on a date.

I should have invited him in. 'Join us for a Campari, darling, why not?'

We should have rocked up to the door in his snazzy car. I had been thinking of Peter, desirous not to hurt my friend's feelings.

Pierre reversed, spun on the track, releasing whorls of grit, while I remained planted to the spot until the fins of his automobile, the lipstick scarlet of the rear lights, had disappeared out of sight. A dot diminishing to nothing, as though the car and he had never existed.

Cicadas were thrumming in the roadside brush, drowning the diminishing hum of the Cadillac's departing engine. My golden carriage had evaporated, evanesced.

Sober, back down to earth, I plodded the last hundred yards of the track, still replaying in my mind the record Pierre had slipped into the car's 8-track tape deck as we had jetted the higher coastal *cols* in silence. Chuck Berry's album, *St. Louis to Liverpool.* The track playing over in my head and humming on my lips was 'No Particular Place To Go'.

Over lunch, I'd asked Pierre where he was staying and he'd replied, 'Just passing through.'

So, that was it? The best-looking bloke I had ever bumped into turns out to be my brief encounter in that summer of '68. 'Too bitter-sweet. Too bad.' I cursed, as I kicked at the dust.

If only it had been the last time I ever set eyes on Pierre.

My days were super-cool, unfolding in languorous lengths, each moment apportioned: eating, swimming, kicking my heels in the sand, dozing on the rocks with a book over my face, jaunts to the village with Peter for baguettes and wine. We would take Agnes's car for a spin and sometimes stop for a dip or make a detour to visit one of the bays I hadn't previously discovered. Peter sought out the isolated spots where no other soul visited. We lay in the sun together, he reading, studying, me daydreaming, getting sticky and covered in sand. We didn't make love, or infrequently. Some days he laid his book aside and rolled towards me, licking at my flesh, but I fended him off, making excuses. 'Let's just enjoy companionable interludes together,' I would say.

' "Companionable interludes"? Why, Grace? What does that mean? What's happened? Don't you love me any more?'

His words, that question, left me bunched up inside, confused, guilty. It was as though I'd missed a whole movement in the music, an act in the play. We had never spoken of love before.

On these occasions, I'd jump to my feet, and saunter off across the rocks to watch the mottled brown fish darting and feeding in the shallow pools. Peter could identify them all: the *saupes* and the *sars*, the groupers and the turtles. It was enlightening, uplifting, being in his company, discovering the flora and fauna. His knowledge was thrilling on so many levels. I wished then, with a deep ache, that I loved him as passionately as he did me, that I could reciprocate his feelings, but I couldn't. The intensity of his emotions was a bit scary. I was changing and I didn't know how to explain it to him without injuring him.

I considered taking the bus back to Marseille, returning to that bar in the hope of bumping into Pierre, but then the image of the big-bottomed policeman returned. If he should find me hanging around on the hookers' corner again, for sure he'd haul me in, question me, maybe find out about Paris . . . So I didn't.

Peter studied in his room most mornings and played tennis in the late afternoons. There was a club in La Ciotat, the small town close by. Twice I accompanied him for a set or two, but in the devouring heat of midsummer, I had no energy for the game. I preferred the beaches and the secluded creeks or doing nothing at all. I was becoming expert at doing nothing. Besides, the crowd at the tennis club bored me.

Agnes was painting from dawn to dusk, transformed into a furious energy. She talked, loquacious as ever, but with brushes in her mouth while her black hair, all disarray, was held in place by paint-stained cuts of ragged old sheets, or bits of string. Trays of paints and utensils surrounded her.

A local Algerian woman turned up most days to make lunch and clean the rooms because Agnes had declared she had no time for the domestic needs of three. After dinner one evening, she invited me, a rather regal invitation, up to her vast studio. High at the top of the house, it faced out over the sea.

It's our bedroom now. Peter's and mine. There still remain traces of her paint, her industry. Her soul.

Agnes wanted to paint my portrait, she said, 'When I return from Italy. If you're still here, of course.'

I so hoped we would be.

'Have you and Peter talked through your plans?'

'Not really.' I shrugged. 'He said – if it's all right with you, of course – we'd stay here for the summer. I start college in September.'

She watched me, appraising me. 'You're very young and so very beautiful.' Her hand reached up and touched my cheek. 'I can see why my nephew is captivated, enthralled by you. Poor dear Peter.'

Her remark made me feel awkward. 'How long will you be gone?'

'Two or three weeks. Back before the end of August.'

Her studio gave off a pervasive smell of turpentine, as did she, when she was painting, and the billowing smocks she wore to work in. Its penetrating odour travelled all the way down the stairs. I found it potent, mysterious somehow, like Agnes herself, and I breathed it in as though it was a Chanel perfume. It was cool up in her eyrie with the windows open wide, facing out in every direction from mountain to sea. On a clear day you could stretch out your arms and let your fingers drift towards the tip of Africa.

Birds had been nesting in the rafters. The remains of their abandoned roosts were still visible, crumbling and dry. Geckos stalked the walls.

Agnes kept a record player up there and when she paused to reflect, to consider the stages of the work in progress, she flipped on an LP and tuned in to the music, humming to it, sometimes jiggling her head about, which caused her hair to fall loose. Sometimes I could hear her bare or slippered feet slapping back and forth. She talked to herself, or to an imaginary someone. I could hear snippets of her voice from my room, through my open window where I would kneel for hours and stare out to sea, dreaming of Pierre, while listening to the strains of musicians as varied as Lester Young, Milt Jackson, Juliette Greco and Bob Dylan. 'The Times They Are A-Changin''. As was I.

On the wall of the winding stairs that led up to Agnes's studio was a portrait of a woman, wearing a wide-brimmed hat, facing left against a muted grey background. A young Agnes, surely. It was signed Romaine Brooks. I wondered if the artist had been a friend of hers.

I was fascinated by my hostess, curiously transfixed by her, her life and all that had gone before. Some days I wanted to be her, to play her in a film, to tell her story, which I still did not know. Mysterious and self-contained, she was. I was overawed by her dedication to her work and the process by which she changed a blank white possibility into vibrant images. Rich, thick, layered oils imbued with the heat of the sun, the generosity of the plants all about us. She trowelled the paints onto the canvas as though she was about to cement a wall and then she dragged the earthy hues, spreading them in all directions until, miraculously, they took shape and form.

'Do you know in advance,' I asked her, when I dared breathe a word in this sanctuary of silence or music or her own mumblings, but always concentration, 'how it will look when it's finished?'

She laughed, a guffaw more than amusement. 'I know nothing, not even the subject. The barest outline only.' She was rubbing a fallen blob of a bright blue oil off one of the wooden legs of the tall easel with a white turpentine-dipped rag. I wondered why she bothered when there were splashes of paint everywhere. Her nails and fingers were an encrusted rainbow.

'Is that you on the stairs?' I asked boldly, one afternoon, when we were alone in the house.

'The portrait?'

'Yes.'

'It's me.'

She must have been so striking when she was young, if the painting was an honest reproduction. Alluring and poised. I didn't express these thoughts, though. I tried to imagine her life. Sometimes I sat on the stairs and stared into the picture, willing it to talk to me. There were no signs of her husband anywhere, or possibly she had those memories neatly bundled away. Out of reach of the prying eyes of busybodies such as myself. I was intrigued. I imagined tragic endings. Broken hearts. And while I was cooking up imagined stories of Agnes's past, I continued to ask myself what had become of Pierre.

'Be kind to our Peter,' Agnes said to me on another afternoon. 'Youth can be cruel, selfish, unthinking, and I'm sure you don't intend any of those.'

'I hope I'm not unkind to him, Agnes. I'm trying hard not to be.'

We were in the bush, walking up behind the house, working our way along a narrow track where spiny plants snagged at my naked legs. Spindly eucalyptus trees reached out in all directions and waved in the cliff-top breezes. The landscape and views she was offering from this isolated spot were stupendous.

It was dry and hot, cicadas making a racket, like an African wind instrument. I expected us to encounter rattlesnakes but she dismissed my concerns as foolish. She was wearing her broad-brimmed sunhat and carrying an empty basket. We drew to a halt close to a clearing, an oasis of her making. Quite unexpected in that spot. The garden was encased by a wall of cacti, tall as skyscrapers, with leaves like huge rubber paddles. They were weighed down with orange and burgundy fruits covered with spikes.

'It's one of my hidden bush gardens.' She smiled. 'I cultivate several up here. Let's sit in the shade and talk and contemplate the view.' She pointed to a trio of home-crafted wooden stools. I feared she might ask me about my home life, where I hailed from, what had driven me south, but she was far more discreet. For her own reasons, I learned later.

Her concerns were for Peter. 'He's very taken with you.'

'I know and . . . I don't want to disappoint him. I'm just not as . . .'

'As what?'

'Committed to everything. Peter's very . . . well, dedicated to whatever he sets his mind to, and I am, well, I'm not sure I have the same depth of loyalty in me. Maybe I'm just shallow,' I confessed, a lump expanding in my throat.

She stared at her espadrilles, tapping her feet. It was a rare hiatus in her speech. 'He is the dearest soul in the world to me, now that I am by myself,' she said, taking my hand and clasping it between both of hers. Her paint-stained fingers scratched my softer skin. 'Any advice I give to you would be imprudent, senseless, arrogant. You will find that commitment, the same depth of love, when the moment arrives, when the person fits. I was seventeen when I ran away from England and I would not have listened to a word from anyone. Fortunately for me, it turned out well. I have been blessed with everything I could have dreamed of, except . . . more time with the one I loved.' She was silent again for a moment, lost somewhere in her own past, in the companionship of someone cherished.

'Peter is . . . ready to give his heart. What can I say to you who are so young and open, wide open in the fullness of her callow beauty, for all life's experiences? You're not shallow, my dear one, but you are hungry for everything. Try not to break his heart, Grace.'

I was shocked. 'I don't want to.'

She patted my hand. 'Remember my words. That's all I ask, dear, glorious Grace.'

Before we left, she donned gardening gloves to collect a small basket full of the spiny fruits she called 'prickly pears' from the cacti. These she said she would serve later to me as a snack.

When we had trekked back to the house and poured ourselves tumblers rattling with ice and freshly pressed juice from oranges the colour of the midday sun, Agnes peeled and sliced the prickly pears with a sharp knife and handed me one to try. Their flesh was rich, fibrous, blood red and laden with seeds. 'What do you think? Very thirst-quenching. You like it?'

'It tastes like bubble gum.'

'Bubble gum.' She tut-tutted but chortled anyway. 'Have you ever eaten figs direct from the branches?'

I shook my head.

'When we've time, Grace, after my exhibition, when

I'm painting less, we'll harvest a great haul of them, fresh from the trees, and boil some for jam.'

Every day was a discovery. I had been seduced. Dreams of future harvests, the months to come. I wanted to stay for ever.

The trauma of Paris was fading, not ever-present now. Even so, since my excursion of two weeks earlier or more to Marseille I had kept away from built-up environments. Even the sleepy fishing village of Cassis made me a bit jumpy. There were days when I got butterflies in my stomach and grew anxious about being arrested in Paris on my way back to England. Perhaps I just didn't want to think about leaving Heron Heights, returning home.

On those days I lay in the grass with a book, eyes closed, listening to the cooing of doves, the humming of bees, or I stared open-eyed at the sky, its vast impenetrable blueness. I watched butterflies flitting between the rose blossoms, the bougainvillaea straddling pillars or I gazed at eagles overhead, small dots circling, growing larger as they descended, before pitching themselves earthwards to trap and tear their unsuspecting prey from its life. I watched them swooping with lilting calls to their enshrouded nests, their open-beaked young.

And I fantasized about Pierre. Pierre and me, here.

Our one afternoon together, our drunken lunch. I wondered where he was now. Fifteen, sixteen, seventeen days had passed. He could be anywhere. I looked out for his car along the back lane. His grey-blue eyes burrowed into my listlessness, my despondency, my longing. But he didn't come back. He never drove our way on the off-chance that I might be out walking the mountain path or meandering through the bush close to where he had deposited me.

I sprawled in a deckchair on Agnes's veranda, rolling cubes of ice across my cheeks and down to my cleavage. I was aroused by the chilled water, trickling from my breasts to my underarms. I listened to the blatter of the crickets while I replayed my months in France, but mostly I replayed that one, not even entire, day with Pierre. Where was he now? Picking up another girl, buying her lunch? I couldn't bear the thought of it. Should I go in search of him?

The Present

I skipped breakfast, left a scrawled word on the table beneath the vines explaining to Peter or whoever found it first that I had driven into Cassis and would be back within an hour or two. I gave no explanation for my absence, feeling unable to write a bald lie.

On the same pad, I scribbled a second message:

George, I am sorry to have let you down. I tried to meet you this morning, to keep my promise. Unfortunately, the boat wouldn't start. Don't think the worst or jump to hasty conclusions. We can and will sort this out. Grace

When I arrived at the Strand, I parked across the way and ran directly to number eleven, Gissing's rented accommodation. The curtains were drawn closed. It was after eight thirty in the morning. I had no idea how long he might have waited for me down at the creek. Might he still be there, pacing the bay, watching for our little vessel, stirring himself up into a frenzied state? It was a forty-minute hike from here, give or take. He should have been back now. I rapped hard with the iron knocker and waited. I hoped he wasn't in. Yet I knew I had to face him again sooner or later. There was no reply. I knocked again, then stuffed the note through the letterbox and hot-footed it back to my car. I sat at the wheel, scrutinizing the house.

No sign of life. I was immobile. Worn out, exhausted. My brain was frazzled. I couldn't go home yet. I needed coffee, space in my head. Replaying over and over my encounters with George. Something felt wrong, was not adding up . . . A memory out of synch.

In Cassis, I sat alone in Thierry's café, cradling a cappuccino, staring out of the window. It was still early. The place was more or less empty. I had a raging headache. The fishermen were docking and unloading their hauls. I watched them without really seeing, my gaze fixed to the window.

A detail was troubling me. Unsettling me. Unspecified. A creeping sense of nausea. About our previous meetings. When George removed his sunglasses, the shock of his disfigurement . . . I was trying to recall, and the pressure beat into my brain . . .

Thierry strolled over to my table, whistling softly, slid a small basket of freshly baked croissants onto the table in front of me. 'You don't look like you've had breakfast, Madame.' He smiled. 'Help yourself. I'll make you a fresh coffee. You've barely touched that one.'

I nodded my thanks absently, thoughts elsewhere. What was I missing? A key, a pointer, overlooked . . . Eyes squeezed closed, I was spooling back and forth, recollecting Pierre when I'd first met him in Marseille. And then the day he'd fashioned his fishing rod . . .

1968

20 August

I watched Pierre whittling, singing to himself as he trimmed a length of pliable wood. 'Blue Bayou'. I loved Roy Orbison. Pierre's voice was different, softer, equally sexy. I longed to join in, to sing along. The cane was pine or another wood of a slightly more solid variety. Young yew? His hand clasped the staff and ran up and down its length, smoothing and gently flexing it. He was carving a rod. A rod to go fishing. I had seen him crop it from a shrub earlier in the day. There was an almost imperceptible tremor in his hands as he worked diligently, lost in a world of his own.

He had a sharp knife, one of those Swiss Army things with dozens of pointy bits, and with that he was shearing off nubs, smoothing inconsistencies. On the rock beside him, weighted by a smooth pale pink stone he had picked up along the shoreline earlier that morning, lay a small triangle of sandpaper. With this he planed the rod. I marvelled at his dexterity and the delicacy of his movements.

Until now, during the last few days since he had been here, he had snorkelled for our fish. The bounty for our starlit, fire-lit barbecue suppers. These we had been consuming as a threesome on the beach, Agnes not with us. She had been working like a fiend: last-minute preparations for her trip. Since Pierre had reappeared, since Peter and I had bumped into him in a portside bar in La Ciotat, he'd been spending a great deal of time with us. I'd wake in the mornings, go to the window, lean out and there he'd be on the beach, bending and rising, amassing debris. Driftwood, stones, shells. He collected his hauls in bags and stowed them in his car. Except the driftwood, which he piled high for fires on the beach.

Peter and Agnes didn't say much. They hadn't commented on Pierre's arrival out of nowhere. What could they say? They didn't own the cove, although, before, it had felt as if they did.

I spent my time observing Pierre, couldn't take my eyes off him, naked in the water. He was so at ease within his body. I scrutinized him, lusted after him. I was besotted. His blue rubber flippers splashing, drumming up and down. The sun beating on his bronzed buttocks and back, rouging his upper arms, his supple muscles. The circles of salt on his shoulders when the sun had dried off the seawater, the blond hair at his armpits soggy, like tufts of flaxen seaweed.

I tried not to lust after Pierre, for Peter's sake.

But today we were alone, Pierre and I. Now he was running metres of fishing line along the stick. He had a hook at the ready, a bob and a sinker. I marvelled at his resourcefulness. His long, slender fingers were nimble, dexterous even when he was smoking a joint. I'd smoked one with him earlier. I was a bit stoned.

The rustle of leaves now from behind where we were seated in the bright sunlight drew my attention. For a moment, I thought it must be Peter returned from Italy but it was a bird that had landed in the foliage. A small songbird. It began to sing. Such a melodious tune. I couldn't have identified it any more than I knew the names of the trees and plants. There were grebes and plovers – Peter had pointed them out to me. I felt sure my present companion could put a name to them all. Agnes, too, would know. I felt sad that Agnes had left us. Off on her trip to Italy, to her exhibition in the Eternal City, jumping with excitement, fizzing with nervous energy.

Was Pierre my companion, or were we merely strangers who had found ourselves in the same place at the same time? He never proffered information about himself. Peter had asked me, 'What's his real name and what is he doing here?' And why is he hanging around all the time, parking his car alongside our land? Peter hadn't worded it quite so brutally.

Pierre inhaled as he dragged on his cigarette, then coughed. I was curious to know what he was thinking during the long silences, lost in a world of his own. Whom might he be dreaming of? A girl back home? Where was his home? I had introduced him to Peter and then to Agnes as Pierre, but he was not French.

'He's English, isn't he? Pierre who?'

Agnes referred to him as a drifter. 'No reason not to be polite to him, though. It was kind of him to give you a lift from Marseille. Invite him in for a drink with us if you wish to, Grace. Make him welcome.'

He wore no ring, no jewellery, no adornments of any sort. Nothing to suggest there might be an attachment to another. A sweetheart. He was a free spirit. Of his time and generation. A hippie? A creature of the sixties.

As I hoped I was learning to be.

I tried hard not to allow my wandering eyes to settle beneath the pale blue sarong he had casually draped about his unclad torso, his smooth golden abdomen, his nipples a darker shade, like two chocolate stars. His bare legs hung loosely apart on the rock where he was perched, the heels of his upturned feet nestling in the sand. Beneath the loose clothing, he was naked. I closed my eyes, forcing myself not to peek at his genitals, his limp penis.

He knew I was watching him. But could he surmise the depth of my hunger? Did I betray myself?

It was love, and it left me weak.

'What's happened to your boyfriend?' He asked the question as though he had divined my lust and was deflecting it, reminding me of my betrayal of the man I had been sleeping with intermittently, but not for more than a week now, not since before Pierre had shown up in the bar and bought us a drink.

In answer to my prayer.

Pierre's voice was husky, tobacco-weathered.

'Peter's not . . .' I wanted to make it clear that Peter and I were not committed to one another. We were friends, companions, who were travelling together and who had shared a bed from time to time: there was nothing special between us. But the words choked in my throat, all too aware of Agnes's words and Peter's deepening affections for me.

But, hey, this was the sixties. Who wasn't sleeping together?

'He's with his aunt,' I muttered. 'He's taken Agnes's car and driven them both to Italy. She's picking up a train for Rome.'

Pierre made no comment.

'He'll be gone all day. Might not be back till to-morrow.'

He lifted his head, half smiling. He crooned a few bars of an Elvis song. Was Pierre asking me to love him tenderly, as the words suggested?

I might have swooned.

There was a sheen of sweat on his forehead, his nose, the upper parts of his cheeks. He had caught the sun.

My breath constricted. I was crippled with longing. That flame in his eyes. I loved him. In secret, in the shadows of my heart.

'So, we have this precious day to ourselves.'

I was skating on thin ice.

The house, the beach, the sea. It was our playground to do with as we pleased. Agnes would not be returning for about two weeks, but Peter was due back by late evening or at the latest the following morning. 'I will only be delayed overnight,' he'd said, 'if I'm held up at the border.'

'Do you like sleeping in your tent?'

Pierre glanced up at me, noncommittal.

'Maybe tonight you could stay at the house, if you want. There are plenty of spare rooms.'

In an instant, the rasp of the crickets and cicadas had grown louder, rising to a crescendo, as if someone had just turned up the sound. Their calls had escalated in pitch almost to screech level, picking into my brains, entering my head. I closed my eyes and replayed that scene from *The Birds* with Tippi Hedren. Those terrifying creatures – the parrots in the cage, the empty staircase and then, don't turn that handle, that final climactic attack.

Was this a warning? An augur, like the chant of a chorus in a Greek tragedy? There will be repercussions. Repercussions for your foolishness, your infidelity.

Make him welcome, Agnes had said. She wouldn't object. She was Bohemian.

Blind to my fate, I dismissed my guilt-ridden nonsense. The overriding emotion was that I had fallen in love and was attempting to draw him closer to me.

As if in response, Pierre leaped to his feet, fit and agile and confident. There were sand clouds clinging to his legs. They fell away like showers of gold as he began to move.

'Are you going fishing now?'

He made no answer. Had he even heard me? Lost in his inner world.

He swiped his transistor from the rock, grabbed his soft pack of Marlboro cigarettes and his coloured shirt and, bearing the newly fashioned rod aloft, strode away. 'You coming?' he called. I stumbled forward and hurried to keep step. My cheeks were flushed, stinging with heat and happiness and desire, but I didn't care. I couldn't have been more elated.

Out on the water, in the distance towards the town, a small flotilla of yachts was scudding across the invisible waves. The sea was glistening, shining in the sunlight, like the dorsal ridge on a diving dolphin.

'Are there dolphins along this stretch of coast? I'd like to watch a pod of them frolicking in the water.'

Carefree I was that day, throughout those hours when

there had been no one but the two of us. And what of the eclipsing shadow of guilt? I ignored it, tamped it down.

'Have you got any gear?' he asked me.

I misunderstood, assuming he was referring to a second set of fishing tackle, but he was talking about drugs.

I shook my head, disappointing him. 'There's a stash in my car.' We glanced up beyond the rise of the beach, beyond the sloped dunes to where his fantabulous Cadillac was parked and, alongside it, his small tent. A tent for one. He hadn't responded to my invitation to move into the house.

'Check the glove compartment.'

'Isn't it locked?'

He scoffed at my question and sent me off in search of the hash, adding, 'Don't forget the Rizlas. I'll be on that rock over there.'

I skipped up the ascent, the sand kicking in whorls about my legs, puddles of joy. We were going to smoke another joint together. An intimate interlude, while waiting for the fish to bite.

Pierre had switched on the radio. I heard strains of Otis Redding, '(Sittin' On) The Dock of the Bay'. One of my favourite songs of the moment. It conjured up summer. Chilling out. My summer of '68, of meeting Pierre, falling in love. A sacred, dangerous love.

I reached the car perspiring, and eased myself onto the leather passenger seat. From where I was sitting, Pierre was within my eye-line. He was crouching on one of the big granite boulders, his sarong flapping lightly in the shore breeze. Fronds of hair rose and fell. I opened the glove compartment and found several white envelopes, all tightly folded. Which to choose? The first I drew out, I unpeeled the flap and found a collection of many coloured pills, dozens of them. Vitamins? Medicines? I scrunched closed the scruffy package and placed it back where it had come from, alongside a battery torch. The next contained the dope he had sent me to collect. A chunk of Lebanese gold, a third the size of Pierre's transistor radio. It was impressive, must have cost a small fortune, its potential a little frightening. Didn't he fear he would get caught? The car's roof was open, the glove compartment left carelessly unlocked.

Did Pierre do drugs all the time, every day, like a habit, or was it because he was on holiday? Hanging out at the coast, getting stoned, watching the ships in the water. Scuba diving. He had a full diving kit in the boot of the car.

Was he on holiday? Or was this his lifestyle? His existence? Driving his open-top, staying with people he encountered along the way, hitchers, like I would have been on the day I met him in Marseille, erecting his tent wherever he fancied . . . And then a thought intruded upon me, flashing its message in strident signposts, momentarily crushing my joy: might this be all I was to him, a girl he had crossed paths with along the way? Or might he be falling in love too? I loved him madly. I was certain. I was crazy about him, obsessed by him, and could think of no one else. I tried not to give space to the guilt I felt towards Peter because this was the sixties and adventure was what I had crossed to France in search of. Peter had to understand that. It was part of the philosophy, the spirit of the age, he and his contemporaries were fighting for.

I closed my eyes for a second, blanking out Agnes's warning to me up in her cactus garden, 'Don't hurt Peter,' and my response, 'I don't want to. I'm trying not to.'

But it was all too easy, it was clear to me now.

I cared for Peter. Deeply. He was my friend. The last thing I wanted was to cause him any unhappiness or pain, but my feelings for Pierre, my emotions, were totally different, and out of my control. I was running headlong with no brake, no controls to fetter them.

I was about to close the glove compartment when, as an afterthought, glancing upwards to confirm Pierre was not watching me, I dug a little deeper, rummaging behind the envelopes. Searching for? A passport? Driving licence? A clue to his real identity? Nothing there. I spun round on my buttocks, tearing my skin. Ouch. The underside of my thighs was puckered and sweaty from the heat and leather. I leaned over to the rear seats where a guitar lay beneath an untidy pile of clothes. Was Pierre a musician like my dad? How cool was that. There was a shirt I recognized, worn on the day I'd first met him. I resisted the temptation to nick it, to hide it under my pillow.

Pierre would be wondering what was taking me so long. I should get a move on. Somewhere there must be papers for the car. I pulled down the sun visor. Nothing but my own bronzed face, bleaching hair, in a small mirror, and then I stretched over to the driver's visor. That was where my dad kept his logbook. No paperwork there either. Curious to have no documentation to hand. Might the car be stolen? What had put such nonsense into my head?

I stepped out and slammed the door.

Might it be that this was not Pierre's car? Who was Pierre with those grey-blue eyes that burned through the lining of my skin, peeling me away from myself, leaving me raw and exposed?

The sand was already scorching beneath my bare feet so I ran on tiptoe, hurrying back to my dreamboat. He could see me even though his back was to me and he was facing out to sea. His newly sculpted rod curved lightly towards the water. Its nylon line gliding, bobbing from side to side with the movement of the shore waves.

'Here,' I called, as I approached.

The music had changed. Otis Redding had been replaced by the Mamas and Papas, 'California Dreamin''. I loved this song too, owned the LP back in Bromley, the original rendition. On such a summer's day, it made me want to dance on the sun-drenched rocks by the waves.

'"I've been . . . to find the hash . . ."' I was waving my arms above my head, moving in step to the music.

'Why don't you roll us a spliff?' he called, concentrating on the water and his task. He had donned a pair of tortoise-shell Ray-Bans. Wayfarers. So hip. As he turned, I caught my reflection in the mirrored lenses. My open shirt billowing, revealing my red and white striped bikini. Me, proffering the crushed envelope. My smile expectant and nervous, with a flash of strong white teeth. My long hair, getting lighter in the sun, flapping like laundry in the salty breeze.

He smiled at me. 'You're beautiful,' he purred. 'Too beautiful.'

My heart swelled, rising out of my breast and soaring skywards. A happiness kite. I was glad now that I had asked him to stay. My guilt and foreboding were nothing but adolescent anxieties.

'I don't have any cigarettes.'

'Here, take one of these.'

The soft-pack was sticking up out of the pocket of his open shirt. I leaned in close to him. He smelt of tobacco, musky, feral, of patchouli oil, which was not a scent I cared for but, mixed with the pheromones of Pierre, it was intoxicating. My head was spinning and I almost lost my balance. His left hand grabbed my wrist tight. His grasp rubbed, burned, as I regained my footing, but I didn't object to the pain.

'Whoa, crazy chick, stay with me. Don't let the wind blow the tobacco and gear away.' He laughed.

I threw my head back, closed my eyes, willing him to lean in to me, over me, silently begging him to kiss me. Waiting for that sweetness, eyes tight shut, tighter, here on the shore . . . He didn't. When I opened my eyes, he was concentrating on his fishing equipment in the water. Lost in his world. I had been forgotten.

By mid-afternoon we had smoked three joints and Pierre had caught four handsome speckled fish. Their skins radiated colours, like oil slicks on water. The Doors were crooning 'Light My Fire' on the radio and I was feeling as though I had been hypnotized.

'You look like Jim Morrison,' I murmured. A god-like creature.

'We need beer,' he announced, carefully wrapping his rod and the fish in his shirt.

'What! That's disgusting! Your shirt will stink!' I shrieked with hysterical laughter. Nothing could have been funnier.

We strode up the dunes, entered the house by the back door and ditched the fish in Agnes's tall refrigerator in the kitchen, where Bruce was sleeping in his basket in a cool corner, and we began rummaging for beers. We found none. While I filled Bruce's bowl with tap water, Pierre tossed his sullied shirt into the rubbish bin, which shocked me. 'Why don't you wash it? I can do it for you.'

'Forget it. C'mon, babe, let's drive to town and buy some beers.'

The dog lifted himself on unsteady, sleepy legs ready to accompany us and then, as Pierre pushed him back with his foot, disappointed, resettled himself among his rugs.

The pretty little town with ochre-coloured houses along the seafront towards the Strand was heaving with tourists. How could the two worlds nestling alongside one another be so different?

'Let's grab a crate of beers and get out of here. I can't take this action. It's doing my head in.'

We pulled up outside a store, an *épicerie*, where tourists stared open-mouthed at Pierre's car, which he seemed not to notice or ignored, and picked up two crates, each of a dozen chilled beers and a litre bottle of vodka. Pierre pulled cash from his shorts pocket and peeled the notes off a thick roll. His funds appeared bottomless.

We had installed ourselves on the terrace at Agnes's fancy house. The beers had been stacked on their sides in the refrigerator and those that wouldn't fit were on the floor by the sink with four chilled bottles at the ready, lined up at our feet. Inside, in the grand salon, one of the two ground-floor living rooms that faced out to the sea, shaded from the light by several shuttered windows, a television set was playing. Pierre had switched it on as we'd made our way out onto the terrace.

'How about that? The screen's in colour,' he marvelled. 'Pretty fancy, huh? She's quite something your posh friend's mother.'

'She's not his mother.'

'Whatever.'

Outside, The Wailers were warbling on Pierre's tranny.

I had taken a shower and changed into a T-shirt and shorts, splashed myself in lavender cologne. A headache was throbbing at the rear of my skull. It was the dope, I felt sure, but I didn't complain, didn't mention it, inhaled a lungful of the fresh sea air, and hoped to clear my fogged brain with a beer.

'Fuck, look at this. Tanks. Those are Russian tanks. They're rolling into — where is this? It's Prague.'

I rose from the wooden rocker, steadying myself, and scuttled inside.

'What does that say?'

I shook my head. 'No idea.'

Someone on the screen was holding up a handwritten message, waving it like a poster. It threw up memories of Paris, of the violence, of the crowds in the streets, but here the people were passive, or those I could see, the few the camera was recording. Standing in front of the TV, we watched what appeared to be a live transmission, watched the tanks entering the main streets of the Communist city. Now, we spotted a few students who were leaping up onto one or two of the tanks brandishing the red, white and blue Czechoslovakian flag, but on the whole the mood was one of shock, of muted disbelief.

'They're bringing down the Prague Spring, taking back control, rescinding the reforms fought for earlier this year. Freedom of the press, citizens' rights . . . Peter should be here. He has to see this. It's all gone wrong. De Gaulle is back in Paris, consolidating his support, having quashed the riots. The students thought he'd be destroyed, his career finished. What did everyone fight for?'

'They're not Communists, they're Fascists.' Pierre shook his head at the screen, then strode from the crepuscular light of the salon out to the breeze on the veranda and our chilled beers.

That was the first expression of emotion I had seen from him, the first demonstration of any unreserved opinion and it surprised me – surprised me that he cared about the politics on display.

My brain was dipping up and down, spinning in loopy circles as though I was travelling in a flying saucer. I was too stoned to worry about whether Peter or Agnes would object to my having invited Pierre into the house. It was not the first time he had seen the interior of Agnes's home – he'd been in a couple of days earlier to share a bottle of wine with the three of us – but the suggestion that he sleep beneath Agnes's roof had not been made and I was too smashed now to reason it through.

'Why not sleep here tonight?' I repeated my invitation while we were staring out to sea, supping our beer from the bottles, reflecting on Czechoslovakia. I was attempting not to slur my words. The prospect of him being only a few rooms away from me had set my heart thumping so fast I thought I'd faint.

Pierre mulled over the suggestion in silence, seeming to weigh it up with some deliberation, until he replied, 'Why not?'

'Let's get your stuff now while it's still light.'

'It'll be light for some time. No rush. You want another beer?'

I shook my head. It rattled like a clogged-up washing-machine. My constitution couldn't handle any more stimulants. 'I feel wobbly,' I confessed.

'Seriously? You want a 'lude?'

'A what?'

'Quaalude. It'll calm your heartbeat.'

'What is it?' I asked, trying not to sound miserable because I couldn't have been happier. I stood up from my chair a little unsteadily – 'Whoops' – and the room began to spin.

'A powerful tranquillizer, sedative. Harmless. You'll feel great. Popped after the deadly white powder when it gets a hold and is a little too intense. When the heart starts beating like a galloping horse.'

I nodded, gripping the arm of my chair. 'Yes, please.' I thought I was going to vomit. I didn't know whether the sick sensation was caused by my desire for Pierre or over-indulgence in unaccustomed drugs. My head was seesawing. I was a spinning top out of control. I allowed myself to sink to the floor. Once there, and stabilized, I drew my knees up tight to my chest to keep myself grounded. The palms of my hands were clutching ferociously onto the rattan rug. Its natural rough fibre was cutting into my flesh, the tender, awkward triangular bit, like webbing, between my thumbs and forefingers.

Bruce was back in his basket, in the corner close to the entrance to the kitchen. His eyes fixed upon me, he was whining.

'I haven't fed the dog,' I mumbled. 'I don't feel well.'

When I attempted to draw myself to my feet again, I realized I was alone. Pierre had gone, and the dog was thumping his tail.

Pierre returned from his car with one of the folded envelopes I had seen in the glove compartment earlier. Was that today, or yesterday? How long had Peter been gone? Had we been snorting cocaine? Pierre had mentioned cocaine. When was Peter coming back? I had lost all sense of time and perspective. I watched as Pierre dipped his fingers into the envelope and pulled out a small white tablet. 'Here,' he said. 'You need water or a swig of beer to wash it down.'

'Water.' I groaned, and said again, 'I haven't fed the dog.'

'Mellow, babe. I'll feed him.'

My heartthrob, knight in shining armour, went in search of a glass while I allowed my head to flop forwards. It felt too heavy for my body; it was unbalancing me. Was it *my* head or someone else's? A tap was running. Popular music was emanating from the television. My lips were trembling and I began to dribble. Bruce was whining again. He padded from his basket and began to turn in circles snapping at his tail. Had he been given drugs too? When Pierre returned with the glass, I was back on the floor, on my knees, holding my head in my hands, squeezing it, trying to silence the cacophony in my brain. This was hardly the image I'd been attempting to project. The seduction I'd hoped to pull off.

'Here.' Mr Gorgeous was offering me a glass of water and an oval white tablet. I took it shakily from between his fingers, trusting him as he bent on his haunches and steadied me with his left hand. 'You look like shit.'

'Thanks for the compliment.' I was trying to sound light-hearted, insouciant, but it didn't come off.

'Swallow it with a slug of water and then maybe you need to lie down.'

'Don't forget to feed the dog, please.'

When I regained consciousness later, spread-eagled on my single bed, my head was splitting. The last thing I could bring to mind was Pierre assisting me up the stairs to my room. Not carrying me exactly, hauling me and directing me with his hands beneath my armpits. Once horizontal, he had pulled off my plimsolls and tossed them to the floor.

How much earlier was that? For how long had I been sleeping?

Gingerly now, I lifted my head from the pillow and glanced down at my body. I was still wearing my shorts and T-shirt. Fully dressed. The door was closed. Pierre had shut it behind him. He hadn't touched me.

I hauled myself up onto my elbows, concentrating, listening for sounds throughout the house. Waves beyond the open windows washed against the shore. In the distance, downstairs, music was playing. Pink Floyd, a track from *The Piper at the Gates of Dawn*. I loved this track. Which one was it? 'Set The Controls For The Heart Of The Sun'. I quite fancied the new bloke, the guitarist, Dave Gilmour. I thought he was pretty gorgeous. Not as much as Pierre, who was more than pretty gorgeous: he was totally gorgeous and such an elegant, cool guy.

And I could, couldn't I, discern the hum of conversation in one of the rooms on the ground floor? Was Pierre singing or talking to himself? He had a guitar. Maybe he'd play to me, like my dad used to. Who was he talking to? Using Agnes's telephone? I had no clock and not a clue where I had left my watch. When had I last worn it? Outside, the light had disappeared. Was it night or pre-dawn? For how long had I been sleeping? I could get up, go and find out. What would Peter say? Peter. Might he have returned from Italy? Pierre could well be in conversation with Peter. I should go back downstairs. My head felt like a kicked football. Tears pricked my eyes. My day with Pierre had been spoiled by my inability to handle a few beers, a couple of joints and loads of other powdery stuff and pills. What an unsophisticated child he must judge me. I dragged myself off the bed. Cold water splashed on face. A shot gulped from the tap. I pulled on a pair of jeans and a fresh T-shirt. All set to go.

Pierre had installed himself in a bedroom further along the corridor. I remembered that.

The house was dark and creaky as I descended the stairs. It was different without Agnes. I missed her. The TV in the living room was still switched on but with the sound muted now. Peter was indeed back: the two men were out on the veranda. Bruce was sleeping peacefully at Peter's feet. The vodka bottle had been opened, one third consumed, and was on a table between them. Peter was cradling a beer between his fingers. They were not conversing. Pierre was rolling a joint. The very sight of it caused my stomach to turn. The wireless was on, now switched to a French news channel. Peter, head lowered, was concentrating on the relay of events from Prague.

'Hey, you're back,' I trilled lightly, unnecessarily.

He turned at my approach. 'We've been waiting for you,' he stated. 'Want some supper?'

I shook my head and shuffled into the space. 'Did one of you feed the dog?'

He nodded, then sighed. 'Prague's been invaded.'

'Yeah, we saw it on the television earlier.'

'I should ring my father.'

'Why?'

He frowned. 'To hear the facts. Britain's position on this. The news reported Harold Wilson's statement. "The invasion is a tragedy not only for Czechoslovakia but for Europe and the rest of the world." There are demonstrations breaking out in London. Several other governments are calling for Russia and the Warsaw Pact nations to withdraw.'

I sighed and curled myself into the rocking chair, like a coiled snake, glancing towards Pierre, who did not acknowledge my arrival.

Later, when we were alone, because Pierre had gone out to his car to close up the roof, Peter remarked upon the fact that I had invited him to stay.

'Do you mind?'

He shrugged, pursed his lips. 'We should have discussed it with Agnes first, but it's too late now,' he replied flatly.

'She said the other day to make him welcome.'

'I'm not happy about the possession of drugs on her premises without her knowledge, and Pierre is very casual about them. They're illegal and this is not my house.'

'So is rioting,' I rebutted. 'Drugs are revolutionary, like fighting the police and the establishment, digging up pavements, overturning cars, burning your draft card in the States. They're all part of your revolution,' I insisted.

'Grace, for pity's sake, you're so naive.' Peter rose from his chair. 'And did it not occur to you that you might want to discuss such an invitation with me before bringing a stranger into our holiday time together?' He strode into the main body of the house without waiting for me to offer an explanation, without a glance backwards. He scratched his neck and rubbed one hand over his face.

'It was only for tonight.'

'Well, make sure he's gone in the morning.'

'Please, don't be angry.'

Peter continued indoors out of sight.

Those were the first cross words that had passed between us, the first rift, the first crack in our bonding, and the cause of it was not the drugs or my juvenile political assessments, as Peter had suggested. It was Pierre.

'Be kind to our Peter,' Agnes had reminded me, as she had hugged me *au revoir.* I felt the sting of her words in my guts. I had betrayed them both.

I asked myself what my reaction would be if Peter insisted Pierre leave. I felt sure that Pierre would not tackle him or resist the command. He would casually pick up the few items he had brought into the house and be on his way. But what would I do? Where did my loyalties lie? I wouldn't be here if it wasn't for Peter. He was my dearest friend, but my emotions were cross-wired. My longings had shifted focus. My desire for Peter had never reached these heights.

That night Peter knocked on my door, apologized for his quick temper and invited me to his room, but I stayed alone again in my monk's cell. I couldn't own up to it: I had no desire left for him. I said I felt queasy and ought to get a good night's sleep.

In fact, I lay awake, my eyes wide open, staring at the light patterns on the ceiling, yearning for Pierre just a few doors down the corridor. I pictured him in his room and the images aroused me, and no matter what I did I could no longer sleep. I had hoped he might come to me. He knew my room. Eventually I kicked off the sheet and made my way to the window, pushing it wide, resting my arms on the sill, chin in my palms. There, I gazed at the moon moving in an arc over the sea, the waves lapping the sand.

I had fallen in love with someone I had barely engaged in conversation. I knew nothing about him, not even his name. It made no difference. Since he had first picked me up, I had thought about little else besides my passion for him. Was I being transformed into a druggie and a sex maniac? A druggie, no. The joints had sent me flying off the wall and made me sick.

Sex with Peter had been fun for a while and I had looked forward to our nights together. So why wasn't it Peter I was crazy about? My confused emotions saddened me. I was a stranger to these complexities, but wasn't this what I had come travelling for? To break through my own barriers and experience life to the full? To stop at nothing?

I got back into bed and lay against my ruffled sheets, curled like a foetus, and gazed out at the sky. It was dark, and the heavens were navy, full of depth and radiant stars. Then I caught a shooter. One, then another, and then so many I could barely count the flights. Oh, my God, this was the Perseid meteor shower zipping across the cloud-less sky. It felt as though the heavens were rotating, as though I was being spun on the axis of the earth. Bright fireballs, long, streaking flights. Showers of light. It was magical, beyond all wizardry. Surely I was being blessed. My wishes were coming true.

Pierre was absent throughout most of the following day. Had Peter sent him packing? He claimed not. Pierre had taken his car and scuba equipment and disappeared without explanation. I crept into his room and lay on his bed out of the noontime heat, reading poetry.

The next night I returned to Peter's room for the first time in a while. He had told me twice during the course of the day that he had been missing me and I decided I must make an effort. He had not turned Pierre away, so I should be more affectionate to him. I waited until we all three had retired to our rooms and then I crept barefoot along the corridor to Peter, knocking softly and leaving the door open when I entered. Had Agnes been in the house I might have been less careless, more jealous of our privacy. Only later, much later, did I ask myself whether I had done it on purpose. The moon was many days from full so the light shining in through Peter's sea-view was shadowy, dim.

When I crept in, he was leaning on an elbow, reading Marcuse. He set the book aside, rolled back the sheet to welcome me and I knelt up on the bed.

'I've missed you,' he purred. I pulled off my T-shirt, tossed it to the floor, lingered a moment, resting the weight of my body on my heels before sinking and sliding deep onto the mattress alongside him. The night was warm, a midsummer heat that had mellowed from the day's harsh sunlight. The windows were wide open. We lay listening to the movement of the waves. The air smelt vaguely saline. Peter peeled back the flimsy sheet, revealing my abandon to the shadows of the night. He ran his left hand across my abdomen and up towards my breasts before turning me slowly, nudging me onto my side.

He was behind me, pressed up against my back and buttocks. I was facing the window, facing the open door. I lowered my eyes as I felt his fingers move to enter me and I bumped my buttocks a few inches towards him, inviting him to make love to me. In that moment I was there with Peter, but I had not forgotten Pierre. As Peter moved within me, I fantasized about the other man down the corridor.

When I lifted my gaze Pierre was there at the open door, watching us. Watching me, watching Peter. Peter's face was buried within the blades of my shoulders. He was inside me, moving gently back and forth, brushing his lips and tongue across my back. Back and forth, like a cat cleaning itself. I was listening to the rhythm of his breathing, his moans growing feverish in my ear. His line of vision was blocked by my flesh, the expanse of my curves.

Pierre and I locked eyes. Engaged. My desire, carnality, was fully exposed to him, his nakedness, both lit by the pale moon from outside. His penis had grown erect. I slipped my hand to my pubic hair, touching myself, thrilling, laughing. My body was weak: slow spasms, vibrations were oscillating through me, like electric waves. I closed my eyes and succumbed, allowing myself to open, to judder to orgasm. When I lifted my head, there was no one at the doorway. It was empty. No figure framed there.

The Present

I led my grandson gently by the hand. Harry's fingers were gripping me tightly as he trotted beside me, coughing, rocky on his feet, both of us in a stunned and battered silence. I felt sure Harry must be replaying in his small boy's mind the disquieting incident to which he had just been party: the man in black who had tried to take him away, who had disappeared. Where had he disappeared to? Over the cliff-side?

George Gissing, who had promised me, no, threatened that if I did not befriend him he would do something 'bad'? He would inflict harm on me and my family.

Was he dead? Finally dead? I felt sick with a medley of emotions: an inability to think straight and rising panic.

Harry and I passed through the front door and into the house. Its tall white walls were cool and safe. He had begun to hiccup, which I took to be an expression of his shock. I rubbed his back and held him tightly. 'Everything's fine now, Harry,' I whispered to him softly.

Noises from overhead. The urgent packing activities were still at full tilt, which I barely registered as I led my favourite boy into the kitchen, settled him at the table and gave him a glass of water while I dished up a large helping of chocolate ice cream. My hands were shaking. Peter was nowhere to be seen on the lower level of the house. I decided not to call to him. In any case, I wasn't sure that I should disclose what we had just lived through. I had no clear idea how I was going to deal with all that had just happened. Should I call the emergency services? Had a man gone over the cliff-side?

My 'big boy' ate slowly, methodically, sucking at his spoon, and making an unnerving humming sound, rather like an irritated bee. I sat alongside him, touching his arm. He was kicking the heels of his trainers against the two front legs of the chair. I wanted to ask him to stop because I thought I might scream, but I knew he was rattled. We were both rattled. My hands were dancing with tremors. All of me was shaking, I realized now, and a white pain was radiating outwards, like indigestion, in my chest.

How much worse, then, for Harry.

Might Harry have an inkling of the consequences of the man's disappearance from the mountainside?

'The mountain that sits on the sea' is the poetry the Provençaux people use to describe those awesome cliffs. How much should I confide to Sam, his mother? Certainly not the man's identity. What precisely had Harry witnessed? Had he seen me wrestle with the man? The pushing and pulling, the loss of footing, the crumpling forwards as though in agony. The nothing to hold onto, no means to break, to disengage the fall . . .

The episode, the tussle, was playing in my mind. Several different renditions, a variety of scenarios. What had actually happened? The details had blurred.

I had to react, do something, call the appropriate services. There was a man missing, possibly a body to report, to retrieve.

I moved out to the veranda to telephone the police and the Lifeboat Rescue service both in La Ciotat and Cassis. My voice felt as though it had been coated in fur.

'He went over the cliff-side, you say?'

'I c-can't say for certain. I didn't actually see him fall . . .'

After I had repeated the circumstances, the reason for my call, spelled out our address several times, I returned to the kitchen and poured a rather-too-early-in-the-day glass of chilled white wine.

Within fifteen, twenty minutes, there was a caravan of cars, some with flashing lights, parked along the lane, up beyond the ascent from our villa.

'We will need to interview you, Madame Soames,' a woman at the other end of the telephone line had fore-warned me, after jotting down my name, address, citizenship.

Sam came hurrying down the stairs, hauling two stuffed sports bags.

'Harry's in the kitchen,' I said. 'Dressed, ready to go. More or less. Can I help?' I was attempting to disguise how agitated, deeply shocked I was. I had almost forgotten that four of our family party were leaving that very afternoon and I was supposed to be chauffeuring them to the railway station in Marseille. I set the half-empty wine glass in the sink, out of sight.

Jenny would have to drive her sister. From where she and her two girls were installed on the beach, they would not have been able to see George's plummet.

George's fall. If . . .

'Listen, Sam, something . . . something rather urgent has come up, not very pleasant. Ugly, tragic, in fact. I need to stay here.'

Sam's back was to me after she'd dropped the cases on the floor and had taken the first step on the stairs. My news caused her to swing back. She was frowning. 'Are you all right?' she asked. 'Goodness, Grace, you look a bit, well . . . green, actually.'

'Someone, a man, disappeared . . . fell . . . yes, off the Soubeyran ridge up towards the Semaphore creek.'

'Oh, my God. Into the sea?'

I nodded. 'I th-think so. The police are on their way. I'll need to remain here and answer a few questions. Er, Harry saw it too. They might want to . . .'

'Harry saw the accident?'

'I had gone to fetch him and . . .' I was deliberating about how much further to go, the details to divulge and decided, wrongly or rightly, to say nothing else for the present. 'Have you seen Peter anywhere?'

'He took the car to the village to draw out some cash.'

'Cash?'

'For me. I'm out of funds. I'll need money for the journey. You know, drinks and . . . God, someone went over the cliff, how awful that you saw it, Grace. And Harry . . . Where is Harry?'

'In the kitchen, eating ice cream. He's fine.'

Sam brushed by me in search of her son.

I was relieved that Peter was not about and I wouldn't be obliged to decide whether or not to confide in him about Gissing. Until this point, I had refrained from revealing that this man, who had identified himself as

Pierre, yes, Pierre, was hiding in the vicinity, that he was alive. Alive, though surely dead now. Again.

To have drowned twice.

Had Peter, my gentle husband, tried to murder Pierre all those years ago? Surely George's accusation was intended to poison me against my own husband. Here was the legacy George was leaving with me. Suspicion. Mistrust. Festering ill-feeling. George's payback for his sad, loveless existence.

Had Peter lived his entire life, a successful public persona, believing he had murdered Pierre?

For the past few days, I had been going crazy, carrying the burden of both men's secrets.

There was a knock at the door. The police, I assumed. In fact, it was Peter. 'I forgot my key. What's all the fuss about up the lane?' he asked, as he stepped into the hall. 'Ah, Sam!' He began to dig in one of his trouser pockets. 'Five hundred euros. My limit at the cash machine. Will it do?'

'Thanks, Dad. Grace says a man went over the cliff.'

'Peter, would you mind driving Sam to Marseille or shall I shout to Jenny? The police are on their way. I called them about the, erm, accident . . .' I coughed. 'And I need to be available for . . .'

'Did you see it?'

'Not exactly. I mean, I saw a man . . .' I exhaled, confirmation enough.

Peter knew better than anyone the trauma it would unlock within me. What he could not have foreseen was the complexity of the trauma. The same man had died here twice.

He stood watching me, puzzled.

'I'll be on the veranda,' I said.

'Perhaps we should postpone our departure. I can call Richard. In any case, I'd prefer to be here for your operation, you know that, don't you, Dad? I hate to go.'

Peter lifted his hand as though he were stopping traffic.

'I'll be on the veranda,' I repeated, and left them to it. I stuck my head round the kitchen door to see whether Harry had finished with his dish. My hand outstretched, I beckoned him to me. 'Come on, big boy, come and sit on Nanny's lap.'

His obedience was instant.

Sunk in one of the rocking chairs with my youngest grandson curled like a squirrel on my lap, his head pressed against my chest, I closed my eyes. We rocked in silence, consoling one another, healing one another with our heartbeats. The certainty of our precious love for one another.

Aside from shock and a tingling numbness, what else did I feel?

Could I mourn the loss of this man? Was there grief, or simply huge relief? And Peter's part in the story, what should I believe? That my husband had attempted to murder another man because he was jealous of my relationship with him? Should I judge Peter, blame him?

I had carried a knife with me when I went to meet George at the creek. Had I intended him harm with my inept weapon? Or had I carried it out of self-defence?

I hadn't pushed George over the cliff, with my rage and violent hammering at his chest, had I? I had held out a hand to him when he was losing his balance. I had attempted to help him . . .

I felt tired, immeasurably weary. Impossible to gauge any more what or who I believed.

'Nanny Two,' Harry gurgled into my breasts.

'Yes, big boy?'

'Was Uncle George unhappy?'

Uncle George? 'He might have been. Did he ask you to call him "Uncle"?'

I felt the confirmation with the brush of my big boy's head against my shirt. 'Did you see what happened, Harry? What happened to Uncle George?'

'Grace, sorry to disturb you, the police are here. They're requesting a word.'

I hadn't heard Sam's approach. I felt as though a very large stone was being settled on me, crushing my strength.

'Come on, Harry, down you get. Let's get you ready.'

'I don't want to go home. I want to stay with Gramps and Nanny Two!' Harry let out a shriek, a piercing sound with a surprisingly chill edge to it. It took me back to George's bird-like call on the cliff. His last attempt at speech? Harry began to stamp his small but powerful sneakered feet. The wooden floor vibrated. This outburst of temper was out of character.

I bent low to him. 'Sssh, don't be upset. I know you're sad to leave us but you can come back very soon. Be strong, Harry. Nanny loves you.'

Harry lifted his thumb and two fingers up to his mouth and began to draw on them as though he were smoking a pipe. 'That man was funny,' he said uncertainly through a mouthful of digits. 'Scary.'

'The police are here,' Sam repeated to me, sotto voce, as she bent and swept her son up into her arms. Harry screeched as though his mother had given him a good swipe. He kicked against her. 'Ouch, stop that right now.'

'I don't want to go,' he yelled, tears like crystal pendants dropping from his eyes.

A middle-aged man, thinning hair, out of uniform, stepped onto the veranda and waited patiently, facing in my direction. I didn't recognize him. In this small community, that was surprising.

Sam, along with Harry, who had fallen silent now, overwhelmed or intrigued perhaps by the arrival of yet another stranger, discreetly melted out of sight.

'Madame Soames? *Bonjour, je suis* Capitaine Bernard Moulinet, from the Marseille National Police corps.'

I gestured to one of the chairs. 'May I offer you a drink or coffee, Capitaine?'

He shook his head and glanced out towards the wide expanse of sea. 'Quite a magnificent spot you have here. I've noticed this property once or twice from up on the high road, wondered who occupied it now. You don't object to the isolation?'

I shook my head and sank back in the rocking chair, in the hope that this would encourage my interrogator to take a seat and a less formal stance with me.

'Wasn't this once the house of the artist Agnes Armstrong-Soames?' He was slowly connecting the dots. The abbreviation of my married name to Agnes's more formal nomenclature.

'Agnes was my husband's aunt. Peter inherited it when she died in 1993.'

'And you reside here permanently?'

'We also have an address in London and Peter still, on occasion, works from Brussels but it's rare now that he's retired.'

'What can you tell me about this morning's incident?' The captain was pulling a rolled-up notebook out of his bomber-jacket pocket. He was wearing grey slacks and brown lace-up shoes, I registered.

'Not a great deal.' I concentrated on his gestures. The way the tip of his finger tapped almost impatiently against the paper. I was fighting to keep my mind focused, to keep my story simple. 'I was standing here, well, out . . . out there, on the grass, scanning the beach areas for my smallest grandson. I looked over in that direction towards Soubeyran Ridge just in time to see someone, a man in black, I think, lose his balance . . . He tripped, I think, and then he . . . must have fallen from the cliff top. Has a body been recovered?'

'He was picked up about ten minutes ago. Dead, as expected. His corpse is being driven to the hospital morgue in La Ciotat as I speak.'

I lowered my eyes, scratched at a fingernail.

I fought back the relief, and then, to my amazement, a tear sprang. I brushed it swiftly from my cheek.

'We will need to find someone to help us proceed with the identification of the body. The gentleman in question, was he in any way connected to you or your husband?'

'Not at all.' I shook my head rather too vehemently and felt the bones of my spine tighten, each vertebra, one after another. My hands were in my lap, clasped tight against my shorts. The palms were sticky. I wanted to lift myself out of the rocker and walk outside for air or to switch on the two overhead fans to break up the wall of heat, but I feared to budge, lest my agitation be construed as a sign of guilt or my body language give away a telling clue. Had I reason to be guilty? Was I culpable? It had all happened so fast. 'Has he been identified?'

'Too soon. I was hoping you might be able to help us with that.'

'I'm afraid not, *desolée*, Capitaine.'

'Did you happen to notice, Madame, if the victim was alone at the time of his . . . fall?'

I dug my nails hard into my palms. The hair at the back of my neck was damp against my flesh. I was desperate to move but I dared not. 'I'm trying to recall. To be honest, Capitaine, my concentration wasn't really with the foreigner. He was merely a silhouette on a cliff. I was . . . looking . . . for my grandson.'

The officer stared at me intently, digesting my words, then scribbled half a sentence in his notebook. 'Think back, please.'

'Yes, he was alone, I think.' I felt the pressure of the lie, like a chain being drawn round my chest.

At that moment Jenny and her two girls arrived from the beach. Sunburned, sandy and rather wild, exuding euphoria, the special sense of liberation that sea air and waves can release.

'Is Sam ready, Grace?' Jenny called, arriving out of breath at the top step, to the rear of her daughters. 'The girls want to drive to Marseille and see them off there. Oh, I'm so sorry. I didn't realize you had company.'

'Nanny Two, there've been lots of boats, did you see?'

'Mummy told us a person fell over in the waves.'

'Oh, Grace, Dad's boat. It was drifting. I think someone had drawn up the anchor. We've had a little jaunt in it and secured it, haven't we, girls?' They nodded dutifully. 'Come on through, then. We can talk to Nanny later.' Jenny, jaunty, bustled Anna and little Christine, both weighed down with towels, spades and flip-flops, through into the main body of the house.

I had drawn up the anchor.

'I'll tell Dad about the boat. Curious about the anchor.'

'Thanks, Jenny.'

As they passed us, sprinkles of sand dislodged and slid from their limbs, out of their swimwear and settled into a pattern of minuscule dunes on the floorboards. I stared at the sand particles, replaying in my mind's eye the final moment just an hour or so earlier when George Gissing had disappeared over the side of the bluff. It threw up a memory, many memories, both joyful and terrifying, of that sweltering summer of '68, so very long ago.

Behind me the police inspector, Capitaine Moulinet, was scrutinizing me. I could feel his eyes on my back while patiently awaiting answers I was unable, unwilling, to furnish to questions that seemed to creep unnervingly close to the fringes of my unravelling mind. From the rooms above us, along the landing and down the stairs, could be heard squeals and thuds of activity. I glanced at my watch. If Sam and her trio were to make the train it was almost time to leave. I shifted my feet and nudged myself forward in the rocker.

'Is there anything else you would like to ask me, Capitaine Moulinet? If not, forgive me, but I need to assist my family with loading the car, and . . .'

He rose, stuffing his notebook, the page almost as blank as when he had first sat down, into his pocket. 'If I need to be in touch again, have we . . . ?'

'My phone number was requested when I reported the . . . incident. Please feel free to make contact whenever you need to. We . . . I will do my best to help.'

I was walking on ahead, leading the investigator towards the main door, situated mountainside, to the rear of the villa. He paused in our small hallway. 'Do I recognize you here in these photographs, Madame?'

'Yes.'

It was not the first time a guest had halted at the bank of framed pictures, highlights from my career, prominently displayed on the wall. Peter's artistry. I would have preferred to leave them in drawers. One had been snapped at an award ceremony and, directly alongside it, there was a publicity shot from a television film series. It was the role that had won me that particular accolade.

I turned back from the open door beyond which the family were piling a chaos of bags into the boot of my Espace. I wanted to be out there with them, in the sunshine, carefree, mucking in, cuddling and reassuring Harry, sharing the heartbreak of farewells.

'I think you must be a very fine actress, wouldn't you say so, Madame?' His gaze was boring into me. In this shadowed, unlit corner, his eyes had an impenetrable yet perspicacious glint to them. 'You're quite sure you didn't know the man?'

'Y-yes, Capitaine, quite sure.'

He doubted me. I sensed it. Had I betrayed myself, made a slip?

Out on the veranda, the telephone began to ring.

'I'd better get that. *Au revoir,* Capitaine. Thank you for your visit. If you are in need of further information, please don't hesitate to . . . Good luck.'

1968

24 August

We were peering into the candescence of the bonfire we had built from the bundles of driftwood I had collected from the neighbouring cove earlier that afternoon. I was listening to the wood crackle, listening to Bruce snoring loudly at our feet. Around us the light was beginning to fade and dusk was gathering, yet still everywhere was luminous, as though it had been brushed with fairy dust.

Pierre, head lowered, concentrating, was rolling another joint. He had been missing for most of the day, taken off in his car without a word while Peter and I were eating breakfast. He was absent for so long I thought he must have left us. Peter had spent the day working, studying. He was writing a paper on Prague, recent events, the crushing of the Spring reforms, its impact on Western rebellions. It was about this time that Peter's interest, later his speciality, had first been drawn to the plight of refugees and those whose rights had been taken from them.

I had been left to my own devices, waiting for Pierre's return. In his room nothing remained but a few loose cotton garments. They smelt of him. I had spread myself out on his bed and fondled them tight against myself.

The flame of the lit joint was rising high. Blue-tinged from the Rizla paper, it sputtered and sizzled softly, an accompaniment to the fire's spitting. Pierre dragged hard on his handmade cigarette, then leaned forward to pass it to Peter, who was reticent about taking it but, after a glance in my direction, accepted it. His expression was clear. He disapproved of the illicit opiate between his fingers. He glanced towards me, to Pierre and then, with little relish, he passed the joint back to Pierre.

'I won't have any, thanks. Grace, let's organize some supper.'

My companions' faces were lit and shadowed by the flames that shimmied between us. The sea and the fire were the shifting forces that surrounded and embraced us. An occasional hooting of a distant owl broke into the tranquillity. Dogs barking. Bruce slept and heaved contentedly, tired out from the long walk he and I had enjoyed and our frolicking in the sea. Drunken screams from a party on a beach some distance towards the town carried on the night air.

'I'm not hungry, thanks. Anyway, there's fish.' I sensed Peter's irritation as he jogged on the spot. 'Later, maybe,' I added, to pacify his impatience.

He dropped back onto his haunches in the sand. Disgruntled.

The sky was turning red, carmine and purple, shot with an aurous glow. It was outstanding. The sea was slicked with gold. The colours were sharp, so vibrant, it was almost unseemly.

We watched the celestial light show while solemnly passing the joint between us, Pierre and I engaged in ritual. I was getting pretty stoned, the rush of dope to my head. My thoughts were slowing, becoming fuzzy, woozy, yet the sounds all about me, the physical sensations and my awareness of them, were expanding, zooming towards undiscovered galaxies. I heard the inhalations, exhalations, of my two silent companions. I heard the lick of waves. The tide was coming in, edging towards us, creeping up the beach. There were bubbles from the curling waves, a foam that was whiter than white even in the descending darkness. I was a part of this universe and I wanted to immerse myself in it.

'I'm going swimming.'

'Don't be silly, Grace.'

'I want to lose myself in the sea,' I murmured.

The moon was beginning to rise, slipping up from beyond the horizon. It made flaxen the light.

Peter rested a hand firmly on my arm to discourage me. I brushed him from me. My skin was warm, itchy. It burned slightly but not uncomfortably. I had been spending long hours sun-bathing. Every inch of my body was tanned. My flesh stung, in a pleasant way. I dug my fingernails into the tissue and knew I was alive. I cut into myself for the sheer pleasure of it, for the sharp, indecent thrill. You don't own me, I wanted to say, but I couldn't face a scene. I was beginning to care less for him. He was square. Controlling.

I dragged on the joint and the tobacco swirled in my brain, sending me on a giddy bend. I passed it to Pierre. Peter kicked his legs and jumped to his feet again, staring down into the fire. The flames had grown higher because Pierre had just added several cuts of wood. Peter's mood was edgy, fuming. He disapproved of the drugs. Or so I thought. I was wrong, too lost in my own preoccupations to appreciate the level of pain he was experiencing.

'The finest Lebanese gold,' hummed Pierre, as he rolled another spliff, blending the crumbs of it, catching each and every one, pressing them, kneading them into a brown paste, mingled with the lighter flakes of tobacco.

Was that where Pierre had vanished to today? Had he taken off to Marseille to score more dope? Had we, during these last days, smoked the other great chunk?

Peter was neither a smoker nor a drug-taker. He preferred 'reality and revolution' as galvanizing forces. Earlier that morning, while making coffee, he had expressed the opinion that Pierre was a dealer, a criminal, and that I'd had no business inviting him into our lives. Into Agnes's home.

'One night, you said. He's overstayed his welcome. I am going to ask him to leave.'

He didn't, though. Had he worried that I might take off with his rival? Did he suspect that over these last days Pierre and I had become lovers? While Peter had been shut in his room, chronicling his thoughts on the revolution, we had been making out on the beach.

Pierre placed his transistor radio upright on the sand alongside his shoeless feet. 'You fancy going swimming? A visit to the caves by night?' he whispered softly.

'It's too dangerous. Grace, you mustn't go.'

'I will, if I choose to. Yeah, I'm up for that.'

Peter let out a breath. 'Come and watch the moon-rise from the dunes.'

We had a favourite spot for sunset-watching. It was beautiful, and we had spent several evenings camped out there with a bottle of wine. The days before Pierre had pitched up.

'Let's go, Grace.' Peter held out his hand. Was he offering me a final opportunity, my last chance to heal the wound? I glanced swiftly at Pierre, who had either not heard or wasn't listening.

I shook my head. 'I want to visit the caves. Pierre's got diving gear.'

'Grace, please listen to me. You mustn't go swimming now, do you hear? The caves can be dangerous even when you're sober.'

'Leave her alone, man. She's fine. I've got all we need. Flippers, snorkels, the full kit. Let her do her own thing. Stop pecking at her as though you own her.'

Peter opened his mouth to speak, then must have thought better of it. He spun on his heels and marched away. I watched him go. Stoned, blinded by my infatuation for Pierre, I watched my friend walk away into the diminishing night. I was impervious to his heartache. Then, with one turn of the head, I dismissed him from my thoughts and returned my concentration to the new lover at my side, who was, almost imperceptibly, swaying to some inner rhythm.

'Music?' I whispered. 'Let's have some music.'

Pierre pressed the cream switch on his transistor and the machine burst into song. The Lettermen were crooning 'Goin' Out Of My Head'. Which was a fair summation of my senseless state.

Stargazing from the dunes, swimming through moonbeams: Peter and I had ventured out from this shore on innumerable previous evenings after a few glasses of wine. Bathed by twilight, starlight, moonlight, deliciously liberated. And there had never been a whisper of threat or jeopardy. Because Peter knew those waters. He had swum in them since his childhood. It was his mysterious aquatic world, alien to me, so we had hugged the shore, dipping, splashing, dunking ourselves in the shallows rather than immersing ourselves in the steely blue-black bowels. Never ranging out of our depth.

'He just fusses,' I muttered, more under my breath than aloud. I was mad at Peter because he'd treated me like a child.

Had Pierre heard me? Was he defending my position or challenging his male competitor? The quondam partner of the woman – no, the imprudent girl – he was having sex with?

I will never know.

Pierre rose to his feet. Letting fall his lightweight clothing, he stepped purposefully towards the foam, posing there, allowing sufficient time for Peter, disappearing along the shore, and me to notice him. The incoming water swirled about his feet as he waded into the shallows. His broad-shouldered silhouette was ebony in the fading light, a powerful upright figure against the horizon's deepening purple and grapefruit-yellow moon. My sight was fixed upon him as he plunged forward, the water splashed around him, and he was enveloped.

Phosphorescence lent a mystical hue, a green tinge under the meadow-yellow glow, as he crawled purposefully out to sea. The muscles on his unprotected back rippled like waves. He was a Selkie returning to his natural habitat.

It was a bizarre, mythical image that I was never to forget.

He paused then, I remember, and scanned the littoral. Settling his attention on me, he raised a hand and, with one crooked finger, beckoned me. I jumped up, unsteadily, shook the sand from between my toes and lurched to the spumy fringe. I was flying, not stepping. My body was an apothecary of consumed drugs. Could I remember how to swim in my present condition? I staggered. The water curled itself about my legs, tucking me in. It was invitingly warm even at that hour. I felt it tickle and lick the skin of my legs, the backs of my knees. Somewhere behind me, I heard Bruce whimper, then bark. I tossed my head back and then, arms outstretched, allowed my body to sink low into the turquoise brink. Propelling myself forward, kicking my feet, I began to swim, easy, crawling speedily in the direction of Pierre.

'Grace! Grace!' Peter yelling at me from further along the shore. I paid no heed.

As I drew close, Pierre wheeled towards the horizon, crawled forth. Was this a game? Had I to give chase?

'Wait for me,' I gurgled. He was too distant to hear me.

His sinewy back, the strength of his arms and shoulders propelling him onwards. In no time he would be a luminous fleck, then swallowed by the watery dead of night.

'Pierre, wait!'

I was fagged out when I finally caught up with him. I

swung myself round to establish the distance to land. Far. Was it still within my reach? I allowed myself to float while I caught my breath. I spied the house, carelessly ablaze with many lights both upstairs and down.

'We're miles out,' I said, or perhaps I only thought it. My thoughts were so loud and clear, echoing from one side of my skull to the other, reverberating in a chamber. It was impossible to differentiate between spoken and imagined. I sensed the depth of the water we were wading in, treading my feet, pumping my legs up and down, as though on a bicycle, because my limbs were beginning to be eaten by cold. This was no longer the warm shallows. I remembered Agnes's warning about the steeply shelving seabed. I shivered, giggled a frisson of fear. Pierre lifted an arm out of the water, drips ran its length, and plopped it back into the sea. He hooked a hand about me and dragged me towards him. I thought he was going to kiss me. He pulled me tighter. 'Let's dive,' he said. 'Sex in the sea. Sublime.'

'No, let's go back now.'

A cloud passed over the moon and, for a chunk of time, all was pitch. It was scary. Actually, it was terrifying. We were too far from *terra firma*. 'I'm getting cold.' I began to panic, clawed at the water, fighting against it, as though it were swallowing me.

Pierre loosened his grip.

'I'm sinking,' I choked.

'No, you're not. I've got you.'

I felt a rush of water beneath me as he kicked hard to remain afloat. 'Hey, I thought you were a game chick who wanted thrills.'

There was an edge, a threat, to his voice that made me want to pull away from him, but his hand was locked around my neck.

'Let go, please.' I pictured my father, hand at my mother's throat. I was gulping water. 'No!' There was no reason to shout but terror was taking hold. 'Let go!'

'Don't be so scared. Wrap your legs round my midriff. Piggyback on me – I'll take you on a ride. To the caves, maybe.'

'We've got no diving gear.'

His back was to me now, nudging me, reversing up towards me. He was my amphibious transport. Both his arms were inching me towards the rear of his upper body, his shoulders, wrapping me about him. My feet poised against his slender waist, his skin sticky with salt, yet slippery. My arms clung tight round his shoulders. Sea was getting up my nostrils. I was snorting it. It stung. I shivered. My eyes, the salt, smarting. My balance was precarious.

'Don't panic. Trust me.'

We took off, riding the ocean like a pair of dolphins. His power beneath me. I felt safe again. More or less. Thighs beating athletically in the deeper blue. I let out a whoop. He swam in a circle, then circled wider and circled again. I was getting dizzy, losing my grip. I slid to one side and pressed my fingers into the flesh of his shoulder blades, attempting to regain purchase.

'Shit!' he cried. 'Don't do that!'

It happened all at once. No sequences. One frame layered over another.

I was beating at the water.

'I'm sinking,' I yelled. 'I can't swim any more.' Then I felt his hand, pulling, tugging at me. 'Don't grab me like that.' My legs were going numb. Reflexes closing down. My head was ringing. I lurched heavily backwards, capsizing into the water, which was dragging me under.

So many pictures, one on top of another.

I was kicking violently, to save my life, and splashing up a storm. As I did so I must have kicked Pierre in the head. I felt the strike, the sole of my foot knocking against something hard, bone.

Images of Paris. A skull splintering. Images of violence. My dad hitting my mum.

'Oh, God. Pierre! Are you all right?'

No response. 'Pierre!'

'Get back to the shore.' His voice ordering me.

There was a deep, long groan, a sound that could have emanated from the underworld.

The moon was breaking through the clouds again, a shaft of light restored, but with it, an eerie jaundice hue. A rounded mass of flesh appeared above the water, like a ghostly leprous hump. Had we crashed against a sea creature? Or was it Pierre's shoulder? Had I struck him?

'Pierre!' I screamed, slurred speech.

'Get back to the shore as fast as you can. Swim. Go.'

'No, I won't leave you.'

How deep were we? I called Pierre's name again. The water was dragging me down. I was going to drown.

'Start swimming. I'm right behind you.'

I kicked my legs, began to swim. A fury, a virago. Breast-stroking for my life. I was pumping with terror. Was Pierre still behind me? I felt the power of movement, of a current. Fear was crawling all over me, like seaweed embalming me. I was engulfed in blackness, a blanket of night all about me. I feared sharks the most. Sharks trailing me, tuning in to the scent of blood. Was I bleeding? I gulped. Salt water coursed down my throat. I began to cough. My brain was a jamboree of questions, of legs and arms and body parts. I was choking on the blood in my mouth. The wound from the Paris riots, the toothless cavity, had reopened. I would be eaten to a skeleton if I didn't make the shore.

Then the shore. In sight. I stopped just short of it, heaving for breath. Crawling, I hauled myself, heavy-limbed, from the sea.

Bruce was there, awaiting my reappearance, barking, barking, jumping up and down. A demented black beast. I heaved myself slowly up onto the sand, panting, and threw myself onto my back. There I lay. Tears were rolling down my cheeks, warm puddles in my ears as I stared skywards, freaking, thinking about my mum and dad, the hand around my throat.

As the fear and emotional jolts subsided, I closed my eyes. What was I doing? Bruce licked my face. His tongue was prickly against my flesh.

Stop that.

He was panting with happiness or relief.

I was done in: cold, wasted and vulnerable. I made my way, half walking, half scrabbling, staggering back to our bonfire. To get warm, to await Pierre's return. The newspaper Pierre had wrapped around the fish he had caught the day before, our supper, had been ripped to shreds and scattered about the beach. The fish were gone. A few bones remained. Bruce had had his fun. I shrugged on my T-shirt but couldn't manage my shorts.

I kept my eyes peeled on the water. I was puzzled by the length of time Pierre was taking. I had thought he was right behind me, following me to shore. I couldn't begin to estimate the number of seconds, minutes I stood there, watching out, shivering and hunched, calling his name. A solitary vigil by our fire, teeth chattering, waiting for Pierre's return, for his muscular form to surface from the waves. Eventually I pulled on my shorts and ran barefoot the length of the beach, looking out for him, for footprints, signs of his exit from the water. There were none.

Night had fallen. It must have hit midnight. The cries from the beach party west of us, close to the town, had died out. Everyone had fallen into bed, dead drunk. I had sprinted to both ends of the bay and back twice, turned in circles till I was giddy, yelling my lover's name till I was hoarse.

Where was Peter? Was he sleeping? Had he witnessed my cavorting? Where the hell was Pierre? He was too strong a swimmer for anything to have happened . . . surely. Should I raise an alarm? Who to call at this late hour? No coast guard available till dawn.

Even though it was late summer and the evening was warm, I continued to shiver. My body refused to calm, to be still. Had Pierre been carried by a current further along the coast and waded ashore some distance beyond the house? That had to be the explanation. There were dozens of inlets and coves to the east and west of Agnes's spot. It would be possible to berth at any of them and not be spotted from our bay.

If I went looking further afield, I wouldn't find my way. It was too dangerous to venture off alone. Better to wait for him here. The lone cliff house with its lights blazing would be his beacon, a guiding star for him to return to.

But I should wake Peter. I hesitated, reluctant to face him.

I should hike to the next bay, cross over the boulders and search. But it was dark and my legs were weak, muscle spasms. I had freaked myself out. Where was Peter? Had he gone to bed, was he sleeping? I returned to the fire. Pierre would return, I was willing it hard.

His pale blue sarong and darker blue shirt remained an ink puddle on the sand. Holding the garments up to my face, I inhaled the smell of him. I leaned forward, switched off the transistor and gathered it up along with Pierre's flimsy clothing. I swayed on my feet, giddy, head unfocused. I was still mighty stoned.

And then I caught sight of him. Thank God. A tall, slender silhouette wading from the saline shallows, some fifty yards ahead of me in the direction I was walking, a fair distance beyond the eastern flank of Heron Heights. I picked up speed, jogging, my breath rasping in my chest. I yelled Pierre's name. Relief surged through me. I knew he'd be safe. I was waving to him as he drew closer until his features converged into another recognizable somebody.

It was Peter. Peter, on the beach, signalling to me. He sprinted in my direction. The disappointment all but felled me. 'Have you seen Pierre?' I wailed.

'I've been looking for you, Grace.'

'I've been here all the time. Where's Pierre?'

Peter swung his body towards the distant bottle-black horizon. His breathing was fast, erratic. His abdomen was pumping as though his pulse was in his gut.

'Have you seen him?'

'He was in the sea. And then . . . then I couldn't make him out any more.'

'Were you with him?'

Peter shook his head. 'I waded in to look for you. I thought perhaps . . .'

'What?'

'. . . you . . . needed some help.'

'Pierre's missing.'

'He's a terrific swimmer, better than I am. He'll be fine.'

'Are you sure?'

'You shouldn't have gone out there in your condition – you'd both been smoking. You were encouraging him.'

His words were broken, covering his heartbreak and anger.

'For God's sake, Peter! Where is he? We need to call someone. Get a search party out.'

'Calm down.'

'Calm down? He's missing.'

'He's not missing.'

'How do you know?'

'He's probably . . .'

'What?'

'. . . returned to the house.'

I stared at Peter in the starlight, praying this was so. 'Did you see him return to the house?'

He shook his head.

'I'll go and look.'

'I'll walk up the beach, kick out the fire.'

'No!'

'What?'

'Leave it.'

Peter hesitated. He seemed agitated.

'Throw another log onto it. A marker for him. If he's surfaced further along the coast – all the bays look the same in the dark – trying to locate where we are, our stretch of land, it'll give him a marker.'

'He can see the house. The lights are on.'

'Please, build the fire up.'

He didn't respond to me, paid me no attention. He was shaking. And dripping wet.

'What's wrong with you?'

Peter glared at me, as though he didn't know what to think or do, as though I was a stranger. He appeared stunned, in shock, frozen to the spot. I began to shake too, trembling all over my goosepimply flesh.

Peter was the one who seemed to be out of it, not me. Our roles had switched. 'Peter!' He was weeping, blubbering. A figure in trauma. 'Grace,' he wept. 'I thought I'd lost you.'

I was taken aback, couldn't understand this ill-timed and rather desperate confession. I pulled off my T-shirt, screwed it into a ball and rubbed his back with it, vigorous movements to calm us both. I hugged him tight, clinging to him, taking comfort from our friendship. The solidity of Peter. I felt guilty and afraid, as though a hand was reaching for my throat. I wanted to retch but there was nothing to throw up, except seawater, pills, chemicals. 'He hasn't drowned, has he?' I rasped.

Peter shook his head. 'Of course not,' he replied flatly. 'He's a strong swimmer. He'll be fine.'

'I'm going to see if he's in the house.'

When I arrived at the veranda, calling Pierre's name as I climbed the last few steps from the beach, I heard the phone ringing. I dashed to lift the receiver.

'Hello?'

It was Agnes from Italy. Even today, I can recall that late-night exchange, the excitement in her voice as she recounted Rome's rapturous reception of her artwork. It was the night of the opening of the exhibition, her *vernissage*, or the early hours of the morning by then, and I was standing in her hallway dripping with seawater, gibbering from shock, out of my skull, petrified by what news we would be forced to face.

That evening was the last time we saw Pierre or heard any more about him. No body washed up. No evidence floated on the sea's surface. No bits of him to put back together. His disappearance was as mysterious as his existence, his identity had been.

The Present

The sun was cooling, moving west, throwing off a golden strip of light across the sea and its island elevations. I was alone on the ridge. Still in shock, I was wearing a pashmina to keep the chill off me even on that full summer's evening. I had been recalling those first days with Pierre, attempting to fit together the pieces of that disastrous night, of the young man of so long ago. Not the one who had disappeared from the cliff-top that very morning. Only this morning? It seemed almost as long ago as my ancient history of '68.

I heard the whine of a car descending the hill. Peter, Jenny and the girls had not yet returned from seeing Sam and the kids onto the train in Marseille, and I was expecting them anytime now. In the end they had all accompanied Sam to the station. Harry had been kicking up such a fuss about leaving that to squeeze them all into the one car, with Peter at the wheel, had been deemed impossible, and too stressful. Jenny had jumped into the fray and offered to drive my car. I would have liked to keep Harry with us but it was out of the question.

When I turned, I saw it was Peter descending the lane. I waved and began to hurry back towards the house to greet him. He looked so tired. I would have preferred he hadn't made the outing but there had been no choice.

'Where's Jen?' I called, as I approached my husband

making his way along the lavender pathway to enter by the veranda.

'She stayed on in Marseille with the girls to buy clothes, I think. They wanted to browse the shops. They won't be far behind me.'

'You look worn out. Have you eaten? I've laid the table on the vine terrace, thought we might have a simple tapas-style dinner. Sound good?'

Peter flopped into one of the rockers and rubbed his face with both hands as though washing off the day.

'The clinic telephoned while I was being interviewed by Moulinet, the police inspector. Your operation has been booked for next Monday. Eight in the morning. We'll check you in on Sunday. There'll be a few pre-op controls, they said.'

He nodded. Today was Tuesday. 'I'll be glad to have the blasted thing behind me. Get on with my life.'

'Shall I pour you a glass of wine? A chilled rosé?'

He nodded without looking up.

'How did you get on with the police inspector?' he asked, when I returned with an uncorked bottle and two glasses. I threw myself into the other rocker.

'I told him what I know,' I lied, feeling my body tense. 'I saw the man stumble while I was calling for Harry.'

'Was he a local or a tourist? They should cordon off that area. I've said it before. It's too dangerous.'

'I don't think they've identified him yet.'

Peter leaned forward and poured our glasses, handing one to me. 'Cheers. What were you doing over there in the falling light with no one about? One wrong foot, Grace . . .'

'Daydreaming, remembering.' I sighed.

'Anything in particular?'

I took a tentative sip of my wine. 'Pierre.'

'Who?'

'Pierre. You must recall?'

Peter frowned, shaking his head, bemused.

'We've never really talked about it. What happened that night all those summers ago.'

'You're surely not talking about the Gissing fellow? Good Lord. Whatever brought him back to your thoughts? No reason to dredge all that up again after all this time.'

I was taken aback. *The Gissing fellow.* Pierre had never revealed his surname to us. I was desperately trying to call back the events . . .

We didn't hear the arrival of my car with Jenny at the wheel. She was in the house before we knew it with the girls, who ran gleefully to their grandfather and almost sent his glass flying.

'Careful there!'

Jenny followed, laden with shopping bags. 'God, it's a relief to be back.'

'We've got new swimmers,' cried Christine. 'Anna's is green and mine is all stripy like a bumblebee.'

A whirlwind of energy had burst into our space and taken over. Peter was lifting his grandchildren onto his lap, laughing, engaging in their worlds. He had forgotten Pierre. Nothing more than a distant figure from our past.

And he knew nothing of his reappearance. Of George.

I went in search of a glass for Jenny before we were caught up in their afternoon's events in Marseille.

Gissing and his final moments were a universe away from this family gathering.

A tapas supper was deemed a terrific idea and Jenny, once she'd taken all the shopping to their rooms and rinsed her hands, offered to help me prepare everything. 'I left your car keys hanging in the hall,' she called back to me, as she pounded up the stairs. 'And I bought you a box of fab soaps. Olive-oil based. I'll leave them on your bed.'

I glanced at Peter. He was smiling, rocking his grand-daughters to and fro, enthralled by their news and stories, admiring the newly acquired glittery rings on their small fingers. He looked tired but at peace, his mind and body preparing for the medical challenge that lay ahead, his thoughts a million miles from the past that had returned to taunt me. Did those days ever return to trouble him? Why would they? In spite of George's insane accusations I still refused to believe that Peter had any reason to reproach himself. Curious, though, that he had used the name Gissing. How could he have known it?

Although Peter was fatigued from the outing and the farewell to his family, once Jenny's girls had been fed and sent upstairs to wash, he happily followed them to their room to read to them. Jenny told me that when she and Sam had been children he had never missed an opportunity to read bedtime stories to them.

Later, over the tapas plates and local red wine, both Jenny and Peter probed me with questions about the day's tragedy. I gave little away but I knew it was only a matter of time before the dead man sidled back into our lives. I dreaded the revelations with which he would be return-ing, and I was still baffled by Peter's casual mention of the name Gissing. Might there be something from our past my husband was keeping from me? Obviously not an attempted murder or an act of violence: of course not. Gissing's accusations had been preposterous. But might there be a missing piece to the puzzle I had never been party to?

1968

Late summer

The waves were landing like metal barrels crashing onto the *plage* before being sucked back out to sea. They were drawn by the current, by rip tides, as Pierre must have been. I recalled Agnes's warning words of some weeks back.

Peter was the only one who really knew this part of the sea, its prevailing winds, its channels and currents within the inlets and caves. He knew how to negotiate a safe course from one cave to the next, from one hidden bay or concealed creek to another. If there was a body, or a man wounded out there, Peter could have found him, surely. We had barely slept, both up at first light. At my insistence, Peter had been back into the sea, in and out, back and forth, tirelessly searching, exhausting himself, but now he had given up.

'It's time to call in the Coast Guard,' I pressed. 'Notify the police.'

He seemed reluctant, but nodded his assent.

All along this coastline, the beaches were emptying. Out on the water, a scattering of distant heads bobbed in the waves. No more sandcastles were being erected and slapped firm with the flat underside of a child's metal spade. I turned my head away from the innocent image, recalling Paris and the street riots. The strike of metal.

Summer was drawing to a close and the tourists were readying themselves for departure. The horseshoe bays and sheltered coves had been forsaken, returned to the sand crabs and the sea urchins, the marine life.

Oceanic secrets.

Our *plage* of the past few weeks was also deserted. I was alone with my bruised emotions and tormented thoughts. I sat on the sand, hunched into myself, waiting for Peter, not knowing where he had disappeared to, listening to the drag and pull of the water. It reminded me of drum rolls except nothing followed. No magic circus act. No reappearance of a missing person, stepping onto the stage to uproarious applause.

I climbed back up to the house.

'Have you called the police?'

'I called the search and rescue operations at La Garde.'

'And?'

'They're sending out a search party. They advised that we need to register him as missing with the local police, but they're not answering the phone.'

Peter had taken our luggage – his case, my backpack – down from our rooms. He'd told me earlier to pack my things. I had misunderstood, thought he was kicking me out. 'It's time to leave,' he'd explained brusquely. 'I need to return to Paris. My parents rang. They're closing the flat, surrendering the lease. I need to vacate my room.'

I had chucked all my stuff haphazardly into my bag, clean mixed with soiled. Towards the middle of the morning, Peter had stacked it in the hall, in preparation for our departure.

'We need to book train tickets.'

'Why are you in such a hurry?'

Peter was dictating this change of plan. 'I've just explained.'

I made vociferous objections.

'But what about Bruce? Your aunt left us in charge of the dog. And Pierre? We can't just go!' I'd yelled.

Peter ignored me, returned to brew coffee, jettisoning out-of-date packets from the fridge. A frenzied tidy-up.

'I'm not leaving. Who will feed Bruce?'

Peter refused to look at me. He had barely held my gaze since the previous evening.

'We promised Agnes we'd feed her dog. She's expecting us to be here when she gets back,' I insisted. 'What's the sudden rush?'

'I told you. My parents need me in Paris. I'll find someone in the village for the dog.'

'If you need to go, go. I can hang on, wait for Agnes.' Wait in the hope of Pierre's rescue, but I didn't voice the thought.

'You can't stay here on your own, Grace. Sorry, no.'

My arguments evaporated. I was not being given the choice and this was not my place, plus I had transgressed the rules. Big-time. I stomped through the television room and out onto the veranda, making my way back down the path to the beach. Hot tears were stirring.

We couldn't simply walk away. Pierre could be beached on some rocky outcrop, fighting for his life. Why was Peter being so resistant?

I sat cross-legged in the sand waiting for the arrival of helicopters overhead, fishing vessels, a Coast Guard steamer tacking through the water, systematic in its search. Had we left this too late? We should have gone to the police at first light, called the water patrol then. The rescue operations.

'I'm going to walk to the police station in Cassis. I won't leave until we've reported his disappearance!' I roared back at the house from the beach, my hair flying in every direction.

Birds landed, strutted for a few feet in the dunes, blanketing our tracks, our bare footprints of the last few days, then took flight again. Herons appeared from a cloudless sky and drifted landward. Their legs unfurled as they settled in between the spiky tufts of Marram grass. Marsh terns touched down in their wake. The wind nudged itself against me. It whistled in whispers. Accusations. Guilty secrets. My heart was broken and I couldn't stop the shaking. I craved drugs, downers, tranquillizers. But I resisted. I stared out to sea. I had lost, misplaced, my sunglasses. As well as my watch. And something far more crucial had gone from within me, had been bitten out of me, hollowing me.

The sun glistening on the water's skin was blinding me. There was no one there. Nothing except wind against billowing waves, and when the susurrations ceased, the surface of the sea became calm again. Calm as glass, calm as a mirror, an ice rink. And through the stillness his face was reflected, in giant form, Cinerama, as far as the eye could see. As though he, from below the surface, was looking up, outwards, skywards. Calling to me.

Was he calling for my help?

It was insanity to expect his head to break the surface, to part the waters, for him to indicate his whereabouts, alert me, us, to the reality of his miraculous survival.

It was too late. Was it too late?

How many hours had it been now?

I had lost count. People can survive days out at sea.

No body had washed up. No discovery had been reported by the local TV station. I had kept an eye on the screen. No corpse had been sighted floating, bloated eyes pecked out by the gulls, hauled on board by a fishing boat or cruiser, and ferried back to shore.

Nothing but silence, and emptiness.

We walked the four kilometres into the town together. Trudged along the rocky shoreline, navigating the great stones, exchanging nothing more than a few intermittent words. Our thoughts were elsewhere, both of us in vastly different places. Still, I found it comforting that Peter was at my side. For months now he had been at my side, and I found it soothing how deserted the beaches were along our stretch between Agnes's remote house and the fishing town. Busier, though, as we approached habitation. The previous week families had been sheltering from the heat of the sun beneath coloured parasols, sunk into the sand at angles.

The walk seemed longer than it did habitually, enervating for a body running on empty: no sleep, next to no food. No drugs in my system now but several shots of alcohol had been my fluid intake. I had raided Agnes's bar in the night, after talking to her on the phone, depleted her vodka stores.

The sun burned hotter than it had since the day we'd arrived there. Or was it because we had spent the earlier carefree days floating in the Mediterranean at the water's edge, lying in hammocks in the shade, making love in a shuttered room that I had not correctly evaluated the intensity of the heat?

When we arrived Cassis was silent, like a ghost town with its pastel-pale irregular-shaped houses. Its spookiness fitted my mood.

Peter pointed out the police station nestling down a side street, discreetly set back from the main tourist area. Crime had no place among the holidaymakers was the message. When we reached the old building, we found the door locked. A sign to the left, hanging from a lace-curtained window, read *Fermé*. I pressed my face to the glass. It was more reminiscent of a country-house sitting room than a police station.

'Shit. Now what?'

'Don't swear, it doesn't suit you.'

There were moments when I silently hated Peter. He could be such a prig. Now was one of those moments. 'Someone's drowned, for heaven's sake, and you're at me about swearing.'

'He hasn't drowned.'

'Well, where is he, then?' My drowned angel. I heaved a sigh, bit back tears. 'Even if he didn't want to spend more time with us, decided he'd had enough, why would he leave his car? He would certainly have been back to collect that.' *And he'd be after his glove compartment's treasure trove, which I had emptied. The contents were secreted beneath the sink in my bathroom. The guitar case had also been hiding drugs. Cocaine.* I didn't mention any of this aloud. 'Why would he just disappear on us?'

'We'll have to wait to find out.' Peter glanced at his

watch, not listening to me. It read two fifteen. 'I don't know why I didn't consider that everything would be closed for lunch. Nothing opens again till three. There's no point returning to my aunt's. I need a cold drink. Come on, let's go.' He scratched at his hair and fidgeted with his face. I noticed then that he hadn't shaved. Out of character. The five o'clock shadow didn't suit him: it made him look scruffy and surly. Our friendship was souring. It saddened me. I had let him down.

Every bar we walked by was deserted. The remaining summer population was either on one of the beaches we hadn't traversed or having lunch elsewhere out of the blazing sun, while the permanent residents would be settling to a siesta behind shuttered windows. I felt tiredness sweep over me.

I was overwhelmed by grief, by the loss of all that would never be. A man I had made love to, but knew almost nothing about, not even his name. Desolation threatened. It was the prospect of never seeing Pierre again, although what future I had expected or dreamed of I could not have put into words. It was the bleakness. The thought of the dull, commonplace life I would lead without his presence was washing through me in waves. Pierre, with all his glitz, had made the difference. Corny as that might be, I had felt alive in his company. I glanced across at Peter, who struck me then as ramrod rigid. He had been tense, uptight, since before Pierre had disappeared. My feelings, worn too openly, without discretion, were at the root of this change in his demeanour. Agnes had divined them. 'Don't hurt him,' she had warned. I felt rotten, guilty as hell that I had let her down. But I hadn't asked Peter to get so involved with me. I mean, we weren't anything permanent. We hadn't made plans, promises for the future.

I was sixteen, for goodness' sake.

How could the best days of my life be over at sixteen?

We found a bar, also a bistro, but neither of us had an appetite. It was set back in a leafy pebbled courtyard. We were seated at a small iron table with, shading us from the sun's harsh rays, a white scalloped parasol decorated with fat green bottles. Bulbous bottles. They were advertising Perrier, a popular mineral water. Somewhere beyond my sightline, water fell in a steady trickle. The flowing fountain cooled the air but attracted mosquitoes. One landed on the upper part of my wrist. I slapped it dead and drew my hand away quickly. The squashed black-brown body remained, its blood streaking a thin uneven line across the back of my hand. I felt disgust. I hate the sight of blood. It reminded me of home.

One other couple, lost in their own intimate conversation, their four hands entwined against the surface of their table, were seated almost out of sight in a deep shady alcove, our sole companions. They seemed so in love.

A waiter appeared.

'We'll have two Perriers, and one large whisky, *s'il vous plaît*.'

I made no comment. Peter rarely drank spirits. He must have been suffering the same grief as I was, the same glaring reality that our lives, as we had known them, innocent and blameless, were over.

*

The police officer was a local man, who spoke with a thick twang and ringing consonants, like the clopping of horse's hoofs, iron against cobbles. I was growing accustomed to the Provençal accent and was beginning to break through its maze to decipher partial meaning. He was tall and bronzed, how I pictured an Australian outback ranger. The long-limbed, loping style of someone who has grown up out of doors and practised many sports, who looks as though he is too tall for his bed. He expressed little interest in us or our story.

'A tourist friend has gone missing, you say?'

Peter nodded.

'Whose relative was he?' The man coughed, realizing his faux-pas. '*Is* he, I should say.'

We shook our heads. 'He wasn't related to either of us,' confirmed Peter. I noted that Peter was also using the past tense.

After that, a roll-call of questions.

Who was the man? What was his name? The officer let out a sigh as he prodded at a biro from which no ink was flowing. He wore no jacket. An overhead fan spun lazily. Even so it was stifling in the cramped cubicle that acted as Reception. And there was nowhere for us to sit down. I stared at a black-and-white portrait photograph of de Gaulle hanging on the wall.

'His name was Pierre,' I said.

'French, then?'

'We don't think so.'

A frown from the inquisitor. 'His surname?'

Peter harrumphed. He glanced at me. I pursed my lips.

'Pierre was the only name he gave us,' I said.

'We met him in a bar.'

The lawman squinted, considering the facts, or lack of them. Peter was watching me as though I might be shielding the answer, burying a truth. I shook my head. 'I don't know his surname.'

'But he was staying with you?'

'Yes.'

'No.'

We both spoke at once. I had answered in the affirmative, Peter negative. 'He was sleeping in his tent close to my family's villa.'

'After you met him in a bar?'

'Yes.'

Should I admit to hitching a ride with Pierre from Marseille?

It was later, in La Ciotat, we had bumped into him in the bar. Quite by chance. Pierre had spotted us sitting together at a corner table, raised a hand in greeting and approached.

'Oh, look, that's *him*,' I'd squealed. 'It's the bloke I met in Marseille, the one I told you about with the car.'

Peter had let out a groan of dissatisfaction. In spite of the music from the loudspeakers I had heard it distinctly.

Cradling a tumbler of whisky, Pierre, in loose linen slacks, had strolled towards us, made himself comfortable at our table, without invitation, and offered to buy us both drinks. He had pulled from his back trouser pocket a rolled wad of crisp five-hundred-franc notes, the new francs with the head of the French mathematician, Blaise Pascal, on the back. This was more money than I'd seen in my life.

Peter turned his head away in disgust. He had been

raised to despise such displays of ostentation. Nouveau riche would have been his silent judgement.

'Age?' asked the ranger-type, bringing me back to the present.

Again Peter spun his head in my direction. Had my intimacies with Pierre given me an insider's knowledge? Who knew of those intimacies?

'Older than us,' I offered. 'Twenty-five possibly.'

'Do you have any photographs?'

We shook our heads again. I had no photograph to remember him by.

'Any idea about his profession?'

I bit my lip. Tricky. Pierre had surely been peddling drugs. Drugs stashed in an otherwise empty guitar case? I hadn't known about them till this morning. I had planned to ask him to play the guitar for us one evening.

I tried not to dwell on the fact that he was a dealer because I wasn't comfortable with it, but it would explain his casual wealth, his super-duper car and the other stash in the glove compartment. His lifestyle, too. I never confirmed Peter's suspicions. That would have felt like a betrayal of Pierre. If Pierre was a dealer, he was discreet about it. Possibly why he hadn't revealed his identity. We were three strangers, three travellers, enjoying a summer in the South of France. Indulging our senses. I was sure he was English. The lilting accent. He must have been born in the north and moved south at some point during his childhood, softening the Yorkshire in him.

I shook my head. 'He never mentioned his work.'

'Well, what do you know about him?' the officer enquired, a little tetchily.

I watched, as he attempted several times to get the ink in his biro to flow so that he could complete the lengthy form he had placed on the cluttered desk in front of him, where papers flapped as the overhead fan turned. Alongside the paperwork there was a black Remington typewriter. He swore under his breath. He had already opened and closed several drawers in his hunt for carbon paper to make the required number of copies of the missing-persons report. The carbon paper was as elusive as the biro was intractable.

'Nothing, really.'

Everything and nothing.

'And he wasn't staying with you? Where did you say you are staying?'

'My aunt's house is situated overlooking the beaches and coves west of Figuerolles. The missing man, Pierre, was a stranger to us. He was sleeping in a tent that he had pitched close by our land. We knew little else about him.'

Why was Peter lying? To protect Agnes?

'Anything else?'

Both heads turned to me.

He liked to fish, enjoyed dancing to Jamaican Ska music when he was stoned. He was always stoned to one degree or another. He'd introduced us to Ska. 'One Love/People Get Ready', Bob Marley. The Wailers. He was softly spoken. You'd melt in his presence. Occasionally, in the evenings he wore mascara. In the mornings when he woke, the black make-up had smudged beneath his eyes. His tanned face was bewitching. Tanned body. Firm limbs. Most of the time he was dressed in a batik wraparound and open shirt. Or loose floppy cotton pants that tied with a string at the waist. Almost always topless. He rarely wore anything more than an open shirt. His skin was smooth, his chest hairless. His head hung with long golden locks. And sex with him was transcendental.

They were staring at me, stony-faced. These two men.

I shrugged. 'Nothing else.'

The officer reached for a map of the coast. One of those detailed ones, the Ordnance Survey variety. They show every nook and cranny, every wiggly path, whether it leads somewhere or nowhere.

'Can you put a cross, please, at the point where you say he entered the water to go swimming at midnight?'

'It was earlier than midnight,' I insisted.

Peter took the pen and obliged.

'You mentioned he had a car. Where is that now?'

'Still parked alongside my aunt's villa.'

'Do you have the key?'

Peter pulled the key from his pocket and slipped it uncertainly onto the desk. 'I was thinking we should leave the car a day or two, in case he returns to collect it . . .'

The police officer looked at Peter, confused.

'Of course, if you can arrange for it to be towed away, then, thank you, yes, that would be helpful. I would prefer it's gone before my aunt returns.'

Afterwards, the policeman requested that we stay in the area, saying he'd be in touch.

'We're leaving tomorrow. I can give you my parents' contact details in Paris. This man, Pierre, was not with us, you understand. We've taken it upon ourselves to report his disappearance because it's possible, more than likely, that we were the last to see him before . . . before he went swimming.'

'It would be most helpful if you could delay your departure, please. I might need to ask you one or two more questions. Leave your telephone number with me before you go.'

And so we stayed.

When we woke the following morning, Pierre's snappy green 1963 Cadillac Eldorado Biarritz had gone. The police must have collected it.

I walked the beach with Bruce. He became my loyal companion, best friend; his company calmed me. Peter and I skirted round one another as though afraid to make physical contact. There was no more sex between us, little affection, even. He had stopped inviting me to his room, which I was relieved about.

The ghost of Pierre stayed with us. Perhaps more so than when he was alive. You see? I said it. *Was*. By then I was facing the brutal reality, the fact that Pierre was dead, his body languishing at the bottom of the sea.

I dug out tomes of poetry from Agnes's library. Oscar Wilde, Yeats, Pablo Neruda, E. E. Cummings. I immersed myself in others' heartache, their longing and love stories. I wrote my own lines but threw them away. All the while we, or I, waited for the phone to ring. Nonsensical, unrealistic were my hopes for the police to solve the mystery of the missing body and return Pierre to me.

The Present

Gissing's identity

Two days later, Capitaine Moulinet was back at our door. It was sooner than I might have expected. I was intending to pop to La Ciotat to buy pyjamas for Peter's upcoming hospital stay. He and I had always been in the habit of sleeping in the nude and he didn't own a single pair.

'*Bonjour, Madame.* A couple of small points, if I may . . .'

'Yes, Capitaine?'

'Did the victim, the foreigner' – Moulinet emphasized this word heavily – 'who went over the edge, speak to you, say or shout out anything before he took his life?'

I shook my head. 'He was quite some distance from here. Even if he had shouted, I doubt I would have heard him or been able to distinguish anything more than a noise. No, there was no call that attracted my attention.'

'You mentioned on the day in question a description of the dead man.'

'Did I?' I was struggling to recall. 'Oh, yes, that he was dressed in black.'

'You described him as "a foreigner", which, in fact, is accurate. He was English. I was wondering what made you arrive at this conclusion.'

My head was beginning to spin. Giddiness caused me to take a step backwards.

'Would you prefer we go out onto your veranda where it's breezier and you can sit down, Madame? Perhaps the fresh air might jog your memory.'

Without a word, I led the way. Moulinet took a seat and pulled out his tattered notebook. I remained standing, looking out to sea. My legs were jelly and I wasn't sure I could sit down with confidence or ease. I took a few deep breaths. An actor's training to alleviate stage fright before setting foot on the boards.

'What made you describe the deceased as a foreigner?'

'The majority of people who stop at that spot are tourists. I assumed that he must be . . .'

'Do you know the identity of the dead man, Madame?'

'You have asked me that question and I told you that I do not.'

'It's curious, puzzling me, because your name and address were found in the house where the dead man was staying. Written in ink on a sheet of paper torn from a notebook. Can you explain that?'

Such a possibility had never crossed my mind. I shrugged and shook my head. And what of the notes I had handwritten to George? On both I had signed my name. 'Was there anything else, or . . . only those details?'

'Nothing else so far. The deceased's name, according to a passport found in a side pocket of his hand luggage – his suitcase stored in his wardrobe is locked and we haven't yet found the key – was George Andrew Gissing. He was born in Bradford in the United Kingdom. Does that mean anything to you?'

Andrew, not Peter?

I shook my head, wondering, after all these years,

where the Christian name 'Pierre' had come from. Were Peter, Agnes and I the only three ever to know him as Pierre?

'I wonder how you knew where he was staying,' I said casually, to deflect the conversation away from me.

Moulinet shrugged. 'We found several English coins in his raincoat pocket, the soggy remains of a London train ticket. It was not hard to track him down after a few enquiries at various lodging houses and hotels.'

I nodded.

'I have spoken with Madame Celeste Gurnier, the proprietor of number eleven The Strand, and she confirms that the house had been rented for an open-ended period of time to an Englishman bearing that name.'

'I see.'

'She has no idea why Mr Gissing was visiting this part of the world. He did not strike her as a typical holiday-maker and he had little luggage for a gentleman planning on a lengthy stay, but then again, who can say? He hadn't booked the house on the internet or by telephone or agency. So, no traces there. It appears he just turned up in the village looking for a place to "stop for a few weeks". At least, that was his explanation to the barman, Thierry, at the Café du Port. He enquired there for rentals and was given Madame Gurnier's address by the proprietor.'

'Unusual,' I remarked, for want of something more elucidating to add.

'And you are unable to shed any further light on the matter, Madame? Do you know from where he had found your name and address?'

I lifted my hands as though to give an explanation,

make a gesture, to offer some trumped-up clarification and let them fall heavily back by my sides.

'He might have died with the key to the suitcase on his person. It fell out of his pocket, perhaps, as he plummeted. The case will be forced open and, with luck, the details of his presence here and the reason for his death will be explained before the week is out.'

1968

Summer's end

I was on the upper floor of the villa, in Agnes's studio and bedroom, with its semblance of quietude, keeping myself out of sight and sequestered from the tensions that were Peter's and mine. My gaze was locked on a trio of men and one woman who were busying themselves on Agnes's beach. Uniformed police. Police Nationale. Pressed back from the frame of the window, a shadow hovering beyond the shutters, I reminded myself of Judith Anderson as Mrs Danvers in Hitchcock's film *Rebecca*.

I watched sneakily as they cordoned off the area where we, all three, had spent our last evening together. Agnes's cove. Our playground. All those fabulous evenings. Stoned, music, barbecues. Sex when Peter was not about. Evenings of falling in love under the stars, watching for shooting stars. Days discovering his flesh. A love hidden by me, cherished beneath wings.

One of the lawmen was donning a pair of rubber gloves. He was poking about in the ashes of our last bonfire, using an instrument, which, at this distance, resembled a giant pair of tweezers. I couldn't imagine what clues he might be looking for. The dog-ends of our spliffs? If he unearthed any, were we going to get busted? Was I to be arrested for the second time that summer?

I was getting seriously panicked about the boundaries of our involvement, our obligations. How far would we be implicated? We should have called the cops hours sooner, but Peter had stubbornly resisted the idea. Why? He'd said it was unwise, that Pierre would be fine and he wasn't our responsibility. Why involve ourselves? Why bring the law snooping about? 'Wasn't your first skirmish with the police sufficient for one summer?' he'd reasoned. His words had stayed with me, put the fear of God into me.

Yesterday afternoon, Peter was called back to the police station in Cassis to 'answer a few unsettled queries'. He was monosyllabic when he returned and refused to engage in conversation. Neither would he tell me what the 'unsettled queries' had been.

While he was gone, I took Pierre's drug stash out of my bathroom cupboard and put it in Agnes's studio, tucked among the chaos of her paint pots and cleaning materials. I was intending to dispose of everything, every last tablet, but hadn't yet worked out how or where. I was dreading a raid on the house. An exhaustive search. I realized it had been judicious of Peter to insist that Pierre was not staying here when he drowned.

A police motor boat out on the water was rounding one of the four islets of Riou and crossing our bay yet again. It reminded me of one of those train sets where the train just keeps turning in loops on the tracks. The cruiser had been out there since morning. The nag of its engine, even up here in the eyrie, had been taunting me since daybreak. I'd taken refuge in Agnes's sanctuary where Peter wouldn't think to look for me.

As soon as Agnes returned, I was planning to set off for London, to take the train from Marseille to the Gare d'Orléans in Paris. And then a Métro to the Gare du Nord where I would board the first boat-train I could secure a seat on. I knew that I was abandoning the last shred of hope that Pierre's body would be recovered.

I didn't intend to stay in Paris with Peter. I told him honestly that I wanted to return directly to England. No matter how adamant or persuasive my arguments, nothing I said destroyed his illusion that we would spend time together in the city. He continued to harbour the hope that I would have a change of heart, would soften towards him, even after I'd advised him, repeatedly, that our relationship was over. How could it not be over after everything that had happened?

'You can't leave me,' he'd said. 'Not now.'

Pierre's tent had collapsed, fallen in the wind or been knocked down by Bruce. No one had bothered to right it or pack it away. It had been blown into the scrub. It was caught between bushes, torn and damaged. His belongings, a simple cloth bag, floppy, stuffed with his few articles of clothing, I had cleared out from the room he had barely slept in and thrown away. I regretted that hasty gesture, that I hadn't held on to something for myself. He seemed to own so little and I was left with only memories, no souvenirs. I recalled his Hawaiian shirts, short-sleeved tropical fantasies. I recalled his bronzed arms, his movements. His softly spoken voice. That smile, the splinter of broken tooth. Rolling joints.

The days advanced. No corpse was retrieved.

A phone call came from a police investigation office in Marseille to inform us that we were free to leave at our leisure. I was on the veranda, a book on my lap, another volume of love poems.

So, that was that. Peter was champing at the bit to get on his way. 'Go ahead,' I told him. 'I'll hang on.'

There was nothing to remain for, besides the care of the dog, until the return of Agnes, due any day now.

'We'll both hang on.'

I longed to stay for ever. To be alone at the place I had grown to love, but with everything still perfect as it had been. I sat cross-legged on the soft sand, imprinting every image into my brain so that I would never forget the cliff house, the bay. Never forget falling in love with Pierre.

We met Agnes at the station: she arriving, loaded down with shopping bags from Rome, we departing with our luggage. All three of us embraced fondly, hugged and wept a little. Then Peter handed her the keys to her car, to her home.

'But why must you leave?'

'Father's beckoning, getting himself into a right stew.'

'What a bore that brother of mine is. Come back soon, both of you. Grace, make sure to come with Peter. I'll be expecting you.'

The train to Paris was packed. The *wagons-lits* had all been reserved. This was the beginning of the end of the holiday season. *La rentrée*: the return north for families with children, readying themselves for the start of the school year. We were obliged to stand in a crowded corridor, awaiting the chance of a seat at the next station.

'Will there be a stop before Paris?'

'Yes.' Peter nodded, stroking my hair. 'Avignon.'

We were feeding ourselves on packets of biscuits Peter had bought at the station, although I had little appetite. I had lost weight and felt sick most of the time. When I was exhausted and looked as though I might fall over, Peter propped me up. He put his arms about me and pinned me against the window. His caring, his insistence that nothing between us had changed, exacerbated my loss, my grieving for another. Still, his kindness helped me hold it together. On that long journey towards home, the end of my summer of '68, Peter was all I had.

Was I all he had? Had we brought misfortune upon one another? I knew I had saddened him, and it tore at my heart.

I didn't choose for him to fall in love with me or for me to fall for Pierre.

I replayed in my mind's eye the crawling fear, the panic, the knowledge that Pierre and I were drowning, although both of us could swim, those last moments in the water with him as I clung to him. Had he been fighting for his life? Was he having a fit? A drug-induced heart attack? The kick – did I knock him unconscious? Had I caused his death?

'Swim. Just swim, don't look back. I'm right behind you.' Was that what he had called? My brain was furring up, the details growing foggy. He had still been alive when he shouted those words. *Right behind you.*

And then what had happened? What had become of Pierre? The questions never left me, never let me go.

*

The tablet. My first of several. Pierre had called them 'tabs' – 'Let's drop a tab' in that persuasively velvet voice of his. I hadn't known what it was, what it contained. LSD. Acid.

My hesitance there on the beach. His open hand proffered, palm upturned, visibly sticky from the heat, holding what looked like a small square of blotting paper. Pink-tinged, innocuous. I was ignorant of the trip that tiny pellet, a 'tab', had the power to unlock.

'I don't know,' I'd said. 'I never have.'

There was an almost invisible trembling of his hand. I remembered that from when he had fashioned his fishing rod.

'All the more reason to. Life is about broadening your horizons.'

Wasn't that why I was in France, to broaden my horizons? A hip chick of the sixties.

'You'll see the world through new eyes. It'll be as though you were once blind. Opulent colours. A roller-coaster ride of self-discovery, and the sex is transcendental.'

'"Once I was blind, but now I see."' I giggled coyly, propelled by temptation. I was sixteen. My clothes, a loose shirt over a bikini, were flapping in the wind, like a grounded bird.

'You'll fly,' he encouraged.

'What about Peter?' I'd asked, turning my head without focusing on any point in particular. Was I to take this pivotal journey alone, without Peter? Why couldn't it be the three of us, like in *Jules et Jim*? I hoped it would be mind-blowing, life-altering, but not solitary. I had wanted Peter to be present, to share the experience with us.

'He's walked into town. He'll be back. There's plenty left for him. My supplies are limitless.' Pierre had winked.

'What about you?' My eyes pierced his.

'I'm with you.'

'Shall we share one? I'll start with half.'

He shook his head, grinned, that roguish broken-faced smile. Like a cherub yet not remotely saintly. His long blond hair flew upwards and stood high above his head. A halo against the horizon and the baking ball of the afternoon sun.

'It's all or nothing, Grace. There's little point in taking half. That's not what it's about. Shall I go first?'

I was apprehensive, hesitant, yet I wanted whatever he wanted. I hungered to be a part of him. Would our minds meld? Would we enjoy 'transcendental' sex?

My left arm holding my weight, my outstretched body, in the sand began to give way. I was subsiding, collapsing. The backs of my bare legs were reddening, stinging from the burning sun.

He lifted the 'tab' towards his mouth, leaned forward and kissed me softly. The tip of his tongue worked its way between my lips, excavating, hollowing a space. I closed my eyes. His fingers were at my chin. The drug was on my tongue.

I wanted the high, but I wanted Pierre more. I would have done anything for him.

'Swallow.'

I obeyed, then opened my eyes, as though startled, waiting, expectant. It tasted of nothing special, a tiny bit fizzy, rather like weak sherbet. Nothing was happening. He must have seen the puzzlement in my eyes.

'It's not working.'

'Be patient.'

'What about you? Don't let me do this alone.'

He drew an envelope from the breast pocket of his open Hawaiian shirt. It must have been folded a dozen times. Scruffy worn paper, disintegrating into powder at the edges. Deftly he opened it. Secreted within were tablets of varying colours and sizes. A paper purse of pills. Uppers and downers, including several more tabs of acid. With nimble fingers he drew one out and popped it into his mouth before folding away the envelope. His navy and red striped shirt was blowing, like a Phoenician sail, in the wind.

'Come on, let's go.'

We strolled along the beach. Once or twice, I glanced backwards, looking for Peter.

'Don't worry about your friend. He'll find us. There's no one else here. Two lone figures in the distance. He'll know it's us.'

I allowed myself to be led, went happily. Docilely. I was beginning to feel light-headed. We walked for a while, feet sinking into the soft, warm sand, spilling through my varnished toes. Fifteen minutes, three-quarters of an hour, I couldn't have gauged it – time had melted away – until we neared the end of the bay, approaching a cluster of magisterial granite rocks that would need to be scaled if we were to continue onwards at the water's edge to the next set of coves. I marvelled at the smoothness and roundness of the giant stones in the sunlight, the delicate patches of damp that made them darker, and the dried salt trapped within the perforations and crevices glinting like smuggled stars.

'These are so beautiful,' I crooned. I stretched out my arm to brush my fingers against the first boulder, to experience its texture, its formidable age. It might have been a giant sleeping seal from a fairy tale. My touch might awaken it. Its outlines began to shift, to change shape, oscillating, rippling, breathing. 'It's alive.' I hooted. 'This is incredible.' I repeated those three words over and over. Mind-blowing. Corny. I screeched with laughter and was bent double with my spaced-out chortling.

We made love. It was not just sex. Stripped in the sand. The scent of him. Pierre's words had been more than accurate. *It was transcendental.* Every touch was as though he were switching me on, as though I was coming alive for the first time. In slow motion. He awakened me to countless sensations.

He was turning me on.

I'd love to . . . excite you . . . blow your mind . . .

To . . . *Aaaaah.*

It was before we had gone swimming for the first time that day that I spotted Peter, thought I caught sight of him, high up near the house looking down to where we were prostrate on the beach. He must have returned from town, was looking for me. And then he was gone. Or possibly I imagined him.

Don't think about Peter.

'Pierre, where are you going from here?' It was the first time I had broached the future, the possibility of a relationship.

Pierre nuzzled his mouth close to my ear. 'Who knows? Morocco maybe for the winter, take the motor down through Spain. Why? Want to come with me?'

'Seriously?'

He laughed loudly. Was he mocking me?

I don't know what had happened to our clothes. At which point had we discarded them? Bare-skinned, bronzed. A hip young couple, we were, strolling, idling, holding hands, drinking in the view across the horizon, discovering nature, seeing everything through the eyes of a tripping psyche. Me, for the first time. Branches, roots, crabs, the glint of sand, every stone, every flaw in every stone: all was a revelation. A new perspective, as Pierre had promised. What a gift he was offering me: a lustrous universe, vivid and intense. Life through a magnifying glass. In tight close-up. The world about me was pulsing, palpitating. Even the rocks, it seemed, had a heartbeat. Every object and creature throbbed with life. Within everything was memory, a recording. A witness.

I was a girl climbing out of a closed box for the first time, happening upon a sky that was not blue, but BLUE, vigorously tinted, fervently, thrillingly blue.

We paused to embrace, to kiss, before he laid me on the seashore. My bed of particles warm and itchy beneath my buttocks. Our legs stretched out, intertwined. 'Amazing Grace,' he whispered, his hands pressing into me. I have never forgotten his hands. He had long, elegant fingers. On one hand, the left, I think, yes, the left hand, there was a small wart and to me on that day it was possibly the most beautiful blemish I had ever clapped eyes on.

His sparse body hair was golden. His flesh smooth. He was an Adonis, and for that brief, precious time, he was mine. I was his. On that wide-open, wild, deserted beach, I forgot Peter.

*

'You're crying.'

I shook my head. 'No, not crying.'

Someone was watching us, a portly man who laid claim to a few limp strands of dark hair combed from one side to the other across his scaly pate. He was scrutinizing me. Eyes screwed up. His was a cruel look with a downturned lip, as though he had a sour taste in his mouth.

'That man is watching us.'

His red face, polished and sweating.

'What's he looking at?'

'Your tears have drawn his attention.'

I turned in the crowded train corridor, swivelling awkwardly on my feet, pressed my cheek against the window-frame and stared outwards, recalling our arrival in Marseille. My heart once full of hope and joy.

'How long have we been travelling?'

Heaven knew where my watch was. I seemed to have discarded so much over the summer, been careless with myself, my possessions, profligate with my emotions, with no memory of where the pieces had been abandoned. The shards of me.

My breathing had calmed. I heard the rhythm of the train's wheels and the movement no longer alarmed me.

We were out in the countryside. It could have been anywhere. French farmland. Prettier than English rural scenes. Vines, rows and rows, heavy with darkening fruits. September harvests. A field of goats. Another of donkeys, their tails flapping at the flies on their flanks. We flew by villages with church spires. We had long left the coast behind us.

I recalled Pierre's open-top Cadillac, banked against

the dunes, on the verge of the wild beach with its tall, spiky grasses. Above which, high in the Mediterranean scrubland, I had eventually buried his stash of drugs, every incriminating package, banking and cramming them into an underground tunnel, heaving huge stones to close off the aperture of the abandoned badger's sett. Stones so heavy I was obliged to roll them into place, so that Bruce could not sniff them out, dig up the illicit substances and kill himself on an overdose. He wouldn't be able to shift those stones. Over time, the earth would drift and settle, swallow the breach. The vegetation would grow. No one would ever be the wiser.

We were flying over a bridge, a broad, densely brown river wending its way beneath us. I lifted my eyes heavenwards, pressed my nose against the glass. The sky was china blue. I remember that blue. A hue that offered serenity. The vista was bucolic, unthreatening beneath that sky. A sky that had watched over the events of our summer. I had been carefree, never knowing there would be a price to pay.

The train braked, juddering to a halt between two stations. This was unscheduled. Passengers turned their heads towards the windows demanding an explanation. A child began to bawl loudly. Some muttered, exchanged glances. Everybody was disgruntled and tired. An old woman rummaged in her shopping bag, pulled out half a baguette cut into a lengthy sandwich with slices of charcuterie hanging loosely from between its two halves. Pink and floppy, like a dog's panting tongue. Bruce. I'd miss him.

'Where are we?' I murmured. I was thirsty. Tired. Out of sorts.

Peter did not hear me. I glanced sideways in his direction. I would have liked to rest my head on his shoulder, to take comfort from him, but I had gambled away our relationship. His face was locked in a frown, as though he was puzzling over a problem. I saw him – us – in Pascal's studio, making love on the floor. Outside were street-lamps and Paris. It seemed a lifetime ago.

The sun's heat through the glass was making me giddy. A sickness rose up within me.

I'm sorry I've pained you, I wanted to whisper into his chest, *so sorry*, but I kept my mouth shut because I knew, if summer lay ahead of us again, I would make the same choice.

The train had not moved on. Its engine agitated, then settled and remained silent. The passengers were growing restless. Children were crying, fretting, hungry, fidgety.

I needed to pee.

Uniformed men were standing alongside the tracks. Police officers. Half a dozen climbed aboard. Was it they who had intercepted the train? My heart began to race.

They were combing through the compartments, apparently in search of someone. I felt the skin on my back begin to spike. My spine stiffened. A stranger's feet, plonked either side of mine, shuffled nervously and resettled.

Were we, every one of us, guarding a guilty secret? Skeletons in our cupboards? Had we, all of us, a reason to dread the intervention of the law?

Who were they looking for? The uniformed officers penetrated the length of our carriage surveying faces. Face after face. Some travellers hung their heads to avoid the intrusion, the scrutiny.

A police officer outside, beyond the exterior of the

window on the pebbled siding, paused, hovered close by us, glanced my way, frowned, then continued walking onwards. Sweat was breaking out around the back of my neck. My urge to urinate was becoming desperate. I was spooked by the intrusion and wanted to leap from the train and take off. Peter, at my side, remained calm. His body gave off no signs of fear. No animal scents of one who was threatened. He had nothing to rebuke himself over, no reason to feel remorse. Unlike me: I had kicked a Parisian police officer, escaped from an arrest, buried drugs in the south . . .

A quartet of officers in our carriage, walking in a crocodile, were hustling a path, drawing close, pushing their way slowly, methodically, through the bunched crowds. Head swimming, I recalled Paris, the demonstrations. The batons, the violence. My instinct was to run, to shoulder my travelling companions roughly aside and hotfoot it off the train, fleeing out of the door. I needed an escape route.

The train was beginning to move. It shunted forward a yard or two and was then at a standstill again.

The first officer had arrived alongside me. He took a step sideways, to position himself directly in front of me, his eyes upon me. I lowered my gaze.

'Name?' he demanded. The decibel level of his voice was low but charged.

I muttered my response.

'Are you travelling by yourself?'

My body went rigid. Peter, a hair's breadth at my side. I nodded. I noticed a furrowed brow. The man with the bald head who had been watching me. He knew I was lying. Might he chirp up? Betray me?

Why had I lied? Because I did not want to give Peter hope. I wanted him to understand that it was over. It had to be.

A second member of the force had drawn up behind his colleague, glaring at me from over a navy blue uniformed shoulder, while the other pair of the four had continued on through the train passing into the next carriage. The train was picking up speed, rolling as it advanced.

The interrogator swung his attention to Peter. 'Are you travelling alone too?' he demanded. There was an undertone of sarcasm in his voice.

'We are together,' replied Peter, with his impeccable accent.

The man's attention was back with me, a whip of a turn. He lifted his hand, open palm. 'Identity papers.'

I reached inside my pocket, fumbled for my passport and handed it over. I was fighting not to blurt out the question, 'Is this about Pierre? Have you found him? Is he alive?'

The man was studying my passport, turning the blank pages back and forth as though puzzling at their emptiness.

'British,' stating the obvious. 'How old are you?' He was not asking me. He looked for his answer within the passport, flicking back to the identity page, and then lifted his eyes to mine. Yellow-tinged eyes that drilled into me.

'Sixteen,' he spat, pushing the passport back to me. 'Young to be travelling alone.' He pulled out a pad and paper. 'Will you be staying in Paris?'

'Returning directly to London,' I murmured, sensing the balance of Peter's body shift.

The officer considered my reply, accepted it and turned his attention to my companion. 'Passport.'

Peter delivered it without a word.

'You are also returning to London?'

Peter shook his head. I observed the tiniest bead of sweat on his temple, smaller than one of the spots on a ladybird. 'I live in Paris,' he informed the men. 'My father is employed at the British Embassy.'

Passport returned, the officer glared at Peter. With a gesture of his head, he ordered his silent underling to pass on through the carriage. He followed a step behind him.

Everyone was watching us. Dozens of eyes upon us, as though we were criminals. I turned my face to the window attempting to reel in the chaos of my private world, remembering a fishing rod. I closed my eyes. Was Pierre alive? Might that be the reason these men were prowling the train? Or had they found clues to something sinister or illegal in his car? A weapon? Some trace that had led them to us?

A tear swelled. I felt its warmth as it slithered like a snail down my cheek to my chin, from where it fell to my T-shirt.

'Stay a few days with me in Paris,' Peter pleaded, barely audible.

I shook my head. I knew I was skewering him, but I was too wretched, too engulfed in my own misery, self-pity and nausea to consider anyone's feelings but mine. Selfish, odious creature that I was. 'I need to get out of France.'

'Why don't I travel to England with you? For a few days. I don't need to register at the Sorbonne till early October.'

I shook my head, begging him to desist.

'Grace, look at me, please. We can't simply drop everything, lose contact. We need time. We need to clear this mess up.'

I felt the sharpe edge of his heartbreak and I did nothing to alleviate it. What could I do? I shook my head again.

I was pushing him away, dismissing him. I didn't deserve his love and kindness. I should have hated myself for my behaviour towards a young man who had been my best friend, so generous towards me.

But I had fallen in love and lost my special one. In spite of the drugs, the crazy seesawing emotions and the escapades, beneath had lain a real depth of emotion. I had fallen in love with Pierre and now he was gone. Sunk, drowned, dead, disappeared. Gone.

I was sixteen years old and I wanted my life to be over. Finished with. The grief was all-encompassing, more than I could tolerate. I wanted to drown myself in my own misery, to sink to those watery depths where I could reconnect with Pierre.

1968

London, November

It was bleak and bitterly cold with a wet wind that penetrated my skirts, my skimpy inadequate jumpers, stinging my legs and rattling at my broken heart as I prowled the streets in search of a past that was fading, while trying to get to grips with the present. The heating in my rented room was woefully inadequate. It was a gas contraption into which I had to feed coins before its faint blue flame would fire up, sliding the Queen's head into a green metal box attached to pipes to supply a miserly quantity of heat. I spent chunks of my spare time traipsing in and out of the local shops, shivering, in search of shillings. The shopkeepers were getting fed up with me. I caught that glazed look in their eyes when the doorbell clanged and I stepped over the threshold calling, 'Any change?'

The house where I had my digs was a three-storey Victorian terrace on Grafton Road in Kentish Town, north London, a five-minute walk from the drama school where I was midway through my first term. My room was on the ground floor, one window with limp net curtains. The view was a grey-brick garage across a narrow street. Grey London. How I missed Heron Heights, my 'cabin', with its whitewashed walls, its terracotta floor tiles and the blue-green sea enclosed by giant spherical rocks.

My landladies, Moira and Ashley, were a pair of middle-aged, ginger-haired witches. Seriously. Or so they confided. There were cats everywhere. The house seemed to undulate with fur. 'White witches we are,' Moira qualified, as I dragged my bags and my sorrows through the front door and they watched, like a couple of dragged-up imitations of Les Dawson.

It was a far cry from Agnes's idyll.

I baptized the place Witches Court.

'We'll cure you,' promised Ashley.

Did they know? Had they sussed that I was pregnant? I was approaching twelve weeks gone, but it was too early to show. No bump in sight. In fact, I had lost weight from all the movement classes at college. We began every day with an hour and a half of stretching and strenuous exercises. I stupidly assumed that my lack of menstruation was due to the change in my lifestyle, a new departure with plenty of physical activity and a gnawing sense of misery.

Such a moron not to have twigged my condition.

It was Pierre's – his last and most precious gift to me – but it made no odds now. I could not keep the baby. It was out of the question. I hadn't got a penny to my name, was struggling to feed myself. I had only the rented room in Grafton Road to call home. Soon I would be approaching the close of my first term at drama school. I was a fledgling and too raw to throw myself out into the professional world of film and television in search of an agent, and even if a theatrical agency took me on, I would not have been able to earn my own living, let alone feed two of us.

Too, too, too everything.

Christmas was approaching. A new year cometh.

I had promised to spend the two weeks' break at home with my parents in Kent. Dad would be out most evenings, gigging, so I was looking forward to keeping Mum company, cheering her up, offseting her loneliness while concealing my own.

The last time I'd seen them was when I'd stayed for a couple of weeks after I returned from France. It had been the standard living-at-home experience, my home, at least, with flashes of happiness, flashes of laughter, and then a descent into arguments, threats and, occasionally, violence. It meant that I was able, more or less, to keep my own heartbreak under lock and key. Mum looked desperately sad when I took off with my belongings for a new life in London. I wished I could confide in her, a female chit-chat, come clean with one another. It was the first time I had ever stopped to ask myself what had attracted her to my father in the first place. Had she been as besotted with him as I was with Pierre? Had she ever suspected there was a violent streak within him?

But such intimacies were out of the question.

I had no choice but to handle this alone.

To terminate my pregnancy was not the decision I wanted and I did not arrive at it lightly. It was not what I would have opted for had there been any choice. I was cornered. I didn't want to, absolutely couldn't, share my condition with my parents. My mum had more than enough on her plate without trouble from me, and I had no friends in London, the Big Smoke, nobody to see me through this.

I had bonded with one of the blokes in my year at drama school, Connor. If I had an ally, it was him. We went to the pub together, spent hours nattering about our ambitions in the Sir Richard Steele on Haverstock Hill. Connor was gay, yet seemed comfortable in my company, as I was in his. He invited me to the theatre to see *Hair: The American Tribal Love-Rock Musical* in the new year. 'I've got two tickets. A belated Christmas present,' he said.

'Wow, fantastic,' replied I.

It was playing at the Shaftesbury Theatre, had premiered in September a few days before I began college, soon after I'd got back from France. Tickets were gold dust but Connor boasted he had scored stalls seats, 15 and 16, row C, for Wednesday, 22 January. I was pretty excited and a bit chuffed that he had chosen me as his theatre date.

Or I would have been if I hadn't been facing the pregnancy nightmare.

I knew I had to go through with the termination and sooner rather than later. The days were sliding by and I wanted it over and done with as soon as possible. I couldn't bear to contemplate the notion of a life taking form within me. Looking at it from a practical angle, I needed someone to collect me and sit with me in my room for a few hours, to keep an eye on me, possibly overnight. It involved taking a day off college. I was asking myself whether I could persuade Connor to be that someone. It was a huge favour to ask, even if termination of an early pregnancy was legal now. At least I wasn't hauling him in as an accomplice to what some would have judged my 'sordid crime'.

The prospect of what lay ahead, how to organize everything by myself, was doing my head in. I needed funds, a doctor ... What else? Could I count on the National Health Service? Alone in my flickering gas-fired room with, as company, the curled pages of a Tennessee Williams play lying untidily on the candlewick bedspread, I started to cry. There were rivers of tears to offload and I sobbed uncontrollably. I was scared out of my wits, grieving, missing Peter's friendship and cursing myself for the mess I'd made of everything. My summer of '68 had gone drastically awry. Looking at it from another angle, the positive aspect, I had tripped off to France in search of new experiences and I had returned with a zillion.

'All well in there?' A knock on my door. It was Moira.

'Yes, just learning some lines, rehearsing, thanks, Moira, working on a scene, bit dramatic.' I managed the lie with barely a quiver in my voice. Eventually, more out of exhaustion than anything saner, I pulled myself together, rolled off the single bed, crouched on the smelly old carpet and put the kettle on. I wasn't the first to face this and I would, could, must get through and rise above it.

I made the appointment or, more precisely, a kindly Kentish Town doctor I registered with the following morning arranged everything on my behalf, including the requisite two signatures of approval. Moira gave me his name as I was dashing out of the door puffy-eyed.

'Here,' she'd said, 'pop in and see this chap before you go to college this morning. Get yourself sorted, lass.' She knew. They both knew. Witches, they were. Kindly souls.

I was booked to go in, fasting, at nine a.m. on Friday, 8 November. I refused to allow myself to dwell on Pierre. It was his child. I had been over the dates a million and one times. The idea that he had said farewell to this planet, and now his child, our child, was not destined to survive . . . That was the thought, the reality, that sent me spiralling into desolation.

For a moment or two after I regained consciousness, I couldn't work out where I was. Then it all came crashing back to me: the South London Hospital for Women alongside Clapham Common, a red-brick monolith of 1920s design and not dissimilar to a prison. The 'bloody deed' had been accomplished and I had been trolleyed back to the ward.

It was dark outside. A blizzard had blown up needles of snow. Through the window to the left of me, I could see trees illuminated in patches by streetlamps. They were waving and swaying. The wind was abating but the snow continued, closing out the light. Evening had fallen hours ago. It was past six o'clock, and visiting time was upon us.

One or two men in coats and lace-up shoes shuffled onto the ward with magazines under their arms, *Woman* and *Woman's Weekly*. It was so reverentially silent that I could hear the squeak, like rubber toys, of their creeping shoes. They perched, still in their outdoor garments, on wooden chairs at the bedsides of their wives, looking out of place. Trilby hats, flat caps in laps, they coughed awkwardly, glancing about as though fearful of being caught in there. From brown-paper bags that crackled when opened they delivered bunches of dark-skinned grapes.

The hospital gave off an air of being involved in

something illicit, something preferably not alluded to within decent society: *women's matters.*

An order had been sent down to the ward to keep me in overnight due to a complication. I had suffered an excessive loss of blood. I had not prepared for that, and was lacking toothbrush and face cleanser. A little while after, a nurse bustled up to my bed and provided me with two sanitary towels in a slender white box – I was still bleeding, lightly 'spotting', the lady gynaecologist had called it when she'd popped in to see me – toothpaste and brush, a flannel and a bar of musty-smelling soap. The nurse, who had green sparkly eyes, rested a hand on my shoulder, stroked my hair off my face and smiled. 'Try to rest, Grace,' she said comfortingly. 'It's all behind you now.'

Dinner had been and gone. I had barely touched my tray. The food was unpalatable, congealed baked beans and a strip of gravy-sodden, unidentifiable meat that looked as though it had been hewn from a cable-stitched beige cardigan. It tasted like string. To be fair, I didn't have much of an appetite. My throat was parched and I was persistently thirsty even after having downed several jugs of water refilled at regular intervals and left on my bedside cabinet by the kindly emerald-eyed nurse.

I felt overwhelmingly sorry for myself. My emotions were in bits and pieces, like a jigsaw puzzle that had been tossed across the floor. My insides felt as though they had been vacuum-cleaned: the last vestiges of summer had been wrested from me. I closed my eyes and recalled Agnes in her brightly coloured smocks smiling, chattering, singing, paintbrushes in both hands. I pictured the view from her attic. Such serenity and visual opulence. I refused to allow myself to brood upon images of Pierre at the bottom of that sea. I yearned for someone to take me in their arms, hold me and reassure me with words whispered into my hair that everything was going to come back together.

The dull, raw ache in my abdomen was throbbing, like a heartbeat, which was an illusion because the heart, along with the foetus, had been removed. What had I done? The act that I had consented to was irreversible. There was no bringing that life back.

Two deaths.

Had someone, a hospital staff member, notified Connor that I was not going to be discharged that evening? I hoped he was not sitting in Reception waiting for me. My legs were too unsteady for me to walk downstairs. In any case, there was the trickling blood. I had no means of contacting him. I looked about in search of a nurse but saw none.

And then, as if by osmosis, Connor materialized at the door of the ward. I gave a sheepish wave. He spotted me – third bed to the right – and made his way to the chair at my side, a cheery smile lighting his handsome, eager face crowned with a head of ginger curls. He could make his fortune shooting shampoo commercials, I was thinking, but would never have told him so because he would have been affronted at such a prospect.

He was never going to sell out. Neither of us would. We were both Committed to Our Art. True warriors of our trade and dreams.

'Sorry. Have you been waiting downstairs?' I asked,

feeling a bit embarrassed that I was greeting him in a nightie and no make-up, with wild, uncombed hair.

What a pal.

I was more used to seeing him in a leotard during voice and movement classes than in his rather natty outdoor clothes. I knew his ambition, which was as bold and naive as my own, and a few of his weaknesses. His fear, for example, of emotional exposure, revealed during drama classes. Was it because he was gay? Did his parents know? Had he confided in them?

He had never discussed any of that stuff with me.

Homosexuality between consenting males, adults of twenty-one years and over, had been legalized in Britain eighteen months earlier, gaining Royal Assent on 27 July 1967. But Connor had not yet reached twenty-one. Any sexual act he performed could have landed him in prison. The Abortion Act had come into effect in April 1968, a mere nine months earlier. Every time we smoked a joint we risked arrest. Not that I was doing drugs any more. Not a puff since the summer. Even so, Connor and I, in our different ways, were both living on the edges of legality and acceptability. I quite liked that, though: it made me believe we were truer artists, and bonded.

To keep me company for a bit and lift my spirits, Connor recounted an anecdote or two from his day at college. We both managed another chuckle, then he lifted himself from the chair. 'They said to collect you in the morning, about ten. Shall I come back at about nine thirty, help you with your bag?'

'It's Saturday,' I replied, as though that should relieve him of his duty. 'Maybe you have something on.'

He shook his head and grinned. 'But I'll be on my way now. I've got a date.' He winked coquettishly. 'See you in the morning.'

I nodded, deciding then, even with my eyes cast away from his open face, that Connor would be my best friend for ever. Once upon a time, not so long ago, I recalled, I had thought the same about Peter . . .

Peter. For the first time in a while I thought of him and wondered how he was getting along. 'Wherever you are, Peter – Paris, I suppose – I hope you've met someone lovely, someone who treats you better than I did, and that you've filed me away in the box labelled "That Disastrous Past".'

January 1969

Hair: The American Tribal Love-Rock Musical.

Our seats were perfect, so close to the front we could almost touch hands with the performers. I felt so involved, so much a part of it. My age, my generation. Well, the actors were a little older than us, but by less than a decade in most cases. Connor and I sang along to the tunes, all of which we both knew by heart. Every single line. Connor had the LP. He had lent it to me before Christmas, to get me all excited about this evening, he'd said, but in reality to cheer me up after my hospital stay.

The show *really* cheered me up. My companion had proved himself such a stalwart since my operation. At the end of the evening the audience in the stalls rose to its feet and swarmed towards the front of the stage. We were literally swept along with the joy. Alongside the orchestra pit, we danced and sang with our arms above our heads, swaying from side to side. I felt so positive and alive. For one fleeting moment I was reminded of Paris, of rue Gay-Lussac, the night we heard the nightingale sing. And I shoved that memory to the back of my brain.

Many in the audience were wearing long beads and hippie clothes, flowered shirts and bandanas round their foreheads. I glanced up to the dress circle, then to the gods. All the way to the very top level of the theatre, the spectators were on their feet, chorusing and clapping, raising the roof. A tear pricked my eye. We are the generation of hope, I said to myself. Or those a little older than me are. Get out of Vietnam. Free love. It had just turned 1969. We were creeping towards the end of the swinging sixties, but America's longest war still lingered on, haunting and shocking us on TV news programmes, and last year's Paris riots had come to what? A handful of changes at the end of the day, with a price of violence too high.

Where and why had it gone wrong?

I still wanted to change the world.

The cast reprised 'Aquarius' four times. They stayed on stage for a while, chanting and clapping along with us, and it was tantamount to a party, like a peaceful, rapturous prelude to a revolution. I felt high on the atmosphere, elated, and yearned to be up on the stage with the actors. I threw back my head, laughing. Hope had been triggered. I was fired by potency, reminding myself, while singing my lungs out, what I was training for. Theatre can have an impact on the world, even if the dreams and revolutions of last year's riots, marches and protests across the planet had not effected the reforms we all dreamed of. We artists could make a difference through our work. I looked up into Connor's beaming face, his fantastic singing voice rising towards the ceiling. 'Thank you for this,' I yelled. His head was nodding and keeping time with his dancing feet.

There was every reason to be optimistic. Paris was behind me, but my future was not.

*

A couple of days after Connor and I had been to see *Hair*, I was called to the college secretary's office. Such a summons usually portended bad news. One poor student had already been asked to leave. The reason given: not suitable for the rigorous training. It had put the fear of God into all of us in my group. Securing a place there was far from sufficient. The commitment and work ethic could not let up, but my desire to work was, always had been and remained tenacious.

The reason for the summons: the pinched-face bat, with her sallow skin and primly pinned hair, was in possession of a letter addressed to me.

'This arrived for you, Grace. I'm not sure why your mail should be delivered to this establishment. We are not a *poste restante* service,' she sniped, as she passed the envelope across the desk.

I was puzzled.

'Please refrain from using this address in the future. I work alone and am too busy for such nonsense.'

I nodded an inarticulate promise that I would make sure it didn't happen again.

Outside in the corridor, I took a deep breath. It hadn't been the guillotine, thank the Lord. College was my only lifeline. My future dreams were the banisters holding me steady as I climbed. A lifeline that my work provided.

The envelope was white, of quality stationery. I turned it over. French stamps. Oh, God. I needed a chair but not in the coffee bar. Privacy. I glanced at my watch. I had a voice lesson in four minutes. Late arrival to class achieved a black mark. I stuffed the letter into my embroidered shoulder bag and thundered down the stairs. It would wait, though my heart was beating as if someone had just rewound it and forgotten to stop.

It was evening before I pulled the missive out of my bag. I was in the girls' changing room, bracing myself for the brief walk back to my digs. I sat on the bench and stared again at the envelope. My name and the address were handwritten with black ink, a bold, elegant script. Nothing on the reverse gave me any indication as to the identity of the sender, although I had an inkling.

Pierre? An impossible, improbable, out-of-this-world flight of broken-hearted melancholic fancy. How could it be? Pierre, who had never known my surname, never enquired it, as I had not known his, was decomposing in his bottom-of-the-sea resting place. Or had his body been recovered? Was that the purpose of this communication? Cassis police station contacting me to return for another interview, or . . . ? I peeled open the triangular flap and pulled out the folded letter, which was four single sheets, each handwritten only on one side.

The author of the letter was Peter. I would have put my money on it being from him, if I'd had any, even if he had never been given the address of my parents or this college.

Dearest Grace,

Please don't be angry with me for tracking you down. You had mentioned on one occasion in Paris the location of your future conservatoire. After that, it needed no Sherlock Holmes to discover the full address.

Don't throw this away! Please, I beg you to read on. Hear me out.

There is so much I want to say to you. If only you were here at my side. My heart is full.

Those last few days at Agnes's eviscerated me, after such a splendid time together, so many months of discovery and happiness. You arrived with the spring and brought fresh life to me. And when you left, winter had crept our way early.

I fell in love with you from the moment you sat down in that little café on the Left Bank across from the Sorbonne on that early April morning, Friday, the fifth. The date is imprinted on my brain. That first sighting of you, dragging your bedraggled self and backpack in off the street, so lithe, so beautiful, your long auburn hair swaying with the effort, your kooky outfit. I watched you and prayed you would choose the table beside mine. You did. I knew it was Fate watching kindly over me. It seemed to me then, on that first spring day, that you were, you are, my destiny. Please don't let these words frighten you.

And when I watched you at the barricades, working all night, brandishing your faith, your newly won enthusiasm with such gusto and courage, I was overcome with pride. You seemed to understand what I — we were fighting for. I knew then that we had so much to share, a life ahead of us.

Agnes adores you, as I knew she would. And she has warned me and I have understood that you are not yet ready for commitment. But there is time, Grace, time. We have all the time you need.

And then into our summer came that man. An individual who seemed to have no purpose but to make money from peddling illegal substances. I could have tolerated his arrival, pitching his tent and car close to Agnes's land — who was I to turn him away? But I lost you from the moment he arrived. How did I lose you?

You seemed dazed, bewitched by him. And your invitation to him
to stay in the house with us, how could you not have seen the
rejection that would cause me? All the way, during my drive back
from Italy, I had been relishing the prospect of the two of us alone
for ten or so days, there in that idyllic setting. Agnes's gift to us.

I was gelded, not only by his presence in our lives but by the
manner in which he seemed to take you over and deprive you of
your reason.

The door to the changing room opened and I instinctively shoved the letter onto the bench and slid it beneath
my bottom, looking up apprehensively, guardedly. It was
Tom, the kindly old caretaker. 'Sorry,' he said. 'I thought
you girls had all gone off for the night. I was about to
lock up.'

'I'll be out of here in two minutes, Tom. S-sorry to
have held you up.'

'Don't you fret yourself, Grace.'

I shoved the letter back into my bag, pulled on my coat
and hurried home. Peter's words had churned me up.

Back in my room at Witches Court, I had no small
change for the gas heater so I curled up on the carpet,
huddled tight against the bed with my leopard-print coat
draped over me, like a rug, retrieved the letter from my
bag and continued reading.

I saw you. Yes, I saw you, and if I could unsee it, I would gouge out
my eyes in exchange for the peace of mind I have lost. Even now
when I picture that first witnessing of the two of you lying wrapped
in one another's embrace in the sand . . . You, my darling, naked
in his arms . . . I went directly to the house, broke down and cried.

I couldn't speak, couldn't have faced you. You would have noticed that evening, if you'd had eyes for anyone besides him, which you didn't, that my mood had changed, my confidence withered.

Let us not talk about what happened when you went into the sea . . . his drowning. I shan't write about that night. It haunts me, and it always will. Those last few days of you and I together haunt me. If only he had never entered our lives . . .

With a little distance, do you feel the same? Do you see now that he was an intrusion, a menace? A stranger from another seam of life?

My parents are back living in Knightsbridge at my grandmother's house. I think we talked about it once in Paris. I am still studying at the Sorbonne, soon to have my master's. The next time I am in London, which will be mid-February, can we meet? Please say yes.

I have a small studio now near place Maubert in the fifth arrondissement. You would be welcome here too, if you fancy a weekend back in Paris. The address is at the top of the page. At least, let us meet in London. Let us try to pick up the pieces.

Je t'aime énormément.

Peter

I read the letter several times. How could I have allowed myself to wound him so profoundly, 'gelding' and 'eviscerating' him? I was racked with shame for my behaviour towards him.

I folded the letter back into its envelope and slid it beneath my mattress. I would keep it. I did not want to dismiss his words. I needed to be reminded of them. I had been thoughtless towards him, horribly selfish. However,

I would not reply, not even to apologize. Nor would I agree to see him again. At this remove of several months, had my perceptions changed towards Pierre? Had he been an intrusion? I still ached for him. A part of me was deficient without him.

The kindest gesture I could offer Peter was to keep my distance, to ignore his invitation, to remain silent. At some point he would meet another girl to fall in love with and he would forget me. I had caused too much damage already.

After that letter, the days and weeks grew long and dark. A wet, endlessly drawn-out winter compounded my misery. I yearned to be somewhere else, a different place, but where? To return to our beach? No: a location concocted from my imaginings, rich and exotic, imbued with the hues of Agnes's canvases, a warm and sunny location where Pierre was attentive at my side. Work was my solace. I lived and breathed through my work.

I received one more letter from Peter in March '69, inviting me to share his twenty-first birthday celebrations in London with him, along with a group of his friends and his parents. I ignored it, as I had ignored the first communication. I asked myself whether he had received any news of Pierre – and if he had, would he inform me? I doubted it.

I was determined to move forward along my solitary path, learn my craft, build my career, wall in my heart and shelve all retrospection of that summer of '68. The chapter was closed. I threw myself into the characters I played with a ferocious energy. To be anyone but Grace.

The Present

The heather was blossoming – full-blown summer had trumpeted its way to our doors. Hands clutching a mug of coffee, I was sitting outside at the back, having carried out one of the kitchen chairs. I was facing the mountains, not the sea. For many reasons, I couldn't look to the horizon today.

There was too much at stake.

The first Sunday in June. It seemed so much hotter, clammier, for this season than in recent years. On the hillsides, the cicadas were deafening, with their raucous mating calls, drowning the arrival of a car yet to appear down the lane and in view. Cream and citrus-yellow butterflies were making the most of the nectar-rich scrublands beyond the house. I was tuning in to nature, to the environment, as I so frequently do when I am alone and need support.

Alone. Peter in the clinic. His operation scheduled for eight the following morning. I had said my goodbye, my *au revoir*, and I wouldn't see him again until he regained consciousness. It was going to be a long, solitary twenty-four hours.

Sweet-natured Jenny had set off with her two daughters on Friday from the station in Marseille, returning to the UK. I drove them myself, waved them off. She would have stayed on, willingly, but Peter had requested that he and I were by ourselves for the upcoming weeks of convalescence.

Last night, as the sun was beginning to dip and the air

was busy with dragonflies, gnats and geckos on the walls coming out to feed, my husband and I had sat together, side by side, looking out across the calm sea. Slender deep-green lizards were darting between wall crevices and the safety of flower pots.

Peter took my hand. His fingers stroked mine. A finger-tip settled on my wedding ring as it had done possibly a thousand times before but on this occasion the gesture carried an enhanced significance. He said, 'Grace, we both know there's a risk to this wretched procedure. Ssh, don't be agitated, it's a small-percentage risk but it exists and we shouldn't shy away from it. So, ssh . . . let me say what I need to, please. Should the unthinkable happen, my will is prepared and you know all about that . . .'

My throat was knotted. I felt a treacherous tear well up and begin to fall, but I didn't move my hand from his to wipe it away.

'What I haven't previously mentioned is that I've left an envelope locked in the top drawer of my chest of drawers. You know where the key is. It's addressed to you. Confidential, to be opened only in the. . . well, the worst-case scenario.'

'An envelope?'

'A letter I've written to you.'

'What does it say? Is it not something we can discuss together? Let's discuss it now, this evening, while we have time and are quiet.'

'Not now, Grace, please. Bear with me. Let me handle this my way.'

I nodded, at a loss and disquieted.

'The essential point is the following. You are the very best thing that has happened to my life. I've loved you since I first set eyes on you. You know that, of course you do. There wasn't a day when I wouldn't have done whatever it took, any damn thing, to win your love.'

I let out a feeble laugh. '"Any damn thing"? Surely, Peter, there was not an act so terrible you can't divulge it to me now.'

'Let's leave it there for tonight, Grace, please. I'm not proud of that moment in my past.' His face grew flushed.

'So ashamed that you can only write it to me?'

'The letter is there, Grace. Let us hope that . . .' He sighed. He appeared to be troubled.

Tears began to fall and my throat felt as though I was being strangled. I doubted anybody could have loved me with more passion, generosity and loyalty.

If your Peter hadn't tried to kill me . . .

I had dismissed Gissing's accusation as nonsensical. Words from the mouth of a man who was bordering on lunatic, who was a blackmailer and . . . My head was turning in circles. Gissing had led me in circles. I was tired and afraid for Peter, of what lay ahead for both of us.

Had Peter's love for me, his young hot-blooded heart, pushed him to such a fever pitch of jealousy that he had attempted to kill for me?

My decent Peter whose moral compass never faltered?

I couldn't confront him with Gissing's accusation, flood him with the troubles of my heart. Not tonight, when tomorrow he would be facing the precipice.

Gissing, who had drowned in these same unpredictable waters.

I drove Peter to Marseille, to the clinic, this morning. He insisted on being much too early, which meant a long and rather draining wait in Reception clutching one another's sticky hand. After he had been checked into his room and the first of the most minor of the examinations had taken place, I sat at his bedside with him for a while. We spoke little. Blood pressure, heart rate, the basics had been ticked off, functioning as expected. Later, when the consultant dropped by to talk his patient through his upcoming procedure, a nurse requested that I leave. Peter and I kissed goodbye in the presence of the medical team. A witnessed moment, not an intimate *au revoir*. I love you, I mouthed. He nodded. So much more not said. The thought was not lost on me that this was our final moment of intimacy that side of anaesthetic, operation, recuperation period and return to consciousness. Unless a slip, an arrest of the heart, stole him from me for ever.

I had intended to stay in a hotel close to the clinic in the old part of the city of Marseille, to spend today visiting a museum, keeping my thoughts occupied, dinner somewhere down by the port. The hotel was booked and paid for, but the room was bleak, the city full of ghosts, and I felt so afraid for tomorrow's outcome that I checked out, got into the car and drove back here. I decided that I'd stay at home tonight, in our bed, and return to Marseille early tomorrow morning. The hotel booking was still available should an emergency arise and I was called back to the hospital.

I had rarely felt so edgy. Everyone had assured me that there was nothing to worry about, that the operation – I hate the word 'procedure' – was straightforward, yet no one had denied the percentage of risk, which, though slight, still existed. Who knew where the finger of Fate, of miserable Fortune, of a surgeon's split-second loss of concentration might deal its blow?

A motor's engine pulled me back to the here and now.

It was Sunday. I wasn't expecting anybody. I rose from the chair to watch the unfamiliar Peugeot draw to a halt a few yards along the lane.

Out stepped Moulinet. He was dropping by, he apologized for the intrusion, with information regarding the contents of George Gissing's suitcase. 'I hope I am not disturbing you?'

My apprehension rose at his approach.

Aside from a few items of clothing, a change of underwear, Gissing's case contained a rather substantial collection of photographs.

'Really?'

'Most are portraits of you, Madame.'

I stared at the man now seated opposite me, who had refused the offer of a coffee or cold drink.

Two were of Peter and me together. They had been cut out from newspapers, articles reporting on our marriage.

'On these two, Gissing, or perhaps it was someone else, had drawn a circle with a black felt-tip pen round your husband's head. Through the circles he had made in each a cross.'

An act of annihilation of Peter's identity? Retribution?

'Do you have any idea why?' Moulinet asked me.

I shook my head, alarmed. The timing of this revelation was ghastly.

You're surely not talking about the Gissing fellow?

'You have stated that you were the only witness to the victim's fall. Is that correct?'

Still lost in my musings on what this was all about, recalling Peter's recent words.

You're surely not talking about the Gissing fellow? Whatever brought him back to your thoughts? No reason to dredge all that up again after all this time.

'Madame Soames, you seem to be in a world of your own.'

'Apologies, excuse me. As I explained to you when we first met, I didn't actually witness his fall. I saw him stumble and then . . . then he was gone.'

'Are you certain that Gissing was alone, that he was not pushed?'

'Pushed?'

My heart was in my mouth. Might I be accused of pushing George when he lost his balance? He stumbled because we were fighting.

'No, no, he stumbled. He stumbled and I . . . think he – he fell, though . . . I . . . I . . .'

'At some distance, was how you originally described the circumstances to me. Where was your husband, Madame, at the time of Gissing's plummet to his death?'

My mouth fell open. 'Peter? He has nothing . . .'

'It seems rather possible, judging by the photographs, that Gissing was harbouring a vendetta against your husband. Any idea why? Was your husband personally acquainted with the victim?'

I was speechless.

'Did Gissing visit your property either on the day of his death or beforehand?'

'No . . . no, he never came to our house.'

'Can you be sure of that, Madame?'

'Sure? Yes, yes, I'm sure.'

'Is it conceivable that your husband was in the company of George Gissing during those last minutes of the man's life? A row ensued and a man was pushed?'

The Early Nineties

New Year's Eve, 1989

New Year's Eve 1989: the eighties were making their exit and, along with them, the twenty-seven-year-old Berlin Wall had fallen.

I was arriving at a party in Hampstead, squeezing sideways along the hall and through into the high-ceilinged rooms packed with partygoers, sliding by corners where bodies hovered, whispered, laughed. Filming had wrapped in Dublin on a low-budget picture in which I had played the principal role. I had returned to London the week before Christmas, spent a few days with my widowed mum, then kept myself in hiding for a day or two.

I had been filming in Prague when my father died, three years earlier: a stroke had taken him within hours. It had obliged me to get myself back to the UK and, as an only child, offer all the emotional and practical support I could. The loss of him, which touched my mother more deeply than I would ever have expected, had reinforced the natural bond between us. Two lone women closing the gap.

It seemed to be a lively crowd present tonight, made up mainly of theatricals: thespians, some household names, lesser-known actors still hoping for that longed-for break, designers, production folk, directors. Friends from drama-school days, others I had got to know or encountered along the way. Mostly I had been looking forward to catching up with Connor – terrific to see him again, or I thought it would be.

I had been anticipating some convivial time in his company, chit-chat and laughter, having enjoyed snatched conversations only by telephone on a few occasions throughout the closing year. My schedule had been hectic but I'd had an uncomfortable feeling I'd neglected him. I knew his last, short-lived, relationship had ended. He had mentioned it on the phone several months earlier but I was not aware, until I set eyes on him now, that it had affected him so profoundly. My heart sank when I glimpsed him. He had lost weight, was gaunt and so much paler. Never had his light skin against the ginger-red hair appeared so blanched. He was as dapper and well turned-out as he habitually was, but something about his bearing had taken a turn for the worse, as though the confidence had been zapped out of him.

He clocked me from across the room a few minutes after I had elbowed my way through to the dining room, in search of a decent glass of wine. I was cradling two unopened reds in my arms and needed to dump them somewhere. He called my name, took a few steps towards me. His opening line: 'I thought you might have decided not to put in a show. Standing me up again.'

'Would I ever?'

'If someone gorgeous came along, like a shot.' This and similar quips were the basis for perennial jokes between us, given that lovers, any who lasted more than a couple of months, were few and far between in my life. My excuse: career woman, dedicated to the job.

Jolted up against one another by an unsteady reveller, we both smiled, a little shyly. I don't know why. We knew the bumps and curves of each other's bodies almost as well as our own. 'Someone gorgeous. Like who? Name him and I'll hunt him down with ruthless endeavour,' I joshed, picking up a glass from the table, lifting the bowl to eye-level to confirm it was clean before I poured myself a generous measure of Rioja. It was the best on offer other than my gifts, but I couldn't be bothered to search for a corkscrew.

Connor was watching me, scrutinizing me.

'Want one?'

He shook his head. I intuited something, an energy shift. I couldn't put my finger on it. I took a slug of wine and smiled. 'Hey, that's no way to say hello.' We laughed, embraced, hugged hard, kisses brushed against cheeks. I inhaled his sandalwood cologne, with notes of mandarin and another I could not identify. Patchouli. I hadn't smelt that one in a long time. It took me momentarily back to the sixties. God, the sixties, how long ago was that?

I felt safe within Connor's radius. Always had. His humour, his hidden vulnerabilities, his ability to love and care for those close to him. His steadfastness.

My back was to the wall, Connor's to the room where behind him a few couples were dancing lethargically to Simply Red, 'If You Don't Know Me By Now'.

We broke apart and Connor stepped to the right of me, opening up for me a better view of the carousing crowd. A friend waved. I raised my glass, nodding an acknowledgement.

'How was the filming?'

I lowered my head, recalling the exhilarating yet tough

working sessions I had been enjoying over the past few months. I was cautious, though, about expressing too much enthusiasm, all too aware of how indifferently the profession had been treating my dearest friend. Was that at the root of what was bringing him down? In two decades he had clocked up a few classy commercials, one film in Rome, which had sunk without trace, stints of modelling for *Vogue*, both Italian and British, photo shoots for high-ranking fashion houses, and a few lines here and there in plays in London's West End. Since, it had all dried up. And in the modelling game, age was against him. I was thirty-eight, Connor forty. His rich-red curls were greying at the edges and now cropped short. It suited him but the dreaded shift towards middle-age roles was creeping inexorably towards us both. We would soon be competing in different markets, obliged to rethink our presentation. Even tougher for women, of course, but I, thankfully, had built a reputation. I was 'recognized'.

'Fun, good people, an important subject,' was my brief appraisal of my three months' work in Dublin. I flicked a glance in Connor's direction, noted how tightly he was fisting his drained glass and the flaky, papery aspect of his ghostly-white skin. He was uncharacteristically tense. His sea-green eyes, as I viewed his profile, darted about the room anxiously. 'And you? What trouble have you been making?' I asked, attempting light-heartedness.

'How much time have you got to spare?'

I frowned. 'For you, as much as you need.'

'*Connor*, darling!' a female voice squealed. A woman, thin as a paper clip, swathed in black with dyed-black shorn hair: Betsy, a set designer Connor had worked with on several *Vogue* shoots, wriggled and gesticulated her way towards us. Others approached, encircling us, screaming with seasonal and theatrical jubilation. Our private moment had been swallowed. We were both engulfed, dragged off in different directions and barely set eyes on one another over the next couple of hours.

Some time after midnight, as I was standing alone in a bedroom piled high with coats, a photographer I had bumped into here and there over the years pushed open the door and made his way towards me. Into the room burst the vocals of Carole King crooning 'Will You Still Love Me Tomorrow?'.

'You're not leaving?'

I nodded.

'It's a tragedy for a beautiful woman like you to be going home alone on New Year's Eve, no one to escort you.'

'Is that a proposition, Laurie?' A stupid thoughtless off-the-cuff wisecrack made after a couple of glasses of wine, which I immediately regretted and wished I could bite back down. Laurie had been married to a mutual friend of Connor's and mine, a production manager called Bonnie, but he had serially cheated on her over the years until finally she'd got sick of it and kicked him out, much to resounding applause from all her friends. Now he haunted our social get-togethers, as a guest once removed, because he had been invited into our crowd by virtue of his marriage to Bonnie. Whatever, when he came too close I felt my skin crawl. From the start, I had not much cared for him. He gave me goose bumps. He was pressed close against me now and lust was radiating from his slippery bedroom eyes.

'Don't even think about it, Laurie.' I spoke the words commandingly with the timbre of one centre stage. I had been there too many times before, with too many unsavoury men. I grabbed my knee-length leather coat, a recent present to myself, and swung right by him. His hand, fast as a gunslinger's, reached out, barring my exit with iron muscles pressed firmly across my midriff.

I took a beat to maintain control. 'Just let me pass, Laurie, and we'll say no more about it.'

He hesitated. My intention was clear. His gesture was violent, intrusive, misogynistic.

'You've become a bitch, you know that? Hard as nails. Everyone knows it. I wouldn't fuck you if . . .'

'Goodnight, Laurie.' And with that I was out of there. His parting shot, just audible as I pulled the door to was, 'I wonder what all your adoring fans would say if they knew the true you.'

The true me.

I sighed, clicked tight the door, closed my mind, glanced everywhere in search of Connor who, I deduced, must have disappeared without looking for me to say goodnight. No problem, we were scheduled to meet in the morning. A New Year's Day ritual we had adhered to since year three at drama school, broken only by stints of pantomime in far-flung repertory theatres. In the kitchen I gave our bedraggled hostess a hug, kisses and thanks, wished her once more a happy new year, then braved it out into the cold, long night. In the distance, drunken shouts, and a late firework was set off. 1990 was upon us. A new decade. Promising what?

My car was parked a couple of streets away in Keats

Grove. I descended the wrought-iron stairway at the side of the capacious Victorian house converted into three fashionable and ludicrously expensive flats, worrying about Connor. I stood alone on the stone path that led to the gate, debating whether I had drunk too much to drive. The answer was almost certainly yes, even if I had taken it steady by the standards of the majority of the other guests. The cops would be everywhere, crawling the streets, waiting to breathalyse. I would never be able to hail a taxi on this night at this hour. A glance at my watch told me it was close to two a.m. I lived in Primrose Hill, a hike from the nearest Tube station – in any case at this hour there were no Tubes running – so I was in for a fair walk. It was chiefly downhill and I was in no hurry. There was no rain or snow and, as Laurie had cuttingly observed, there was no one at my home waiting for me, nor had there been in a very long while. My forays into romance had been ill-fated.

Was I a bitch, too tough, demanding rigorous standards? Or was I just trying to get along alone?

I strode out beyond the gate, pulled up the lambswool collar on my leather coat and turned right. I'd return and pick up the car in the morning before I met Connor.

When we were flush, Connor and I had frequently lunched or dined together at Lemonia, a family-run Greek taverna in Primrose Hill, our friendly neighbourhood hangout. It reminded us both of our early post-drama-school era. Eating Greek in Primrose Hill was a bond with our history, with our youthful carefree days, of early twenties angst let off the leash for a few hours when our grants, or dole cheques, had arrived and we'd had a few bob in our bank accounts for fifteen minutes. It was Connor who had called yesterday morning and left a message on my answer-machine suggesting this much-cherished location for our first lunch of the year. It was he who had made the booking.

The place was buzzing when I walked in. Connor was seated at our favourite table deep in the restaurant. He had ordered a bottle of Mega Spileo, a Greek merlot that we had both grown to appreciate over the years. I wasn't sure I had the stomach for alcohol after a long night, but preferred to raise no objections. Once the wine had been uncorked and poured, Connor lifted his glass. 'Zorba the Greek' was playing on a stereo in the background. It usually was.

'Happy new year, darling,' smiled my gorgeous pal.

'And to you. Let's hope it's a winner.'

And then, almost too swiftly, 'I've got news.'

'Great.' I grinned expectantly, enjoying the tease of mystery as I lifted my glass to my lips.

'I tested positive.'

It took me a moment. And then another. A small dish of hummus was plonked on the table between us, along with a basket of warmed pitta bread.

'I assume we're not talking screen tests,' I returned drily.

'HIV, to you and me,' he replied, downing his wine in two long draughts. He had always drunk too fast.

'Oh, Connor.' My brain was signalling to me that, above everything else, I must keep my composure. I could not break down, must not let him see what a body blow this news was. Worse, totally worse, for him, but he was the only true ally I'd had for the past two decades. He was more of everything than a boyfriend or partner. We had seen one another through every kind of trauma, rejection and stint of impecuniosity life had thrown our way. He was my best buddy. Better than a husband, better than any lover I had been involved with. We had even given being lovers a disastrous shot, but we had laughed at our ineptitude. In those drama-school days, when anything went and I was the most determined and studious girl on the block, we had bonded and, for a crazy moment in time, I had arrogantly, ignorantly, believed I could 'turn him straight'. We had cried together, covered each other's backs, been there in the late nights, laughed ourselves to stomach-ache over jokes that were hilarious probably only to us. If ours was not a definition of fulsome love, I don't know what was.

From the autumn of '68 onwards, he had been my mainstay and I his. The only secret I had never shared with him was all that had come to pass during my summer of '68 in Paris and the South of France, having brushed it off as 'a hippie and rather risqué summer on the French Riviera'.

This last year, however, I had been jumping on and off planes, running to rehearsals, sitting in make-up caravans with scripts on my lap, weekends on late-night chat shows, awards ceremonies, and I had dropped the stitch. When he'd most needed me.

How many times had I played mock-shocked at his promiscuity, been silently amazed at the unstoppable tenacity of his libido? Mutual friends, fellow actors were dropping like flies. Ian Charleson was dying from an

Aids-related illness. The gossip on the grapevine was that he didn't have much longer to live. Others within our broad circle and across the pond were going down fast, yet I had never, never for one moment believed it would hit home, not this close, not to my Connor. He was indestructible for Heaven's sake.

My mind flipped back to those three years of drama-school days. The parties, the nights in the pub. Groups of us piling back to someone's pad in Belsize Park, clutching paper bags containing bottles of cheap Hungarian wine. Bull's Blood. Sleeping on floors. His affairs, the casual liaisons. Connor dragging himself to his feet from one or other overcrowded bedsit.

'Where you going?' I'd ask drunkenly, pulling at his shoes or ankles.

'Never you mind.' He'd winked. He was off to get laid, a street pick-up, or wherever he found those casual sexual partners. The loneliness for me, dragging myself back to Grafton Road with no bed companion of my own. I lived like a nun after Peter and Pierre. My highs were my work, the challenges, the applause. Connor and I had even joked about getting married. The perfect arrangement. He'd do all the fucking and I could get on with my career without being hassled by men who judged me for being alone, branded me a lesbian or frigid.

We could have been the perfect match.

Two copious plates of lamb kebabs and rice appeared before us. I had lost what little appetite I'd had. 'But not full-blown Aids?'

He shook his head again. 'And I intend to keep it that way. I'm strong and healthy and I will beat it.'

'Here's to that,' I said. 'Here's to us lunching together when we're sixty.'

Sixty? Ian Charleson died five days after our Lemonia lunch and Connor lingered barely six months more.

Late July 1990

'Yesterday' was the tune, the magical accompaniment, I most remember from Connor's cremation, which took place on a Thursday afternoon in a sweltering late-July heat wave during that summer of 1990. Paul McCartney led, then was joined by the raised voices of hundreds, literally hundreds, of mourners in the chapel and spilling out into the courtyard and gardens beyond. A chorus of inconsolable voices, many professionals straight out of London's West End musical scene, and a forest of waving arms were raised in celebration of my darling friend, Connor.

Why had I lost him? Why had he gone? Why Connor? I had no answers.

I was numb, broken-hearted, desolate and exhausted having spent most of the previous three weeks camping at his bedside in the hospice in Hampstead where he had breathed his last. I had lost my big love. That was how he signed every note and every card he had ever sent me, scribbled to me, 'Big Love, Connor'. Followed by a crookedly drawn star.

For the celebration of his life, I had booked two rooms on the upper floor of the pub we had frequented all our lives in Haverstock Hill, the Sir Richard Steele. 'Nothing too swept-up, darling,' he had insisted on several occasions, during those last few weeks when he was thin as a twig, fighting for oxygen and his face had caved in. 'Let the *Vogue* lot slum it.'

The drinking, talking and speeches, the eulogizing of Connor, continued till the small hours, including a series of gloriously bawdy tales and anecdotes from friends of his I had never met, never even heard of before. Those from the side of his life I had never been a part of. A few I knew from our theatre excursions but others were part of his cruising days, the saunas, alleyways, the lonely nights of searching for companionship, fulfilment or just a quick screw. How had they all found themselves here? Who had passed on the word? He was so loved, so revered, held with immense tenderness. His generosity, his big heart were cited repeatedly. Connor had belonged to so many. I was one small part, a precious link in his life, but others glistened equally brilliantly.

Somehow the realization embedded my loneliness deeper. I suddenly found that I loved him even more than I had ever known.

Love is so short-lived, and oblivion endures for an eternity.

The Present

The following morning I was woken by my mobile a little after seven. It was out of character for me still to be sleeping at such an hour but I had suffered a restless night, the phone next to me on Peter's pillow. Just in case.

'Hello?'

'I wanted to let you know how much I love you. And, all being well, I'll see you this afternoon.'

All being well.

'Peter, morning. How are you feeling?'

'I'm hugely looking forward to seeing you later.'

'Me, too. I'll be there,' I offered brightly, attempting to cover up the army of misgivings plaguing me. 'The nurse said you'd be under for about three hours and then two hours sleeping off the anaesthetic. I'll be at the clinic for one o'clock. See you later. I love you. The very best of luck.'

The phone went silent.

Had anxiety impelled him to make the call? Was he doubting the outcome? Needing reassurance, to hear my voice one more time? For the very last time?

I chided my negativity. This day would end well. Peter was going to rally, to survive.

I slipped out of bed and hurried to the beach. There was not a soul about, no boats crossing the horizon, no dogs barking. I might have been the last person living in this corner of the world. Even so, the beach was full of ghosts.

Peter's absence, Moulinet's erroneous assumptions and my worries about my husband's ordeal were crippling me. I waded into the water but felt too queasy, too physically afraid to swim, turned from the sea and, wet feet gathering sand like small bootees, climbed back to the safety of the villa where I brewed a pot of coffee and took a shower. I wished I smoked. I wished it wasn't too early to calm my nerves with a drink. Should I come clean with Moulinet, admit that Gissing had made contact with me? Confirm to him that Peter had played no part in any of it?

My plan was to leave the house well in advance of Peter's return to his ward, at about eleven. Even facing the worst Monday traffic on the outskirts of Marseille, I would be at his side when he regained consciousness.

Those few hours passed at a funereal pace. I could set my mind to nothing. I returned upstairs to the attic to shower and dress.

On my way down, I hesitated on the first-floor landing, the guests' level, at the far end of which, with views to the mountains, was Peter's office. It was rare that I entered his sacred foxhole. I pushed open the door and took a tentative step. The room smelt of cedarwood and sandalwood, the reassuring scents of Peter, his aftershave. It gave me a sense of him welcoming me in, bolstering my courage. There were two or three used coffee cups forgotten on the desktop. His computer was switched off. Pages of notes lay beside it, his Mont Blanc pen, a Christmas present from me, on top of them. His chest of drawers, a mahogany piece inherited from his parents, stood on the far side of the room. The key to the top drawer was in its hole. I turned it to the right and pulled the metal handle. The drawer slid open. I felt a stab of guilt. This was trespassing.

Many documents were neatly stacked in folders. And there, in the back left-hand corner, was the white envelope. As he had promised, the letter for me. I reached in and plucked it out. It wasn't heavy. Two, maximum three, foolscap pages? Written on its front, I read in my husband's fine, flowing hand: *For Grace. To be opened in the event of my death.* On the back was one word: *Confidential.*

I felt the blood pumping through my veins.

What message was so intimate that it could be revealed to me only after my husband's death? Surely I had a right to know its contents. And yet what an abuse of his trust to rip this – what was it, a confession? – open now. A confession, yes, surely. A disclosure of some nature, or why make such a mystery of it?

A revelation that could revise for ever the way I perceived my husband, erase my love for him, make me despise him? Was there any single act that could wipe out at a stroke the respect and deep attachment I felt for Peter?

I am not proud of that moment in my past.

Violence against another? An attempted murder?

George Andrew Gissing's face, twisted, riddled with failure and despair, stared up at me from the unopened envelope. 'Look at me. Who did this? Who wanted me dead and gone?'

No, no. I don't believe it. Not Peter.

I thrust the envelope back into exactly the same corner I had found it and pushed closed the drawer. My heart was pumping hard. I was not sure I could think straight but I knew it was not my business to open any of those documents, not without Peter's agreement, and he had spelt out his instructions clearly.

'In the event of my death'.

But Peter wasn't going to die, was he?

November 1990

The months after Connor's death – I hate the euphemism 'passing' – were some of the most challenging for me. I was in a play in the West End. A Coward revival. *Private Lives*. Wit and flamboyance night after night. Some evenings it was a tall order. I was returning to the theatre, the boards, after years of television and film work. Still living in Primrose Hill where so many ghosts resided along with me. Otherwise alone. No relationship, no big-love mate. My life was my work. I fed everything into it, wholeheartedly, meat into a mincer, repudiating the void within me.

Each night after the curtain had fallen, and I was in my dressing room cleaning off my stage make-up, I'd listened to the footsteps on the stone stairs of actors leaving the building, their calls of 'Goodnight', or 'Catch you in the pub' or 'Fancy a quick half, Jack, before you head home?'

I had said no to the other cast members so frequently they rarely bothered to invite or include me, these days. After Connor, I had set socializing aside, ironically when I needed the company most.

The backstage areas were usually resoundingly silent by the time I was heading off for home. The emptiness rattled and my footsteps echoed as I made my way to the exit, locking my dressing room, dropping off my key as I wished a good night to old bald-headed Fred, who had been manning his stage-door cubicle there for more than half a century and could, and would, given half the chance, recount stories of all the theatrical greats – Johnny G, Larry O, Ralphie and his motorbike – who had trodden these boards, passed this way before us.

Outside, in the bleak winter night, feebly brightened by the lights from Soho, a spattering of patient 'johnnies' hung about at the stage door, waiting for my autograph. 'Stage-door johnnies': I don't know where that expression was coined. After a while, you got to know the faces of some. They turned up wherever you were performing. You didn't remember their names but their sad, eager expressions, the cold red cheeks, noses running, greased hair, the worn-to-threadbare overcoats, hand-me-down cloth shoulder bags that carried the autograph books and the albums of photos now clutched to their breasts.

'Hello, Grace, you're out late. You're the last, then. Sir Donald stopped, gave me his autograph. Said tonight's performance went well, full house. Said you were still inside . . .'

Books, pencils, cheap Bic biros at the ready, proffered in my direction. The exhalation of their breath rose like smoke in the night air. Sometimes the hands trembled, from cold or illness or nerves. I always tried to take the time and trouble to sign each and every piece of paper or book, to answer their questions, hear the short tales of their journeys into town or where we had last met or whatever it was they stuttered to impart. To please the fans, give them their money's worth, as my musician dad, my much-missed late dad, used to say. 'They put you there, love.'

Even the lonely souls who rarely bought seats for the shows, I suspect because the ticket prices were astronomical and way outside their meagre pay packets, if they had jobs at all.

It was on one such night, November, with all the meretricious glitter of Christmas appearing in the shops and streets around Shaftesbury Avenue, the scent of roasting chestnuts drifting along the narrow lane, that a different voice from among the thin clamour caught my attention.

'Grace. When you're done, if you fancy a drink . . .'

That rich timbre, the lilt of the well-spoken voice was familiar to me. It set my blood racing. An upsurge of rather tangled emotions came flooding back and I wasn't convinced I wanted to revisit them.

I lifted my head from the faded pink page I was scribbling my name on, peered into the darkness to identify the speaker. There, a shadow from a streetlamp hiding the features of his face, three or four heads back, was a tall, elegant man dressed in an expensively cut navy suit. Hair flecked grey about the ears. He shifted a step and I saw him more clearly. Familiar eyes aged with a few, not unattractively placed, wrinkles. Mid-forties, at a guess. For a moment I was so flummoxed that I could not recall his name, though I knew it, knew him. Had known him intimately.

I dropped my attention to the disintegrating autograph book and continued signing the others, responding by rote to a remark here and there, scrawling felt tip onto the TV and film annuals, on the pages open to my photograph. I was buying time. When all were done, the few questions answered and the hunters drifted away, I stood with my head still crooked.

'You don't remember me,' he began. 'Well, it's been a very long time, Grace. How well you look. Forgive the intrusion.'

'Of course I do.' I was trembling. 'Remember you.' The

cold was eating into my marrow. My history was creeping up my spine. 'It's Peter.'

'Well done. I'm delighted.' His voice softened, washed with relief. 'Apologies if I've butted in. You certainly have a legion of fans. To be expected, of course.'

I lifted my eyes hardly daring to look, unwilling to expose the rawness of the diminished inner me. The man was more handsome than the boy had been, the vigorous stripling, who had fought for Paris, who had loved and protected me, and from whom I had fled without any forwarding contact and denied access to my company even once he had tracked me down. What was he doing here after all these years? All these years.

'You look like you could use a stiff drink.'

I nodded. It had been a tough year. A thought I didn't share. I eschewed proposals of the Ivy and the Groucho where there would be too many familiar faces, drinking late after shows, and we settled on the Rivoli Bar at the Ritz, within easy walking distance of Shaftesbury Avenue.

The unadulterated luxury enveloped me as soon as we sank into the leopard-print bucket chairs. Peter waved over a waiter and ordered champagne without waiting to hear what, if anything in particular, was my preference.

An image flew right at me. Paris, April 1968, a small café on the Left Bank. New to the city and I knew not a soul. 'What's your name?' He had been too impatient or preoccupied to wait to hear my response. In that, he did not seem to have changed.

I tuned in to the tinny sound, like dice rolling, of a shaker preparing cocktails at the bar behind me, the clink of cubes,

the sluice of ice being crushed, a hissing coffee machine –
who drinks coffee at this late hour? A table of Saudi
Arabians in white *thawbs* tucked into a corner – while Peter
and I familiarized ourselves silently with the shock of
being in each other's company after all this time, creatures
reacquainting themselves with the other's scent, reaching
back, picking through spoor from a bygone decade.

I had glimpsed his photograph from time to time,
grainy black-and-white images or distant portraits, in
newspapers, as he might well have spotted mine. Still, we
were twenty-two years further along the road of life and I
had no idea what he was doing here now, or why he had
come looking for me.

He had grown so tailored. Always neat, spruce, yes, I
recalled that, but now expensively so, bespoke surely,
nails professionally manicured. Hair chic but not trendily
styled. Everything in its place. Reassuring in appearance.
Handsome, very, in a clean-cut fashion. Even the ears
that I had once found so attractive, had nibbled.

What had become of that hot young revolutionary?
Peter had learned that revolution is most effectively handled from within the system, he told me later. He was a
highly esteemed human-rights lawyer whose office was in
Brussels, and he was engaged almost full-time by the EU
and the European Court of Human Rights. He was sought
after. And he was at my side.

Had he come in search of me or had he been strolling
along Shaftesbury Avenue after a restaurant dinner with
friends, clients, spotted my name on the illuminated bill-
board outside the Apollo and thought, for old times' sake,
why not pop backstage and say hello?

How often during the ensuing years had he thought of me, if at all, remembered our summer, blissful and ultimately tormented? Those letters – did I still have them stored somewhere? – in which he had poured out his heart to me, baring his soul, recounting the sorrow and anguish my deception had caused him?

He wrote fine letters, sentiments well expressed, I remembered that.

I smiled silently.

He had claimed eternal love for me but what had that meant back then at twenty? We had been callow fledglings. Emotionally charged but our energies, mine anyway, undirected.

I, in my coltish credulousness, had held fast to the dream that the long-gone Pierre had been The One. How foolishly I had wept over his mysterious disappearance for too many wasted years. If he had lived, he would doubtless have proved to be a misjudgement. The lifestyle of a dope dealer would have palled very quickly.

Ribald laughter from the table of Saudis drew me back to the here and now. I glanced in Peter's direction. He was watching me. A soft, appraising look, his handsome head tilted to one side.

I felt my defences lock down. The past was not to be reinhabited. Certainly not mine. I would make this sweet and short.

The Ruinart arrived.

Illuminated by the light of a single candle, it glowed the colour of liquefied wheat. Two flutes, delicately iced, were placed on the round polished mahogany table that marked the scant distance between us. Peter's legs were crossed.

One hand, his right, lay across his thigh. The other was loosely poised across the arm of his chair. The immaculately presented waiter, with slick black hair, removed the bottle's cork. It slid from its glass throat with barely a sough. Glasses semi-filled, he back-stepped discreetly out of our space. Peter lifted the first flute and passed it to me. Then, taking up his own, he raised it towards me, and smiled. 'Our very first aperitif together was champagne. Spring in Paris. Cheers.'

'So it was.' I smiled at the memory. '*Santé*. It was also the very first glass of champagne I had ever drunk.' I lifted my flute to meet his and the crystal rang one against the other.

We sipped the fine wine.

'This is quite a surprise, Peter.'

'Yes, it's been a very long time.'

'Any particular reason why tonight?'

'Several, actually, but let's do justice to the Ruinart and we can get there all in good time. Unless you have to be somewhere?'

I shook my head and the small hard stone within me, the nugget of loneliness, lodged itself tighter in the sphincter of my gut. I sensed him observing, studying me.

Peter's presence evoked swimming in calm waters, the saline scent off the warm sea, the sun burning my back in a pleasurable abandoned way, until I forced myself to push away where these snippets of reminiscence would take me, to the memory of a drowned man. If there had been no Pierre, would Peter and I have maintained our friendship? Might we have formed a more permanent liaison? Absurd questions after twenty-two years.

He must have sensed me starting to slip away, to sink to a place beyond the present. 'Grace . . .'

'How are your parents?' I butted in. A trite question. I hadn't thought of them in donkey's years and, in truth, I didn't care. 'And Agnes? The wonderful vibrant Agnes. How I adored her. Is she well, still painting?'

'Parents both gone, alas. Father died of a heart attack almost ten years ago and Mother drank herself to an early grave all the while socializing with her AA pals. Agnes is splendid and gloriously successful. I still visit her regularly. The girls adore her – well, they would, wouldn't they? Who can fail to? – and she them.'

'Girls?'

'My daughters.'

I hoped he could not see the surprise settle like winter within me. What had I expected? That he wouldn't have married, built a happy life without me? I had wished that for him. 'Congratulations.' I bent to my glass and took a long sip. 'How many?'

'Twins. We got it behind us all in one shot.'

I nodded.

'Beautiful girls. You'd fall hook, line and sinker for them, Grace. Everyone does.'

His pride shone like a beacon, sparking violet eyes.

'And you . . . live . . . in London, or Paris?'

'London. A couple of times a month, I commute to Brussels and I'm frequently in Strasbourg. It's a peripatetic existence, which suits me rather well at present. For many years, a decade or more, we've been resident in the UK. About the time my father died. Angela hated Paris. She wanted the girls to have an English education, my mother was alone, so we found ourselves a house and . . .' he paused, and let out a sigh '. . . set down roots here.'

'I know how you cared for your life in Paris.' I pictured him back on the barricades, sweating, arms raised, fired by vision and the determination for a more ethical future. He seemed – what? – sober now by comparison. Restrained, subdued? But, then, we were no longer teenagers, youngsters with our lives ahead of us and none of the car crashes behind us.

'And you?'

'What?'

'Children?'

I shook my head, recalling the women's hospital, the wretched winter of '68. My pal Connor. The loss of Connor, our shorthand with one another. Loneliness, grief swirled within me. 'I chose not to. I've devoted myself to my career,' I said softly, hoping to keep the desolation, which was a surprise to me, a new note, out of my voice.

'And what a career,' he replied. 'I've followed your successes, watched you on television. You're very good. Born to it, Grace.'

I laughed. 'Moulded myself.'

It was all there was. Affairs, a relationship or two, of course, one that had staggered on for three or four years, off and on. It was work, though, that had seen me through, sustained me. Since that summer of '68, and Pierre, my career had been my lifeline. But it would be ludicrous to claim still to be in love with a man who had been dead for more than twenty years. A golden if tarnished figure, resting at the bottom of the sea. My love for him had long since evaporated. Blurred to extinction, that imprudent infatuation. I'd come to my senses, realized it would never have worked between us – with hindsight, that much had been clear. Still, Pierre had lit a flame within me that had never been outshone.

Or might that be a half-arsed excuse for my hopeless failure at building a life with anyone else? The fact was, in all probability, I was too single-minded, too ambitious for relationships. Better off alone.

'And your wife?' I asked, out of politeness and to deflect my dreary late-night maudlin ruminations. I should finish my drink and hail a taxi. It was pleasant, though, to be in the company of a warm soul, to encounter Peter again. A young man who had been so overwhelmingly good to me.

'Angela? What about her?'

'Does she work? Have a career?'

Peter shook his head. Suddenly he was the one who seemed spent by life. 'We're separated, have been for a little over a year now, though the writing had been on the wall for some time. No, she never worked. I suppose she might consider it, once the divorce has been finalized, although she does have the girls living with her' – he let out another sigh, a note of regret: mourning the loss of his permanent place alongside his beautiful children? – 'and the pair of them are fairly full on. Bounding with energy and drive. You never married. Never gave it a shot?'

I shook my head and realized the first pulsations of a headache were settling in. I preferred not to go to wherever this conversation might be leading.

I should be on my way, get some sleep. I had an early-morning recording to get to. A dubbing for a foreign film that I wished already I had not accepted. Too late now but tiredness would damage my voice, cause it to crack and croak. Not an acceptable image, and the dubbing company in question gave me some of its best opportunities. In any case, this polite exchange was a little straining for a loner such as I had become. Foolish to romanticize the past.

'Are you staying here? No, of course not. Peter, forgive me, I doubt I'll be able to help you polish off this magnificent champagne. Twenty years ago, I'd have guzzled the lot, but not tonight. I have a reasonably early start tomorrow and I'm out of the habit of late nights.'

'No, it was thoughtless of me. You've just finished work. I should have taken you to supper.' He placed his glass on the table and made as if to get up.

'No, please, there's time to finish our glasses at least.'

'Can I give you a lift or do you have a car in town?'

'I come in by Tube or sometimes take a taxi. I rarely drive to the theatre. Rush hour, parking . . .'

'Still in Primrose Hill?'

I frowned, puzzled. 'Yes, how clever of you.'

'I read it somewhere, a newspaper cutting or an interview with you. Let me give you a lift. Finish your glass, and whenever you're ready I'll drive you. You look worn out. My fault for imposing myself.'

'No, please.'

Such a waltz of manners.

Outside my maisonette, set one street back from Regent's Park, we sat a moment in the leathery warmth of the Mercedes with the engine humming, the heater on. A streetlamp illuminated our faces.

'Thank you,' I said.

'It was good to see you.'

'Yes, you too.' And, surprisingly, I meant it. I put my hand up for the door as Peter leaned over to open it for me. Even replaying this moment today, I cannot recall which of us reached for the other. It was simultaneous and completely unexpected. He drew back, switched off the engine and returned his face to mine. Kissing in scarves and overcoats, a handbrake between us, never easy but we were not daunted. I had no idea I had longed for this. Or, yes, in the abstract. Sex, a lover. Passion.

'Will you invite me in?' he whispered in my ear, gently brushing his cheek against mine.

And I did.

The front door's inner lock remained unturned, barely closed, shut carelessly with the heel of my stiletto. Our clothes were abandoned everywhere, on the stairs, the dining-room floor, shoes kicked off at the bedroom door. Such a rush of longing, of desire. Pressed tight against one another, leaning on the wall, a springboard to the bed. He, disrobed from the waist upwards, I almost from the waist down. Tearing at the last of our outdoor garments. Until we landed on my counterpane. The sex was rushed, furious and greedy. A thought flashed through me that it was me who had been so starved. In fact, it was both of us. Each of us devouring the other. We were strangers and yet there was a palimpsest of familiarity, a movement here or there that recalled a grungy floor in Paris, a summer bedroom in the Midi in glaring sunlight.

We lay in one another's arms, breathing hard, hearts pounding. As though we had been running, fleeing memories, fleeing. I felt the trickle of his juice on my upper thigh. I opened my eyes and stared upwards into the darkness, asking myself what had come to pass. From where this passion had arisen.

'You cannot know how often I've thought of this,' he whispered, into the ball of my shoulder.

I felt my body go tense. He sensed it too and laid the palm of his hand across the flat of my exposed stomach. His fingers stroking me angled themselves towards my pubic hair. 'Don't,' he said softly.

'Don't what?'

'Push me away. Don't run from me again.'

I was afraid of this, of intimacy, of bold confessions. I had walled myself in with supreme efficiency, hidden behind many roles both on and off screen. Peter had known a girl, a foolish girl called Grace, with wide-open eyes and an undamaged heart. She, who had been bursting with dreams and optimism. But she had long since faded away, taken her exit bow; she had vanished and could never be resurrected. This was foolhardy. A mistake. I could only reassure myself with excuses there in the dead of night. Weakness, sexual hunger, my grieving for Connor had broken my reserve, resolve, washed away at me, allowing me to become vulnerable again.

'Listen,' I began, my voice cracking after a show and being up too late and . . . 'I have an early start ahead of me.'

'You said. We should get some sleep.'

'No, no, you should go, Peter. Better you go. I'm not in the habit of sleeping alongside anyone. I won't get any rest. I need to . . .'

His hand was over my mouth. 'Spare room?'

Slowly I swivelled my head to face him, to search out his violet-blue eyes in the midnight gloom. The heating, a radiator, began to click, to flame up. I could see so little but I knew that he was smiling. 'This is . . . well, out of the blue and I'm not . . .'

'Don't send me home, Grace.' His hand slid to my buttock and he dragged me, inched me gently towards him, the few remaining millimetres that had separated us were being filled in . . . by me, as my body squeezed up against his, his limp cock hardening again, swelling to life, and his hand pressed into the small of my back.

'Do you know that I love you still, always have?'

'Peter!'

'Sssh, stop. Don't move. Stay like this for a few more moments and then I'll let you go. I'll sleep on the couch or in the spare room, if there is one. Or, if you cruelly insist, I'll leave, reluctantly. But stay like this in my arms, so close to me for these moments. Please don't resist or reject me.'

I was pinned to him. My instinct was to break the moment, to let fly an arm, escape, but I remained static. I tamped the resistance down, breathed his tempo and allowed myself, my opposition, to melt. I lifted a leg to wrap around his thigh and within seconds he was entering me again. This time at a leisurely pace. Moving slowly in rhythm with him, I felt my head swim and my body turn to liquid. He rolled me onto my back and rose up above me. A tear ran down my cheek. I buried my face in my arm. Jesus, I was crying.

Why? For my departed father, whom I felt such judgement towards, whom I had fought with myself to forgive, to understand, and whom I still missed every day, for Connor, who still walked beside me every inch of the way but not quite close enough for me to feel the caress of his hand, and for my own bunched-up inadequacies. It was cold, but I was smiling, crying and smiling – it felt good to let the demons free – and for the first time in as long as I could remember, I surrendered. I gave myself up to another. It was fitting that it should be Peter.

When I opened my eyes, I smelt the brewing coffee. The clock read 8:30 a.m. It took a moment before I realized that, yes, I was in my own bed, this was my familiar chamber, and I was running a little late. I was alone and I was wet. Damp, sticky. Crumpled pillows next to mine. A radio was playing in the kitchen downstairs. BBC voices in debate. Peter was in a towel, making toast. The table had been laid with yoghurts and a few bits of fruit from the fridge. I entered my own well-protected space gingerly.

'You said you had an early start so I thought I'd organize breakfast. You still begin the day with coffee?'

Peter had set up his domicile in a twenty-square-metre, professionally furnished studio-flat a few streets back from Victoria station. A short let contracted out by the month, renewable from week to week. After he and Angela had split up, the girls and their mother had remained in the family home and he had moved out, taking with him only the minimum. The Brussels legal firm, Human Rights Lawyers for Europe, provided him with a base in the European capital, a rather elegant one-bed, he described it, which met his requirements. Until the house was sold, he was managing and had no reason for complaint. He expressed no bitterness or regret and said he was not intending to fight over assets or possessions.

By the weekend of the following week, ten days after his appearance at the stage door, he had moved in with me. I warned myself repeatedly that I was treading an unwise and potentially precarious path. It was me who offered. He accepted and we kept smiling. He arrived with almost nothing so I was little inconvenienced. There was no need for me to move over, to shift the space on the shelves, divvy up corners of the wardrobe. I allocated a drawer for his socks and underwear, shirts were hung on hangers and he worked on his laptop at the big square kitchen table. He rose before six most mornings while I slept on. When I returned of an evening from the theatre, a light meal was waiting, a bottle of wine breathing. I felt as though I was on holiday from my own life, but that this would pass because it was too good to be true.

Our free days we spent walking together, frequently hand in hand, on Primrose Hill, contemplating the beauty of the city that unfolded before us, the rustling of leaves, a shaft of light, smiling faces, or roaming across Hampstead Heath, then home to read books, scripts, legal documents by the fire. We dined once or twice at Lemonia, and I poured out my sorrow at the loss of Connor.

Sharing. I was sharing. I had lost the knack of it, I'd thought.

I was in love. I had fallen in love with the same man, the juvenile beau who had taken my virginity more than two decades earlier, and I was having a job coming to grips with that reality. It was all so sudden and improbable that I mistrusted such a turn of Fate. Even so, the happiness flowed out of me, like a beneficent fountain. When I was alone, I had to stop myself calling out his name to the four walls that surrounded me. My fellow actors commented on the lightness of my being, the gaiety of my demeanour, the agility of my step. Even the audience must have picked up on my state of mind, of heart, because the laughs were louder, the responses more positive, the applause more resounding and the show was two minutes shorter. My energy was driven by a turbo-jet, and it was called Love.

Every now and again, I stopped short and silently warned myself that this could not last.

'We could have done this twenty years ago,' he remarked, one Sunday morning over oven-warmed croissants and the *Observer*.

'You wouldn't have had the girls,' I replied instantly. The girls I was yet to meet. We had talked about it but I had taken fright at the prospect of a pair of adolescents, twins, who doted on their father, being confronted by an almost forty-year-old actress who knew zilch about parenting and had until this point been pretty poor at relationships altogether. 'Let's give it time, see how it goes,' I'd vacillated.

Peter accepted my shilly-shallying until the approach of Christmas, when he put his foot down. 'Family time,' he insisted. 'And Angela and I are not intending to play charades or masquerade as a happy twosome or reunite for the holidays for the sake of our daughters. We did it last year as it was only weeks after our separation and it was a disaster.

Besides, I want you to meet them. I want them to love you and to know that you are now the woman in my life.'

I listened without argument.

'You always were, Grace.'

I couldn't decide whether this was going too fast for me or I wanted to charge in, like a starved insane brute.

'The spare room,' he said adamantly. 'They won't mind sharing a bed for a few nights. They might pretend to be grown-ups in front of their school pals but they're still kids at heart and sharing a bed is fun. They can discuss you with their heads under the blankets. Share their thoughts and opinions. Twins complicit. They'll love it. I'll organize a Christmas tree and you can get their room ready.'

'What about Angela? Won't she want her daughters with her during this season?'

'She'll thrill at the possibility of time out. Skiing with her pals.'

'At Christmas? Don't they have families of their own?'

'Well, her . . .'

'Lover?'

Peter had not touched upon what had caused the dissolution of his marriage and I had not asked him. I had no desire to delve and pry. Naively, I had just taken it for granted that they had drifted apart. The presence of another, a lover, had not crossed my mind. So Peter would still be there, in his perfectly well-set-up married life, if Angela had not asked him to go, I was now learning. Where did that leave me, us? Might I be the fill-in, the understudy, while Angela had her fling, saw it through to its conclusion, then turned back, remorseful, to her long-standing, patient husband who adored his daughters and had been comfy in the family home? I kept this to myself, warned myself to rein in my foolishly overflowing insecurities, and drove to John Lewis to buy new bedding. And presents. Gifts for thirteen-year-olds. Thirteen-year-olds I had never met. I didn't have a clue. I spent far too much in a bid to be liked, willing their words to be kind during those hours when they put their heads together, complicit, breathing in the fresh scent of new pillowcases. I chose neat leather shoulder bags, same style, different colours: yellow and pale pink. Heart-shaped silver lockets. Were they twin twins, identical in dress codes as well as features? I was trying to recall the photos Peter had shown me. Peter was in Brussels. I needed to do this alone. He was intending to collect them on his way back from the ferry.

I was still in the play, Noël Coward until January, and there was talk of an extension of the run. My agent had called me. 'If they want three more months, Grace, what are your thoughts?'

I had been looking forward to time out, possibly to spending a few indolent days with Peter in Brussels, a few short city trips with him, long weekends in Europe, a rare interlude from my full-on working life. Now I was hesitating. When all else failed, when life had caved in, it had always, always been my work that had seen me through. It had been my rudder in choppy waters, guiding me in the best direction. I should accept the extension, lock myself into the show, and secure another offer for afterwards in the spring. Book myself up, cement myself in. Secure my safety belt because, sooner or later, this affair would be over, and I would be alone, back to my secure solitary existence.

The Present

Eventually, a little after ten thirty, unable to stay put in the empty house for any longer, I reversed out the car and turned up onto the high road. My heart was thudding. I began to count the fallen pine branches along the verge from the recent storm. Anything to keep my mind occupied, to keep at bay the invasion of negative thoughts. The bell of the phone on the seat at my side caused me to jump. I almost skidded off the cliff. I pulled over into one of the many parking bays offered for contemplation and picture-snapping of the numerous beauty spots along this stretch of the coast. The sea was glinting aquamarine way beneath me.

It was a local number, commencing with 04. A Provençal landline. Please, God, don't let it be the clinic. Don't let there be a hitch, an unforeseen problem.

'Hello?'

I had one hand clutching the steering wheel while the other held the phone with such force I might have squeezed it out of shape.

'Madame Soames?'

A man's voice. French. A nurse? The consultant? Please not.

'Yes?' I was barely able to form the one-syllable word.

'It's Capitaine Moulinet.'

A sigh of relief followed instantly by a jab of concern. '*Bonjour,* Capitaine.'

'Is this a good moment?'

'No, not really, I'm driving. I mean, I've pulled over. No, I'm on my way to Marseille to . . .'

'Excellent, I am in Marseille. I wonder if you would spare me half an hour of your time?'

'Today?'

'As soon as is convenient, if that's fine with you.'

'My husband is . . .' I glanced at my watch. I didn't want to be late. I was keen to be at Peter's side when he opened his eyes.

'Your husband is in the operating theatre. Yes, I know.'

'I'll call you later.'

'By all means. A short interview this afternoon. I would be most grateful.'

'Is it . . . urgent?'

'A couple of points to clear up.'

'I'll contact you later.'

'Much obliged.'

Had Gissing kept hold of my two notes suggesting meetings with him? Both signed 'Grace'. Thoughtless of me. Had the police discovered them? If they had, I was implicated. I had lied. Would I be forced to disclose the whole story?

I didn't know the whole story.

Traffic down at the port delayed my arrival. The usual city parking nightmares. I locked the car, ran to the clinic and took the lift to the second floor, hurrying breathlessly along the corridor to the rest-and-recovery area. Another woman was there, seated patiently. I had spotted her the morning before. She was in the waiting room, going through the same ordeal perhaps. Her head was bowed. She looked puffy-eyed as though she lacked sleep or had been crying. I muttered, *'Bonjour,'* but she did not register my presence.

I sat on the opposite side of the room for a few minutes. This corner of the clinic was empty, lacking activity. Silent, eerily still, save for a distant hum of machinery. No nurse passed by. I glanced at my watch. Ten past one. I stood up, paced to the window, returned to my chair and then, without taking my seat again, exited the *salle*.

A staff member wheeling a trolley was ambling in my direction.

'Excuse me.'

'Yes?'

'My husband should be up from the operating theatre by now. I was in the –'

'You need to press that buzzer and give your name.'

I did as instructed.

'Yes?'

'Peter Soames,' I announced, into the speaker alongside the bell. 'I'm his wife.'

'Just a minute, please.'

I heard a click. I waited. Nothing. No one.

I pressed the buzzer again.

The same woman. 'Please be patient. I am trying to find out what has happened.'

'Is he there?'

'Apologies, but he has not been brought up for recuperation.'

My knees went weak. I almost collapsed against the wall. 'Do you know why?' I pleaded.

'I was trying to find out. Hold on, please. Just wait. Don't buzz again, please.'

I remained half leaning against the green-painted wall.

'Madame Soames?'

'Yes?'

'Your husband is still in the operating theatre.'

'Why?'

There might have been a delay at the start of the operation. I was trying to calm myself. A million details, preparations, anything might have held them up. Consultant couldn't park. Overslept. I didn't believe any of these excuses.

'I am not at liberty to give out the information. Apologies. I suggest you make your way to his room and try to find his nurse or a member of staff on ward duty. They should be able to help you.'

I tore along the corridor. My mouth was parched as sandpaper. I peered through the glass cut into the door of Peter's room. Empty. No nurse. Only his bed, made ready for his return, banks of machines. It was a private occupancy.

I heard laughter from the far end of the corridor. Peals of laughter, like small silvery bells chiming. A nurse exited from where the sounds had arisen. I bolted towards her.

'Mr Soames,' I was calling. 'My husband.'

She shook her head.

'Someone must know what's happened to him,' I had to force myself not to yell, all too aware of others sleeping, convalescing, dying perhaps. Not Peter, please, not Peter.

'My husband has not been returned to the recovery suite. Has something gone wrong?'

She looked at me and must have registered the terror in my expression. Gently she took my arm and led me back to the nurses' den. 'Does anyone know what's happened to Monsieur Soames?' she asked. They all looked so young, so unencumbered. Life and death were not intruding upon their afternoon. One young blonde was sitting on a desk, her feet perched on the seat of a chair, scrawling on the screen of her mobile.

Another picked up a telephone receiver – an internal phone, I assumed. 'Just a minute,' she said. A short dialogue was exchanged and she replaced the phone.

'The operation is taking longer than expected. He is still in the theatre.'

'Why?' I cried. 'Did he go down late?'

'Sometimes it works out that way. Would you like a glass of water?'

I shook my head, fighting back tears.

'Why don't you sit in his room? One of us will come and get you when he's up from theatre.'

I nodded and retreated.

In Peter's room, on a chair at the foot of the bed, I was silently praying. Desperate measures. It was now almost two o'clock. If his operation had begun at eight, as had been programmed, it meant he had been under anaesthesia for six hours. The worst of everything was flashing through my mind. Escalating hysteria was interrupted by the ringing of my phone.

'Hello?'

'Madame Soames?'

'Yes?'

'I am waiting for your call.'

'Capitaine, unless this is extremely urgent, I'm very sorry, but I – I can't talk now, apologies.' I closed the phone.

Moments later the door opened and a young nurse popped her head in. 'Madame Soames?'

'Yes?'

'Your husband is being brought up to the recovery room now.'

'Thank God.' I leaped to my feet. 'Is everything all right? May I see him, please?'

'Everything's fine, but he will be under intensive surveillance for the next two hours and then, when all is well, he'll be brought back here. You must wait. Why not pop down to the cafeteria and grab a coffee or a sandwich? There's nothing you can do for the next couple of hours.'

I needed air.

Christmas 1990

Peter was delayed by inclement weather in Belgium, which also caused snow in Kent. It meant he was late collecting the girls from Angela and I couldn't wait in. I had to get to the theatre. A rigorous ruling of my own: I was always in my dressing room a minimum of an hour and a half before curtain-up. It gave me time to collect my thoughts, settle my mind to the world of my character, shed my own habits, concerns, and prepare myself for immersion in another universe. This discipline had been informed by my training and I had adhered to it since the beginning. Even the prospect of holding Peter in my arms again did not dent my routine.

I scribbled a note and left it on the dining-room table. *Welcome back. Feed everyone. Fridge groaning. Home directly after show xx*

The girls were in bed when I returned after eleven.

'Shall I call them down?'

'Let them sleep.' I yawned, stretched my legs, pulling off my overcoat and slinging it over a chair, tired.

'Hungry?'

I shook my head. Peter poured me a glass of red wine. We sat holding hands across the table, not having seen one another for more than a week.

Behind me, the door creaked as it opened slowly and I heard bare feet squeaking across the wooden floor.

'I couldn't wait till tomorrow,' the girly voice said. 'May I come in, Daddy, please?'

Peter rose. Protective in his manner, eyes beaming with love. 'Come and meet Grace. Grace, this is Samantha, though she prefers to be known as Sam.'

I swivelled on my chair and the loveliest of girls, a teenager with a head of lustrous dark-brown hair, stepped towards me and bent low. She wrapped her arms about me in an unheralded bear-hug. 'Fab Christmas tree, Grace. Thanks for inviting us.' Muffled words in my ear.

I smiled. She smelt of Chanel Number 5, my perfume. She must have been in my bathroom. They had their own alongside the spare room but evidently mine was more inviting. 'It's a pleasure. I've been looking forward to . . .'

Samantha, or Sam, pulled herself back from me and stood gazing into my face, appraising me. Her almond eyes – must have been inherited from Angela's side – and confident expression quite startled me. She seemed older, far more self-assured, than her thirteen years.

'Come and sit down, sweetheart, and let Grace relax and enjoy her wine.'

Sam swung herself into the chair between her father and me. I was looking for the resemblance.

'Are we coming to see the play?' she asked. 'I told Dad it's what I want for Christmas.' She smiled the smile of a beauty, wide and trusting. A future heart-breaker.

'No need to waste an opportunity for presents on tickets to the show. I'm sure I can organize them without any difficulties. Middle of next week suit you both?'

'I think it's amazing you're an actress. I've seen you on TV. Mum doesn't work and I think it's partly what makes her so bad-tempered.'

'Sam, hush now.'

Fortunately, at that moment, Twin Two crept through the door. She appeared to be a shyer child, more hesitant. Her hair was lighter, less dramatic in colour. She was slighter of build and moved directly to Peter, wrapping herself about his shoulders from behind. From there she looked across at me and then to her sister.

'I'm Jennifer,' she announced hesitantly.

'Hello, Jennifer, or do you prefer Jen or Jenny?'

And with that, she began to cry, head nuzzled in the nape of her father's neck, her body heaving. 'I want to go home,' she sobbed.

'Now, now, that's not very kind to Grace, is it?' Peter drew his weeping daughter to him and coaxed her onto his lap. Her face buried in his chest, her body settled itself between his strong arms. A small person secure in the fork of two branches of a solid, much idolized tree.

'Stop it,' ordered her sister. 'Stop whinging, Jen.' The force of Sam's command rather took me aback. It was hard to believe they were twins. Sam behaved with a bossier, more self-possessed maturity. This, I was to learn, was an erroneous observation on my part. They switched emotions constantly, one opening up as the other closed down, both expressing warmth towards me for one instant and then, within the blink of an eye, anger or, on one or two occasions, hostility. Never were their emotions in synch. When one rejected me, the other embraced me with open arms, and for a while during that rather fraught festive season, I began to suspect that their shifts were a game, a ploy they had cooked up to unnerve me, a scam to tease or rattle me. A punishment for stealing their precious father.

Nothing could have been further from the truth.

They were adolescents, adoring daughters coming to terms with the break-up of their parents' marriage, with the fragility of all they had held precious and indestructible. I had to learn to let their mood fluctuations bounce off me. Their overt criticisms and occasional judgements were because they perceived me as the agent of change within their young lives.

It was not an easy holiday period. I felt tense much of the time, yet there were moments when it was utterly joyous. Children, youngsters, in my life for the first time. It was a new world. They crept into our room, perched on the two sides of the bed, peeped through the crack in the door and ran off giggling. They quizzed me with impossible questions, personal details, delved into my wardrobe, strutted about in my high heels, offered to make us tea in bed, and delivered bundles of gifts to us on Christmas morning – beautifully wrapped, in Jenny's case, or thrown untidily together in Sam's. Jenny was the more artistic of the pair, Sam curious, questioning, penetrating in every detail. Both were volatile.

I soon learned that it was vital to treat them individually and not as a pair. They were not joined at the hip, were not identical and had very different interests and characters.

They stayed with me – us, I should say, I was still getting used to the notion of 'us, the couple' – until the new year when Angela returned from her trip to Switzerland. In any case, it was soon time for school, time for Peter to return to Brussels. Peter saved me the business of meeting up with his wife then by driving the girls to the family home in Paddock Wood, near Tunbridge Wells in Kent, before continuing to the Channel ferry.

'It's probably for the best that I'm away for a few weeks.' He smiled shyly. 'Give you a chance to catch your breath.' He was looking dishevelled, which was unlike him. Hair tousled, one collar point of his blue denim shirt tucked inside his V-neck cashmere sweater, the other out. All our lives had been turned upside down, and we were, all four of us, attempting to get used to it.

'I'll call you when I reach Brussels before I fly to Poland.' He had an interview scheduled with Lech Wałęsa, the newly appointed president. Peter had been working on a case that involved the violation of a Polish prisoner's rights after an arrest in Belgium, ill-treatment while held in custody. The man, an illegal immigrant, was claiming physical abuse. One of the obstacles was that his own past record was a little on the shady side. Still, Peter was confident that he could achieve results. He specialized in assisting those with troubled histories.

'Good luck.'

'See you soon.' His lips brushed lightly against mine. A squeeze of the arm – *je t'aime* – and he hurried down the front steps, disappearing into the car.

The curtain had risen on 1991. I had played a central, if sometimes awkward, role within a ready-made family. Now, my single-inhabitant maisonette was returning to its emptiness, its lack of chaos, its silences and polished creaking floorboards, videos and CDs neatly in their jackets, soap and loo rolls not on the floor but where they were intended to live, a fridge containing only the basic necessities, empty Nutella jars ready for the bottle bank. Besides preparing for the evening's show, I was at a loose end, not knowing what to do with myself.

When my agent telephoned me early in the new year to know whether I was going to accept the prolongation of my contract, I told him no. I needed a bit of time out.

He was momentarily silenced, surprised, never having known me turn down good work for no alternative.

'Is there something you want to whisper in my ear before I read it in the press?' I heard the smile in his voice. 'Don't shock me,' Ken joked. 'I'm too old, Grace. I only want to hear good news. The happy stuff. And if it's delightfully effervescent, let's do it over a new-year lunch and a bottle of something refreshing and expensive.'

He'd caught me off-guard for a moment. The new-year lunch. Connor. So occupied had I been with the Armstrong-Soames trio, I had mentally missed the first New Year's Day without my 'big love'.

'No, there's nothing juicy to share, Ken. When there is, if there is, you'll be the first to know it, I promise.'

The Present

Two hours. I had two hours to kill.

I could make a rendezvous with Moulinet, get this blasted situation behind me, but I hadn't the stamina, the guts for his third degree now. It was preposterous of Moulinet to insinuate that Peter might have pushed Gissing over the edge, as I well knew. If anyone had had a hand in the man's death, it was me.

It was as preposterous as Gissing's accusation that Peter had tried to murder him all those years ago.

In my mind's eye, I lifted out the white *Confidential* envelope from Peter's drawer.

I am not proud of that moment, Grace.

Oh, Peter, my darling, we all have moments we aren't proud of.

By keeping silent about my encounters with Gissing, I was shining a false shadow of suspicion over my own husband. Why not admit the truth and put an end to the nightmare? What was it that I so feared?

Outside on the clinic's forecourt, the sun was shining. I inhaled the day, the waves of heat. I might as well make the most of it. I decided to stroll to the port, perch by the boats, watch the remainder of the night's catch being unloaded.

Within fifteen minutes I was at the old harbour.

I found a bar and settled at a table half in, half out of

the shade. I ordered, quite out of character, a beer. My throat was dry, scratchy. My thirst was demanding. I changed the order to a bottle of San Pellegrino and a small beer. Clusters of fishermen were at the quay's edge repairing their rafts of nylon nets. Pleasingly, even in this day and age, the old method continues. I sipped my drink and allowed the sun's heat to calm me. The operation was over. Peter was in recuperation. The worst was behind us. Wasn't it? We had a good life ahead to look forward to. As I sat, idling, watching the comings and goings of the harbour life, the many tourists, the screeching passage of traffic, I realized that I had chosen a seat directly across the water from the bar where I had first met Pierre. I wasn't precisely sure which one it would have been – today it was either a pizzeria, a cocktail bar or a Mediterranean bistro.

I picked up my phone from the table and re-dialled Moulinet's number. It was a switchboard not a direct line. The receptionist put me through to him.

'Sorry to have been abrupt. My husband is in a clinic –'

'Yes, I know, and you are in Marseille.'

Was Moulinet craftily monitoring Peter's recovery process? Was he waiting to pounce? On an innocent man?

'What can I help you with, Inspector?'

'There are a couple of matters I wanted to run by you.'

I closed my eyes, and gave Moulinet the name of the bar.

Within twelve minutes he was settled across the table from me. From a file tucked under his arm, he pulled out the damaged wedding photos.

'I wanted you to see these because, well, there is a violence about them that begs an explanation.'

I glanced at the disfigured cuttings. I could offer no explanation for the black crosses.

'Gissing: a man who was jealous of your private life?'

I shook my head, an expression of bewilderment rather than a repudiation of his hypothesis. I had no handle on truths any more.

'A fan, perhaps?' Moulinet proposed.

Photocopies of Gissing's birth certificate and passport accompanied them.

The date registered on Gissing's birth certificate was 10 April 1958.

My jaw dropped. This man, George Andrew Gissing, born in Bradford, would have been ten years old in 1968, according to the passport details given by Moulinet.

Eyes: hazel.

George's eye colouring had been perturbing me for days. Not immediately noticed due to his sunglasses and damaged features, which drew one's attention instantly. Alone in Thierry's bar, when I had failed to keep my rendezvous with George, I had struggled to recall.

Pierre, when I'd loved him, that summer of '68, was in his early to mid-twenties. Denim-blue eyes.

Gissing was not Pierre. Gissing was a stranger who had posed as Pierre. He was not my ex-lover at all. Yet . . . he seemed intimate with so many details.

You're surely not talking about the Gissing fellow?

There had to be a connection.

'Any thoughts, Madame Soames? Does his identity ring any bells?'

I shook my head. 'I'm as confused as you, Inspector.'

'A rather misguided admirer. A menacing stalker?'

'That must be the explanation,' I concluded, without certainty.

I left coins on the table alongside my unfinished drinks and began my re-ascent from the water. I was eager to be in Peter's room when he was wheeled in.

When I arrived back on the ward, there was no update on his condition. I made myself comfortable at his empty bedside and pulled out my Kindle, which I did not open. I stared out of the window. Eventually Peter was delivered on a gurney by two orderlies. He was still unconscious. I had expected him to be awake.

'Any idea how much longer?' I asked.

It was now nudging four in the afternoon.

They shrugged. They had no idea. Gently, they lifted the rather alarmingly flaccid body – one had his shoulders, the other his ankles – onto the bed and folded the light cover over him. A nurse arrived and he was clipped up and connected to a number of machines, all of which began bleeping or flashing. The hardware was formidable. There were two drips delivering liquids into his arm.

I was shocked by Peter's appearance. His head flopped to one side as though he had lost muscle control – had he suffered a massive stroke? – and his throat was horribly swollen. He reminded me of one of those frill-necked lizards you find in the southern hemisphere.

When he regained consciousness would he still have full control of his faculties? Had he suffered a seizure? Might there be brain damage?

A second nurse appeared, carrying a clipboard, which,

after nodding to me, she hung from the metal bar at the foot of his bed. 'Feeling calmer now, Madame?'

'Is everything, you know, as you would expect?'

She frowned.

'Nothing untoward occurred during the procedure?' I beseeched.

She shrugged, 'Too early to know the full details,' and rested a reassuring hand on my shoulder, smiled and started to check the machines, making notes of the various figures on display, then disappeared from the room.

My long vigil began. Peter was snoring loudly. Almost trumpeting. This pleased me greatly, made me giggle to myself. Every sound he made was a sign of life, one heartbeat closer to his recovery.

Otherwise the time passed sluggishly and, because I could not concentrate on my book, the ticking seconds were long and boring. Time stagnated. I stared at Peter, at the walls, at the machines, none of which I could interpret.

Occasionally, the door opened and one of the nurses stepped in. Each acknowledged my presence, checked that the bottles had not drained, that my husband's temperature was normal, that his heart was still functioning, and then she was gone again.

Around six o'clock I was beginning to flag. I had eaten nothing since the previous evening. The schedule the clinic had foreseen was that Peter would be released the following morning. However, one of the nurses now warned me that his discharge could be delayed by a day, maximum two, due to the length of time he had spent under anaesthesia. The consultant would decide once he'd examined Peter the following morning.

'Do you have somewhere to stay, Madame? All visitors must vacate the wards by seven p.m.'

'May I please stay here in the room or do you have a visitor's sleeping area nearby?'

'All the rooms are booked, I am sorry.'

'How much longer before he wakes?' I begged. 'I had wanted to be here when he comes round.'

'I am sorry but it is a rule of the clinic and they are very strict about it. Health and safety and stuff like that.'

'Yes, of course.'

I couldn't face the drive back. I was utterly exhausted, drained, and decided to check into a hotel, not the one I had booked before. Another, with more life.

Before leaving the clinic at seven, I wrote Peter a note and left it at his bedside. When he opened his eyes, he'd know I'd been waiting.

There was a sketch I had dashed off, something silly and personal between us. And I left a small bear he had brought back for me from a trip he'd made years ago. It was a tiny worn-out skeleton of a thing that had occupied my various handbags for more than twenty years. It lacked most of its fur and was smaller than my hand, but had become very dear to me. It sat now propped up against a tumbler of water at Peter's bedside and, I hoped, as I could not be there to greet him back into our world, it might be the first thing he focused on when he opened his eyes.

Underneath the bear, I had written on a strip of paper torn from the back of my cheque book: *I love you, Grace xx.*

April 1993

Agnes's gift

The news of Peter's windfall was brought to us by Royal Mail. It plopped through the letterbox of my Primrose Hill flat, forwarded by Angela, Peter's first wife. Peter was home that morning and I carried the letter through to him at the breakfast table.

He opened it without a word.

Accompanying Angela's scribbled note was a large printed envelope. It contained a letter and a document of several pages signed and stamped by a French *notaire*, whose address was given as La Ciotat.

'Darling Agnes has died,' he muttered, frowning, squeezing finger and thumb into his eyes, brushing back tears. No one could have doubted how close they had been. He read the contents of the letter twice, then placed it alongside his plate, sullied with toast crumbs and the remnants of a spoonful of raspberry jam.

'She was taken to the hospital in La Ciotat and died in her sleep two days later. She survived to the grand age of eighty-seven. That was three weeks ago. I wonder why no one tried to contact me.'

He moved his attention to the thick document that had accompanied the letter.

'Agnes's will.' He sighed.

We sat opposite one another in silence, both of us lost in our memories.

For me, the mention of Agnes always recalled that hot, calamitous summer.

'I should have visited her more regularly.' He was talking to himself more than addressing me, flicking back and forth through pages dense with print. I sat across the table pouring coffee, watching him.

Although I had not set eyes on Agnes for twenty-five years, I could still picture her. Her vibrant energy. I had loved and admired her. She was a rare bird, brave, exotic and talented.

'A handsome financial gift has been bequeathed to each of the girls held in trust till their twenty-first birthday. Otherwise, dear sweet Agnes has left me pretty much everything, including Heron Heights.'

It was late April 1993 when that letter popped through our door. A quarter of a century beyond the summer of 1968 and the demise of Pierre. I had just turned forty-one. Peter and I had been cohabiting, although our careers kept us apart, sometimes for weeks on end, for a little over two years. His divorce only recently finalized, I was not pushing for a legal endorsement of our newly rediscovered love. I was still blissfully dazed by our reconnection.

'The solicitor says the house needs a fair amount of structural and renovation work. Hardly surprising. I don't suppose she's touched it in decades.'

'Remarkable that with her increasing age she was able to continue living on that steep hillside, though I remember her as super-fit.'

'I'll need to go, Grace. I can't deal with all this long distance.'

Tension rose within me. I had no desire to return to that past, to the horrors of that night, and Peter was all too aware of it.

'There's no need for you to come along. Before I leave London, I'll make an appointment with her solicitor – who sent through all this paperwork – sign all the relevant documents when I arrive, and put the property on the market with a couple of the local estate agents. I'll sell it in its present condition. I'll be back here within a week. Ten days at the outside. Or we can do this together . . .'

I said nothing, fingers fiddling with a knife slicked with honey. Sugary fingertips. I licked them clean, fiddled with a spoon, avoiding Peter's gaze.

'We could break the spell.' From across the table, Peter stared hard at me. 'You aren't still holding a candle for him? Reassure me, please, Grace, that you're not.'

'How could you even ask such a question?'

'Then don't you think it's time to let it go?'

'I have let it go.'

'I'm not so sure. Every time over the past two years that I suggested a visit to Agnes, you reeled off excuses.'

'Are you going to blame me because –?'

'Because you adamantly refused to accompany me when I suggested paying a visit to my enfeebled aunt? Foolishly, I allowed myself to listen to you and in the process I now feel I rather neglected the one family member who cared for me with an open heart.'

'That is grossly unfair, Peter. You spent weeks with her,

even driving the girls down with you for their summer holiday last July and August. You and I barely saw one another during two months, and you know very well I was working in the West End and couldn't have joined you even if I'd wanted to.'

'Come with me now.'

'Don't insist, please.'

'Mull it over, give me your answer at the weekend. I'll make no plans till then.'

It took me those days, of disturbed nights, of innumerable memories recalling the heady scents of lavender and wild yellow broom drifting across the hillsides, of seaweed clinging to my flesh or beached and sulphurous in the dry heat, of the acrid inhalation of tobacco smoked with hashish, of the anguish.

After a quarter of a century, my head was once again flooded with that summer past. The banks were breached. To be there, in the present, could only be kinder than the return of misgivings. Peter was intending to make the trip whether I accompanied him or not and so, hesitantly, tentatively, I agreed to go along.

'Splendid. In that case I won't rush in and out as I originally planned. We'll make a holiday of it. Or what would you say to a honeymoon?'

I was pulling glasses from a cupboard and stopped in my tracks. 'Is that a proposal?'

'Do you know? I think it is.'

We were in the kitchen, heating lazy Sunday pizzas. Peter had been uncorking a bottle of red. He put it aside and stepped towards me. 'Stop,' I cried, laughing, as he began to bend to one knee. 'There's champagne in the fridge.'

'Is that a yes?'

'Do you know? I think it is.'

Because we were going to be two now, Peter judged it 'no fun' simply to hop on a plane and hire a car at Nice or Marseille airport. He loved France, always had – it was his spiritual home – and here was an opportunity to indulge all his senses in the land of his youth. 'We'll take my car. Ferry from Dover to Calais and from there south.'

A leisurely drive from Primrose Hill, dedicating a week to the journey itself, a few days at Heron Heights or, if that proved emotionally too disturbing or the house was too dilapidated, we'd check in to a small hotel portside in Cassis or La Ciotat, sign all the necessary documents with the *notaire* and hand over the required sums to settle the legal fees and the death duties. The letter informed Peter that 148,200 French francs remained in a bank account in Toulon. Sufficient to cover all costs. In fact, even beyond the trust settled on Sam and Jenny, there was plenty more, but it was a while before we traced those accounts.

After the legal matters had been set straight, we'd find an estate agent, *une agence d'immobilière*, put the house on the market, and then a swift drive north to the ferry with only one more overnight in France.

We hadn't factored in the spell that spun us both into its web.

Our dates were set for May, full spring, the perfect season for a register-office wedding in Hampstead, which the press had got wind of: a few photographers showed up to snap and congratulate us. And the following morning we were off. To France.

Our crossing was smooth, the ferry agreeably deserted on the mid-week morning. Once the boat docked, we disembarked in a jiffy and drove on through, bypassing Calais town, and found ourselves a rather attractive *auberge* entwined in ivy on a secondary road that headed in the general direction of Rheims and Troyes, which was to be our chosen route. Not the route of our May '68 days, but another further east.

Our itinerary was not planned. One decree only: keep clear of the motorways and stick to the *routes nationales*. This made for a slower trajectory but offered us the countryside and an ample choice of modest hotels, *auberges* and bistros along the way.

Peter had fixed his rendezvous with the solicitor in La Ciotat for the Wednesday of the following week. Aside from that, the time was ours. Day after unfolding day of birdsong, of pastoral landscapes, crisp, green-leaved vineyards and, by evening, the serendipity of off-the-beaten-track overnights with delicious dinners accompanied by fine wines. Nothing booked in advance. Pot luck and my husband's sharp eye. The roads were blissfully empty. Traffic jams were farmers with their tractors. The driving we took in turns. Winding roads, small towns, humpbacked bridges, riverside picnics. *La France*, lulling me into a state of calm. Those were perfect days. Spring breaking out. Leaves unfurling. Our honeymoon and we were mellow, serenely happy in one another's company.

However, as we drew closer to the Mediterranean, my anxieties began to increase. Peter sensed my apprehension.

His presence at my side remained steady. He was calm, confident, discreet, but even he couldn't have envisaged the magnitude of Agnes's gift and, once we had arrived, her villa's healing power.

We spent the last night of our southbound journey in a *pension* in La Ciotat. Early the following morning, Peter collected the keys from the solicitor and, without delay, we wheeled off along the upper road where the scenery had changed not a jot since my first stay, thanks to the fact that most of this altitudinous coastline had been designated national parkland.

Almost as soon as our car drew to a halt I felt the shift, as though I had been lifted out of myself, craned to a higher plane of reality. The energy, the stillness, the immensity, the awesomeness of the surrounding nature. The villa, cleaving to its cliff, beckoned; a haven in its panorama. I stepped slowly out of the car, not because I was afraid, as I had prepared myself to be, but because I wanted to relish this moment, the return. Standing high above the building, I drank in the view, its boundlessness, while Peter walked on ahead to open the empty house.

I understood then that this spot, this environment, this refuge was broader, more magnanimous than my fears. It was forgiving.

I imagined I heard the barking of a dog, Bruce, charging forth to welcome me. A shadow, a soul brushed close against my shoulder: Agnes. 'Welcome back, Grace, to where you belong. Your spiritual home, remember, as it has always been mine. And now yours. You're family. Your nymph's wish upon the stars to come back has finally been granted.'

Agnes was omnipresent. I felt her drifting through the rooms, running up the stairs, batting along the mountain tracks, nattering sixteen to the dozen, and it was always a kindly energy, forgiving and sparky.

When we began our scouting, every room offered a trove of unexpected gifts and discoveries. Dozens of her paintings were stacked in cupboards, piled high in corners, tucked in uninhabited bedrooms. My little 'cabin' from all those years earlier was occupied by cobwebs and canvases. On the floor leaning against the wall that faced out to sea, beside 'my' little bed, was a rolled canvas held tight with a brown ribbon. I unfurled it. The portrait caught my breath. *Grace, 1968.* My own image, sixteen years old. I lifted it up to the light, perched on the mattress and peered into it. I stared curiously, as into a mirror, at the soft eyes looking out at me, and I understood that part of me had always been here. Somehow, Agnes had known or intuited that fact. She had kept hold of, jealously guarded, a part of my heart. The heart intact. The portrait in oils, unframed, was dated November 1968.

What Peter and I found in all the other rooms were mostly lesser works. Those that perhaps she had chosen not to exhibit or sell? They would be of interest to the market, to her collectors now. Some were valuable, others remarkable, a few were simply fun. Fun as in a collection she had put together of rare children's pop-up books from the thirties and forties. All were signed LW.

'Who's LW?' I asked Peter.

'No idea,' he replied, leafing through brilliantly designed pages.

Elsewhere, sketches, studies for paintings that she, Agnes, had never completed.

414

Dozens and dozens of watercolours, oils – many were of the surrounding views and yet each was different. The light was a new experience with each canvas. The view from her studio out to sea, always shifting, transforming. Sometimes by moonlight, while other studies were cloud-covered. The sea featured in so many of the landscapes: angry, turbulent, calm, glistening, seductive. The sea talked to her in all its temperaments.

Had it divulged to her the secret of Pierre?

We settled our cases on the top floor in her attic. We made no decision on the subject. It seemed the natural place to park ourselves. Agnes's bed, her space, now ours. The view through the windows she had gazed out upon for more than half a century. In this room, her precious private space, we uncovered her heart. Her photographs, boxes, decades of them, fading black-and-white images, of the woman she had met in Paris, fallen in love with and remained with until the early death of Lyn Woolfden. LW. An American, a renowned ceramicist and a beauty, judging by the pictures and canvases. Lyn had died at the age of forty-two in Nice. On the back of one photo in Agnes's purple lettering: *I close my eyes and see you still. A*

Peter's father's sister, the formidable old 'spinster' who had lived alone 'for centuries', or so Peter and the family had always assumed. Even as a boy holidaying in the South of France, he remembered Agnes as a solitary, indomitable figure planted within her ocean-view eyrie, now our bedroom, smearing great daubs of paint across sweeping canvases. Working obsessively, tirelessly. Labouring through her loneliness, her loss of her lover-partner, Lyn, and her isolation.

Oils were her passion, her *façon de parler*. Seascapes, these mountains, towering skywards from root beds plunged deep into the sea, eruptions of limestone and scree. To these she brought, with a flick, turn, dab of her brush, the minutiae of the region's unique flora and fauna: a golden wing in flight; an eagle hunting, a red breast disguised within the scrub. Carmine skies, purple and orange sunsets; bustling or abandoned ports. Her relationship to the Provençal light, its movement, its dispositions and humours, had brought her the attention and recognition of the Royal Academy. The London she had fled from had welcomed her into the bosom of its artistic elite. She would have been tickled by the irony.

'I can't sell this house, Grace. Whatever was I thinking?'

I shook my head. 'Of course not. It's Agnes's gift to you, it's our wedding present.'

It was as though Agnes had been waiting for Peter to return with me as his wife.

During those weeks, because we extended our stay, our newly received legacy healed me. The trauma of those long-past events was leached out of me by the magical surroundings, the warmth and peace, the colour and joy, of Agnes's bewitching villa and the power of Peter's love for me, which had never felt more ardent than when we arrived back at Heron Heights.

The Present

Gissing's past

It was afternoon, hot and sticky. I was still waiting for Peter's release from the clinic, which was now scheduled for the following morning.

Capitaine Moulinet was already at the bar, waiting, when I arrived. 'Sorry to be late.' I smiled as I took a seat opposite him.

'You are looking more rested, Madame Soames. Better than when we met the day before yesterday. I hear your husband has passed through his ordeal with flying colours?'

'It seems so. He was in excellent form this morning when I visited him,' I answered, still fearful of a last-minute turn of fortunes.

Moulinet and I sat in the sun in silence after our initial exchange. I glanced about. It was a rather trendy joint he had picked, and was conveniently close to the newly opened MuCEM, the Museum of European and Mediterranean Civilizations, where I had wiled away my morning, drinking in the beauty of the seascape, relaxing, knowing that I was soon to be driving my man home with me.

'Thank you for your time again,' Moulinet began. 'I know these have been taxing days for you.'

I nodded. Nothing to add.

He said no more. I waited.

'You mentioned there were one or two outstanding matters you still want to clear up.' I was keen to get this episode behind me. To begin anew with a clean slate.

'Peter Gissing. Name mean anything to you?' Moulinet asked, in a surprisingly casual tone, while signalling to a waiter to bring us a jug of water and two espressos.

My heart momentarily stopped. 'Don't you mean George?' I corrected nervously.

'No, not George. His corpse is being repatriated to the United Kingdom for burial with his family. I am speaking of Peter Gissing.'

I shook my head stiffly.

Pierre.

Moulinet dug into a small brown leather bag with a handle strap, one of those bags southern European men frequently carry. From it he pulled out a red passport and slid it across the table to me. It was a British EU passport. I stared at it, puzzled.

'Open it.'

I did as requested, turning the document to the second page, the page of identification. I swivelled it with my hand on the table so that the photograph was upwards. The passport was stiff, barely used. There, staring out at me, was the face of Pierre. Pierre in late middle age. I peered hard into the gaunt face with its crow's feet and pleated wrinkles. A steely, weathered face, full of sadness and regret.

The name to the right of it: Gissing.

Underneath: Peter Thomas.

British citizen.

Date of birth: 22 Jan 1946.

It was Pierre. Indubitably. Pierre was alive.

The passport had been issued in London in 2004.

My heart felt as though someone had just punctured it with a knife and its contents were flowing out. I glanced upwards, fighting back a surge of emotions. Fifteen minutes from where I was sitting now, across the water, was the spot where I had been picked up by the younger incarnation of this stranger whose picture glared at me from the table.

I had so many questions I didn't know where to begin.

'Who is he?' My voice sounded as though it had been soaked in caustic soda.

'George's older brother.'

My spine and neck felt as though I had slept in a car.

George was dead, but what of Pierre? What had become of Pierre? Was he here too, somewhere in the vicinity? The passport was out of date.

'What about him?'

'A criminal, a serially convicted drug dealer. First picked up in Spain in 1973, sent back to the UK, served a short prison sentence. The first of several, I'm sorry to say.' Moulinet's gaze was fixed hard on me.

'And?'

'Twelve years his recently deceased brother's senior. The younger boy's hero.'

Our coffees arrived, along with a jug of water, ice clinking in it. I splashed some into a glass and gulped it down thirstily. I was hard put to sit still, to remain upright. I felt as though someone had just unplugged me, flipped open the little stopper that keeps the air trapped in an inflated beach toy. Deflated. Deflating. Pierre must have confided everything of our affair to George.

'Does Pie– Peter, does this erm . . . relative, this Peter

Gissing, want to meet with me? To help with his brother's death, or . . . ?' I cleared my throat. 'I'm not sure where this is leading, Capitaine.'

Had he sent his younger brother to find me? Was that why George had been begging me to return with him?

Could I meet up with Pierre again now, after all these years? After everything, could I face him?

'What I mean is . . . I mean does he need to . . . to talk to me . . . about his brother's . . . accident?'

Moulinet shook his head. His eyes locked on mine. 'He can't meet with you.'

'He's in prison?'

'Peter Gissing died two months ago, in late April.'

My hand rose to my mouth.

'He suffered from dementia, Alzheimer's to be precise. He had been living in a home, receiving medical care, for the past three years, according to the file sent through to us.'

'The result of a surfeit of drugs, perhaps,' I murmured. I recalled Pierre, a golden Apollo, striding the beaches. I had been lucky. Mine was a fleeting indulgence, a brief flirtation with the dark side. My work had pulled me back, given me direction, a lifeline.

'As far as we can ascertain, he was George's sole remaining relative. It seems George had worshipped him. A father figure, of sorts.'

I tried not to, but I thought of Pierre's child. Lost so long ago.

If Pierre had sent George to find me, for what reason?

'According to his police and medical records, Peter Gissing claimed to have been attacked at some stage, an assault on his life. His assailant, bizarrely, rather incomprehensibly, was cited as your husband, Madame Soames.'

'What?' I swallowed and fidgeted with my fingers, tapping my glass. 'But how is that possible? Peter was studying at the Sorbonne in the sixties.'

Moulinet scrutinized me, furrowed his brow. The thumb and forefinger of his right hand were pulling at his lower lip. 'The sixties?'

He had made no mention of *when* Peter Gissing had been assaulted. I was digging my own grave. Peter's grave. Peter, who was battling for his life.

I pictured the letter locked in his study drawer.

I coughed, took a deep breath. 'I assumed you . . . w-were referring to – to the years before I met my husband.' I felt as though the sweat breaking out all over me was pouring like a waterfall. I was tired, on edge. Better to keep my mouth shut. Yet I didn't. I wanted to bay at the moon. Mourn for lost lives, for the passing of time, for the fact that Peter, my loyal partner, was in hospital and I had dreaded losing him, the one person who had loved me so tenderly.

And now this.

If Pierre had lived, and for how many dark lost hours had I grieved his passing, I would have wished him a decent life.

Not this story. Not an incarcerated, dead-end existence.

'Please tell me what this is about, Capitaine. Is the family making some kind of claim against my husband, who, as you know, is unwell?'

'Not at all. But it might explain the aggression in the photo cuttings.'

'So, if . . .' I rubbed my forehead with the palm of my hand. 'I'm rather . . . worn out, a little shredded, to be honest, and I'm confused about who this person is and how my husband would have been involved with him.'

'Your husband was his lawyer.'

'I'm sorry?' My arm dropped to the table.

'When Peter Gissing was picked up in Spain, somewhere close to Barcelona, penniless, convicted of peddling drugs, without the means of legal representation, your husband stepped in and took care of all his requirements. Soon after Mr Armstrong-Soames had completed his studies and been called to the Bar, he represented Peter Gissing whose sentence was lighter than it might have been if he had faced a term of imprisonment in Spain, ruled by a dictatorship at that time.'

'Peter helped this man? But how could he have . . . ?' I was stunned, speechless. 'And what of the accusation against Peter? It doesn't add up.'

'It went nowhere, was never followed up. It was deemed the imaginings of a disturbed mind. It is not uncommon for such troubled souls to turn against the one who has been their champion. Both brothers were, at one time or another, treated for episodes of mental disorder. However, scant details have been sent across from UK services. I have only the bare bones of the information to hand. You had better ask Monsieur Soames yourself. I wanted to make you aware of all this because, had anything untoward happened with your husband's health, given the rather unfortunate episode of the younger brother's death so close to your property, I thought you should know of your husband's kindnesses. His reputation is well earned, well deserved.'

I lowered my head to the table, attempting to grasp these extraordinary facts, recalling Peter's words to me: *I am not proud of that moment in my past.*

Moulinet downed his coffee in one and dug in his pocket for coins. I remained where I was, trying to pull myself together.

'One last question, if I may, Capitaine?'

'Of course.'

'George Gissing's face, that scar. Do you have any idea what happened to him?'

Moulinet, who had been in the act of rising from the table, halted halfway, smiled and stood to his full height. 'You saw the scar on his face, did you, Madame?'

I froze. 'I . . .'

'The boy George spent his childhood in and out of care homes and, later, prison, frequently in secure wards. Petty crimes at first, then theft, followed by an armed robbery conviction. There was a brief sojourn in a mental asylum. He partnered with his brother in the drugs business for some years until they were both locked away. As I said, there was a long history of violence and mental instability. Low-income upbringing. Episodes of truancy. Parents divorced. Not much of a family life had they been given, the Gissing brothers. Neither of them formed any lasting relationships. As for the facial scar, George got into a fight with some fellow detainees. There was a crowbar, broken bottles, not an uncommon story of prison life.'

Pierre had never spoken to me of his childhood, his life in England, as I had never spoken of mine.

'Alas, neither of these men left much of a legacy to humankind. Unlike your husband. George's autopsy report, by the way, states that he died of a heart attack. He was dead before his body hit the water.'

I closed my eyes, reliving those final minutes on the cliff-top with Harry and George.

'He was grieving the loss of his brother, his only surviving relative. I suspect he was in your vicinity because he hoped to make contact with your husband. I surmise the only person George Gissing felt he could turn to, after his brother's death, was the man who had shown kindness to his brother. Your husband. There was no one else left and not much of a horizon out there for him.'

I pictured George on the beach at dawn. His words: *There is only you, Grace. You are all that's left. Over the years, I dreamed that when we eventually met, as I always knew we would, you would be the one to unchain me. To make me whole again.*

Pierre must have spoken kindly of me then. Could I have helped George? I doubted it. But if I had known the whole story, the real story, might I have been able to assist him, to offer him some compassion, consolation? What had he hoped for?

'I'd best be on my way. Give my regards to Mr Soames, wish him a speedy recovery. It is unlikely I shall need to trouble either of you again. However, I will look out for your films. It's been a pleasure, Madame.'

Recovery

I was perched on the foot of our bed looking out to sea, trawling through the past. The past and the recent events. The Confidential Letter to Grace was in my left hand. I was tapping it gently against my right.

I should tear it up, shouldn't I? Peter had made the request on our journey home from the clinic. 'The letter I left upstairs for you, Grace . . .'

'Yes?'

'Tear it up, will you, please?'

'I was rather hoping . . .'

'No point in keeping it there.'

'Don't you want to tell me what's in it?'

He shook his head. 'It's not necessary for the present,' he'd said.

Was it connected to our old story? To Pierre? To George Gissing? I wanted to ask him about Pierre but I swallowed the question. Patience. In time, I would learn whatever it was he had to tell me.

Peter was dozing, resting, out on the veranda where I had made up a bed for him. It was cool there, thanks to the two overhead fans. He preferred, he said, to be close to the outdoors, where he could watch the sea. It was also advisable, until he was stronger, to avoid the exertion of two flights of stairs.

He was weak, but he was alive and home with me. His upper left leg and groin were covered with spectacular bruises from where the consultant had punctured the skin to connect up the apparatus that had sent a catheter on the journey through one of Peter's blood vessels to his heart. I thought of little Harry and smiled at how proud he had been of his bruises. I pictured Gissing lifting the child to safety from the prison of rocks. I pictured Gissing tumbling to his death. Might death have been a blessing for him?

I had not mentioned my meetings with Moulinet or Gissing to Peter. It was too soon. He needed peace of mind.

Peter had survived a far more arduous operation than the medical team had originally anticipated. More importantly, miraculously, his heartbeat was back to normal, averaging sixty-four beats a minute. The risk that his heart might simply pack up due to over-exertion had been controlled and, according to his consultant, 'There is no reason why he should not live a normal life for as long as any of the rest of us.'

After two or three weeks of rest and recuperation, the clinic had promised me, my husband would be fighting fit again.

I prayed so.

I had spoken at length with both his daughters, on several occasions over the last few days, filling them in, reassuring them. We had agreed that they, along with their families, would return later in the summer, in August, by which time Peter would, if all went according to plan, be as fit as he had ever been. This time Sam hoped that her husband, Richard, would accompany her and then it would be a full house all set for a family holiday.

There was nothing else for me to concern myself with, aside from the weekly check-ups at the clinic for the next month, then once every three months for the first year. Modern medicine. A miracle.

It was evening. The swallows were swooping in a gold and hyacinth sky. Peter was perched in one of the old rattan loungers that had been part of the furniture as far back as Agnes's tenure. I had a glass of white wine to hand, Peter was sipping weak tea. We were watching the sunset, allowing the tensions of the last few days to drain out of us. Imbibing nature's beauty, side by side.

On the small table to my left, alongside my wine, was Peter's Confidential letter.

I hadn't destroyed it.

'Any reason why you haven't torn that darn thing up, as I requested, Grace?'

'I thought you might want to read it to me. Or tell me what it says. It's on my mind, you see.'

George was on my mind. Pierre, too.

There was a long silence while Peter deliberated.

'Hand it over.' He leaned a few inches towards me with his arm outstretched and I passed the envelope to him. Without opening it, but head bent to it and one hand fingering it as though he were reading braille, Peter recited softly:

My darling Grace,

Now that I have gone from your life, or stepped aside while I wait for you to join me elsewhere, I feel that it is only right that I fill you in on a few facts.

This is a story that goes back in time. It involves a man, Peter Gissing. I believe you loved him and loved him deeply. You knew him by the name of Pierre. Remember him? Actually, I rather hope you have forgotten him.

I have kept a secret from you for all these years . . .'

'Stop, Peter, please.' I lifted myself from my seat, leaned over to my husband and placed a hand on his, the one holding the envelope. 'Tear it up, Peter. It's the past. We don't need to go there.'

He lowered his head, dropping the letter into his lap.

'The fellow had filled you with so many drugs, Grace, I feared for your life when you went into the sea. He was encouraging you, playing with you. I had seen you both together, making love in the sand. I believed, persuaded myself, he didn't care for you in any profound sense, not as I did. My jealousy knew no bounds. I swam out after you . . .'

'But he didn't die. You didn't kill him, you know that. You do, don't you?'

'Yes, I do, Grace, but how do you?' He turned to me. 'Were you in contact with him?'

I shook my head. 'I shouldn't have interrupted . . . Please continue.'

'I swam out after you,' he repeated softly. 'Once I'd released you from his grasp and sent you back to shore, I had intended to follow directly, see you to safety, but Gissing grabbed me, pulled at my arm. "Leave the fucking chick alone," he growled at me. I turned back to him, fighting to release my arm, which I thought he would break, such was the force with which he was holding me. I was kicking to

428

stay afloat. I lifted a leg and booted him in the stomach or possibly the crotch. He let out a long groan. We began to fight, tussling in the water. I was calling out to you to swim fast. There was blood in the water. His, mine, yours?'

Peter stopped speaking, as though he had run out of battery.

I had believed it had been Pierre calling to me. So stoned, I hadn't differentiated between their voices.

'He's dead, Peter,' I mumbled. 'I don't need to know any more. We don't need to take ourselves back to those unhappy yesterdays.'

He waved me to silence, lost somewhere in that other life.

'Gissing fought his way to the surface and grabbed me by the head, bending me backwards by the neck. I punched him hard. It carried all the weight of my disgust for him and the torment I felt at having lost you to him. It caught him in the face. I heard something crack. Had I fractured a bone? His? Not mine. He sank beneath the water in the darkening night. I was terrified. Had I killed him? Surely not killed him. I waited for him to resurface. I waited until my blood turned to ice, my limbs heavier than ballast, and then I waited no longer but turned and crawled fast for the shore. I abandoned him because . . . because . . . I wanted him dead, or gone from us, at least, but I was certain, almost certain, that he would take care of himself. He was the best swimmer I had ever encountered. He understood the sea better than I did.'

'And so he made his way back to shore?'

'No, no.'

I waited, attempting patience.

'No matter that I loathed every cell in his corrupt body, I couldn't leave him to drown. I turned seawards. He possibly would have died if I hadn't gone back for him. He was in a mess. I hauled him ashore some distance from here, swimming, dragging him half-conscious. It was slow going. I berthed him in a cave in one of the coves half a mile or so from our bay. I stayed with him some minutes and then . . . then . . .'

I took a sip of wine, waiting, holding my breath.

Peter, his head lowered, appeared to be crying.

'I threatened him. If he came anywhere near you again, I'd turn him over to the police for what he was. A drug dealer. I told him the keys would be in his car and I wanted him and his belongings gone, out of the house, out of my sight by morning.'

We sat in silence.

'I'm not proud of myself, Grace. I lived with that guilt added to the loss of you for five years.'

'But you saved him.' It was not as George had claimed it. How could I have allowed him to feed doubt against Peter, even for a moment?

'When the car was still there in the morning, I feared he had perished overnight or, at best, had decided to make a getaway on foot. I had no idea why he didn't come back. All I cared was that I had you.'

'But . . .'

'But you were gone. My threats to him had been in vain. Your heart had turned from me. I'd lost your love, and then you vanished from my life entirely. I need a drink, please, Grace.'

I rose, unsteadily. 'What can I bring you?'

'Better make it water.'

I hurried to the kitchen and returned with a full glass. Peter drank thirstily, draining it.

'More?'

He shook his head.

'Five years later, Gissing was arrested in Spain. He gave Agnes's name – well, this address and our names – as a contact. Damn cheek of him. To stand bail, money or . . . I'm not sure why now. The Spanish police contacted her. She remembered him, not fondly I might add. It seems that after you and I had left for Paris, somebody broke into the house and helped themselves to a few valuables. Of course, Agnes had no proof and didn't mention it to me until he reappeared in our lives.'

'Oh, God, I'm so sorry to hear that.'

'Agnes telephoned me in Paris. My first reaction was profound relief. I was bloody glad the blackguard had survived. I flew to Barcelona where Gissing was awaiting trial. Blackmail, I think, was his intention, a threat against me for violence. He wanted money. I refused but offered to act as his legal representation for no fee. I believed I owed him that. I managed to secure his deportation. He served a short sentence in the UK and then was at large to get on with his insalubrious life.'

We sat in silence. I was asking myself what I would have done differently if I had known that Pierre was alive. 'You have nothing to berate yourself for,' I said eventually.

'He asked after you, Grace.'

'In Spain?' I was listening to the sea, breathing slowly.

Peter nodded. 'He accused me of destroying his chance of happiness with you. I told him, quite truthfully, that I didn't have a clue where to find you. I told him that you were settled and that your life had moved on. I warned him off making contact with you.'

I let out a long slow exhalation. *Pierre had asked after me.* Might he have cared for me as I had him? He had spoken of me to George. That was evident. 'Is that it?' My voice was quavering.

'He got in touch with me once again nine or ten years later, requesting large sums of money. He said I'd ruined his life, that I'd kept the two of you apart. He'd go to the police, he said, report me for attempted murder. I told him to go to hell. I never heard from him again.'

I took a breath, asking myself what if Pierre had found me, what if I'd taken him in?

'So, there you have it, Grace. The whole rather sordid story. If I couldn't have you, I was determined you wouldn't throw yourself away on him. You had too much to offer. Arrogance and jealousy on my part.'

If Pierre had found me . . . It would never have come to anything. Our worlds were universes apart.

Peter lifted the last page of writing – his hands were shaking – and read aloud,

'Grace, my darling, you have been the best gift my life has given me. Even in the years when we were separated, you were always an essential part of me. I would have done anything to win your heart.

There are two Peters. Both within me. I hope you will remember the best of me and find it in your heart to love me, and to forgive the other.

Yours for ever, Peter

'That is what I wanted you to know, Grace.'

Tears were dropping down my cheeks. I felt so deeply grateful that Peter was there to relay his written words and that I was not alone on this deck, in mourning, reading the letter in silence to myself. My life had been blessed. With the miracle of Peter's recovery, and with his unswerving love.

I sipped my wine while Peter tore the envelope and its contents into tiny pieces.

I placed my glass on the small table between us and rose to my feet, brushing the damp from my cheeks with the back of my hands. Night had fallen. In the distance, far out to sea, a boat was making its silent passage to its destination. Its lights shone on the water, creating a small pool of silvery brightness, a beacon of hope widening as it moved. I stood behind my husband and rested my arms on his shoulders, bending low into him, my cheek brushing his. I kissed his head softly, nudging my chin through his grey hair.

He lifted his hands to take mine.

Somewhere, inland, a nightingale began to sing, while on the beach beneath us the waves rolled and pounded as they had done for as many millennia as this powerful, magical sea had been in existence, guarding its subaquatic secrets.

And here we were, in this weather-worn old house, Agnes watching over us, bearing witness to nature's force and magnificence, grateful to be in one another's company, in silence, with, on this remarkable night, no particular place to go. Except onwards, surviving, hand in hand, side by side.

Acknowledgements

My very special thanks go to my team at Curtis Brown literary agency, led by Jonathan Lloyd. Curtis Brown is an exceptional 'home' and I am honoured to be counted among its clients. Thank you for helping me put my writing out there. Special thanks to Alice Lutyens, Melissa Pimentel and everyone in the Accounts Department.

At Michael Joseph Books, Penguin, I would like to say a huge thank-you to my editor and publishing director, Maxine Hitchcock, and her two editors, Matilda McDonald and Clare Bowron. Your enthusiasm has been a terrific buoy. My copyeditor, Hazel Orme, and I have now worked together on several books, and I so appreciate Hazel's clarity and beady-eyed brilliance.

There are so many others on the team at MJ whom I do not always have the opportunity to meet so I would like to say *un grand merci* to those of you who work within marketing, sales, publicity, Nick Lowndes, who is overseeing the proofs, and design for *The House on the Edge of the Cliff*.

As always, there are friends who have been there for me throughout the writing process, offering me meals, a bed when I lacked one, laughter and a patient ear when I needed to talk things through. I am raising a glass to us all. Special thanks to Jane Thynne, who has allowed me to use the Philip Kerr quote at the top of the book.

Last, but certainly not least, my very special husband, Michel Noll. *Je t'aime.*

Reading Group Discussion Points

1. Discuss the role of the settings in the novel. For example, why do you think the author chose Paris and the student demonstrations as the backdrop to young Grace's early encounters with Peter?

2. What role does the house on the edge of the cliff play in the story?

3. How do you think Grace's character changes and develops over each time period of the novel?

4. Do you think Grace should have confided in Peter about Pierre/George's reappearance? In what ways might it have changed the outcome for the three of them?

5. Discuss the societal norms of the sixties which are touched upon in the novel. Do you think the sixties were liberating for Grace, or not?

6. What do you think drew Grace to Pierre in the sixties?

7. Discuss the theme of family in the story. How does Grace's upbringing affect her subsequent relationships? How does Peter's family shape their marriage?

8. What role does Agnes play in the story? What influence, if any, does she have on young Grace? How are the two women similar?

9. What are the political influences on the novel? How does the political scene in each time period impact on the lives of the principal characters?

10. Do you think George was responsible for his actions towards Grace and Harry? Did you think they should sympathize with him, or fear him?

Also by

Carol Drinkwater...

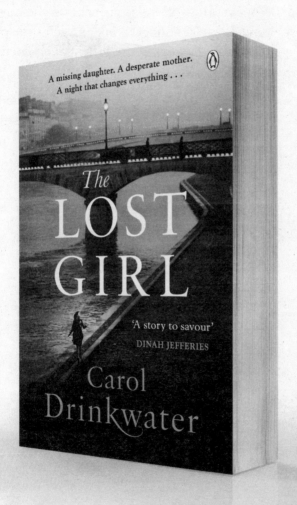

Available now

Also by
Carol Drinkwater...

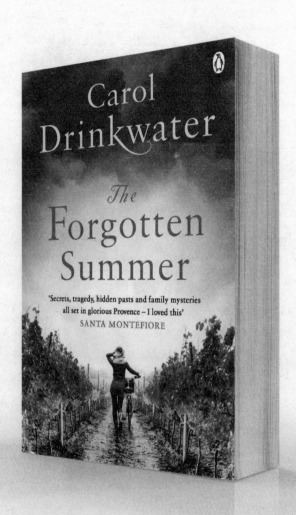

Available now